BERKLEY UK

MAGIC TO THE BONE

Devon Monk has one husband, two sons and a dog named Mojo. Surrounded by numerous colourful family members, she lives in Oregon. She has sold more than fifty short stories to fantasy, science fiction, horror, humour and young adult magazines and anthologies. She has been published in five countries and included in a year's best fantasy collection. Visit her website at: www.devonmonk.com.

Magic to the Bone

DEVON MONK

an imprint of
PENGUIN BOOKS

BERKLEY UK

Published by the Penguin Group
Penguin Books Ltd, 80 Strand, London WC2R 0RL, England
Penguin Group (USA) Inc., 375 Hudson Street, New York, New York 10014, USA
Penguin Group (Canada), 90 Eglinton Avenue East, Suite 700, Toronto, Ontario, Canada M4P 2Y3
(a division of Pearson Penguin Canada Inc.)
Penguin Ireland, 25 St Stephen's Green, Dublin 2, Ireland (a division of Penguin Books Ltd)
Penguin Group (Australia), 250 Camberwell Road, Camberwell, Victoria 3124, Australia
(a division of Pearson Australia Group Pty Ltd)
Penguin Books India Pvt Ltd, 11 Community Centre, Panchsheel Park, New Delhi – 110 017, India
Penguin Group (NZ), 67 Apollo Drive, Rosedale, Auckland 0632, New Zealand
(a division of Pearson New Zealand Ltd)
Penguin Books (South Africa) (Pty) Ltd, 24 Sturdee Avenue, Rosebank,
Johannesburg 2196, South Africa

Penguin Books Ltd, Registered Offices: 80 Strand, London WC2R 0RL, England

www.penguin.com

First published in the USA by Roc, an imprint of New American Library,
a division of Penguin Group (USA) Inc., 2008
First published in Great Britain by Berkley UK 2011

1

Printed in Great Britain by Clays Ltd, St Ives plc

ISBN: 978–0–241–95661–8

www.greenpenguin.co.uk

Penguin Books is committed to a sustainable
future for our business, our readers and our
planet. This book is made from paper certified
by the Forest Stewardship Council.

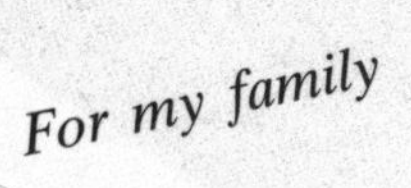
For my family

Acknowledgments

This book did not come into the world without the guidance of many talented, hardworking people. I owe my deepest gratitude to my outstanding agent, Miriam Kriss, who took a chance on me and then made magic happen. Without her, this book may not be in your hands. My heartfelt thanks to my superb editor, Anne Sowards, not only for believing in this book, but also for putting her time and incredible energy into helping it become the best it could be. And thank you also to editorial assistant Cameron Dufty and all the people at Penguin who have worked so hard to make this book a reality.

Thanks to my amazing cheerleaders and first readers, Dejsha Knight, Dean Woods, Deanne Hicks, and Dianna Rodgers. You have been an unfailing source of strength and joy. This book would be so much less without your insightful comments. I owe you each a drink. Or twelve.

Thank you also to my dear friends Mickey Bellman and Sharon Elaine Thompson for listening to my earliest stories without cringing; Eric Witchey and Nina Kiriki Hoffman for your encouragement and friendship; the Wordos for all those nights at the table; and

Loren Coleman for the rejection. If this had remained a short story, it may never have been a book.

Thank you, Mom, Dad, my brothers, sisters, and the rest of my family for showing me that the best way to get through life is with hard work, wild stories, laughter, and togetherness. The words I write wouldn't be half as bright without all of you in my life.

And lastly, to my husband, Russ, and my sons, Kameron and Konner. You are the three most wonderful men I know. This book would never have been written without your years of patience, love, and support. Thank you for being not just a part of my life, but the very best part. I love you.

Chapter One

It was the morning of my twenty-fifth birthday, and all I wanted was a decent cup of coffee, a hot breakfast, and a couple hours away from the stink of used magic that seeped through the walls of my apartment building every time it rained.

My current fortune of ten bucks wasn't going to get me that hot breakfast, but it was going to buy a good dark Kenya roast and maybe a muffin down at Get Mugged. What more could a girl ask for?

I took a quick shower, pulled on jeans, a black tank top, and boots. I brushed my dark hair back and tucked it behind my ears, hoping for the short, wet, sexy look. I didn't bother with makeup. Being six foot tall and the daughter of one of the most notorious businessmen in town got me enough attention. So did my pale green eyes, athletic build, and the family knack for coercion.

I pulled on my jacket, careful not to jostle my left shoulder too much. The scars across my deltoid still hurt, even though it had been three months since the creep with the knife jumped me. I had known the scars might be permanent, but I didn't know they would hurt so much every time it rained. Blood magic, when improperly wielded by an uneducated street hustler, was a pain that just kept on giving. Lucky me.

One of these days, when my student loans were paid off and I'd dug my credit rating out of the toilet, I'd be able to turn down cheap Hounding jobs that involved back-alley drug deals and black-market revenge spells. Hell, maybe I'd even have enough money to afford a cell phone again.

I patted my pocket to make sure the small, leather-bound book and pen were there. I didn't go anywhere without those two things. I couldn't. Not if I wanted to remember who I was when things went bad. And things seemed to be going bad a lot lately.

I made it as far as the door. The phone rang. I paused, trying to decide if I should answer it. The phone had come with the apartment, and like the apartment it was as low-tech as legally allowed, which meant there was no caller ID.

It could be my dad—or more likely his secretary of the month—delivering the obligatory annual birthday lecture. It could be my friend Nola, if she had left her farm and gone into town to use a pay phone. It could be my landlord asking for the rent I hadn't paid. Or it could be a Hounding job.

I let go of the doorknob and walked over to the phone. Let the happy news begin.

"Hello?"

"Allie girl?" It was Mama Rossitto, from the worst part of North Portland. Her voice sounded flat and fuzzy, broken up by the cheap landline. Ever since I did a couple Hounding jobs for Mama a few months ago, she treated me like I was the only person in the city who could trace a line of magic back to its user and abuser.

"Yes, Mama, it's me."

"You fix. You fix for us."

"Can it wait? I was headed to breakfast."

"You come now. Right now." Mama's voice had a pitch in it that had nothing to do with the bad connection. She sounded panicked. Angry. "Boy is hurt. Come now."

The phone clacked down, but must not have hit the cradle. I heard the clash of dishes pushed into the sink, the sputter of a burner snapping to life, then Mama's voice, farther off, shouting to one of her many sons—half of whom were runaways she'd taken in, all of whom answered to the name Boy.

I heard something else too, a high, light whistle like a string buzzing in the wind, softer than a wheezy newborn. I'd heard that sound before. I tried to place it, but found holes where my memory should be.

Great.

Using magic meant it used you back. Forget the fairy-tale hocus-pocus, wave a wand and bling-o, sparkles and pixie dust crap. Magic, like booze, sex, and drugs, gave as good as it got. But unlike booze and the rest, magic could do incredible good. In the right hands, used the right way, it could save lives, ease pain, and streamline the complexities of the modern world. Magic was revolutionary, like electricity, penicillin, and plastic, and in the thirty years since it had been discovered and made accessible to the general public, magic had done a lot of good.

At first, everyone wanted a piece of it—magically enhanced food, fashion, entertainment, sex. And then the reality of such use set in. Magic always takes its due from the user, and the price is always pain. It didn't take people long to figure out how to transfer that pain to someone else, though.

Laws were put in place to regulate who could access

the magic, and how and why. But there weren't enough police to keep up with stolen cars and murders in the city, much less the misuse of a force no one can see.

Things went downhill fast, and as far as I can tell, they stayed there.

But while magic made the average Joe pay one painful price each time he used it, sometimes magic double dipped on me. I'd get the expected migraine, flu, roaring fever, or whatever, and then, just for fun, magic would kick a few holes in my memories. It didn't happen every time, and it didn't happen in any pattern or for any reason I could fathom. Just sometimes when I use magic, it makes me pay the price in pain, then takes a few of my memories for good measure.

That's why I carried a little blank book—to record important bits of my life. And it's also why four years at Harvard, pounding tomes for my masters in business magic, hadn't worked out quite the way I'd wanted it to. Still, I was a Hound, and I was good at it. Good enough that I could keep food on the table, live in the crappiest part of Old Town, and make the minimum payment on my student loans. And hey, who didn't have a few memories they wouldn't mind getting rid of, right?

The phone clattered and the line went dead.

Happy birthday to me.

If Boy had been hurt by magic, Mama should have called 911 for a doctor who knew how to handle those sorts of things, not a Hound like me. Suspicious and superstitious, Mama always thought her family was under magical attack. Not one of the times I'd Hounded for her had her problem been a magical hit. Just bad luck, spoiled meat, and, once, cockroaches the size of small dogs (shudder).

But I had done some other jobs since I'd set up shop here in Portland. Every one of those sent me sniffing the illegal magical Offloads back to corporations. And nine times out of nine, even that kind of proof, my testimony on the stand, and a high-profile trial wouldn't get the corporation much more than a cash penalty.

I rolled my good shoulder to try to get the kink out of my neck, but only managed to make my arm hurt more. I didn't want to go. But I couldn't just ignore her call, and there was no other way to get in touch with her. Mama wouldn't answer the phone. She was convinced it was tapped, though I couldn't think of anyone who would be interested in the life of a woman who lived in North Portland, in the broken-down neighborhood of St. John's, a neglected and mostly forgotten place cut off from the magic that flowed through the rest of the city.

I tipped my head back, stared at the ceiling, and exhaled. Okay. I'd go and make sure Boy was all right. I'd try to talk Mama into calling a doctor. I'd check for any magical wrongdoing. I'd look for rats. I'd bill her half price. Then I would go out for a late birthday breakfast.

A girl could hope, anyway.

I walked out the door and locked it. I didn't bother with alarm spells. Most single women in the city thought alarm spells would keep them safe, but I knew firsthand that if someone wanted to break into your apartment badly enough, there wasn't a spell worth paying the price for that could keep them out.

I took the stairs instead of the elevator, because I

hate small spaces, and made it to the street in no time. The mid-September morning was gray as a grave and cold enough that my breath came out in plumes of steam. The wind gusted off the Willamette River and rain sliced at my face.

Portland lived up to its name. Even though it was a hundred miles from the Pacific Ocean, it had that industrial, crumbling-brick-warehouse feel of the working port it still was, especially along the banks of the Willamette and Columbia rivers. The Willamette River was practically in my backyard, behind the warehouses and the train and bus stations. Without squinting I could see four of the mismatched bridges that crossed the water, connecting downtown with the east side of the city. Over that river and north, close to where the Willamette and Columbia met, was Mama's neighborhood.

I zipped my coat, pulled up my hood, and wished I'd thought about putting on a sweater before I left.

A bus wouldn't get me to Mama's fast enough. However, the good thing about being a six-foot-tall woman was that cabs, few and far between though they may be, stopped when you whistled. It didn't hurt that I had my dad's good looks, either. When I was in the mood to smile, I could get almost anyone to see things my way, even without using magic. True to the Beckstrom blood, I also had a gift for magic-based Influence. But after watching my dad Influence my mother, his lovers, business partners, and even me to get his way, I'd sworn off using it.

It wasn't like I had wanted to go to Harvard. I had Juilliard in mind: art, not business; music, not magic. But my dad had severe ideas about what constituted a useful education.

I waved down a black-and-white taxi and ducked

into the backseat. The driver, a skinny man who smelled like he brushed his hair with bacon drippings, glanced in the rearview. "Where to?"

"St. John's."

His eyes narrowed. I watched him consider telling a nice girl like me about a bad side of town like that. But he must have decided a fare's a fare, and a one-way was better than none at all. He pulled into traffic and didn't look back at me again.

In the best light, like maybe a sunny day in July, the north side of Portland looks like a derelict row of crumbling shops and broken-down bars. On a cold, rainy September day like today, it looks like a wet derelict row of crumbling shops and broken-down bars.

Crawling up from the river, the neighborhood had that rotten-tooth brick-and-board architecture that attracted the poor, the addicted, and the desperate. Unlike most of the rest of Portland, it stood pretty much as it had been built back in the 1800s, except it had one other thing going against it—there was no naturally occurring magic beneath the streets of North Portland. The city had conveniently forgotten to add the fifth quadrant of town into the budget when running the lead and glass networks to make magic available, so now the rest of the city largely ignored the entire area, like a sore beneath the belt everyone knew about, but no one mentioned in polite company.

The driver rolled the cab to a stop just on the other side of the railroad track, and I couldn't help but smile. He must have heard of the neighborhood's rules and rep. Outsiders were tolerated in St. John's most days. Only no one knew which days were most days.

"Want me to wait?" he asked, even though he probably already knew my answer.

"No," I said, "I'll bus home. Will ten cover it?" He nodded, and I pressed the money into his hand. I pushed the door open against the wind and got a face full of rain.

I stepped onto the sidewalk and got moving. Mama's wasn't far. I took a couple deep breaths, smelled rain, diesel, and the pungent dead-fish-and-salt stench off the river. When the wind shifted, I got a noseful of the sewage treatment plant. Then I caught a hint of something spicy—peppers and onions and garlic from Mama's restaurant—and grinned.

I didn't know why, but coming to this part of town always put me in a better mood. Maybe it was a sick sort of kinship, knowing that other people were holding together while everything was falling apart too. There was a certain kind of honesty in the people who lived here, an honesty in the place. No magic to keep the storefronts permanently shiny and clean, no magic to whisk away the stink of too many people living too close together, no magic to give the illusion that everyone wore thousand-dollar designer shoes. I liked the honesty of it, even if that honesty wasn't always pretty.

Or maybe it was just that I figured it was the last place my dad, or anyone else who expected me to do better by myself (read: do what they wanted me to do) would ever expect to find me. There was something good about this rotten side of town. Something invisible to the eye, but obvious to the soul.

Except for piles of cardboard and a few rusting shopping carts, the street was empty—a hard rain will do that—so it was easy to spot the motion from the doorway to my left. I didn't even have to turn my head to know it was a man, dark, an inch or two taller than me, wearing a blue ski coat and black ski hat. From the stink of cheap cologne—something with so much pine overtone, I wondered if he had splashed toilet cleaner over his head by mistake—I knew it was Zayvion Jones.

He was new to town, maybe two months or so, and so unpretentiously gorgeous that even the ratty ski coat and knit hat couldn't stop my stomach from flipping every time I saw him. I knew nothing else about him except that he liked to hang around the edges of North Portland, didn't appear to be dealing drugs or magic, or doing much of anything else, really. Since he'd shown me no reason to trust or distrust him yet, out of convenience I distrusted him.

"Morning, Ms. Beckstrom," he said with a voice too soft to belong to a street thug.

"Not yet, it isn't." I glanced at him. He had a good, wide smile and a high arch to his cheeks that made me think he had Asian or Native along with the African in his bloodline.

"Might be better soon," he said. "Buy you breakfast?"

"With what? The fingers in your pocket?"

He chuckled. It had a nice sound to it.

My stomach flipped. I ignored it and kept walking.

"Maybe dinner sometime?" he asked.

Mama's place was a squat two-story restaurant with living space on the top floor and eating space on the bottom. It was just a couple blocks down, a painted brick and wood building hunkered against the broody sky. I stopped and turned toward Zayvion. Now that I looked closer, I realized he had good eyes too, brown and soft, and the kind of wide shoulders that said he could hold his own in a fight. He looked like somebody you could trust, somebody who would tell you the truth no matter what and hold you if you asked, no explanation needed.

Why he was following me around made me suspicious as hell.

I thought about drawing on magic to find out if he was tied to someone's magical strings. Even though St. John's was a dead zone, Hounding wasn't impossible to do here. It just meant having to stretch out to tap into the city's nearest lead and glass conduits that stored and channeled magic, or maybe reach even deeper than that and access the natural magic that pooled like deep cisterns of water beneath all the other parts of Portland.

But I had sworn off using magic unless necessary. Losing bits of one's memory will make those sorts of resolutions stick. I wasn't about to pay the price of Hounding a man who was more annoyance than threat. Still, he deserved a quick, clear signal that he was wasting his time.

"Listen. My social life consists of shredding my junk mail and changing the rat traps in my apartment. It's working for me so far. Why mess with a good thing?"

Those soft brown eyes weren't buying it, but he was nice enough not to say so. "Some other time maybe," he said for me.

"Sure." I started walking again and he came along with me, like I had just told him we were officially long lost best friends.

"Did Mama call you?" he asked.

"Why?"

"I told her Boy needed an ambulance, but she wouldn't listen to me."

I didn't bother asking why again. I jogged the last bit to the restaurant and took the three wooden steps up to the door. Inside was darker than outside, but it was easy to see the lay of things. To the right, ten small tables lined the wall. To the left, another three. Ahead of me, one of Mama's Boys—the one in his thirties who spoke in single-syllable words—stood behind the bar. The only phone in the place was mounted against the wall next to the kitchen doorway. Boy watched me walk in, looked over my shoulder at Zayvion, and didn't miss a beat letting go of the gun I knew he kept under the bar. He pulled out a cup instead and dried it with a towel.

"Where's Mama?" I asked.

"Sink," Boy said.

I headed to the right, intending to go behind Boy and the bar, and into the kitchen.

I stopped cold as the stench of spent magic, oily as hot tar, triggered every Hound instinct I had. Someone had been doing magic, using magic, casting magic, in a big way, right here on this very unmagical side of town. Or someone somewhere else had invoked a hell of a Disbursement spell to Offload that much magical waste into this room.

I tried breathing through my mouth. That didn't make things better, so I put my hand over my mouth and nose. "Who's been using magic?"

Boy gave me a sideways look, one that flickered with fear.

Mama's voice boomed from the kitchen, "Allie, that you?" and Boy's eyes went dead. He shrugged.

I pulled my hand away from my mouth. "Yes. What happened?"

Mama, five foot two and one hundred percent street, shouldered through the kitchen doors, holding the limp body of her youngest Boy, who had turned five about a month ago. "This," she said. "This is what happened. He's not sick from fever. He hasn't fallen down. He's a good boy. Goes to school every day. Today, he doesn't wake up. Magic, Allie. Someone hit him. You find out who. You make them pay."

Mama hefted Boy up onto the bar, but didn't let go of him. He'd never been a robust child, but he hadn't ever looked this pale and thin before. I stepped up and put my hand on his chest and felt the fluttering rhythm of his heart, racing fast, too fast, beneath his soccer T-shirt. I glanced over at Zayvion, the person I trusted the least in the room. He gave me an innocent look, pulled a dollar out of his pocket, and put it on the bar.

What do you know, he did have money.

Boy, the elder, poured him a cup of coffee. I figured Boy could take care of Zayvion if something went wrong.

"Call an ambulance, Mama. He needs a doctor."

"You Hound him first. See who does this to him," she said. "Then I call a doctor."

"Doctor first. Hounding won't do you or him any good if he's dead."

She scowled. I was not the kind of girl who panicked easily, and Mama knew it. And she also knew I had college learning behind me—or what I could remember of it, anyway.

"Boy," Mama yelled. Another of her sons, the one with a tight beard and ponytail, stepped out of the kitchen. "Call the doctor."

Boy picked up the phone and dialed.

"There," Mama said. "Happy? Now Hound him. Find out who wants to hurt him like this. Find out why anyone would hurt my boy."

I glanced at Zayvion again. He leaned against the wall, near the door, drinking his coffee. I didn't like

Hounding in front of an audience, especially a stranger, but if this really was a magic hit, and not some sort of freak Disbursement-spell accident, then the user should be held accountable for Boy's doctor bills and recovery.

If he recovered.

I pressed my palm against Boy's chest and whispered a quick mantra. I didn't want to stretch myself to pull magic from outside the neighborhood. So instead, I drew upon the magic from deep within my bones. My body felt strange and tight, like a muscle that hadn't been used in a while, but it didn't hurt to draw the magic forward. Four years in college had taught me that magic was best accessed when the user was close to a naturally occurring resource, like the natural cisterns beneath the west, east, and south sides of the city, or at an iron-and-glass-caged harvesting station, or through the citywide pipelines.

What Harvard hadn't taught me was that I could, with practice, hold a small amount of magic in my body, and that other people could not. People who had tried to use their own bodies to contain magic ended up in the hospital with gangrenous wounds and organ failure.

But to me, holding a little magic of my own felt natural, normal. I couldn't remember a time when I didn't have the deep, warm weight of small magic inside me. When I was six I'd asked my mother about it. She told me people couldn't hold magic like that. I believed her. But she was wrong.

I whispered a spell to shape the warm, tingling sense of magic up into my eyes, my ears, my nose, and wove a simple glyph in the air with my fingertips. Like turning on a light in a dark room, the spell enhanced my senses and my awareness of magic.

No wonder the stink of old magic was so heavy in the room. The spell that was wrapped around Boy was violently strong, created to channel an extreme amount of magic. Instead of a common spell glyph that looked like fine lacework, this monster was made out of ropes as thick as my thumb. The magic knotted and twisted around Boy's chest in double-back loops—an Offload pattern. This spell was created to transfer the price of using magic onto an innocent—in this case, a five-year-old innocent. It was the kind of hit that would cause an adult victim's health to falter, or maybe they'd go blind for a couple months until the original caster's use of magic was absolved and the lines of magic faded to dust.

This was no accident.

Someone had purposely tried to kill this kid.

That someone had set an illegal Offload bothered me. That they had aimed it at a child made me furious.

The Offload pattern snaked up around Boy's throat like a fancy necklace, with extra chains that slipped down his nostrils. I could hear the rattle of magic in his lungs. No wonder the poor thing's heart was beating so fast.

I leaned in and sniffed at his mouth. The magic was old and fetid and smelled of spoiled flesh. A fresh hit never smelled that bad that fast. Boy hadn't been hit today. He probably hadn't even been hit yesterday. I realized, with a shock, that the little guy had been tagged a week ago, maybe more.

I didn't know how he had hung on so long.

I resisted the urge to lick at the magic, resisted the urge to place my lips briefly against the ropes that covered his mouth. Taste and smell were a Hound's strengths, and I could learn a lot about a hit by using them. But no one wanted to see a grown woman lick someone's wounds—magical or not. I took another deep breath, mouth open, to get the taste of the magic on my palate and sinuses at the same time. The lines were so old, all I could smell was death. Boy's death.

I muttered another mantra, pulled a little more magic, and traced the cords across his chest with my fingers, memorizing the twists and knots and turns. Some of the smaller ropes lifted like tendrils of smoke—ashes from the Offload glyph's fire.

Every user of magic had their own signature—a style that was as permanent and unique as a fingerprint or DNA sequencing. A good Hand could forge the signature of a caster, but the forgery was never perfect, and rarely good enough to fool a Hound worth their salt.

And I was worth a sea of salt. I retraced the spell, lingered over knots, and memorized where ropes crossed and parted and dissolved into one another.

I knew this mark. Knew this signature. Intimately.

I jerked my hand away from Boy, breaking the magical contact with him. No wonder the signature was familiar. It was my father's.

It had been deconstructed to try to hide his distinctive flare, but I knew his hand, knew his mark. The room was suddenly too hot, too small, too close.

Boy was sick, dying, and my dad was killing him.

"Get him a doctor." My voice sounded thin and far away. I swallowed and clenched my hands, digging nails into palms until I could feel the pain of it.

"Mama," I said, "this is bad. A big hit. And it's old. He needs to get to a doctor right now."

"Who did this?" Mama asked. "You tell me who. We make them pay."

But I couldn't say it, couldn't wrap my brain around what my father had done, couldn't understand why he would do such a thing. Boy was only five years old.

Not too far off, a siren wailed.

"Is that an ambulance?" I looked to Boy—the one with the beard—who stood in the doorway to the kitchen. "You did call an ambulance, right?"

He gave me a level look and a sinking feeling hit my stomach. He hadn't called an ambulance. Probably hadn't called anyone. I guess they trusted doctors as much as they trusted magic. Or they didn't have the money to pay a hospital bill. Maybe they thought Hounding would take care of it, would magically make Boy better.

Sweet hells.

"Give me the phone," I said.

Mama waved her hand. "We call, we call."

That was a lie. I took two steps toward the Boy by the phone, wondering how fast I could dial 911 before he dragged me away. Both Boys—the one from the kitchen and the nonspeaker—crossed their arms over their chests and stood shoulder to shoulder in front of me, blocking the phone.

"Get out of my way," I said. "I am using that phone."

"Allie girl," Mama warned.

"He could die, Mama."

"You tell me who did this and I call."

"I already called," a deep voice behind me said.

I stopped and looked over at Zayvion, who was still leaning against the wall, coffee in his hand.

"Before you got here," he said. "They're on the way." As if to illustrate his point, the distant siren grew louder.

Convenient, that. But should I take his word for it? I opened my mouth to say something. Mama beat me to it.

"You have no right here, Zayvion Jones." Mama's voice was sharp, and heavy with that muddy accent I could not place. She was more than angry. She was furious. In all the years I'd known her, I'd never seen her so mad, not even when she'd been robbed for the third time in a month. "My family. My home. My street. Not yours, Zayvion Jones. Not one of your *kind*."

Zayvion stiffened for the briefest moment. He suddenly seemed much less the harmless drifter and much more a figure of authority. He shot a look at me, those brown eyes calculating something. Maybe trying to decide if I was friend or foe. I don't know what he came up with, but he leaned back and that edge of authority—of power—was gone, leaving him just a harmless drifter again.

He shrugged. "Then you can tell them to leave when they get here. Tell them there's nothing's wrong with your son."

"No," I said, not wanting Mama's anger to override her reason. "The ambulance is a good idea. He needs a doctor—someone who can break an Offload pattern or set a Siphon to bleed away the strength of this spell." I walked back over to Boy, the youngest, and rested my hand on his too-quickly beating heart.

I wanted to help the kid, wanted to tear the ropes of magic from him. But the magic fed off him as if he were the caster. That is the power of an Offload: it makes someone else pay for magic they have not used. I did not have the training to break such a strong spell without risking Boy's life.

"Who, Allie?" Mama asked again.

I shook my head, angry at my father and his company for thinking they could get away with something like this, and worried that Mama might do something stupid—like send out a half dozen of her Boys with guns to even the score. I didn't want her to do that. Not until I had a chance to do it first.

"It was a corporate hit—an Offload for magic used in the city. A lot of magic. For something big. I'm going to trace it back to the caster. I'll let you know when I find out for sure. Call the cops and tell them."

I strode to the door, angry and a little dizzy. I hoped the Boys would take care of things and see that Boy the youngest got to a doctor, even if Mama was too angry or too stubborn to do so.

"I want them to hurt, Allie," Mama demanded. "I want them to pay for my poor boy. Tell them we'll go to court, go to news channels, tear them down. Tell them they will pay."

"They'll pay," I said as I brushed past Zayvion and straight-armed the door open.

I was half a block away when the ambulance turned the corner and headed straight to Mama's. I glanced over my shoulder and saw Mama standing on her front step, waving them down.

Maybe Boy still had a chance.

Anger took me a long way, down the street and five more blocks before I hailed a cab. Anger made me not care it was raining, made me not care Zayvion followed me and held the cab door open and slid across the vinyl seat next to me. Anger even made me tell the cabbie to take me to Beckstrom Enterprises as quickly as he could.

"You okay?" Zayvion asked. When I didn't answer, he put his hand on my arm—the one with the scars. And his hand felt good there, soothing and warm like winter mint.

I pulled away. I didn't much trust him, though I had to give him points for calling the ambulance back there. Boy could very well have died if he hadn't. "I'm fine."

He frowned. "Allie, your neck. It's bruising."

Great. I'd forgotten to set a Disbursement spell when I cast magic to Hound Boy. That meant I didn't get to choose how magic would make me pay for using it.

Lovely.

"It's fine." I pulled my coat collar closer to my jaw. I hated being around people when I hurt. But I'd done this to myself. I always paid my own price for using magic, mostly because I didn't want to be indebted to a Proxy. If I had remembered to cast a Disbursement spell, I could have chosen how the pain would manifest: a two-day migraine, a week of insomnia, even flulike sickness—something fairly dramatic that I could get over quickly. I hated the slower Disbursement route some Hounds took. Sure it made for a less immediately painful price, but one that lasted much longer and took a harder toll. I'd seen too many Hounds end up blind, deaf, and insane. That is, if the pain pills, booze, and drugs didn't kill them first.

I glanced at the back of my hands as new bruises darkened, and tried to take a deep breath but couldn't because of the sharp pinch of pain beneath my ribs. Great. I was probably bruising inside and out, and wouldn't be able to move in about an hour.

The good news just kept coming.

Zayvion made a small *tsk* sound. "You didn't forget to set a Disbursement, did you?"

"Bite me."

The cab screeched around a corner and I realized I had forgotten something else. I had forked over my last ten bucks for the cab ride to Mama's and was now completely and totally broke.

Fantastic.

I licked my lips, which also hurt, then looked over at Zayvion. He watched me with a Zen sort of expression. He didn't say anything. Just sat there like he had all the time in the world to wait for me to say something.

So I said something. "That dinner you asked me about."

He tipped his chin down and raised an eyebrow.

My stomach did that flip again.

"Yes?"

"You think you could spring for cab fare instead and we'll call it even?"

"Will you tell me who put the hit on Boy?"

"Are you related to Mama?" I asked. "Are you a cop? Do you have her permission to receive that information? Then no. My work is confidential. I don't even know why you're in this cab with me."

"Maybe I'd like to get to know you better." He gave me that nice smile again, and it did more than just make my stomach flip. Even though he was wet and slouched against the grimy seat of a cab, and even though I had just told him to mind his own business, I found myself thinking about what that soft mouth of his would taste like.

What could I say? I was a sucker for guys who made solid decisions during a crisis, and weren't afraid to step up and help people, especially little kids. But what I couldn't figure out was what stake he had in this.

When I didn't say anything, Zayvion looked out the window, calmly watching the streets whiz by at an alarming speed. We were heading downtown fast, the buildings going from gray concrete to glass and iron and steel.

"I'll figure out who did it when we get to wherever we're going, you know," he said.

"Maybe. But why do you care? Do you think you can cash in on this somehow? Are you a reporter slumming for dirt?"

"No."

"Are you one of Mama's Boys?"

"No."

"A cop?"

The cab swerved, laid on the horn, and made a nauseating left-hand turn. I brushed my hand over my forehead, wiping away sweat. I suddenly wasn't feeling so good. Not nearly good enough to be stuck in a cab that smelled like curry and gym socks with a guy I couldn't get a good read on.

"Allie?"

"Listen," I said, trying to be reasonable. "It doesn't matter who I'm going to see. I could be picking up my dry cleaning for all you know."

"We'll see, won't we?"

"There is no 'we' in this, Zayvion."

He shrugged. "That could change."

Great. A guy who liked girls who played hard to get.

"Is this how you usually pick up women?"

That made him smile again. "Why? Is it working?"

If I weren't feeling so sick, and so mad at my dad, I might actually enjoy this sort of situation. But not today. Today I had to face a man I hadn't seen since I was eighteen and had suddenly found myself leaving for Harvard. My father is good at magic. Very good. It took me two years to shed the mind-numbing grip of Influence he had cast. Two years of attending the school he wanted me to attend, learning the skills he wanted me to learn, and becoming the thing he wanted me to become. Two years of being his puppet. And now I was going to stand up to him and tell him I wasn't going to let him get away with hurting a little kid.

"I'm just not interested right now, okay?"

The cab stopped at a light, gunned through the green, and jerked to a stop double-parked across the street from a high-rise. The building was forty-eight floors of rough, black stone and dark, reflective windows. Elaborate lines of iron and steel twisted like gothic vines to web the entire structure. At the very top of the building was a spire supporting a massive gold-tipped Beckstrom Storm Rod. There was absolutely no mistaking that the entire building was a harvesting station for the rare storms of wild magic that hit the city.

"Leave the meter running," I said. "I'll be right back out to pay." I pulled on the door handle, opened the door, and groaned. I felt like I'd just lost a fight with a bulldozer.

The cold air felt good, then it felt too cold. Shivering made my entire body hurt. Still, I made it through the lead-lined glass front doors, across the cavernous lobby, sparsely decorated with wedges of black marble against white marble, and to the elevator without drawing much attention from the business-suited comers and goers within. Maybe my bruising wasn't as bad as Zayvion said it was.

My father's office was, of course, the entire top floor of the building. And Zayvion, for no reason I could understand, followed me across the lobby to the elevator.

"What part of *not interested* don't you get, Zayvion?"

He held up a hand. "I have an appointment on

the top floor. I also paid for the cab. You owe me ten bucks."

"How thoughtful," I drawled. "And the top floor? Isn't that interesting?"

The elevator door opened on a polished wood interior—a warm contrast to the rest of the Art Deco marble and iron decor of the lobby. Zayvion put his hand out and held the door. He waited for me to enter the elevator.

I hesitated. What if he was part of the hit on Boy? He didn't smell of old magic, but right now, hurting and angry, my Hound instincts were seriously off. Even if he wasn't part of the hit, getting in an empty elevator with someone who might turn out to be only an everyday sort of stalker, wasn't exactly on my "good girl, you get to live" list of smart choices.

Cripes. I could take him. Even sick. Even sore. Even in an elevator.

I walked in and pressed the button for the top floor. Zayvion made a little "what a surprise" sound and stood on the other side of the elevator, his hands folded in front of him.

The door slid closed and suddenly the elevator seemed way too small for the two of us. I took a good deep breath, trying not to think about the walls closing in, the ceiling pressing down, the floor mashing up, until there was no air, no space. My palms were wet with sweat.

This was not working. Think of happy. Think of good. Coffee was good, even though I hadn't had any yet today. Flowers were good—flowers in big open fields. Big open fields like Nola's farm were good. It had been too long since I'd seen her. I'd only been to her big open farm with big open fields twice since her husband, John, died.

Death was not good. My chest tightened. That wasn't good either, so I went back to thinking about flowers and big open fields, and the coffee I wished I'd had this morning.

I hated that I had to see my dad. It had been seven years since he and I had been in a room together. I wished it could be seven more. And having to see him like this—because of what he had done to Boy—made me really mad.

The one thing Harvard got right was this: anger made using magic impossible. For everyone. No exception. It was good because it simplified some things, like whether or not murder via magic was premeditated. Quick answer: always.

I worked on thinking calm thoughts and whispered a mantra, drawing upon the remaining magic within me. This time I intoned a Disbursement, and traced the glyph in the air with my fingertip. Magic was invisible to the unaided eye. And unless you were really good at reading finger motions—a lot like reading lips—you never knew what people were up to, so I wasn't worried about Zayvion seeing that, in about two days, I'd pay for this little magic jaunt with a doozy of a headache. Right now, all I wanted was ten minutes of my father's time. And maybe his blood.

The elevator door opened.

I escaped the coffin on pulleys and walked across the lush burgundy carpet to the single rosewood reception desk, where a fresh-faced eighteen-year-old D cup manned the phone behind a sleek computer console.

"May I help you?" she asked.

I leaned down and put my hand on the edge of her desk, which hurt, but also got me a clear shot at eye contact, something essential for Influencing. "I hope you're having a wonderful day." I smiled and mentally intoned a boost of magic into my words.

Her eyes were light brown and lined with green makeup that looked really nice on her. She was pretty, innocent-looking, and with that hint of Influence behind my words, she already resembled a deer caught in a floodlight. No wonder why Dad hired her. He always picked the ones who were easy to bamboozle.

"I'd like to see Mr. Daniel Beckstrom now," I said. "Please show me in."

"Of course. This way." She gave me a giddy smile and practically skipped down the hallway—no easy feat in heels on carpet—eager to please under the sway of Influence.

Hells. How could I go months resisting the lure of using Influence, and as soon as I was in the same building with my father, it was the first thing I did? I swore and tried to do some damage control.

"Are you sure he has time?" I asked. "I could wait to see him."

"Oh, no. Of course he has time for you." She glanced over her shoulder and nodded, and I worried that she might run into a wall. "This is it." She looked forward again, and managed not to hit her head on the wide, dark wood door of my dad's office. She held the door open for me and smiled like I was a rock star on tour.

"Thanks," I said.

She practically gleamed.

I stepped into my dad's office.

Time, seven years, to be exact, can change a lot of things. The furniture, all steel, wrought iron, and smoked glass, had been upgraded, maybe the carpet had too, but there was still an acre of black marble desk spread in front of the panoramic view of the city, including the river and mountain, when it wasn't raining so hard. And standing behind that desk, immaculate in a suit that cost more than the building I lived in, was my dad.

My height or better, my dark-hair, pale-skin looks or better, he held a cup of coffee in one hand and seemed genuinely startled to see me walking toward him. I was going to play that advantage for as long as I had it because the man hadn't gotten to the top of the magic harvest and refinery technology business thinking slow on his feet.

"Allison," he breathed.

"You're killing a five-year-old kid in North Portland with an Offload the size of a small city. If you don't pay for a doctor to mitigate a Disbursement spell, set a Siphon, and everything else, including hospital stay, rehab, and mental and emotional damage for the boy, then his family is going to drag you through court and publicly expose Beckstrom Enterprises' reckless Offloading practices. My testimony will be in their favor."

He blinked a couple times, then looked away from my face to the rest of me, slowly taking in my cheap clothes and bruised hands. The corner of his lips tightened like he'd just bitten into something sour.

I'd seen that look on his face ever since I turned nine and told him I wanted to play jazz tambourine when I grew up.

"What happened to her?" he asked someone behind me. I looked back, and who should stroll in through the door but my old buddy Zayvion.

"She Hounded a hit and forgot to set a Disbursement spell," he said.

I put two and two together and shook my head in disgust. "You bastard. You work for my father?"

"One contract." He held up his hands like maybe I was going to hit him. He had good instincts. "I did one contract for him."

"For what? To spy on Mama?"

"To look out for you, Allison," my dad said.

Oh.

What girl doesn't want to hear those words? What girl doesn't want to believe her daddy is always going to be there to look after her and keep her safe?

But I could taste the honey-sweetness of magic and Influence behind his words, could smell the bitter tang of something that was not sincerity in his tone. He wanted me to believe him. Too much.

"Really," I said.

"I heard you had been Hounding up on the north side of town," he said. "There have been so many cases of illegal Offloads over there, I was worried you'd get hurt."

He sounded sincere. He looked sincere. This, from the man who had manipulated and Influenced every choice I'd ever made in my life. For all I knew, a man who still believed he could continue doing so.

"Bullshit," I said. "Save it for the court, Mr. Beckstrom. I'll see you there." I intended to spin around and exit dramatically, but I hurt too much. Even the bottoms of my feet were swollen. So I settled for a long, dignified stroll toward the door.

"Allison," my dad said gently. "It is the truth, even if you are too stubborn to believe me. It has been a very long time since you've seen how things work around here. Laws have been passed—you know that. There are more checks and balances and outside watchdogs Hounding the details of business and magic transactions than there ever were before. We use magic sparingly at this company—at all levels—and

Proxy the Offload through approved channels, such as the penitentiaries and prisons."

I wasn't buying it. I just couldn't fit the idea of a kinder, gentler man inside the skin my father owned. I kept walking.

"If it would help you to believe what I'm saying," he said, "you have my permission to draw Truth from me."

That sort of magic involved blood, and drawing Truth, in particular, only worked between people who carried the same bloodline. I hated blood magic. Then again, I felt a powerful need to stab somebody right about now, and a girl shouldn't turn her back on opportunity.

"Fine." I walked back to his desk and held my palm out for a needle. I hoped he wouldn't have one on him because the ornate letter opener on his desk looked more my speed. He must have caught some hint of that in my gaze. He raised one eyebrow and pulled a very thin, very gold straight pin out of his lapel and dropped it onto my hand.

I held it with my fingers and intoned the mantra for Truth. I placed my other hand on the desk. The desk frame was iron and carved with the patterns that allowed access to the magic held in the building's storage network. I intoned a mantra to call the magic up through his desk and into my hand, and felt the electric tingle of magic against my palm. I pricked my middle finger, wove a glyph in the air with my bleeding finger, careful not to let the blood fall, and said a few more words. Then I took hold of my dad's hand and pricked his finger. He leaned across his desk and so did I. We were both tall enough that we could place our fingers together, palm to palm, blood to blood.

This was the closest to him I'd been in the last fifteen years. It was the longest he'd actually touched me too. He smelled of wintergreen and something musky and pleasant, like leather. The scent of him triggered memories and feelings from a time when I was young enough and stupid enough to believe he was a good person. A time when I thought he was my hero.

"Did you, or your company, Offload into North Portland or onto a child during the last six months?" I asked.

"No." His gaze held mine, and that word vibrated in my chest as if I were the one who had spoken it. He was telling the truth as he believed it.

"I don't want to believe you," I said.

He nodded, feeling my truth as I had felt his.

"I'm sorry, Allie." His regret, of things between us, things neither of us could find a way to speak of, filtered back through our blood. Other memories stirred within me. Memories of his infrequent and surprisingly deep laughter, of his hand briefly touching my forehead when I was sick, of the time he made pancakes on Sunday morning.

I pulled my hand away from his. The spell broke. That was as much truth as I could stomach.

I stuck my bleeding finger in my mouth and felt like I'd just lost a game of chicken.

My father pulled a soft white handkerchief out of his suit jacket. He offered it to me. I shook my head. There was no way I was going to leave any more of my blood with him. Truth was the mildest of the blood magics.

I squeezed my thumb tight against my bleeding finger and put my hand in my coat pocket.

Dad pursed his lips again, disapproving, and pressed his finger against the cloth.

"I don't know how you rigged a Truth spell," I said, "but I know your signature. I Hounded it on that Offload. I don't make mistakes."

"Come now," he said. "You are not infallible. None of us are." He smiled, but there was no warmth in his eyes.

"I am reporting you and Beckstrom Enterprises to the authorities," I said.

"I wouldn't expect anything less from you." He tossed his handkerchief on the desk between us. "But I'd like you to reconsider. You've had your fun, Allie. You've proved you can survive on your own without any help from me. And you've had time to cool off—we've both had time. There is still a place for you in this company. I think you should think about where your talents and training can best be used and applied."

He smiled again and those light green eyes of his sparkled. He was happy, his voice comforting, encouraging, safe. I wanted to hug him and tell him I missed him and ask him why he couldn't just be my father instead of my boss. I wanted to let him make all the hard things in my life go away. And something felt very wrong about that.

"Come home, honey," he said, with the unmistakable push of Influence behind his words.

I was tired, hungry, cold. I hurt, inside and out, and yeah, I woke up every day afraid I might have lost a little more of my memory, and that magic was taking a harder toll on me than I thought, and that I wasn't going to make rent on my crummy apartment. Maybe my dad knew all that. Knew I was broke, and scared, and alone. But what he didn't know was that I would happily endure fear and uncertainty, and even pain, if it meant I could live my life free from his manipulation.

"No. Thanks." It took everything I had to say those two words, to push them past the weight of Influence he'd just used on me.

And those two words were enough.

His face flushed dark, angry. "I have asked you politely, Allie. Don't think I won't force the issue."

"I wouldn't expect anything less from you." I dropped the pin on his desk.

"There are legal actions I can set into motion. If you agree to come back to the company now, it will save us both a lot of time and effort."

I nodded. My dad was all about efficiency. And things going his way. I'm sure he knew exactly how he was going to make my life miserable since I'd said no to him. "See you in court."

I walked across the room, past Zayvion, to the door. Made it this time. Got all the way to the receptionist's desk, then across the half mile of burgundy carpet to the elevator that was wooden and small, too small, far too small, but fast, and even a fast coffin was better than my slow feet right now.

Once I hit the lobby, I broke into a jog, needing to be through the lobby in a hurry and gone from here, away from my father who seemed to have found a way to lie in a blood-to-blood Truth spell—something I'd never thought possible. I wanted away from the memories of what I wished he could be, and away from the reality of what it meant to fight him for my life. Again.

I pushed through the big glass-and-iron doors and stopped outside the building, under a dark awning that caught the rain. The cab was not waiting, and I remembered Zayvion told me he'd paid the guy.

Great.

I couldn't decide where I should go next or what I should do.

The police sounded like a good idea, if I could find someone who wasn't bought off by my dad. A lawyer sounded like a good idea too, but had the same drawback.

With any luck, Mama had already called the cops and told them I was Hounding the hit back. With any luck, they would already be starting their investigation.

Someone had put a hit on Boy, and I knew my dad's signature was on it. His real signature, not a fake. He had a part in this regardless of the Truth spell.

Maybe I hadn't asked the right question. Maybe someone had erased his memory of what he'd done. Memory manipulation was against the law, and deservedly so for how dangerous it was. No, I couldn't imagine him ever letting someone mess with his mind.

He must have found a way to lie, to manipulate the Truth spell so even blood magic couldn't detect it.

That terrified me, but I believed he could do it.

He was good at magic, my dad. One of the best.

I couldn't figure out what he would gain from putting such a heavy hit on such a little kid, though. It didn't make sense.

Zayvion strolled up and stopped next to me, standing so close we were almost touching. His heavy pine cologne smelled really good now, not nearly as strong as before. People wrapped in dark coats and scarves moved around us in a hurry. Zayvion didn't say anything, didn't move. Just stared out at the muddied traffic and hazy gray rain like I did. Strangely, knowing my father hired him to tail me made things a little easier—at least I understood why he was following me around.

"Still on the clock?" I asked.

"Nope. Quit today." He held up a check, tucked it in his coat pocket. "I don't get involved in family disputes."

"Right," I said.

He was quiet, still, patient. I decided I liked that about him.

"Buy you lunch?" he asked.

"Not hungry."

More quiet, except for the traffic and constant city sounds. A cab pulled up, and it made sense I should take it home. Instead, I just stood there while a short blond woman in a dark green trench coat appeared from the next building and scurried into the backseat. She looked vaguely familiar, but I couldn't put my finger on where I might have seen her before. I clenched my fist around the little book in my pocket where I wrote the things that I didn't want to forget. I needed to record the hit on Boy and the meeting with my dad so I could add them to my files.

I stopped trying to place where I'd seen the woman and instead watched the cab drive away.

Zayvion said nothing.

My whole body was stiff, and standing in the cold wasn't making anything better. I couldn't bring myself to give up and go home to my empty apartment. Not yet.

Could I have been mistaken about my father's signature? No, I just felt vulnerable right now because dear old Dad had used Influence, and Influence always made me jumpy. I was not going to let him get the best of me like that. Besides, it was still my birthday.

I looked over at Zayvion. Okay, so he worked for

my father. We all make mistakes. At least he had the sense to quit. And he was standing here, beside me right now, not in there with my dad. That suddenly meant a lot to me.

"How about we get a cup of coffee?" I said.

He looked a little surprised, then smiled that nice smile. "How about we do."

I tucked my hands in my pockets and we headed down the sidewalk toward a deli I knew about. The coffee wouldn't be as good as Get Mugged, but it would be hot and dark. Right now that was all I needed.

While we were there I might even have a chance to find out what Zayvion knew about my father. I owed it to Mama and Boy to follow this trail as long as it was fresh. Going out with Zayvion was all about following the trail, I told myself. This was not a date.

At the crosswalk, I glanced at Zayvion and decided he looked good in profile too. A strong nose to go with those high cheekbones, and an angle to his jaw I found intriguing. Okay, maybe it really was a little bit like a date.

He caught me looking. "What are you thinking, Ms. Beckstrom?" he asked.

My stomach flipped.

"Nothing," I lied. And we walked the rest of the way in silence.

Chapter Two

Cody did not like the man who came to visit him. The man stood by the door that would not open. The man watched as Cody sat on the floor and rocked. Rocking was good. Rocking made Cody happy. But the man did not make him happy. The man was quiet and had not moved for a long time. And even though Cody tried not to look, he could see what was underneath the man's skin. Something wriggled and twisted there. Something like worms, but worse. Something bad.

Cody rocked and rocked and looked at the gray floor. He could not remember how long he had been here, in the room that was just ten steps by ten steps wide. He did remember why he had been brought here. He had been bad. He had used magic wrong. He had used magic and pretended to be somebody else, somebody important and powerful and rich. And he had hurt someone.

It had been fun to be a powerful man. But it had been wrong. He had to talk to a lady in a black robe. He didn't tell her that the man by the door had told him he would hurt his friends. He hadn't told the lady in the black robe the other things the man by the door had made him do with magic. Didn't tell her all the other people the man had made him pretend to be. Cody was really good at pretending to be people with magic. He was really good at keeping secrets too. Better than any of his friends at home.

The lady in the black robe had said he was guilty. So now he lived here, in this room. He missed home, and missed his friends who lived with him, and missed bus rides to the park.

He missed the sky and grass and the wind and the sun. He missed the sun the most.

But rocking made a little wind. And it made him a little warm, like sitting in sunshine. So he liked rocking. Rocking made him happy.

He rocked for a long time, but the man did not go away. Pretty soon, Cody couldn't help himself. He peeked at the man and saw the man's quiet outside and his twisting, angry inside. The angry thing inside the man looked back at him. It scared him and he didn't even know what it was.

A snake, the older, smarter part of him said.

Cody smiled. He liked it when the older, smarter part of him talked because he was always right. The man was a snake inside. Snake man. Snake man. Snake man. Cody sang it inside his head and he was so happy, he sang it with his mouth too.

"Snake man, Snake man, bake a cake man."

But that was a bad idea because the Snake man heard him. And the Snake man moved.

Cody rocked harder, faster. He rocked even though it made his back hurt and he hit his head on the wall behind him and he had to breathe with his mouth open. He rocked faster so he could get away. Get away from the Snake man who was walking now, walking toward him, walking with soft, slow steps, bending down so he could see all the way into his eyes, so close, the Snake man could bite him. The Snake man was angry. But Cody had been really good. He hadn't told anyone about the Snake man. He had kept all the secrets.

The Snake man reached out and put his hand on Cody's shoulder. His fingers squeezed.

Cody didn't want to stop rocking. He liked the heat, he liked the wind. He didn't want to stop and have to just be here, in the room that didn't have a sky. But the Snake man's hand made him stop rocking. It made him stop breathing hard. It made him stop everything.

Don't look, the older, smarter part of him said.

But Cody had to look. The Snake man made him look, all the way into his snake eyes. All the way into the twisting, burning magic under his skin. And he could not look away.

"Hello, Cody. Do you remember me?"

Cody did remember him. He remembered everything about him. He nodded.

"Good." The Snake man smiled, but only on his outside. On his inside he twisted and burned.

"You did such a good job keeping our secret. Now I have a surprise for you."

He reached into his pocket and pulled out a very small, gray kitten.

"Oh," Cody said, happy now, happier than he ever had been his whole life. He unlocked his hands from around his knees.

Don't, said the older, smarter part of him.

"Go ahead," Snake man said. "She's yours. A friend." Snake man held the kitten out a little more and Cody touched the soft gray fur on her head.

The kitten mewed and Cody pulled away.

The Snake man's voice got silky. "See how happy she is to meet you? She said hello. You are going to be best friends."

"Friends?" Cody asked. He remembered his friends back home, and he missed them. Missed them maybe more than the sun. Yes, more than the sun.

"Of course she's your friend. Your new friend. Your best friend. Do you want to hold her?"

No, said the older, smarter part of him. *No. Rock. Just rock.*

But Cody did want to hold her. He wanted very much to hold her. He wanted to hold her more than he wanted to rock.

He nodded.

"Good boy," the Snake man said. And then he put the kitten in Cody's hands. The kitten mewed again.

Cody smiled and drew the kitten close to his chest. He bent his head over her to keep her warm and to keep her safe. "Hello," Cody said. "Hello." The kitten's fur was softer than the bunny they had for a little while at the home. It made him happy to have a friend again.

"You did a good job keeping our secret, Cody," the Snake man said. "I'm proud of you. And because you've been so good I'm going to let you keep the kitten."

Cody smiled up at the Snake man. Maybe not all snakes were bad. Maybe Snake man wasn't bad. "Mine. Mine now?" he asked, just to make sure.

"Yes, she is yours," Snake man said. "But first you need to do one more thing for me. Can you do one more thing for me, Cody?"

Say no, Say no.

"No," he said.

Snake man looked surprised. "Oh, that's too bad. Then I have to take her away."

Cody tried to hold on to the kitten, but the Snake man was fast. He snatched up the kitten and took her away.

"No!" he cried.

The Snake man stood. He was tall, and powerful, and angry. He held the kitten out by the back of her neck. Kitten twisted and mewed and shook. "That was a bad answer, Cody," Snake man said. "You've done a very bad thing. And since you don't want a friend, I'll have to kill her now."

The Snake man put both hands around the kitten, one all the way over her head. He twisted his hands.

"No!" Cody jumped up and grabbed for Kitten. He was almost as tall as Snake man, but Snake man was faster. Much faster. He pulled the kitten out of Cody's reach.

"If you want Kitten to live, you must do magic for me. You must pretend to be someone else again."

No, no, no, no!

The kitten gave out one small mew, muffled by the Snake man's hand.

"Please," Cody said. "Don't hurt her. Please?"

"Do magic for me."

No!

Somewhere inside the Snake man's hands, the kitten mewed, but she did not move. She wasn't fighting anymore. She was doing what Snake man wanted her to do.

"You can have a friend, Cody. She's right here. All you have to do is say yes."

No!

"Yes," Cody whispered.

"Good, Cody, good," Snake man said. "I'm proud of you. You did a good thing." He took his hand off the kitten's head, but still held her tightly in one fist. Kitten shook her head and sneezed, and Cody might have laughed about that, but he was too sad. He knew Snake man wanted him to do a bad thing. He knew it would be another secret he had to keep. He didn't want to keep any more secrets. He didn't want to be bad again.

"Now, I'm going to hold the kitten so you can use both your hands, okay?" Snake man said.

Cody nodded. What else could he do? He didn't want his friend to die.

"Good." Snake man walked over to the door. There was a chair in the corner, and on that chair was a little box that could fit in Cody's pocket. The box was made out of black metal and glass and had so many loops of wire wrapped around it, it looked like a square of spaghetti.

Snake man pushed the chair with the little box on the seat over to Cody.

"Remember this little box, Cody? It is very rare. The only one of its kind in the world. Do you like it?"

Cody liked the little box. He knew it was full of magic. But that was part of what made it bad. Cody was not supposed to touch magic. Not back at the home, not in the park, not anywhere. Usually, he didn't mind. Sometimes his guardians would do little things with magic, like help a seed sprout, make the lightbulbs turn a pretty color, or snap their fingers and make a spark. But Cody only did bad things with magic, which was why he couldn't touch it anymore. That was okay, because magic made his head itch on the inside.

But this box was special. The magic inside of it was easy to touch and easy to use. The Snake man said it was a very rare box, and the wires around it were rare too. Cody thought rare meant good. He secretly loved the box because the last time he touched the magic inside of it, he didn't feel tired, and his head didn't itch.

"Now," Snake man said. "You and I are going to play again. I am going to make a picture of a man, and he is a bad man. You are going to be strong and brave. You are going to make the bad man fall down."

"Like the bad little boy?"

"Just like the bad little boy. This time you are going to pretend to be a girl when you make the bad man fall down." The Snake man held out a picture of a lady with short dark hair and pretty green-colored eyes. She was wearing a dress and standing next to a man who was a little bit taller than her, and older than her, but looked a lot like her. He was wearing a dark suit and tie and wasn't smiling.

"Okay," Cody said, even though he didn't want to be a girl.

"Can you see what her magic is?" Snake man asked.

Cody took the picture and held it in both his hands. He looked at it for a really long time. It was hard to see the magic inside of people in pictures. It was much easier to see the magic inside of people when he was close to them. But Cody could do it. He had done it before. It was just hard.

He looked at the smiling girl for a long time. Looked at her until her outside went away and all that was left was her inside.

"Oh," he said. "Pretty."

"Good," Snake man said. "Can you pretend to be just like her?"

Cody nodded. "Easy, easy. Like me."

The Snake man made a surprised sound. "Are you sure? Look at her again, Cody. Make sure you can do this just right."

Cody looked up at Snake man. He knew he could be just like the girl because she was like him. Not on the outside, but on the inside, where the magic was. "I can do it," Cody said.

The Snake man smiled. "That's good. I'm counting on you to do your best. Kitten is too." Snake man reached down and pulled the lid off the little box.

Cody smiled. He could really feel the magic now. It made him think of water, clean and cool and wet; it made him think of sunshine, and he missed sunshine. He wanted to touch the magic.

No, the older, smarter part of him said. *It is wrong. Don't do this for him.*

"Do it for Kitten," Cody said out loud.

"That's right," Snake man said, even though Cody hadn't been talking to him. "Do this so Kitten can be your friend."

Cody licked his lips and looked at Kitten in the Snake man's hand. He could do this. It was right to help a friend.

He dropped the picture of the lady on the floor and sat down in front of the chair. He reached out and dipped his fingers into the box. His fingertips brushed across three cool metal circles that felt like big coins. It wasn't the box that held the magic, it was the coins.

But oh, the magic was wonderful. It was cool and soft and thicker than water. It filled him up, and he liked it. The older, smarter part of him reached out for him, and he reached back and he could see all the wonderfulness of the magic in his hand and had all the words he needed to describe it. He could make the magic do anything he wanted it to do.

"Remember the girl, Cody. Make the magic look like her magic," the Snake man said.

Cody could do that. He could pretend he was the girl. It would be easy. He breathed in the magic, and memories of his life before this place came back to him. Yes, he was good with magic. He was very good. He was an artist—a Hand. He had infused art with magic and he had made a lot of money. But he had lost a lot of money and gone in debt with the wrong people.

To pay back those debts, he had forged magical signatures on Offloads for them. Untraceable signatures. He was so good at it that he started making money. A lot more money than he'd ever made off his art.

And he had made the wrong people angry.

But right now those memories were inconsequential compared to the rush of having magic, of using magic, of finally being able to create with magic again.

He flicked his fingers and magic, in ocher, gold, plum, and sparks of sapphire wove up his fingers, laced around his arms like metal ribbons. He used his fingertips like brushes and painted the woman's strong, confident signature, creating an intricate glyph that glittered above the box like a necklace of sparkling jewels.

"Good," the Snake man said. "Now give it to me."

Cody was rapt, caught by the complexity of the woman's magical signature. She was different than him in ways that were intriguing. He had thought she was an artist, a Hand, but she was much more than that. Her signature carved a picture of a woman whose strength ran deep. Magic burned fiercely bright within her, but she was fragile in unexpected ways. She wasn't a Hand like him. She was something he'd never seen before. He traced his fingers along the trailing edge of the glyph, trying to see what it was about her that felt so different.

"Cody, take your hands away from the box."

The kitten mewed and Cody remembered why he was doing this. He had to save the kitten. Something seemed wrong about that, but magic was flowing through him, and he didn't want to let it go. Then a hand pressed down on his shoulder, and he was suddenly very sleepy.

"Give it to me." Snake man let go of his shoulder and took the little box away from Cody. The Snake man dumped the coins into his hand and something else fell out with them. A bone. A little bone that Cody knew had belonged to a child—a girl who had been good with magic when she was alive. But now that she was dead, her bone contained traces of a different kind of magic. Something dark. Something bad.

The Snake man held Kitten in one hand, and the coins, bone, and a knife in the other.

Cody didn't know where the knife had come from, but there was blood on it. Blood in the hand that held Kitten. Blood on Kitten. Cody whispered a mantra to release the signature spell and the Snake man caught the glyph up quickly with the bloody tip of the knife.

For one disorienting second, Cody thought the Snake man had killed Kitten, but she mewed.

Then Cody worried about something else. The Snake man carved a wicked pattern of magic and blood into the air with the tip of the blade, the knife weaving through the signature spell Cody had created. The Snake man muttered a guttural mantra Cody had never heard before.

This was not blood magic. This was darker. A spell that seethed with anger and pain, and grew stronger with every drop of blood that fell to the floor.

Dark magic, death magic. Forbidden. No one could force magic to follow such fouled and tangled glyphs and survive the casting. Magic had its own natural laws, and one of them was that it only followed certain patterns or combinations of patterns. Forcing magic to follow lines contrary to its natural patterns carried a price so high that magic would lash back and consume the user before the spell was complete.

Maybe the Snake man didn't know that.

Or maybe he was counting on it.

The knife slashed through the air just as the Snake man lunged for Cody. Cody threw himself back, but was not fast enough. The bloody knife sliced across Cody's stomach.

The Snake man changed the mantra, lifting his voice to cover Cody's scream.

Cody's blood and Snake man's blood flowed over the coin and over the little bone that the Snake man pressed into Cody's wound. The coin's magic, the Snake man's magic, and the signature glyph mingled and poured into the bone. And then all that magic mixed up to become something else. Something wrong that was so cold, it burned.

Death magic.

The Snake man yelled the last word of the mantra and released the spell with such force and hatred, it left the bitter smells of chemicals and burned skin in the room.

Cody moaned. He couldn't think. The memories of what he had been, of who he had been, were gone, and the older, smarter part of him was silent. His head hurt. His whole body hurt. He wanted Kitten. He wanted the pain and the coins and the bone and everything to go away.

He felt the box close around the coins and the bone, felt it because his blood was in there too. He didn't like the little box now. Didn't like it at all. Still the pain did not go away.

He wanted the sun. He felt all alone and lost. Cody began to cry.

Everything was quiet in the room. The Snake man took a deep breath and let it out. "You did good, Cody. You did very good." The Snake man helped Cody stand, and then helped him take a few steps and lie down on the bed.

"Did you get hurt?" the Snake man asked.

Cody nodded. "You hurt me."

"No. You got in the way of the magic, Cody. You shouldn't have gotten in the way." The Snake man smiled on the outside and hated on the inside. "It's not too bad though. You're lucky you didn't die. Let me make it better." He reached down for Cody's T-shirt and Cody pushed his hands away.

"No."

"I can't make it better if you don't let me look at it," Snake man said. "Here, you can hold the kitten." He put the kitten on Cody's chest.

Cody scooped her up close to his neck so she wouldn't get messy with his blood; so she would be safe and far away from the Snake man.

Snake man went over to the door, and when he came back, he pulled up Cody's shirt and cleaned off the blood with a soft cloth. Then he sprayed his stomach with something that stung a little and made the cut go numb. The Snake man put a bandage over the cut.

"There. Not too deep at all. You did good, Cody." Snake man brushed his fingers over Cody's hair. He held the box with the coins, the bone, and the knife in his other hand. "Just rest now. I'll be back soon and take you for a ride, okay? Just me, you, and Kitten."

Cody tried to smile. A ride sounded good. Maybe to the park. Maybe to someplace that had sunshine.

The Snake man pressed fingers that were mostly clean on Cody's forehead. Cody felt heavy and tired. He wanted to get the kitten some water, or maybe some food, but he could not move, and even though the kitten mewed, he fell quickly down into darkness.

Chapter Three

Zayvion held the deli door open for me. Old-school chivalry. Nice. I walked into the heat of the deli, into the smell of soup and spices and Parmesan crisping in butter. My stomach knotted with hunger. No surprise there; I hadn't eaten since yesterday.

A small wood table by the window was empty, so I threaded between the early lunch crowd to get to it. Once there, I paused and took a deep breath, preparing for the unique aches in store for me as I tried to take my coat off.

"Want any help with that?" Zayvion asked.

"I got it." Actually, I had already worked up a sweat just unzipping my coat. Getting my left arm out of the sleeve without dislocating something or having all the muscles down my back cramp into one solid knot was looking pretty grim.

Zayvion moved behind me, silent even on the hardwood floor, and gently tugged on my cuff.

"It's okay," I said. But I liked the sensation of him behind me, so close I could feel the heat of him.

"Mmm." Zayvion held the left cuff until I extracted my arm and then he sort of slipped to the side, leaned close, and pulled my coat the rest of the way off. He draped the coat over the back of a chair before I could come up with a comment about him keeping his hands off my outerwear.

I didn't know whether to be attracted or worried. I didn't like it when people invaded my personal space, and liked it even less when I was hurting. But Zayvion had been helpful, and hadn't touched more than my coat.

It was a really nice thing for him to do.

We stood there for an awkward moment while I breathed far too heavily for just a coat unzipping—I mean, I'd walked several blocks in the rain to this place and done okay.

My stomach did more than flip; it rolled and cramped, and a wave of nausea washed over me. The heavy smells of garlic, salt, grease, beans, wet coats, cologne, and hair spray, not to mention the gritty stink of diesel and oil from traffic outside, made it pretty clear that instead of being attracted, or confused, I was going to be sick.

The sweat on my skin went greasy cold and Zayvion got a worried look on his face. He put his hand on my arm. "Okay. Why don't you sit down, Allie. I'll get you some water."

I'm not the kind of girl who does what someone tells me to do, but my vision was going dark around the edges and little sparks of light were doing the cha-cha in front of my eyes. I carefully sat in the chair and propped my forehead against the cool window, not caring what the people beyond the glass or around me thought. I stared at a spot on the wooden window-sill, two carved zeros that were not quite connected enough to symbolize eternity, and breathed very evenly through my mouth, telling myself I was not going to throw up in the middle of this deli like some drunk in a soup kitchen.

A cool, light cloth draped the back of my bare neck.

"Do you need a bucket?" Zayvion asked from behind me.

"No," I gritted.

He lifted what I assumed was a wet towel. I felt the sticky heat of the diner on the back of my neck again, then the coolness of the other side of the rag. As he turned the towel, his fingers rested against the back of my neck, at the base of my skull.

His fingers were cool, like mint. I opened my mouth to tell him to leave me alone for a minute, but instead of words all that came out was a soft moan. That cool mint feeling from his fingers spread up my neck to cradle the back of my head and quench some of the fire there, then worked down the back of my neck and spine and wrapped minty-cool around the hurt in my ribs and stomach. The pain eased off enough that I could think. And what I thought was, I was in pretty bad shape.

How stupid could I be to not set the Disbursement spell when I Hounded Boy? And how stupider could I be to go out for a cup of coffee with a man my father paid to stalk me while magic used me for a punching bag?

"Breathe," Zayvion said, so softly I knew he must have leaned forward to speak near my ear. I would have done almost anything so long as he didn't move his fingers away from my skin. He should be bottled and sold for migraine sufferers.

I took a slow, deep breath and the sick in my stomach let up a little more.

"Good," he said. "Now exhale."

I did that too, and moaned again as the nausea drained away, leaving me tired, achy, but functional. Then his fingers were gone, the cool wash of mint gone. I felt stiff and bruised, inside and out, but not as bad as before he touched me.

Zayvion sat on the other side of the table and picked up a cup of coffee I hadn't seen him bring over.

He glanced out the window, his eyes narrowing against the gray-white light, and took a drink.

"Thanks," I said.

He tipped the cup away from his lips. His eyes were brown, flecked with a gold I don't remember seeing before. "Sure," he said. "Any time."

I put my hands on the table and discovered there was a second cup of coffee and, next to that, a little saucer of individual cream pots and packets of sugar. I picked up the coffee and took a sip of it. Black and bitter, it washed the sour taste of spent magic out of my mouth and filled my sinuses with a sharp but pleasant burned smell.

"Nice trick," I said.

Zayvion blinked once, slowly. "Trick?"

"You set a Siphon to mitigate some of the pain from the price I'm paying for not setting a Disbursement spell, right?"

"Ah," he said. "That trick." He followed up that nonanswer with a Zen-like look.

But his eyes. Gold flecks burned where there had only been brown before, and an intensity flickered through his calm gaze. He had done something, something more than setting a Siphon—not that setting Siphons was easy. It took two full years of specialized education to be able to cast and set channels that slowly bled used magic back into the raw magic that pooled beneath the city. And not everyone who studied hard and practiced harder mastered that trick. The few who did were usually into the more advanced fields of body-magic integrations, people like doctors and the regulators who set tolerance levels for legal Proxies.

I'd seen Siphons set. I put a year of study into it myself before my professor told me I might as well waste my time failing at something I enjoyed. But I remember the basics. Enough to know that Zayvion had not set a Siphon. He'd done something else. Something that took even more skill.

"I'll be damned," I said. "You Grounded me."

Grounding was another matter altogether. It was equivalent to acting as a lightning rod for someone else and was usually done while the original caster was drawing on magic. It allowed a larger amount of magic to be accessed, and a smaller price to be paid by the original caster. The Grounder often bore a heavier burden of the pain—trying to match another person's magical style and ability was very difficult and dangerous. As so was using Grounding to mitigate the pain of using magic.

Zayvion's eyebrows went down and he tipped his chin to one side. "I'm not sure I follow."

"What are you?" I asked. "Master's level?"

He shook his head and took another drink of coffee. "I didn't go to college for magic."

"What did you go to college for?"

"The women." He smiled. "Oh, we aren't being that honest? Economics."

"So you're an economist who stalks people for money and just happens to have mastered the rare art of Grounding?"

"What can I say? I'm a complicated man. And I didn't Ground you."

I took another drink of coffee. He was so lying. "All right. Let's go with that. If you didn't set a Siphon, and didn't Ground me, how come I feel better?"

"Acupressure," he deadpanned.

"Acupressure?"

"Pressure points. It's a kind of massage that helps with muscle tension."

"I suppose you went to college for that too?"

"No, but maybe I should have. I've been told, on more than one occasion, that I have good hands."

I gave him back what I hoped was one of his blank stares. "Do you really expect me to buy that?"

That got a smile out of him, and damned if it didn't make me smile back. "Well, you don't have to buy it, or lunch," he said. "Both are on me. I've already ordered and paid, so no argument."

As if on cue, a girl came over with a platter that held two bowls of soup—beef vegetable, with what looked to be real chunks of fresh vegetables floating in the thick broth—and a side of sourdough bread.

My mouth watered so hard I had to swallow.

"Anything else?" the waitress asked as she put down the soup, bread basket, and two sets of napkin-rolled cutlery.

"Some water," Zayvion said. "For both of us, please."

She left and I stared down at my soup like I'd never seen food before.

"It's soup," Zayvion said. "Beef and vegetable. Oh. You're not a vegetarian, are you?"

"I love soup." Then I remembered he probably already knew that. He'd been working for my father and following me around for I didn't know how long. He probably knew a lot of things about me. Probably even knew what kind of underwear I wore.

Which begged the question. Was he a boxer or brief kind of guy?

Come on, Allie, I thought. *Stop being such a sap-*

head. This wasn't a date. Zayvion wasn't a friendly neighbor. He was someone to dig information out of. Information about the hit on Boy. Information about why my dad was suddenly so interested in pulling me back into the company and under his control.

I sat up a little straighter and unrolled the napkin and spoon. Zayvion might be a liar, a snitch, a stalker—whatever. I wasn't going to turn down a free meal or a chance to find out what he knew.

"How long have you been following me?" I said it as if the meeting had just been called to order and his sales performance were under review.

He already had his spoon in his hand and had taken a big bite of soup. He left the spoon in his soup, reached for the sourdough, broke off a fist-sized section, then dipped it in the broth. So he liked his bread without butter. Not really the kind of information I had hoped to get out of him.

"About two weeks."

Better.

I thought back on what had happened in the last two weeks and scooped broth in my mouth. Oh, good loves. It was perfect, salted and thickened with tomato and hints of basil and peppers. I wanted to lick the spoon, lick my fingers, then dive in face-first and lap up the entire bowl. Zayvion did not appear to be watching me. He was already through his first piece of sourdough and moving fast for a second.

I reached over for the bread, got there just before he did, and pulled the soft and warm center piece out of the loaf.

"Ha!" I held up the chunk of bread with the tips of my fingers. "Still warm." I snatched up a foiled pat of butter and spread it over the bread with my finger.

He didn't look concerned at my victory. "Only half

a loaf left? I suppose we could split it. Oh, wait." He took the remaining bread, dropped it in his soup, and smiled. "Maybe I'll just eat your share."

"What, no more Mr. Nice Guy?"

"Nobody gets between me and fresh sourdough."

"Bread fetish?"

"How about less talking, more eating?" He didn't wait for my reply before digging into his soup.

I took a bite of the buttered bread and then I didn't care what Zayvion did so long as he didn't get between me and the soup and bread. I put my spoon into action and devoured the soup. Hounding always makes me hungry—using any kind of magic usually makes me hungry—and I'd been cutting it pretty tight on grocery money lately. Actually, now that I thought about it, this was the first meal I'd had in the last month that wasn't a cold sandwich, cold cereal, or cold microwaved pizza.

But even hungry, I kept an eye on the door, and the people who came in and out of the deli in a steady stream. I didn't think my dad would go so far as to send the police to haul me in, but I wouldn't put it past him.

The waitress came with our water, refilled our coffee, and dropped another basket of bread on the table.

"Thank you," Zayvion said. I nodded my thanks. I would have said something, but my mouth was full of hot vegetables. I tore into the bread loaf, thought about keeping it all for myself, and knew I'd be sorry and probably asleep if I ate too much too quickly. I split the bread in two, handed half to Zayvion, and got busy buttering my portion.

"Why did my dad hire you?" I asked. "What did he want you to find out about me?"

Zayvion had finished his soup and sat back, coffee

in his hand. I watched him change from a flirty sourdough aficionado into a calm, expressionless man. Interesting. So the Zen bit was his professional mode. It made me wonder what line of business—besides poker—required that strong a poker face.

I took the last chunk of bread and ran it around the inside of the bowl to get any bits of soup I'd missed, sopped up the broth at the bottom, then popped the bite in my mouth.

The deli was getting crowded, full of lunchgoers content to stand and eat if it meant dodging the rain. With the growing noise and heat, my head and body aches were coming back.

Zayvion sipped coffee and watched me with that cool expression. I planted my elbows on either side of my bowl and laced my fingers under my chin. "What?" I said, pitching my voice so he alone could hear me over the crowd. "No quick answers? Talk to me, Zayvion Jones."

"About what? Weren't you the one who was telling me business matters are confidential? How would breaking that confidence be good for my reputation?"

"You have a reputation?"

He shrugged one shoulder. "I make a living."

"Stalking?"

"Not much money in stalking."

"So you're what, a detective? An economic spy? Why would my father hire an economic spy?"

"The only reason your father had one of his men approach me was because I know the neighborhoods in North Portland and he knew you had done some Hounding jobs there." He went back to staring out the window and drinking coffee.

He was lying. I could smell the sour tang of it on his skin. Plus, I knew my dad wouldn't do anything, not in his personal life, not in his business life, not in any other part of his life, so haphazardly. He didn't even choose his socks so casually.

Any sane woman would have cut her losses and called it a day. But it intrigued me that he would tell such an obvious lie, and then look away like he was sort of sorry when he did it. He didn't strike me as a stupid man. As a matter of fact, I was sure the harmless-tramp bit was a ruse. He had to know I was familiar with my father's fastidious attention to detail in all matters of business. So why lie?

"How many years have you been working for him?"

Zayvion did me the favor of eye contact. Then, quietly, "Four."

That smelled closer to the truth. I nodded. "Just me?"

He shook his head.

"Gonna tell me who else you tailed?"

He took a drink of coffee. "Buy you dessert?"

Back to avoidance mode. "How sweet. Tell me about the hit on Boy."

"What makes you think I know anything about Boy? You Hounded the hit. You tell me." Those eyes were all brown and fool's gold, and my stomach flipped.

Sweet loves, he was good-looking.

It would be so easy to put some Influence behind my questions and pry the truth out of him. Well, except I hurt, and was fatigued from using magic. I'd probably blow a vein if I tried to use any kind of magic, even the easy stuff that was most natural for me.

I rubbed my hand over my lips, which were still swollen.

"Listen," I said, changing tactics. "I'm tired. I want to go home and get some sleep. I'm not going to be able to do that knowing that a five-year-old child is dying because my father decided to Offload magic on the poor kid. You've been following me around. If you're any good at what you do, you know I think Mama is a decent human being. You know how I feel about Boy, and you probably even know exactly how I feel about my father and his business practices."

"Everyone knows how you feel about your father and his business, Allie. Dropping out of college, publicly disowning any contact with him, then going into hiding for the last few years paints a pretty clear picture."

Like I needed to be reminded of any of that. Still, it prickled. I just sat there, wondering how he could get under my skin so fast.

"So there's no mystery about how much I hate my dad." I smiled and told myself he didn't know, could never know, what it was like growing up under my father's Influence. There was a reason my mother changed her name and lived overseas, and hadn't ever tried to contact me. There was a reason he'd married and divorced four times since then. People in my father's life were commodities to be consumed and discarded. And I, his only child, was tired of being recyclable goods.

"Since you just quit your job and no longer work for Beckstrom Enterprises, I don't see any reason why you shouldn't tell me what you know about the hit. Why they did it and why Boy was the target."

He frowned and looked down at his hands.

"Zayvion," I said, "I don't want the kid to die. I'd like to think you're the kind of person who wouldn't want a little kid to die either."

"You Hounded the hit," he said. "Are you sure it was your father's signature?"

"Yes."

He looked back up and there was a fierceness in his eyes. "Do you think it could have been a forgery? Or someone else's signature? Something magically forged?"

"I know my father's mark intimately." End of discussion.

Zayvion glanced back out the window again, and I wondered if he were watching for someone, or maybe if he thought he was being watched by someone. Economics, my ass. This man was either a PI or an undercover cop.

"I don't know what to say," he said. "I have no idea why your father would Offload illegally. It seems like there would be too high a risk that he would be found out. He's a careful man."

That was an understatement.

"You know him better than I do." He looked back at me. "Why would your father do such a thing?"

And hearing someone else ask it brought a dozen answers to my mind. Maybe he knew I'd been nice to Mama and wanted to hurt me through her. Maybe Mama was indebted to him and had agreed to let him do it. Maybe he thought hurting the kid would get me storming into his office after seven years of avoiding him.

Maybe he'd done it for no reason at all.

I wanted to take the easy way and just believe my father was thoughtless in his cruelty, but I knew that wasn't true. He wouldn't have put a hit on Boy without weighing the risks and deciding the odds were on his side. And there was no way it could have been a random mistake—he was not that sloppy.

But what did he have to gain from Boy dying?

I shook my head, frustrated. "Do you think I'd be

sitting here having lunch with you if I knew the answer to that?"

Zayvion's expression went carefully blank. "No," he said, "I don't suppose you would."

I rubbed at my eyes and regretted it because they started to water. My head was pounding.

"Sorry. Don't take it personally. I wasn't kidding about having no social life. I'm a little rusty on the finer points of polite conversation. But tell me this: you weren't going to really help me, were you? Because you're still working for my father, right?" It was a hunch, but I was pretty sure I was right.

"I told you I quit."

"You told me you quit tailing me for money. Didn't say you quit working for Beckstrom Enterprises."

A little bit of sadness, or maybe guilt, seeped through the cracks of his calm expression. "No, I didn't."

"That's what I thought." I stood. It took me some time and effort to put my coat back on without grimacing, but I did it.

Zayvion didn't help me, which was smart since I would have smacked him if he touched me with so much as a single pinky. I should have known better than to like him. When people spent too much time around my father, they tended to get infected with his rotten morals and scruples. Too bad Zayvion hadn't gotten out when he had the chance.

"You should go see a doctor, Allie," he said softly.

"Is that you or my father talking?"

He just shook his head.

"Good-bye, Zayvion Jones." I zipped my coat. "Thanks for lunch."

I walked between the tables and made it out to the sidewalk, into the smell of smoke, oil, and wet, dirty concrete. People on their way to or from lunch moved around me, and I tried to decide if I could sweet-talk a cabbie into a ride home. I had zero money on me, zero money in my bank account, and my crappy apartment was miles away in Old Town.

Lovely.

I stood there, sore, hating the rain, hating my father, hating Portland. But mostly hating that someone who was nearly a stranger to me could make me like him so much in so short a time.

One thing I was clear about—I was a good Hound. One of the best. I knew how to do my job. And no soft-talking, mint-fingered Zen economist was going to convince me that I was wrong about that hit. My dad was behind it.

"Taxi!" Zayvion called out.

I hadn't even heard him come up beside me. That man was quiet when he wanted to be. "Don't bother," I said. "I can find my own way home."

Like magic, a cab appeared out of nowhere and pulled up to the curb.

Zayvion turned to face me. We stood almost eye to eye. I was tall but he still had an inch or so on me. "You might be a good Hound, Allie," he said. "And you might have your dad figured out, but you got me all wrong." He grabbed my wrist, turned my hand over, and pressed cab fare into my palm.

I should be angry. I should tell him to keep his money. I should pull away.

Instead, I took one step closer. I don't know what I was thinking—okay, I did know what I was thinking—I liked him, was drawn to him, despite my reservations, like a magnet pulled to steel. A jolt of hot, electric pleasure sparked through my body as I pressed against his warm, strong chest, hip, thigh. The smell of his cologne and the musky male scent of him filled me. Warm waves of need rolled beneath my skin. I could not think. I did not want to think. And I did not want to let him go.

So I kissed him.

I think he was surprised. Frankly, I was a little surprised too. But I was not disappointed.

What I thought would be a quick kiss stretched out into a lingering moment of discovery. His lips were soft and thick, and I sucked at them gently, pleased when his mouth caught mine in an even deeper embrace. I bit, but not hard, and he answered by drawing the tip of his tongue so slowly along the bottom of my lip that I could feel the echo of it vibrate through every pore of my being.

More, I thought.

But he pulled back, pulled away, and suddenly the rain, the noise, the city, and the world returned.

"Be careful," he whispered. He walked away, hands in his coat pockets, stocking-capped head bent against the falling rain. It took a blink, two, before he was swallowed by the crowd, hidden from my sight, gone. It took several more before I could think again.

The cabbie powered down the passenger-side window. "You want a ride, lady?"

I opened the back door and got in. "Fair Lead Apartments," I said.

The cab pulled out into traffic, and no matter how hard I looked out the rain-fogged windows hoping to catch a glimpse of Zayvion, he was not there.

Chapter Four

My apartment building is a dump. When it rains, it is not just the appearance of the building that reeks. It is also the walls.

I was halfway up the climb to my fifth-story apartment. With each step the smell of old magic got worse. Thirty years ago, when the technology was being developed to harvest wild magic, people thought all it took was a lightning rod—well, a Beckstrom Storm Rod—and some copper tubing to channel the magic throughout the city.

That could not have been further from the truth. Channeling magic through anything but iron, lead, and glass pipes that had each been carved and molded with very specific kinds of glyphing and holding spells made the channel useless, rotten, and dangerous.

This old building was lousy with rotten magic. The useless copper tubing was set inside the walls, as was the fashion thirty years ago. The idea was people wouldn't want to live in a building that looked like a birdcage. The result was having to tear the building down to access the tubing and not only reglyph the holding spells, but also replace the copper with something expensive and patent-permit laden. The owners of the Fair Lead didn't go out of their way to replace lightbulbs. So we dealt with the smell that always got worse when it rained.

By the time I reached my room on the fifth floor, I had to hold my hand over my mouth to keep from smelling, and worse, tasting the wet, rotten magic seeping out of the walls. It was a health hazard, I was sure of it, but if a few cockroaches could be ignored by greasing the right palm, then so could old magic. Even though it'd been thirty years, the law hadn't caught up with the use and misuse of magic.

I walked down to my apartment, put my key in the lock, and opened the door. The smell was twice as bad here. So bad that my eyes started watering.

Great.

A small flash of green halfway across the room told me there was a message on my answering machine. I crossed the room and pressed play.

"Hi, Al!" My best friend in all the world, Nola's warm, happy voice piped out of the machine. "Happy birthday! When are you coming out to the farm to visit me? I sent you a birthday present. Check your bank balance. There should be enough there for you to come out for a week. Leave a message at this number and let me know if you take the train or bus, and I'll meet you. I mean that. Oh, and Jupe says hi!"

The machine beeped and the sudden silence, along with the heavy smell, was just too much.

This birthday sucked.

But it was still my birthday. Three o'clock. I rubbed at the back of my neck. If I weren't feeling so bad, I'd go out, see a movie, maybe take some of Nola's gift money and treat myself to a pedicure. But it would be at least the rest of the night before the magic stopped hurting in me, and despite Zayvion's insistence that I go see a doctor, I knew a nice long bath and ten hours of sleep would get me through the worst of it. And that wouldn't cost me money I didn't have. But the smell in the house was unbearable.

Come on, Allie. Time to think smart and find a warm, odorless place to sleep for a few hours.

My hand hovered over my phone. Who could I call? Nola's farm was in eastern Oregon near Burns, a town almost three hundred miles away, at least a five-hour drive from here, so that wouldn't do. Who else did I trust? Ex-boyfriends came to mind, but there was a good reason each of them was an ex. I hadn't kept in touch with anyone from college, and being both unemployed and doing freelance Hounding jobs, usually at night, hadn't exactly created a close-knit social network. Sure, I knew a few of the other Hounds—Pike, for instance. But I didn't think an ex-marine who Hounded for the cops would put up with my whining. Other than Pike, not a single person came to mind.

I had to laugh. There were times when being a sour, distrustful, jaded young woman didn't make my life easy.

I could call my dad.

Not in a million months of never.

Mama. Though I didn't love the idea of ending up right back where I'd started the day, I figured she'd let me stay late at her restaurant, might even offer me a cot to sleep on if I paid her, or did dishes or something. Or maybe we could trade the Hounding job I did on Boy for a bed. Besides, I wanted to know if Boy was okay. Wanted to know if she'd called the police and what they were doing about the hit. They might even need to talk to me.

I picked up the phone and dialed Mama's number even though I knew she never answered the phone. Still, maybe this once. When the phone rang for the twentieth time, I gave up. If she said no, maybe I'd just get a cab to the bus station, and head out to Nola's. Fresh farm air sounded good right now. It wasn't a perfect plan, but it was a plan.

I grabbed a backpack—a hideously pink and green thing with a cow on it that Nola had given me years ago—and packed a change of clothes, an extra sweater, my tennis shoes, a brush, deodorant, and toothbrush. I left the apartment and the building as quickly as my swollen feet could take me down the stairs.

I caught a cab, told him to take me to the nearest ATM machine, and checked my balance while the meter was running. I was expecting maybe fifty dollars from Nola, but she had sunk three hundred bucks into my account. Maybe things were looking up.

I knew she made pretty good money for selling her certified nonmagically grown alfalfa. The horse-racing circuit considered any magical influence into the sport—including spells for pest removal, mold retardant, or growth enhancement on the alfalfa that fed the horses—to be as illegal as performance-enhancing drugs. Still, it wasn't like Nola was rolling in the dough. A hard rain at the wrong time could ruin a year's worth of work on a field, and the nonmagic eggs she raised didn't make up for those sorts of things. This was a generous gift and I owed her big-time.

I pulled out a hundred and got back in the cab. I hugged my jacket closer around me and watched the city fall apart the closer it got to St. John's. The ache in my head was getting downright migrainal. Even more fun was that I dozed off, or maybe blacked out. When the cab came to a stop I slugged out from under the lead blanket of sleep that weighed me down.

"Here it is," the cabbie said in a halfhearted stab at English. "I stop here."

I rubbed my eyes and still had trouble focusing. It looked like the right part of town. The problem was, every time I blinked it felt like it took forever to open my eyes again. All the running around in the rain, jogging of stairs, and most of all, the stupid payback for not setting a Disbursement spell, were finally catching up to me.

Either that, or Zayvion had poisoned my soup.

"Sixteen bucks," the driver said.

"Sure." I looked down at my hands, hoping for a purse or something, and realized I had a wad of bills clenched in my fist.

Smart like a rock, I am. My hands were the color of steamed grape leaves. Nice bruise, that. Then the driver's voice cut through the fog again.

"Sixteen dollar. This is the end."

And wow, that sounded really ominous, like if my life were a movie, this would be the part where the cabbie turned into a serial killer, pulled out the knife and hockey mask he kept in his glove compartment, and did me in. But not, of course, before he collected on his fare.

I giggled at that, and a small part of my mind, perhaps my common sense, started to worry. I was not thinking so straight. That was a bad thing to do anywhere in the city, and really bad—the dead kind of bad—in this neighborhood.

"Here." I put my money in my jacket pocket and gave the driver a twenty. He watched me from the rearview mirror. "No round trip," he said.

"Right. Thanks." I opened the door, got out into the rain. I tugged my neon backpack onto my shoulder, but didn't do it very well, because it made me really dizzy.

I staggered and caught myself on the edge of a trash can.

Lovely. I probably looked like a drunk just waiting for someone to roll me.

Come on, Allie, I thought. *Suck it up. It's not that far. Just a couple blocks.* I needed a bed in the worst way. Maybe I should have just put up with the stink back in the apartment. It was no worse than the stink coming out of the trash can I was holding on to. Too late to go back to my apartment now. There was no way I'd make it that far without passing out. But if I had anything to say about it, I wasn't going to sleep in the trash can either.

I lifted my head and held still as vertigo rocked the street beneath my feet like a hammock in a strong wind.

Just a couple blocks. I could do that.

I pushed away from the trash can, pulled my shoulders back, and took a deep breath. Even though my vision was spotty at best, my nose was still working. I caught the fish-and-salt stink off the river, the rust and oil from the train track and river traffic, and the pungent barf smell coming from, oh, I don't know—everywhere. The sweet smell of tobacco and charcoal, hinting of a wood fire down on the shoreline, wafted through the air. Along with all that, I could also smell the acrid tang of magic being used behind me, from the city proper. To get to Mama's all I had to do was walk toward the smell of old wood and hot grease and something kind of dirty, like wet dog and barf. Those smells.

I knew better than to show how bad I was feeling. So I set a confident stride, kept my head up, and looked around enough to signal to any circling predators that whatever they wanted from me, they were going to have to fight me for it.

I made it to Mama's without having to risk my life over my crummy backpack, walked up the three wooden stairs, and was winded like I'd just done a few record-breaking laps through quicksand.

Boy, behind the counter, watched me walk in. He frowned, glanced over my shoulder, then brought his hand up empty from where it had just been on the gun he kept there.

"Is Mama in?" I asked.

He nodded, but didn't do anything else for me.

Nice.

I walked the rest of the way into the restaurant. I eyed the spindly wood tables to the right and left and considered sitting down. But I knew, once I stopped standing I wouldn't be doing it for at least twenty-four hours.

"Listen," I said as I leaned my elbow, carefully, on the counter in front of Boy. Leaning felt good. Felt real good. Maybe I could just put my head down on the counter and let Boy figure out the rest of it. Surely I couldn't be the first woman who'd passed out on this counter. Probably wasn't even the first woman to do so this week.

I blinked, my chin dipped, and it took effort to fight my way up out of the quicksand that was dragging me down, especially since I was pretty sure I was still wearing my lucky lead coat.

Boy had a funny look on his face. Something between amusement and disgust.

Oh, good loves. I knew what he was thinking.

"I'm not drunk," I slurred.

Fabo. That sounded convincing. "I'm . . . I'm hurt." And I hated saying it, hated admitting it, hated hurting in front of him, in front of anyone. "I need a place to stay. Does Mama have a cot I could rent for the night? I have cash."

He raised his eyebrows and a wicked glint lit his eyes.

Oh, good going, Allie. Tell a man who is never three inches away from a gun that you have cash in your pocket.

"Not much," I amended, "but I could pay something." He just stared at me. Said nothing. I tried to remember if this Boy was mute. "Is Mama here?" I asked.

"I'm here," Mama's voice said from somewhere to my left.

Oh, it was going to take a lot to actually move my head. I weighed my options, and decided to go for broke. I turned my head and the room blurred. Little silver sparks wriggled like tadpoles around the edges of my vision moving in closer and closer until Mama and the whole wide world were far, far away at the end of a tunnel. Wow. Who needed drugs?

"Allie girl. Who does this to you?" Mama strode over to me. She reached up and gripped my face, her small, cool fingers on either side of my jaw. "This bad. A hit? Someone hit you?"

"It's my fault," I said. "I need a place to sleep. I can't go home."

She gave me a long, steady stare. I wondered what she was looking for in my eyes. Didn't know if it was there. Didn't much care. The room was going black, the tadpoles well on their way to full frogdom, and the pain in my head and bones sort of rattled through me in waves.

Mama's touch was like a cool rag on a fever. Like Zayvion's fingers. No, not like that, more like what

I'd always hoped my own mother would do for me—be caring and soft and make the pain go away when I hurt. Mama's hands created a wall between me and the pain, and I wondered if the pain wouldn't mind staying away for a while so I could get a little shut-eye.

Before I actually dozed off, Mama got tired of looking in my eyes. She lifted her hands from my face and nodded. "You hurt. Stay here. Upstairs. You think you can go upstairs, Allie girl?"

"Sure," I said. It came out a little slurred and slow, but true to my word, I pushed off the counter and let Mama, and her strong hand on my elbow, then her strong arm around my waist, lead me across the room and through the door to a narrow hallway where a zag of wooden stairs laddered up.

I remember taking the first step. The rest of the climb got fuzzy after that, and the next thing I saw was Boy—the one with the beard and ponytail who is usually in the kitchen—looking down at me. I was apparently flat on my back, and I hoped I was in a bed.

"What?" I said. Then Boy moved back and Mama was there. For reasons I didn't really want to analyze, I was really glad she was around right now.

She looked down toward my feet, which I thought rather odd; then she was back in my line of vision and something thick and soft was pulled up over me. A quilt. Oh, loves. It was almost enough to make a distrustful, jaded girl like me weep. Almost.

"You sleep now, Allie girl," Mama said firmly. "You sleep. Mama's here."

I had never been so happy in all my life to do exactly what someone told me to do.

Happy Birthday to me.

Chapter Five

Cody used to like rocking best of all, but now he liked sitting very still and watching Kitten play. Kitten wasn't very good at walking yet, but she could find the plate of water Cody put on the floor for her, and could stay quiet when the guard came by to look inside his room every day and night. She slept under his chin, and he liked that. She was warm, and good, and fun. She was the best friend ever.

Cody didn't know how long he and Kitten had been friends, but the cut on his stomach still hurt and, if he moved the wrong way, it felt hot and stiff like maybe it would bleed again. It didn't feel like it was getting better, and that worried him. But he was shy, so the guard didn't care that he undressed all by himself before taking a shower, and the guard didn't mind when he took a little extra meat from lunch or dinner and hid it in his pocket for Kitten.

Except that he still missed the sun and sky and his friends back at the home, things were really good.

Kitten was sniffing at the bottom of the door that would not open while Cody sat in the middle of the floor, holding very still, watching her. She mewed and ran across the floor to Cody. She still wasn't very good at running, and she tripped and slid.

Cody laughed.

Then he stopped laughing. The lock on the door that would not open clicked, and the doorknob moved. Someone was coming. Not a guard. Not a friend.

The Snake man, the older, smarter part of him said. *Hide Kitten. Hold still.*

Cody scooped Kitten off the floor and put her inside his shirt. She wriggled and poked him with her claws, but Cody bit his lip and did not move.

The Snake man was coming. Coming to get him.

The door opened and the Snake man walked in. He smiled and his dark snake eyes were shiny. He looked happy on the outside, but inside he was excited. Excited to kill.

Cody wanted to cry.

Oh, the older, smarter part of him said. *Go away, Cody. Fast. Think about the sunshine. Think about the sky.*

And Cody tried to. He tried to think about how nice the sunshine was, how warm and pretty. He thought about how it was yellow sometimes, and orange, and red, and white. He thought about the sky, but couldn't remember if it was blue or white or gray. He was scared. Really scared. He held his arm over Kitten, who was under his shirt. She stopped squirming.

The Snake man didn't say anything. He didn't lock the door behind him. Cody knew why. Someone was in the doorway. A big man, bigger than Cody had ever seen.

Death, the older, smarter part of him said.

And Cody knew he was right. That man, that big man was death. And in his pocket were bones, little children's bones full of bad magic. Bones like the one Snake man had used to hurt him.

Cody whimpered.

The big man walked into the room. Just one step. Just one. He looked at Cody for so long that Cody started crying. The big man did not come any closer, but Cody could feel the big man's hands move over his skin, squeezing him to see if he was ripe.

"Well?" Snake man asked without looking away from Cody.

"No," the big man said. "Broken as a shattered jug. Won't be nothing left in him to use. That's a shame. A damn shame. You were someone once, boy. Someone." Then the big man turned and walked away.

But the Snake man did not turn. The Snake man did not walk away. He came closer. And he was smiling.

He pulled a coin out of his pocket—a magic coin—and a little bone. He had something shiny in his other hand too, but it was not a coin. It was a knife.

The Snake man smiled more. "Good-bye, Cody. It's been nice doing business with you."

Cody didn't know which thing would hurt him more, the knife or the magic in the coin or the magic in the bone.

All of it, the older, smarter part of him said. *Reach for me.*

But it was hard to reach to the older, smarter part of him. He had tried to do it a lot before, and never did it right.

The knife flashed up, the Snake man intoned a mantra that was so bad, so very bad. The coin filled the Snake man's words with power and the bone changed it into something worse. Into death. Cody knew he was going to die. In the dark, without sunshine.

No! The older, smarter part of him said. *Reach for the coin, for the magic in the coin.*

Cody was crying now. He didn't want to die. Didn't want Kitten to die. So he reached for the coin, for the warm, pretty magic there. And he took some of it. He took it and the older, smarter part of him reached out for it too, and reached out for him.

Hang on, the older, smarter part of him said. *Don't let go, no matter what.*

Cody held on. Held on while the Snake man finished the angry, bad magic. Held on while the knife came down. Held on while the pain shot through him and made him scream. Held on to the older, smarter part of him, while the older, smarter part of him held on to him and to something else—the magic in the coin. Cody wished he could have said goodbye to Kitten.

The knife pushed under his skin again.

He wanted to scream, but couldn't hear anything except the older, smarter part of him chanting soft words that moved the magic in a different way, painting a picture of sunshine and sky. Then the pain was so big that it covered up the sunshine, it blacked out the sky, and Cody was squished into a dark box where he couldn't see or hear anything anymore, not even the older, smarter part of himself.

Chapter Six

There are reasons why I like to sleep in my own bed. One, I have good pillows. Even though the mattress is too hard, as long as I have enough pillows, I don't care. The other reason I like sleeping in my own bed is because gorillas with baseball bats don't come in the room and bash in my head while I'm asleep.

So when that sudden, explosive pain hit, I knew right off that I wasn't at home. I groaned, opened my eyes, and tried to match where I was to places where I might fall asleep. It was a narrow room lit by a small yellow-shaded lamp in the corner. The walls were painted in we-didn't-even-care-the-first-time-we-painted-it beige. A white and blue quilt spilled over onto a wood floor that had been so worn down it looked more like bark than wood.

But the quilt was clean, thick enough that I suspected feathers inside, and looked homemade. I leaned over, almost lost my lunch to the pounding pain inside my skull, and with much careful breathing pulled the quilt off the floor and back onto the bed with me.

Sweet hells, I hurt. But it was not the same pain I'd

been in from using magic. This was different. Deeper. It made me feel really sad and really alone.

Then, as fast as it had hit, the pain was gone. I wiped at the wet on the corners of my eyes. That had been the worst headache I had ever experienced. I took a couple of breaths, and was relieved that really, all the rest of me was feeling pretty good. But the headache, or maybe the haunting absence of that sudden pain, left me feeling horrible in a different way. I was crying, actually crying, like I hadn't since I was ten. But why?

The wispy fragments of a dream brushed across my thoughts; someone was gone, missing. Hopelessness washed over me like when I'd been told my mom had left the country. I wanted to curl up under the quilt and never come out.

I'd just lost someone or something important to me. But I didn't know why I thought that. I must be tired. Just tired.

I wiped my face on my sleeve and took a look at my hands. Still a little yellow from the bruising, but not the angry black and purple-red they'd been last time I'd looked at them.

The digital clock next to the bed read five a.m. I'd slept over twelve hours. I had better write down the details of the hit on Boy and the meeting with my father in my little book while I had the chance. When I got home, I'd take some time and transfer the notes to my computer.

It was strange to have my entire life, or at least the important bits I didn't want to forget, recorded by hand and backed up electronically. It made sense to do it for the jobs I Hounded, but sometimes when going through the book I ran across a detail, like "always take the right trail in the park" or "parrots don't work" that were obviously personal experiences I no longer retained.

Sometimes I felt like a ghost in my own life.

I sat up and turned on the bedside lamp. Mama had left me in my jeans and tank top and put my extra sweater on me, and had draped my coat over the foot of the bed. I tugged the coat up to me, and dug the leather-bound journal and pen out of the pocket.

The first page of the book had my vital information. My name, birthday, blood type, medical allergies, things of that manner. So far I hadn't forgotten those things, but it was a grim and very real possibility that one day I might. I didn't like to think about it, but it would be stupid to not take what precautions I could.

I thumbed back to a blank page and started with the date and time of Mama's call.

It didn't take me long. I'd had lots of practice, in college and otherwise, to make my notes as short, clear, and concise as possible.

I tucked the book back in my coat and turned out the lamp. But instead of drifting back to sleep for maybe another hour, I tossed and turned, the lingering sadness and loss from the dream filling my thoughts.

For no reason at all, I kept thinking about my father. Not about his anger and manipulation, but about the feel of his blood and mine joined, his regret when he said, "I'm sorry," and how genuine that felt.

I should have stayed away. Stayed away for another seven years.

I finally got up and walked across the dark room to the window. I tugged back a corner of the curtain, not sure I was ready for actual sunlight yet. I needn't have bothered being so cautious. It was not daylight out, not even close. The sky was black as a hangover, and the alley below the window didn't have a light anywhere along it. I was on the second floor, so I could see around one building with windows that were broken out, and there was plenty of light from the other streets, lights that burned brighter the farther away from St. John's they were.

St. John's wasn't like what I expected from this vantage. This early in the morning, it carved a strong ebony edge against the burning yellows and blues of the city, like the mountains against sunrise. And there was a kind of haphazard sense of power in the short, strong buildings that were still standing, a squared-off victory over time, over manipulation, over magic. It survived despite the changing world.

St. John's had power to withstand poverty, neglect, pain. Maybe that was what I liked about it. Because there were people in these buildings who hadn't given up, hadn't tried to be anything other than what they were, hadn't tried to conform to what the world expected them to be. There were other people too, the kind who migrated here like rats to garbage. Even so, good people remained—people like Mama and her Boys. Those deep roots made this dump feel more like home than the penthouse condo of my childhood.

A motion at street level caught my eye. A big, heavy man in a dark trench coat moved down the street, stepping around piles of what I hoped were just garbage and cardboard. He was coming from somewhere farther north, moving out of deeper shadow into faint streetlight.

A chill ran over my skin. There was something about the big man that gave me the creeps. I watched as he strolled along, trying to figure out what bugged me about him.

He was almost out of my line of vision, moving in front of the building that blocked my view farther down the street. I shifted on my feet, curling up so I put some weight on the side of my foot. I drew the curtain back a little more.

The man stopped. It was like watching an old movie where a mime runs into a glass wall. He threw a hand in front of him and looked over his shoulder. But instead of looking back into the darkness, he looked up. At me.

Like I said before, it was dark out, dark in the room, and I hadn't brought a night-light with me. There wasn't a single way he could see me, standing behind a dark curtain, in a dark room, wearing a dark sweater and jeans.

But his face was tilted up toward me. I saw his mouth open, as if he had just said the word no. I could see the shadow-smudged thumbprints where his eyes should be, and I knew he saw me. I stared right back at him, because if there's one thing I won't do it's back down once I'm spotted.

My heart beat hard, and I wished I had on my boots, my running shoes, anything. Instinct told me to run. Instinct told me he was dangerous.

I could handle dangerous. Dangerous and me went back a long way. We did lunch when dangerous was in town.

The man lifted a hand toward me and I felt, very clearly, his fingers, like heated oil, slide down my spine, thump over each vertebra, and then squeeze.

I caught my breath because it felt really real. And it creeped me the hell out.

I let the curtain drop and stepped away from the window. Groping someone without their permission was against the law, magic or no magic. Breaking the line of vision was usually enough to dispel that kind of spell. But just in case, I backed away to the door and made a warding gesture. The sensation of his hand down my back had already faded, so I didn't invoke a spell or draw any magic into that ward, but I rubbed my hands up and down my arms trying to rid myself of the sense of violation.

His touch might be gone, but my heart was still pounding. That had been familiar. That man down there, whoever he was, had touched me before.

I tried to draw up a memory that he fit. A client? An acquaintance? Someone from college? An associate of my father's? But where there should be a name, or a defined face in my memory, all I found was black static.

A chill rattled under my skin and I clenched my hands into fists, then shook them out. That man touched me, bone deep, without my consent. He knew me. And he knew I was here, up here, in this room.

"Oh, hell," I whispered.

There was no way I was going to just sit here. For all I knew, he was on his way up now. I didn't know why, but getting away from him, shaking the scent of him—rot, and something like licorice or honey mixed with the faint whiff of formaldehyde—had become the top item on my agenda for the day.

Okay, I wanted out, out of here, out fast.

I looked for my backpack and found it on the wooden chair by the bed. I picked it up, took the time to shove my feet into my shoes and tie the laces so I wouldn't trip. I pulled on my coat, patting my pocket to make sure the book was there.

The other pocket had money, so I pulled out a twenty and threw it on the mattress. Mama's generosity was a bridge I didn't want to burn.

I wanted to run. I needed to run. I knew he was coming for me. I could feel him moving through the darkness below into the light of Mama's restaurant. I could smell him. Could smell the rotted stink of magic he'd used on me. I had to leave. Now.

I looked at the window, but some practical part of my mind calmly listed the injuries I'd get if I tried to hero it down the outer walls of this dump. Right. Probably best to escape through the door. Any time now. Now would be good. Before he made it up the stairs.

I swung my backpack over my shoulder and hurried to the door again. I listened for footsteps. My heart was beating so loudly that I had to hold my breath to hear. Nothing. No sound at all from the other side of the door.

I opened the door as quietly as I could and checked the hall in the dim light of a couple low-watt bulbs in the ceiling. Just a hall with a few closed doors, and the wooden-railed staircase going down. And that's exactly where I was going too. I closed the door behind me and walked over to the stairs, insanely grateful that I'd packed my running shoes. I looked down the stairwell. Pockets of shadow swallowed whole sections of the stair. Anyone could be in those shadows. He could be in those shadows. I hesitated.

What if he were waiting for me on the stairs? I didn't like small spaces, and especially didn't like fighting in them.

But there were other ways I could defend myself. Like magic. I was a Hound. I had certain abilities at my disposal. All I had to do was calmly draw upon the magic within me and use it to see where the man was. It was even possible he wasn't in the building. Maybe he had just walked on. Maybe this was all in my head and I was panicking for no reason.

I shivered even though it was warm and damp in

the hall. Instinct told me someone was nearby and looking for me. Instinct had never been wrong about these kinds of things before.

I silently recited a mantra, the one that always calmed me down no matter how freaked out I was. A mantra could be anything you could actually remember in times of panic. Mine happened to be the childhood chant Miss Mary Mack. *Miss Mary Mack, Mack, Mack, all dressed in black, black, black, with silver buttons, buttons, buttons, all down her back, back, back* . . . and again, all the while listening for footsteps and keeping a nose out for the smell of him. Finally, my shoulders relaxed and my breathing slowed. Good. Now all I had to do was draw upon magic.

Nothing. I felt as empty as a beggar's pocket. No magic here, not even old copper channels. It didn't mean it was impossible to tap into the magic—that guy out on the street had done just fine. It did mean it was difficult.

The small magic I carried within me seemed like a tiny flicker of its usual strength—a flame about to go out. I was deeply tired, and even though I'd slept, I hadn't really recovered from the price I'd paid. I didn't want to draw magic from the nearest source, which was at least three miles away. For all I knew, that guy out there was a Hound and would spot me the moment I cast a spell.

Fine. I could do this the old-fashioned way.

I headed down the stairs as quietly as I could, my back against the wall. The first landing was empty, and I waited there, breathing through my nose, trying to sniff out a whiff of anything, or anyone, out of place. All I smelled was cold cooking grease, and the tang of meat and onions.

I took the last set of stairs down and paused at the

"I know who it is," I said.

"Who?" The gun came up, casually aimed at my stomach.

"I am not going to tell you while you're holding a gun."

Her eyes narrowed and I knew she was suddenly much more awake than she had been.

"You don't trust me?" She did not put the gun down. "Tell me."

"Not with the gun." I was a lot more awake right now, too.

I could tell it was a hard decision for her. She had, as far as I knew, raised a multitude of boys on her own, in the poorest part of town. Asking her to trust me enough to put down a weapon was like asking magic not to follow a perfect casting, or a river to flow backward.

"Did you do it?" she asked.

Oh. I hadn't thought of that. No wonder she wasn't putting the gun down. I shook my head. "No, Mama. I hate that someone hurt him. He's just a little kid."

And she must have heard the sincerity, because she walked over to the counter and put the gun down. She did not step away from the counter, but she did fold her hands in front of her so I could see both of them, which was thoughtful of her. It would give me just enough time to surrender if she decided to grab the gun and fire it at me.

"Who?" she asked again.

"My father." I'd never told her who my father was, but I figured she knew. I'd spent enough time in the public eye when I was younger, and I looked enough like my father that it was hard to find someone who didn't know we were related. On top of that, Mama was smart. Smart enough to know who she hired to

Hound her personal problems. Maybe she hoped some of the Beckstrom fortune would eventually find its way into her pocket.

Mama scowled. "Why? Why my boy?"

"I don't know. I went to him. I told him we knew. Told him he would have to pay for everything, hospital, damage, and more, but he didn't tell me why he did it."

"He say he did it?"

"No. He denied it. But I know his signature. I know what he can do."

Mama considered that for what felt like a long time. Long enough that I started feeling tired again, started wishing for a cup of coffee down at Get Mugged. Started thinking about the big man I'd seen in the street and wondering whether or not I should mention him to her. Yeah, right. Like telling her a strange and possibly dangerous man was in the neighborhood would be news to her.

"He agree to pay?" she asked.

"I didn't give him a choice. He hit Boy, Mama. And he has the money to pay. You should take him for everything you can get."

I expected maybe a smile out of her. Instead, "You don't care for your own father?"

Good question. Only I had no good answer for it. "I don't know. I don't like what he is." It was the best I could give her.

"Then we sue," she said. "I have lawyer."

"A good one?"

"Good, bad." She shrugged. "I just need hungry."

"Then you shouldn't have a problem." I shifted the weight of the backpack straps again. "I'm going out of town for a while, a week at most. You filed a report with the police, right?"

"I take care of it."

Which meant she probably hadn't. I'd need to stop by the station and file a Hounding report. But not before coffee.

"You really need to contact the police about this, Mama. It will make a difference when you go to court."

"I take care of it." She picked up the gun. "You do good for Mama. I do good for you." She walked over to me, the gun balanced in the palm of her hand, grip toward me, like she was offering it to me.

"No thanks. I don't do guns."

She scowled. "Did I say I give you gun? Think with your head." She said it in the same tone she used with her boys, and for no reason at all it made me happy she would be so gruff with me.

"You are good Hound, Allie," she said, "but you can be more. Better. I see it here." She pressed her fingertips against my sternum. Warmth spread out from her fingers and dug down deep, like roots looking for water. I felt magic—it had to be magic, though I didn't know Mama had ever learned to cast—branch out through my veins, wrap my bones, and then drain away, down my arms, stomach, hips, legs, dripping out my fingertips and the bottoms of my feet.

I felt refreshed. Awake. And suspicious as hell. That magic didn't feel like anything I'd experienced before—too clean, too soothing—and it was gone so thoroughly, it was like it had never happened. I couldn't even catch a scent from it. It certainly didn't feel like the magic stored within the city. Didn't feel like the magic harvested from the wild storms.

But there was no other kind of magic in the world. If there were, it would have been exploited. And if a new kind of magic were going to be found in the world, it sure wouldn't be here, in the rundown section of Portland, a city where every tap of magic was carefully regulated, monitored, and doled out in billable minutes. And it wouldn't be discovered by a woman who, as far as I knew, didn't even have a high school education, much less a higher ed in magic, called all her kids the same name, and wore clothes scrounged from the women's shelter.

"What was that?" I asked.

"I say if you try hard, you be better. Here." This time she poked my chest, and all I felt was her bony fingers. "And here." She tapped my forehead. "Think with your head. Get a real job. No more Hound."

I rubbed at my forehead. "What else?" She knew what I wanted to know. What kind of magic had she touched me with. Or what kind of spell or glyphing had she cast. I wasn't an expert. There were spells I'd never experienced before. "What about that magic you just used on me?"

Mama scowled. "No magic. If I had magic, would I be poor? Would my Boy be in hospital dying? Would I live here?"

I gave her a noncommittal shrug. Mama was smart and tough. Tough enough to take a few hits, or live with less if it meant hiding what she had from those who would want to take it. She was also smart enough not to wave magic around in front of someone she didn't know very well—me.

"I don't know what you'd do if you had magic," I said quietly. "Maybe you would be poor and Boy would still be hurt."

I was very aware of the gun in her hand. And of the fact that she and I weren't exactly best-buddy girlfriends.

"No magic," Mama repeated, flat. Final. But she

didn't smell right. I didn't think she was telling me the truth—or at least not all of it.

The door handle rattled behind me. A key slipped into the first lock and the dead bolt snicked.

I moved to one side of the door. Mama tucked her gun into the pocket of her robe.

"Boy?" she yelled.

"Yes, Mama," said a man's voice. "It's me."

Mama seemed happy with that, but I wasn't feeling nearly as confident. I could smell the man, a heavy musk and spice odor.

I thought I knew all of Mama's Boys, but the man who walked through the door was a stranger to me. Lighter hair than the other Boys I'd met, his dark eyes glittered in the low light, hard and glassy against the deeper tone of his skin. He looked more like Mama than most of her boys. I was pretty sure he was actually her son and figured he was older than me by maybe ten years. He looked like he'd recently taken a shower, and was clean-shaven and polished in a casual corporate way, all the way from his button-down white shirt, dark tie, and gray khakis to his loafers. He smiled and there was a smooth, slick coldness about him that made me think of reptiles. Or politicians.

"I didn't know we had company." He extended his hand. "James."

It took everything I had to put my hand out. I might have been raised by wolves, but I still had social graces. I shook his hand and pulled mine away as quickly as possible. His hands were cold and smooth, and I had a real desire to wipe my palms on my jeans.

"I was just leaving," I said. So what if I didn't give my name. Sue me.

His eyes narrowed and the smile slipped. "That's too bad. You look familiar . . . have we met?"

I got that question a lot, and I had zero intention of telling him I was Daniel Beckstrom's daughter. But here's the thing. He didn't look familiar to me at all. His voice wasn't ringing any bells and neither was his face. But his scent was familiar. I may not have met this man before, but I had been around him. Close enough and long enough that the smell of him—musky to the point of being sour and peppery—was imbedded in my memory. He carried other odors too—he'd been somewhere with organic death, like at the edge of the river, among fish and rotted things. He smelled of sweat too, like he'd recently done something very physical. What creeped me out was that he also carried the slightest stink of formaldehyde, very faint, like he'd brushed against someone or something that carried that scent. Maybe the big man in the street?

Despite the overriding smells, I knew I knew him. Or had known him. But I couldn't remember him.

This is where the extra hit—the random double price magic sometimes takes out of me—really sucks. And there was a bad stretch in college where it happened every time I used magic—pain plus memory loss. I shrugged it off at the time, and yeah, I'd turned to booze and drugs to try to handle it. But it didn't change anything. Unless a person was very diligent about always Offloading to a Proxy, magic left marks. It scarred. And I hated coming face-to-face with my own failings. Knowing I was missing memories, maybe even days or weeks of my life, was the sort of thing that gave me nightmares.

Not to mention the fact that I did not like this man, Mama's Boy, or no.

"No, we haven't met," I said. "Unless you went to Harvard."

He did a fair job of looking surprised and confused. "The college?"

Right. So we weren't going to really find out how we knew each other. I'd had enough of this. "Listen, I don't care what your game is, but tell your buddy out there to keep his hands and magic off me or I will report you both to the police."

From the corner of my eye, I could see Mama stiffen. James' face flushed with a fury he dampened with aplomb. "I don't know who you're talking about. I've been alone tonight. And there is no magic here. Not in this part of town."

"No magic," Mama repeated firmly. "You go now, Allie girl. Go." She shoved me toward the door, and opened it for me.

"No magic," she said. Mama was sweating even though the air outside was cold enough to sting my eyes. She was afraid, or lying. I glanced back at James. He stood with his hands in his pockets, relaxed, cool on the outside and burning on the inside, watching me watch him. He was hiding something. I figured Mama knew too, but for her own reasons didn't want to admit it. I also figured she had a gun and it was time for me to go.

I stepped through the door. Mama closed it so quickly behind me that the doorknob literally hit me in the hip. Every lock snapped into place.

"You go to those men again?" Even through the thick wood door I could hear her yelling at James. "Those worthless men, huh? You go to them? Do what they want like dog to them?"

"My business dealings are my own," James said.

"Your own! What you do, you do to family. To Mama."

"Then you should be happy," James yelled. "I'm the one who's going to get us out of this hellhole. Don't you want that? Don't you want to get away from this rotted dump? Have some money, some power?"

"No. Not if that man hand it to me on gold and diamond platter. There is no paying back his *kind*. They will use you. That *kind* always uses. We are dirt to them. You are dirt to them."

"I'm not that stupid," James said. "I know how to play their game. I know how to give them what they want and take what I want. We all win. We all get what we want."

"Good." Mama lowered her voice, but I could still hear her. "I want smart Boy. Boy who pushes pride away. Boy who breaks ties with those men and is not ashamed of his real family."

There was a pause. Finally James spoke. "Well. Maybe you won't get what you want after all." I heard his footsteps pound across the wood floor, retreating deeper into the building.

"You go now, Allie," Mama's voice said through the door.

So I did.

This was so none of my business. If Mama needed me for the trial against my dad, I'd happily be there. But I did not want to get involved in her personal life.

It was cold out, so I hit the street at a pretty fast clip, heading toward the nearest well-lit street with a bus stop. Luck was on my side for a change—it wasn't raining. Dawn smudged cobalt blue over black clouds and faded to a hazy gray by the time I found a bus stop.

Get Mugged would be roasting coffee beans about now, and I'd be there for the first cup. After that, I'd go down to the police station, file my report on Boy's hit, and then I'd get out of town to Nola's for a couple weeks before the trial started.

I pictured her little farmhouse and the hundred acres she farmed. In my mind's eye it was always summer there—the summer I'd left college and landed on her doorstep trying to sort out my life. Nola and I had met in high school. She married her sweetheart her senior year and seemed happy as pie to move almost three hundred miles away to help him run the family alfalfa farm. But with Nola and me, time and distance didn't matter. She'd always been there when I needed her and I'd tried my best to be there for her too, especially when her husband, John, had been sick with cancer.

There weren't a lot of people out on the street yet, which suited me fine. Even better was that I didn't have to wait long for the bus. I flashed my bus pass and settled into the relative peace of the fluorescent lights and rumbling engine.

It had been a strange twenty-four hours. The hit on Boy, seeing my father again after seven years, working blood magic to find a Truth I still couldn't accept. The feeling of my dad's blood and words still resonated beneath my skin. Maybe they would for a long time. Blood magic was a powerful branch of spell casting, and except for Truth spells, it was all but outlawed.

My father told me he didn't hit Boy.

My father was really good at Influencing people to think what he wanted them to think. He was also an expert caster, and probably knew twelve different ways to fake a Truth spell. But it was hard to believe he could lie so completely held blood to blood.

Twenty-four hours had also gotten me hurt and sick from Hounding Boy and, just to make things even more interesting, I'd also gone on a nondate with a nonstalker my father had hired to either protect me or spy on me.

My thoughts circled Zayvion. There was something about that man that made me stop and want to look. Made me stop and want to feel. It wasn't just the outside of him, which was, I had to admit, pretty nice: shy smile, quiet voice, and a gaze that made me feel like he was looking closer at me than any person had in my life. There were other things, unspoken things, that drew me to him. The long silences. The sense of calm he radiated. His willingness to step in when people were in need, like standing up to Mama for Boy. There was something about him that seemed honorable, and yes, kind. And just thinking about that kiss sent a thrill through me.

Survival instincts said step away and leave the man alone. Something else, something deeper that was probably my heart, if I indeed still had one, told me to draw near and fold into the warmth of him.

The last time I listened to my heart all I got was a mooch of a boyfriend I couldn't get rid of for months.

The bus finally dropped me off a few blocks from my apartment.

I decided not to go home yet, so I turned the corner toward Get Mugged, which was down another five blocks.

Someone was following me.

Dawn spread dove wings across bruised cloud bellies, lending the day some light, but not enough for the streetlamps to switch off. The city was waking up, streets and sidewalks more crowded, but not so crowded that I could easily lose my pursuer. I stopped on a corner to wait for traffic and to try to get a better look at the guy on my tail. Shorter than me, stocky.

Dressed in a practical coat, knit hat, jeans, running shoes. At first I thought it might be Marty Pike, the ex-marine who Hounds for the cops. Then the wind shifted and my follower moved. I got a whiff of him—just the lightest scent of baby powder and soap, and beneath that, the peppery stink of lavender. I was being stalked by a woman.

Interesting.

The light changed and I crossed into traffic. I could lead her on a chase, maybe trap her down the end of an alley and then ask her why she was following me. I could walk to the police station and report her. Hell, I could get a cab, go to the cops, and fill out a report about her, and one about my father and Boy all in one easy trip.

But unless she got up in my face for some reason, there really wasn't much to report about her. And I needed a cup of coffee like nobody's business.

Lovely morning. The snap of cold air on my face, the sound of birds in the trees, the gut-wrenching joy of being stalked. It was great to be me.

The next three blocks went by quickly. I kept an eye on her without being obvious about it, but she was good. I saw her once, then lost track of her at the next crosswalk. Maybe she realized she was tailing the wrong woman. Why would anyone want to follow me around anyway?

Zayvion had followed me. If he were telling the truth, he was no longer on payroll. Maybe this was the new girl on the job. Why my father felt the need to know every step I took was beyond me. I wished he would drop dead and leave me alone.

The wind pushed between tall buildings and I caught a whiff of dark roast. Get Mugged was just a few shops away and I put a little extra length into my stride. Just let me get coffee. One cup. After coffee I would take care of everything. I'd report my dad, report my stalker, contact my landlord about the late rent, and get a train ticket to Nola's. Maybe I'd even call my dad and tell him once again, and firmly, to leave me alone.

Just ahead was a newspaper stand, and I considered blowing a couple of bucks on a magazine to read while I drank coffee and let my stalker cool off. That sounded like a fabulous idea. But as I came near the stand, near enough to read the newspaper headlines, my ears began to ring, my vision narrowed down to a hazy tunnel, and suddenly everyone around me seemed to be moving in really slow motion.

All I could see were blocks of black letters across the tops of the newspapers: DANIEL BECKSTROM FOUND DEAD. BECKSTROM ENTERPRISES CEO MURDERED. INVENTOR OF BECKSTROM STORM RODS DEAD.

Shock is a strange thing. It's a little like dreaming about breathing underwater. I could hear the noise of the city around me. I could feel the press and push of people walking too close to me. I even watched as a man casually picked up a paper that outlined my father's death, read the front of it, and dropped it back on the stand. A flash of hatred that he could be so callous, that he could look at something like that and just throw it away like it didn't matter hit me. I knew I was in shock, knew I wasn't moving, wasn't thinking straight.

And all I could think was: so this is what it feels like to have a parent die. I didn't think it would hurt so much. I didn't think I would feel so empty so quickly. I didn't think I'd feel much of anything when he died, since I didn't like him very much and didn't love him either, right?

Then why did so much of me ache?

Move, Allie, I told myself. So I moved. Forward. To the newsstand. I dug in my pocket and bought a newspaper. My hands were shaking so hard the man at the stand gave me a strange look. I tried to smile, but my teeth were chattering.

"Cold," I mumbled.

He handed me change. I put that in my pocket, almost forgot to take the paper with me, tugged it off the counter, and stepped back into the flow of the crowd. I went blank for a couple seconds. Someone brushed past me, bumped my elbow, and I got moving again. Down the street. To Get Mugged, because I could not think of what else to do. I stopped outside the wood-and-glass door and the smell of coffee was suddenly too much, too strong, too sour, and I thought I might puke if I had to walk in there.

I wanted to go away. Wanted to go somewhere where someone could explain to me why my father was dead.

A woman pushed the door open from the inside and I had to step back to let her out. The practical part of my mind took over, caught the door. I walked in and sat at a table in the back where I could watch the door.

Sitting was good. Really good. I kept my coat on, and my backpack. It was hot in the little brick shop; the coffee roaster must have just finished its job. The air was thick and moist with the heat and overcooked smell of roasted beans. Even so, I was shaking cold. I put the paper on the table. I turned it over so I couldn't see the headline. That was worse. The bottom half of the paper was filled with pictures of my father, dressed in his business suit and smiling. I could almost imagine his voice, low, encouraging. *You've had your fun, Allie. There is still a place for you in this company. Come home.*

My throat tightened and hurt. But it was as much from anger as sorrow. How could he die on me? Why? Why now?

Come on, Allie, I said to myself. *Pull it together. You're a tough chick. You can take it. People die every day.*

People die, sure. But not my dad. Never my dad.

I left the paper on the table and got myself over to the counter to order coffee. The girl behind the bar was bristling with multicolored piercings, including the one through her left eyebrow that had some sort of light worked into it and changed from blue to pink every time she blinked.

"What can I get you?" she asked.

"Coffee, black, with a shot of espresso." My voice sounded a little low, a little soft. It was like I couldn't breathe, like maybe I'd swallowed a whole bag of cotton balls and they had filled up my lungs and stuck in my throat. I cleared my throat, handed her money, and picked up the steaming mug at the far end of the counter.

I thought about leaving, about going back to my apartment, and crawling into bed, like when I was little and didn't want to hear my mom and dad yelling, didn't want to hear my world chipping away word by word. But my apartment was horrible and probably still stank, and I couldn't deal with one more horrible stinking thing right now.

I sat at the table and took a drink of the coffee. Hot, bitter to the point of being sharp. It was like a slap to the face, painful, but kind of good too.

I took a second drink, then stared out the window until I'd finished half the cup. My head cleared a bit, my nerves settled some. I didn't want to read the paper on the table. So I didn't. Not until I finished my coffee. Then I pulled my shoulders back and turned the paper over so I could start at the headline.

The report said that my father had been found in his office, dead, late yesterday afternoon. The receptionist had found him. She'd gone in because he wouldn't answer his phone and had an important call on hold. She'd called the police. The paramedics who arrived pronounced him dead. They didn't list the cause but said it was a suspicious death.

The police weren't willing to announce suspects yet, but they were working some strong leads and wanted information anyone had in connection to the case.

The rest covered my father's life, his highly publicized dispute with Perry Hoskil over the invention and patenting of the Beckstrom Storm Rod that had changed magic distribution throughout the world, his playboy lifestyle, his six wives, one child, and the humanitarian causes he'd been involved with over the years—causes I knew he'd only taken on for the tax write-off.

Neat. Tidy. The entire life and death of a man who was a mystery I had never been able to puzzle out, summarized in a thousand words or less by a stranger.

I stuck the paper in my backpack. I should really go to the cops now. I didn't have much information, although I had been at his office earlier that afternoon. I could tell the police I was there and what we talked about. I could tell them Zayvion Jones had followed me up to his office and could corroborate my story.

As a matter of fact, Zayvion had been in dad's office longer than I had. I rolled around the idea of Zayvion being a hit man, capable of murder. The image of him when Mama had yelled came to me.

He'd seemed angry then, dangerous. But not murderous. Still, I suppose it was possible. The article didn't say how he'd died. But I hadn't smelled blood on Zayvion when he'd come out of my dad's building, hadn't smelled the sour heat of anger or violence on him, nor spent magic.

Zayvion struck me as the kind of person who was good at keeping his cool. Even so, he'd seemed a little jumpy at the deli. And he had spent a lot of time looking out the window at the street.

I rubbed my eyes. Okay. Go to the police, tell them I thought my dad was involved in a hit on Boy, then tell them that I knew nothing about my dad's death even though I'd chosen yesterday of all days to visit him, and sure, I'd been angry at him, and yelled at him and stabbed him while I was there.

Didn't that make me sound like a wonderful daughter?

So much for a trip into the countryside. I'd be stuck in the city, maybe even jail, for the next couple of weeks at the least.

Great. I tightened my backpack straps and left the coffee shop. The police station wasn't that far away and the walk would probably help, right? Maybe help my day feel more normal, mundane—like the day everyone else was having, or at least those people who hadn't just found out their father was dead.

I glanced up at the sky. No blue, just clouds blackened with rain. A drop hit my forehead, then another landed on my bottom lip. Then the sky let loose a heavy rain.

Lovely.

About two blocks into my march, it occurred to me that I could call a cab or catch a bus. I had money in my pocket. But I just kept walking, getting more soaked by the minute.

A woman with very blue eyes strode over from beneath a building awning and stopped in front of me. She was shorter than me, stocky like maybe she'd done some time on the football team back in college. She stank of lavender and was pretty in a desperate I-used-to-be-a-cheerleader sort of way.

"Allie Beckstrom?" my stalker asked, her voice all daisies and lollipops.

"Excuse me?" I said, like I didn't hear her right.

"Remember me? We ran into each other on the Lansing job."

I did remember her. She and I Hounded a hit someone had put on a banker maybe a year ago. She'd been hired by the bank; I'd been hired by the banker's son. I successfully traced the hit back to someone inside the company. Turned out my client's father was threatening to go to the authorities about the corporate magic-use policy. The bank had been "test marketing" low-level Influence and Glamour—spells designed to attract investors—and they'd proxied the use onto the stockholders without the stockholders' permission.

I had gotten an arrest out of it, and the case caused yet another flurry of legislation that fell short of managing business magic. Still, the people who hired Bonnie had not been happy with how it all turned out, nor with her.

"Sure," I said. "Bonnie Sherman, right?"

"Yes!" She smiled wide enough to flash me her back molars, a sight I could have done without. "I've been looking for you."

Her eyes were too wide, her breathing too fast. Even without magic I could smell the hunger on her. She was so hot for a fight I could almost taste the adrenaline on the back of my throat. She was also on something and I figured it was painkillers. One of the other drawbacks to being a Hound—it hurt, often and a lot.

I am not stupid. I know when things are about to go down.

"You working for the cops?" I asked casually while I drew upon the magic I stored in my bones, a magic I was certain she could not detect.

"Oh, sure," she said. "The cops, and lots of other people. I've incorporated, even hired my first employee—an office boy to take care of phones and filing. And you? How is every little thing, rich girl?"

"Well, my dad just died. And I'm on my way to the police to tell them everything I know about it. I've had better days."

She puckered her lips in an unconvincing pout. "That's so sad."

"Yes, it is," I said. "How about you make my day better by getting out of my way?"

She laughed. Not like she was amused, more like she was crazy.

Then she took a step closer to me.

Terrif.

It wasn't like I was in top form right now. I still hurt from Hounding Boy—a lingering ache like I'd just gotten over the flu. So I really didn't want this to get physical. My other option was Influencing her to do what I wanted. It would be easy, seductively so. Which was exactly why I had sworn never to use it again, although I wondered if I should make exceptions for when I was face-to-face with crazy.

"I was asked to bring you in, Allie. So you and I are going to walk a little ways and spend some nice, friendly time together, just like best friends in case anyone is watching." She was nodding, like I was a naughty child and she was explaining the rules of good behavior. "And you're not going to run. You know why? Because I have a gun, and I'd really, really like to shoot you. 'Kay?"

Shit.

"Since when do the police want witnesses bleeding on their floor?"

"Oh, that's funny. I'm not taking you to the police, silly girl. There are other people who are interested in seeing you. People who wouldn't care if I dragged you in kicking, bleeding, or dead. Neat, huh?"

She flashed that crazy cheerleader smile again and I noted she needed some work on a filling toward the back.

"So let's stop standing in this rain, 'kay? And go for a little walk, 'kay?"

Here's the thing. Magic can't be cast in anger, or any other high emotion, including panic or fear.

Here's the other thing. I wasn't afraid of her. For all I knew she didn't really have a gun—I sure couldn't smell one—and if she did, I didn't think she had the guts or the skill to pull the trigger.

Of course, I'd been wrong before. Actually, I'd been wrong a lot, lately.

Like that was going to stop me.

I mentally intoned a mantra, pulled magic into my fingertips, set a Disbursement—a headache or stomach cramp should do it—and pulled one of the easiest, most childish stunts of any first-time magic user.

I snapped my fingers in front of her face and set off a glyph that flashed like a two-second strobe light.

The great thing about childish tricks is that almost no serious adult ever expects them.

Bonnie jerked, blinked.

I hit her in the face. Hard enough to make my hand hurt and remind me that I really should get to the gym more often. Hard enough to give me about six seconds to start running.

These long legs of mine can do a lot with six seconds. Instead of turning and running—a great way to get shot in the back—I dodged past her and ducked into an alley, found a side door of a building open, and ran into the fluorescence of what looked and smelled like a print shop. I thought about grabbing a bottle of toner to rub over myself so I could throw her off my smell, but that kind of trick wouldn't fool a good Hound.

I didn't know how hard those pain pills had rattled her brain, or how good a Hound Bonnie still was, and I had no desire to find out.

I looked through the windows at the street, didn't see Bonnie, and figured she was halfway down the alley by now. I needed to get somewhere, anywhere, fast.

I pushed through the door and stepped into the flow of foot traffic. With a silent apology to Nola, I dumped my neon pink-and-green backpack in a trash can, moved my leather book and my cash from my coat pocket to my jeans pocket, and threw my coat into the first doorway to my left. I crossed the street, ran down a few side roads and jogged through a collection of shops, including a drugstore, candy store, and knitting shop.

How had my life suddenly gotten so complicated, and why hadn't I just taken up knitting as a hobby?

I caught a glimpse of short-and-blonde—she'd taken off her ski cap, probably to use it to wipe the blood off her nose. She was on the corner a block away. I ducked into the next shop—stationery and cards.

I hurried over to the older man behind the counter. I was wet enough that my shoes squished water when

I walked. Must have hit some puddles on my run over here.

"Could you call me a cab?" I asked with all the pretty-please I could manage.

He gave me a considering look over his bifocals, and I realized I was a mess. His eyes strayed to the newspaper on the countertop, then back to me. He pulled a phone out from somewhere behind him—I was a little iffy on the details because I was keeping my eyes on the street beyond the windows.

"Sure you don't want me to call the police?" he asked.

Just then a black-and-white cab pulled up and stopped at the light.

"Yes. No. I got it—there's a cab. Thanks."

I ran out of the store and ducked into the backseat of the taxi.

The cabbie was a heavy man with bloodshot brown eyes and a knitted hat with a red pom-pom on top. "What's your hurry, miss?"

"Just trying to stay out of the rain," I said, a little out of breath.

"Doesn't look like you're doing a very good job of it." He pulled out into traffic. "Don't you own a coat, young lady?"

"Forgot it at home," I said. "It's been a day of disappointments."

He glanced at me in the rearview mirror. "Where to?"

"What? Oh." I had no idea. Where should I go? I had no safe harbor in this town. "Do you go outside city limits?"

"I do if you show me your two hundred dollars in cash."

"Right." I only had about fifty left on me. I so

should have pulled all my money out while I had the chance. Something to remember the next time I was being chased by a crazy gun-toting tackle-back sore-loser drug-sucking cheerleader. I rubbed at my eyes.

"Okay, how much to get me to St. John's?"

"Fifteen bucks should get you there."

"Best offer I've had all day." I leaned back and watched the city go by. I tried not to think too much but my mind kept returning to my dad's death. Every time it did I went sort of numb and random bits of conversations and fragments of my childhood drifted through my thoughts. I tried to think of happy times we had together, and honestly couldn't drag even one image forward. Even the pancake breakfast hadn't turned out well.

He had always been a distant, foreboding figure in my life, and when he loomed near he was the voice of judgment, of disapproval. A figure of authority and fear. The only time I saw him smile was when he was trying to get someone to do something his way. And, of course, people always did.

Except me. I'd done anything I could to not follow his wishes. And now, here I was, running for my life, cold and miserable and hoping I could beg one more day of refuge on the worst side of town. I'd done a bang-up job of making a success of myself, hadn't I?

Maybe I should have gone back and been a part of his company like he said. Maybe I could have been a better daughter. I pushed those thoughts away. It wouldn't have changed what happened today. Nothing I could have done would have changed it.

Or at least that's what I tried to tell myself.

Chapter Seven

The taxi came to a smooth stop.

"Here it is, miss. As far as I go."

Seemed like I'd been hearing that a lot lately. I unlocked my arms from over my chest. I was wet. Cold. Wearing nothing but a thin sweater and jeans. What had I been thinking, throwing away my coat? Sure it would make it a little harder for Bonnie to spot me in a crowd, but if she tripped over me because I passed out from pneumonia, it was going to be a dead giveaway.

I dug in my pocket for cash, found a twenty. I knew I was overpaying him, but didn't want to take the time to ask for change.

"Thanks."

The driver took my money without ever looking away from the rearview mirror. "You gonna be okay?"

I nodded. "Got family down here. I'm good," I lied. I got out of the car, and into the rain. The taxi was already driving away by the time I'd taken two steps.

I wasn't kidding about the pneumonia thing. I felt all shaky and cold inside, and my head was stuffed and numb. Maybe I really was getting sick.

Maybe I grieved a death in the family by going catatonic. Wouldn't that be lovely?

North Portland is no place to wander around while confused or injured. Why then, I wondered, had I been making a point of doing just that?

Because I had no one in my life I could trust. And the one sure thing—the hate-hate relationship between my father and me—was gone now too. I wanted to run from town and curl up in front of Nola's fireplace so bad, it hurt. Instead, I kept my ears and nose open, and headed toward Mama's place. She had a phone. I could call Nola. Call the police. And if not that, at least Mama had a gun.

A man strolled out from under the overhang of a half-plaster, half-brick bar, and made good time crossing the distance to me. The heavy odor of pine wafted through the rain. Zayvion.

He fell into step beside me, and I didn't even look over at him. I didn't know how he knew to find me, or that I'd be here right now, but I was glad.

"I'm sorry," he said.

I sniffed. "About what?"

"Your father."

Silence.

"Allie, I don't think it's safe for you in the city right now. Do you have somewhere else you can be for a while?"

I stopped, turned to look at him. "You don't think it's safe? What do you know, Zayvion Jones? What do you know about my father, what do you know about me, what do you know about that bitch who's trying to kill me?"

He tipped his head a little to the side. "Which bitch?"

"A whacked-out Hound named Bonnie who thinks

it's fun to mess with people who have just had family members die on them." I was angry, frustrated. I wanted to scream. Wanted to hit someone. I wanted to cry. And if Zayvion knew stuff I didn't—if he had an idea how my father died, or why Bonnie wanted me, I needed to know.

He shrugged off his coat—a dark blue ski-appropriate thing with ratty edges and cuffs—and held it out for me. "Why don't we start by getting you warm."

"I'd rather have answers."

"Mmm." He walked around behind me and I slid my arms into the coat while he held it for me. "You can have both."

I shivered at the heat lingering in the fleecy interior. It smelled like Zayvion—like his strong pine cologne and the warm, male scent of sweat and soap. It was good, really good, to be so near him. I remembered our kiss, how surprising and right it had felt. He confused me. But not so much that I wanted him to leave me alone.

His coat fit well enough I could zip it and didn't have to roll up the sleeves.

Zayvion stuck his hands in his jean pockets and somehow didn't look cold in the rain. He still wore the black wool hat, and had on a sweater with a turtleneck under it, so maybe he didn't feel the biting cold of the morning like I did. Or maybe it wasn't all that cold out.

Maybe I was in shock.

Nah.

"I heard about your dad's death on the news this morning," he said. "It's on all the channels, the radio, the papers. I've been looking for you to make sure you're okay." He started walking toward Mama's and

I fell into step with him, because that's where I was planning to go too.

"And you came here to tell me to get out of town?"

"I think it would be a good idea."

"Do you know who hired Bonnie Sherman?" I asked.

He shook his head. "I don't know who Bonnie is. The Hound you were talking about?"

"The Hound with a gun who likes the idea of me and dad meeting again real soon." I tried to make it sound all tough-cop, but instead it just sounded like I was confused and a little hysterical.

Zay was silent a bit. Finally, "I don't know anyone named Bonnie Sherman. But your dad made a lot of enemies over his long business career. A lot of people might want you dead. You are, after all, the heir to his business and fortune, unless he's named Violet in his will."

"Who?"

He gave me a sideways look. Realized I was not joking. "His wife."

"Oh." I'd stopped keeping track after wife number three. "So I could inherit a fortune. That's not news. What else, Zayvion? Did Dad tell you something? About me? Something I should know?"

"He didn't confide in me, Allie. I was just a guy he hired to tail you."

"Just?"

"Just. But sure, I kept my eyes open when I was around him. Listened. He was a careful man. Didn't let things slip, didn't let his emotions show. It's not like he ever sat with me over coffee to share secrets. He wasn't that kind of guy."

"No," I said, "he wasn't."

We walked a little farther, and a truck passed by, the unmuffled engine loud and slow.

"I did wonder if something was happening in the company," Zayvion said once the truck had passed. "Like maybe he was going to launch a new product?" He said the last as a question, as if I, of all people in the world, would know anything about what my father was doing.

"I hadn't seen him in seven years." It came out dead flat, and sounded sad, even to me. It sounded like I regretted it. Regretted my father was such an asshole I couldn't love him no matter how much I wanted to.

I sniffed again and was really glad it was raining hard, 'cause when I wiped my face, I didn't have to explain that the tears were from anger, not sorrow. Okay, maybe sorrow too, but at least I didn't have to explain it.

My nose was getting all stuffy and snotty, and that wasn't going to do me any favors, since I really needed to be able to smell if I was going to stay ahead of Bonnie. I swallowed hard and bit at the inside of my cheek and thought calming thoughts.

You're a tough girl, Allie, I told myself. *Suck it up. There will be time to cry later.*

"Going to Mama's?" Zayvion asked.

"Need to use her phone to call the cops," I said.

"To report Bonnie?"

"Yes. And everything else. I figure just because I haven't gotten a summons, it doesn't mean they won't want to know what I know about my dad's death."

Much better. No sniffling or sad, sobby words. Just calm, confident, practical choices. The Queen of Matter-of-Fact, that's me.

"Hmm," he said.

I looked over at him, but he didn't say anything more.

I stopped walking. "Tell me you didn't have anything to do with my father dying, Zayvion."

He pressed his lips together and nodded, like he was sort of expecting me to say something like that. I watched him very closely, looking for any hint of falsehood, in his words, his voice, his body, his scent.

He reached out and caught my hand, and held it while he looked me straight in the eye. The need to draw nearer to him, to feel the pressure of him against me was overwhelming. So much so that I wondered if there were more than just attraction here—if maybe there were something magical going on between us. I couldn't sense a spell, or Influence of any kind from him. But I ached to be closer to him. I stood my ground, a little worried. It wasn't like me to trust so quickly.

"I didn't kill him." He paused and I knew, as strong as blood magic Truth, that he was not lying to me. "I don't know who did yet. When I find out, I'll tell you."

He did not step back, did not let go of my hand, and the contact, of another human being, of flesh and heat and comfort, was enough to bring the tight, tearful feeling back in my chest.

I knew I should pull away, but I didn't want to.

"You were with him after I left," I said, so softly it was almost a whisper.

"I know. And I'm sorry."

My heart beat so hard I thought maybe he could hear it. "Me too," I said, even though I wasn't sure if I was sorry I'd accused him, or sorry my father was dead.

Gone.

I took a deep breath and cleared my throat. "So you don't think it was just a heart attack?"

"No. They would have mentioned that in the paper."

"Do you think magic was involved?"

He looked down at his shoe, but still held my hand. "Maybe. How much do you really know about your father's business? His past?"

"Not much. When I was a kid, I didn't pay any attention to those things. Then when I was older . . . well, he never sat down with me over coffee to share secrets either."

Zayvion's eyes were soft with compassion. Neither of us said any more. I guess we didn't have to. He squeezed my hand one more time and then let go. The sudden absence of him was cold and sharp. I didn't want him to go—to go away too.

Wow. I was a mess. But a thought occurred to me. "Don't you have a cell phone?"

Zay shook his head.

"But I thought you called that ambulance for Boy."

"I did. From the bar down the street."

I stuffed my hand in Zayvion's coat pocket. "You have something against cell phones?"

"No. They just break when I use them."

I walked up the two wooden stairs to Mama's restaurant. I paused with my hand on the doorknob. "Break?"

"Must be my magnetic personality." He smiled, and I knew it was an act.

"Don't do that," I said.

"What?"

"Lie like that."

Zayvion held very still. He looked surprised, then thoughtful. "I'm sorry," he said, and that I knew he really meant. The calm Zay, the Zen-Zay came back.

"I don't care why you don't have a cell," I said. "I don't have one either."

"Why is that?"

"Can't afford the bill." Huh. That sounded kind of weird coming from a woman who was about to inherit a fortune. I needed to change the subject before my mind went running down a thousand different what-ifs again. "You're not following me around, are you?"

He shrugged his shoulders. "Now I am. You have my coat."

I rolled my eyes and pulled open the door to Mama's.

Boy was behind the counter, and I got to thinking that, except for really early this morning, I'd never seen him away from his post. This time he wasn't drying cups, he was reading a paper.

Great.

The thick smell of onions and olive oil and garlic got through my stuffy nose and did some work clearing my sinuses.

I walked into the restaurant, noted two men at a table to my right, and a woman—not Bonnie—at a table to my left. They didn't glance my way as I walked in, so I didn't spend any more time looking at them.

Boy looked up though. Looked up, and looked shocked.

The question was, why? Because I was walking in, or because Zayvion was walking in behind me?

"Morning, Boy," Zayvion said. "I'll have a coffee. Two?" he asked me.

I shook my head. "I just need to use the phone. Is that okay?"

Boy scowled at Zayvion and didn't answer.

I was at the counter now, in front and to one side of Boy so I had a good view of half the room. Zayvion was directly in front of Boy, holding out a dollar like he was daring Boy to take it and get the coffee he hadn't bothered to pour yet. Something was wrong. Boy smelled like fear, and his breathing was a little too fast.

"Where's Mama?" I asked more quietly.

Mama came out of the kitchen, right on cue. If I didn't know how much she hated technology of every kind, I'd say there was a hidden surveillance system set up. She looked like she was in a rush, her hair pulling free from a clip, her apron stained with flour and grease.

"I told you to go away," Mama said as she hurried behind Boy. She pointed at me. "You. Out." Then she pointed at Zayvion. "And *you*. Out. Out of Mama's restaurant."

She was breathing too hard too. She looked worried, maybe afraid. I'd never seen her afraid. Not even when Boy lay dying on her countertop.

"I just need to use your phone," I said. "I can pay."

"No."

I leaned forward, lowered my voice so the patrons wouldn't hear. "I need to call the police, Mama. Someone's trying to kill me."

She pulled herself up, put on a regal poise. "You leave. Now."

"Why?" I seemed to be asking a lot of that lately. "I just need to make one phone call."

"No public phone." She pointed at the door behind me.

I glanced over at Zayvion. He had put the dollar away, which was probably smart because Boy didn't look like he was pouring coffee for maybe the next century or so. He had gone back to reading the paper and glancing off toward the stairs at the back of the room.

"Are you in trouble?" I asked Mama.

She scowled.

And then the other Boy, James, Mr. City Slick, Mr. Magic-and-Danger-in-the-Night, Mr. Reptile, slunk out of the door from the stairwell.

A couple of things happened at once. Boy stiffened. Mama's mouth dropped open, then snapped closed. Zayvion became so quiet and calm he might as well be a potted plant. James-the-slimy paused, licked his lips, and stared straight at me with a look of sheer terror, then a gleefulness that was frightening. I know 'cause I was staring right back at him and wishing, right that moment, that I was maybe anywhere else.

"Hello there," James practically purred. "How nice of you to come back again. May we help you?"

Mama was quick on her feet. She glanced up at me, her eyes too wide. Then she turned on James like a five-foot hurricane.

"They leave. They leave now. You go do dishes. Dishes!"

James crossed the room, a static smile on his face. "Of course, Mama. I was making sure our guests—" Here he looked from me to Zayvion. And a strange thing happened. His smile drained away and his face became blank, then worried.

"Yes?" Zayvion prompted. "Your guests?"

"Of course, guests," James picked up smoothly. "That our guests wouldn't perhaps like a table? Some breakfast?"

"No," Zayvion said. "We didn't come here for the food."

I knew the dynamics had just suddenly shifted. James was on the defensive instead of the prowl, and Zayvion was looking more like a man who had authority, maybe even power, instead of a homeless drifter.

Sweet hells, I was going to need a scorecard to keep up with this man.

James, however, seemed to know Zayvion, seemed to know Zayvion had the upper hand, and didn't like it. "Why else come by our fine establishment if not for Mama's cooking?" James asked.

"We're here to use the phone."

James shook his head. "It's not working today. Mama forgot to pay the bill."

I knew it was a load of crap. Zayvion probably knew that too, but the thing I couldn't figure out was what these two were really talking about. I got the feeling they were squaring off against each other over old grudges.

For all I knew it could be a drug deal that had gone wrong.

Lovely.

All I wanted was to call the police. And if I couldn't do that here, I needed to be moving, moving on before Bonnie and her gun caught up with me.

James took a step toward me. "I would be happy to help you, maybe drive you somewhere?"

From the corner of my eye I could see Zayvion stiffen, and that sense of authority he emanated became one of danger.

Oh, there was no way I was going to get in the middle of this—whatever this was.

"That's okay," I said. "I got it covered." I turned and started walking toward the door. I glanced at Zayvion, but he did not move to follow me, which was weird.

James laughed. "You don't have to run away, Beckstrom," he called. "I'm sure we can work something out."

He started after me but Zayvion stepped in front of him.

"You know what?" Zayvion said in his calm, slow, Zen-like voice. "I changed my mind. I think I would like a cup of coffee. Be a pal and get it for me."

I kept on walking toward the door. I knew the beginning of a fight when I saw one. I already had a woman out to kill me. I didn't need to add two crazy men to the parade.

"You scared off your girlfriend, Jones," James said.

"She's fine," I heard Zayvion say as I stepped through the doors. "She's just fine."

I pushed through the door into the cold and rain, and got walking. I was not his girlfriend, or at least I didn't think I was. Still, Zayvion was buying me some time. It stung that Mama had turned me away when I told her I was in trouble, but Zayvion was right. I was just fine on my own. Better than fine. The best.

The bars along the street were all closed, and every time a car crawled down the street I expected Bonnie to jump out and shoot me.

My need to find a phone was strong, but the need to not get shot or kidnapped while finding said phone was even stronger. My heart beat so fast I couldn't think straight.

My dad was dead. And someone had killed him.

A truck roared by and I almost screamed. Okay, I was losing it.

I hustled down the next alley and leaned against crumbling stucco. The tears I was holding back were mixing with panic. It was getting hard to breathe around all that. I pressed my hands over my face and bent down, trying to hold myself together.

Don't fall apart, don't fall apart.

I sucked in air around the sob in my throat, and did it again until I could do it silently. I just needed a little time to think. I hadn't been doing enough of that lately and I was making stupid mistakes.

To sum up, I had some problems. One of which was a Hound on my trail. If she were any good, and I had to assume she still was, despite the painkillers, she'd already be sniffing out North Portland.

There weren't a lot of ways to throw a Hound off your trail. One way was to not cast magic so there was no signature to follow. So far, so good on that. Other than the snap of light in front of her face, I'd stayed clear of magic use. The other way was to physically mask your smell. But you needed something really strong and natural to the area to work effectively, to help you fade like an invisible woman into the surrounding woodwork. What around here could mask my olfactory identity?

The wind changed, and I got a strong whiff of the sewage treatment plant and the stink of the river.

Great. Rotten fish, garbage, and sewage. I was such a lucky girl. But I couldn't handle being on the street right now. I felt too exposed. I needed to hide my scent, then find a phone.

I followed the alley to another street, one that paralleled the river, and jogged along it, heading toward the gothic spires of the St. John's Bridge and Cathedral Park nestled along its feet.

There had to be a way down to the water from here. This was one of the older parts of town, and the river was still used for shipping and other industrial things. I shivered, even though I was starting to sweat, and flipped up the hood on Zayvion's jacket. I took the next street that led down toward the river. I felt ridiculously exposed walking alongside warehouses and rusted chain-link fences and empty gravel lots. But I didn't see anyone following me. Cars drove past, tires hissing against the wet street, and I kept my head low, hidden by my hood. Bonnie could be in one of those cars. Bonnie and her gun.

I hurried.

Finally, I saw the shieldlike concrete bases of the St. John's Bridge marching down to the river's edge, green metal cables connecting the spires of the suspension bridge to the earth. I headed to the parking lot, and quickly toward the sparse shelter of bare-branched trees that lined the river. The river smells would be down there, past the grassy field, past the meandering concrete walkways and park benches, behind the screen of brambles and trees. I didn't know if there was a real footpath to the shore, and even if there was, didn't want to take time looking for it.

I jogged along the concrete path, parallel to the river. The brambles thinned out here, not exactly an opening, but maybe a way down.

A car pulled into the parking lot behind me, cruising along the edge, low engine idling, headlights flickering against the rain.

Shit.

I pushed through the wet brush and picked my way down the tumble of rough rocks to the narrow sand-and-gravel shore.

Holy hells, it stank of garbage and raw sewage. I covered my nose and mouth, trying not to gag.

Even though it had been raining, the Willamette River was still low. The shore was covered in garbage and punctured by the remnants of old docks, or maybe piers. Wooden spikes as big around as me speared up through the sand and gravel, catching and holding piles of filth. Half-buried concrete pilings tipped in drunken angles like forgotten headstones. The hiss and snap of the river's small waves blended with the clattering noise of rain, but didn't mask the drone of traffic crossing the bridge twenty stories above me.

Across the river I could make out the lights of warehouses, cranes, and silos all set against the evergreen hills. There were more industrial areas on this side of the river too, but they were up a ways toward where the Columbia met with the Willamette.

The twin red lights on the railroad bridge marked the boundary between the rest of the city and this neighborhood. If I followed the edge of the shore I could come up somewhere deeper in the city without traveling by road. That would get me into town without being seen or scented, and from there, so long as Bonnie wasn't on my heels, I'd find someplace to call the cops and lie low until a patrol car came to get me.

I moved as quickly as I could over the rocks and slime and slippery chunks of trash. It looked like the entire neighborhood kept its garbage bill down by dumping here. Seagulls and crows picked through it, screeching and scrabbling. Most of the trash had fallen close to the land, but broken bags of refuse lay like a putrid avalanche, strewn from the brushy edge of the cliff down to the lapping water.

All the better for Bonnie not to smell me, I reminded myself. My shoes and jeans were covered by a wet slime that stank like the bottom of a hospital's Dumpster. I worked my way up a little closer to the cliff, hoping to stay out of sight and a little drier. It also meant getting cozy with the garbage, but I was all for stinking if it meant staying unshot.

The rocks got bigger here, and so did the stumps of old trees and mounds of garbage. This did not bode well for easy or quick footing.

I clambered along as quickly as I could, glancing frequently toward the railroad bridge to gauge my progress.

A pile of garbage to my left rustled and something small skittered out from it.

Probably a rat.

Neat.

I took another step, keeping my eye out for the rat, and saw instead a small, gray kitten nuzzling the hand of a dead man.

Good loves. Could this day get any better?

I am not a cat person. Not that I hate cats or anything. It's just that I have not been around them much, as my father never allowed pets in my life. I developed a sort of cautious distance from all things four-footed. Especially cats, with their curiously intelligent eyes and sleek, unpredictable motions.

But this little guy was hardly moving and his eyes were closed. He mewed, a tiny, pitiful sound. What was I supposed to do? Leave the poor thing there? Even if all I did was drop him off at a shop or on the street as I ran through town, he might have a better chance of surviving. Maybe someone at the police department could get him to a shelter or something. He was so small; if I left him here, a seagull would eat him for lunch.

Of course, there was the complication of the dead body next to him, and if there was one category I needed less of right now, it was "ten interesting things I don't want to tell the cops about," dead bodies being right up there at the top of the list.

Move on, Allie, I thought. Can't save every little thing in the world.

I took another step and the wind changed, lifting the sulfur and rotten garlic smell of a magical Offload from the mess at my feet. The kitten? Who would use a kitten as a Proxy? Maybe the dead joker next to him.

This was so none of my business.

While I am not a cat person, I am even less a dead-body person. But it's not like I hadn't ever been to a funeral before. I could handle seeing dead people. I didn't much like touching them, but in order to get the kitten out from under his arm, and maybe then to a shelter, or at least away from the dead jerk, I had to move the dead arm.

I took a deeper breath and bent down. I plucked at the dead jerk's sleeve and tried lifting the arm, which was heavier than I'd expected. Deadweight. Ha.

Not funny.

I couldn't get good enough leverage, so I took hold of the jerk's wrist.

Warm wrist. Supple wrist. Alive wrist.

Quite clearly alive, or at least I sure as hell hoped so, because he moaned.

The kitten mewed and I yelped, which, I suppose, was better than the scream I'd felt like belting out.

Hells. Double hells. A dying person was a lot more of a problem than a dead one. I glanced back down the beach. A wall of gray rain blocked my view. I looked up the shore, and got the same—rain.

I wiped my face with the hand that hadn't touched the not-dead guy and bent over again to get a closer look.

He was lying on his stomach and just half of his

face was visible. He looked younger than me, and had narrow features leaning toward delicate. He reminded me of a boy who played violin down the street from me when I was ten. His skin was the color of fog and rain, and his lips were blue. Not dead yet, but not much alive either, I decided.

Thinking about back and neck injuries, and the inadvisability of moving someone who was hurt, I gently pushed him over onto his back anyway.

Thin. Malnourished, and bleeding from somewhere under his shirt.

I tugged his sweatshirt up, and hissed at the gash in his chest.

Someone had gone all stab-happy on him, and recently. The wound oozed a little, but wasn't gushing, which didn't make sense until I placed my finger at the edge of one of the puncture marks.

Magic.

I could feel it, a slight, warm tingle like I'd just stuck my tongue on a battery. There was magic sealing this wound. I glanced at his face—still unconscious—then leaned down close and sniffed his blood.

Magic had created the wound, and magic had sealed it, perhaps keeping it from killing him. I'd never seen someone use magic like that before, though I supposed doctors might during surgeries. It was a beautiful, simple glyphing, and I wanted to trace it with my fingers and see just what kind of glyph could hold a man's soul to his bones, but if I did I would have to draw upon magic and Hound him.

Sure, I wanted to know who had felt the need to stab him with a knife and magic several times. I wanted to know if the person who hurt him and the person who sealed the wound were one and the same.

But now was not the time. Any draw I made on

magic would light me up like a neon "get me" sign, and I needed that as much as I needed an almost-dead guy and a kitten.

I pulled his shirt back down and considered finding a safer, warmer place for him to rest while I found the cops. I stood and looked around. I thought I'd passed a makeshift tarp strung between rusted shopping carts a minute ago.

"Please don't leave me," he said.

The sound of his voice, high, frightened, gave me the instant creeps and sent shivers down my spine.

His eyes, blue as a summer afternoon, were open.

"Please," he said. "I need you." He swallowed. "You and the powerful man. The dead man. I know how. I was there."

The chills just kept coming.

Okay, sure, it might be incoherent babbling. It might be some sort of elaborate trap, though I couldn't believe anyone would go through staging an almost death here on garbage shore just on the off chance I'd dodge by on my way to the cops. No one needed me dead that much.

So if it wasn't incoherent babbling, then maybe the guy knew something. If not about my dad's death, about someone's death. Maybe someone who was willing to stab him and dump him down here to get rid of him.

It could have been a gun deal gone bad, a drug deal, a fight over a girl, a fight over a boy, hell, he could have been fighting with a girlfriend over who got to keep the cat. Whatever had happened to him, it was none of my business. I wasn't a cop, wasn't a doctor, wasn't anybody who was in any kind of position to help him.

"You stay here and rest," I said. "I'll try to get you

some help." I started unzipping Zayvion's coat, figuring I could at least give him some shelter from the rain while I called the cops and probably the hospital now too.

"No," he said, his voice lower and somehow older. "Your father, Bed—Beckstrom. I was there when he died. I was you. I did—" He ran out of breath and worked hard—too hard—to pull air into his lungs.

Holy shit.

"What? What's your name?" I asked him.

When he could talk, when he could breathe, his voice was high again, scared. It was eerie, like maybe I was suddenly talking to someone else behind those baby blues. "Cody. Cody Hand," he said. "And Kitten. Please? Take us. Away."

Take him away? Not likely. Haul his pretty blue eyes down to the cops? No problem.

"This is going to hurt," I said.

"Okay," he said in a small, childlike voice.

I bent and pulled his arm up over my shoulder and heaved back, getting him to his feet. He moaned and whimpered and breathed in loud, raspy gasps. I gave him a minute to get ready for the fun ahead.

"Ready?" I asked.

"Kitten," he said. "Don't leave her."

Hells.

I half bent and held out the one hand I sort of had free. Luckily, the kitten was either too tired or too sick to back away. I picked her up and stuffed the poor thing down the front of my zipped jacket. If she fell out, there was no way I could go back for her. The kid might be slight of build and short—his head barely came up to my shoulder—but his legs weren't working too well, his lungs weren't working too well, and I figured his eyes weren't working well either.

Still, we hobbled along. I took us closer to the water because trying to pick our way over the slime of garbage and shin-bruising rocks wasn't doing us any favors.

So I was out in the open with a mostly dead guy on my shoulder and a cat stuffed down my bra.

Living the good life, oh yeah.

It took some time to get anywhere. The kid blacked out once or twice, and I had to wait until he came to before moving on again. The good thing was I didn't see Bonnie, didn't hear Bonnie, didn't smell Bonnie. The bad thing was the rain never let up and the cat peed on my shirt.

I'd wanted olfactory disguise; I'd gotten olfactory disguise. I smelled like garbage, cat piss, and somebody else's blood. Couldn't have asked for a better cover. A nicer one, yes. But better? Not in a river full of sewage. And I was pretty sure that not even Bonnie would be looking for two people stumbling along the shore like a couple of drunk hobos. She was looking for sporty-me, rich-girl me, long-coat-and-running-shoes me. Not wet, smelly, old-ski-coat-and-half-dead-guy me.

Things were looking up.

Except I was freezing, sweating, worried, stinking, and tired. Hells, I was tired. If even one of the mattresses scattered across the rocks didn't look like a whorehouse reject, I would have taken some time to sit, lie back, rest. Dead guy, cat pee, or no.

It occurred to me, however, that I hadn't a clear idea of where the shore went exactly. My theory was to follow it away from certain death and toward the police in shining armor. But as for how long that might take in reality, in crappy weather with a half-dead guy at my side, nope. Not a clue.

I was pretty sure the kid wasn't going to hold up much longer. He blacked out more than he stayed conscious, and I spent as much time dragging him as shaking him to wake up. I scanned the shoreline looking for another decent tumble of rocks to climb (shudder) or maybe, (please, please, please) a road or alley that wound up to the streets above.

So when a slope of cliff to my left made mostly of flat-topped boulders appeared, I shook the kid awake again and headed toward land.

It was not easy dragging him up the boulders along the embankment, but I managed without doing much more damage to either of us. The going got easier once we got to the top. A narrow gravel road wended away from the river, blackberries and other brambles crowding it on both sides. I could hear cars and buses growling somewhere ahead of us. The constant cry of gulls faded as the road took a bend, leaving the river to the right of us and the rest of civilization somewhere to the left.

Even though I was breathing hard, and the kid wasn't breathing nearly hard enough, I could smell the oil and dirt of the city, the salt and hickory of hot dogs getting the grill, the pineapple and smoke of chicken and teriyaki.

I could smell something else too—the copper and lye of magic being cast, spoken, chanted, channeled, used, like a blanket that smothered the city, every crack, every brick. There wasn't a building or person in the city that wasn't touched, coated, and shaped by the force of magic. It was in our soil, in our air, and in our blood. We breathed it, we ate it, we used it. And even though it used us back, we wanted more.

In my opinion, the fine line between advancement and addiction had been crossed years ago.

I was close to the edge of the city. Close to the train track that divided North from the rest of Portland. Close to magic.

The wind changed directions again, and I caught the black-pepper smell of lavender. Bonnie. Or another woman who smelled a lot like her. And since I couldn't draw on magic to investigate the nuances of that smell, I had to assume it was probably Bonnie coming to shoot me.

I stopped trudging along and wondered how much b-lled like me. Maybe I smelled enough like gar- she wo-ee, and blood to hide in plain sight. Maybe along with expect me to be dragging an injured boy

There had to b the only thing that cam ething smart I could do. But and this kid to a hospital or p mind was getting myself meant car or cab on the other e station quick. Quick tracks. Quick also meant walking straight of the railroad of Bonnie if she tried to get between me and a over the top set of wheels. reliable

We were at the end of the line here—the brambles stopped, and a clear and open road continued between some warehouses and into a mix of small businesses and apartments.

I shook the kid. "Hey. Cody. Come on, kid. We gotta get going."

His head lolled to one side, and I shook him one more time, shifting his weight from where I held him propped by one arm over my shoulders, and my other arm around his waist, thumb tucked tight in his belt loop.

He exhaled, and I swear it rattled like he had just blown bubbles in a cup of milk.

Shit. Maybe he was worse off than I thought.

I lowered him as gently as I could and went down on my knees beside him, taking a hard look at his face. Oh, not good. Not good at all. He was white heading toward a horrible pale blue. His eyes rolled into his head and his eyelids flickered. He jerked spastically, his limbs moving like a puppet's on a string.

"Hey now, you're going to be okay. Hang in there, guy." I pulled off Zayvion's coat. The kitten dropped off my shirt and did not land on her feet, but rath pitifully tumbled onto her side, on top of the k then fell down next to his arm. I tucked my his chest.

What were the emergency things re supposed to do when someone was dying hundred scenes from movies and TV shows ied through my mind, most of them involving meone beating on a prone person's chest and s eaming at them not to give up.

Old informati from high school came back to me, and I pulled off my sweater, leaving me in a tank top, and balled the sweater under his head. I didn't have anything to wedge between his teeth to keep him from biting his tongue, and I debated the wisdom of that, anyway. He looked like he needed all the room he could get just to breathe.

I put both hands on his chest and tried to press his body down gently, tried to still the spasms racking through him.

What the hell was I was doing trying to dodge a Hound, get to the cops, and take someone to a hospital all on my own?

What choice did I have? My father was dead and this kid might know who did it. Might know who I could make pay for killing the man I wanted dead and somehow couldn't handle living without.

I wanted to scream, but Bonnie was still
If she heard me, she would find me and shoo
was enough to make a girl paranoid. Or furious.

I decided to go with furious.

But unless I wanted to pull on magic, there wasn't anything else I could do. It wasn't like I could turn bullets if someone pulled a trigger.

This would all be a hella different if I had a damn cell phone.

Or if my father hadn't died.

Or if I had taken his advice and finished school and gone to work for him.

Or if this kid and his cat hadn't gotten stabbed.

"P-please," the kid rasped.

I about jumped out of my jeans. I thought he was way past being able to talk.

"I'm right here, kiddo. Hang in there, you're going to be okay."

"H-hand," he said.

I didn't know what he wanted, but took both of his hands in my own.

"M-magic."

I bit the inside of my cheek. I couldn't. Sure the magic was close enough, maybe a couple blocks away at most. But I couldn't draw on the magic to do so much as add pressure to his wound or make the air he breathed richer in oxygen because Bonnie would spot me. And I certainly didn't have enough medical experience to save him, with my hands or with any of the spells that could ease pain at an exorbitant cost to the caster. If I drew on magic at all, I was screwed. I could smell Bonnie and the reek of lavender getting stronger by the minute.

"P-please?"

ew Bonnie. If she was so determined to kill
d just have to get in line and wait her turn.
kid didn't have any time left.

I took a calming breath, even though I was freezing and soaked through my tank top and really freaked out. I set a Disbursement spell, deciding, even though I didn't like it, I should take a long and slow pain this time so I could remain functional—maybe something along the lines of a bad sore throat or a recurring stomachache over the next couple weeks. I held tightly to the kid's hands and thought about the soil beneath us, and below the soil, beyond the train tracks, to the magic pooled there deep under the city, caught and held by ironworked conduits.

I spoke a mantra, a jingle from a cereal commercial, and called for the magic to come over to this side of the tracks, coaxed the magic, invited the magic into my body and into my hands.

To my surprise, the kid managed to pull my hands, still clasped with his, down upon his stomach, over his wounds.

Kneeling next to him, I was close enough to see his eyes, blue, unfocused, looking at me, or maybe through me, close enough to see his lips and see that he, too, was chanting.

Holy hells. Soft as a whisper or the brush of a butterfly's wing, the kid reached out for the magic I drew upon, and used me like a channel, like an ironworked conduit. He pulled the magic he wanted through me, not through the ground or through the channels. That shouldn't be possible. People were not conduits of magic. Magic killed the people who held it inside their body for any length of time. Magic could only be channeled by lead, glass, iron, and glyphs.

And, apparently, me.

Like a breeze stoking a flame, the small magic I carried within me flared to life and the magic the kid drew upon mixed with it. I filled with magic, more magic than I'd ever held before. Like an artist mixing paint beneath my skin, the kid guided the magic to blend and move, connecting the magic beneath the city to my flesh, to my bones.

This couldn't be good.

But it felt good, very good. Magic shifted and changed in me, and I realized my eyes were closed. Instead of darkness, I saw lines of magic that pulsed in jeweled colors, connected in contrasts of sharp angles, and softened like a watercolor. I could suddenly see so many possibilities in magic, so many things I could use it for. Things I'd never thought of. Like a balm to soothe pain, or a thread to stitch flesh.

"Oh," I whispered. I didn't know it could be so easy to heal someone with magic.

But I did now. I used one hand and drew a glyph for health—the sort of thing that might reduce the effects of a head cold, or revive a wilted plant. I could see how the glyph would fit around the kid, and how it would sink inside him, like a tattoo of color and magic on his bones. It would stay there too, supporting him, healing him. I worked the magic inside of me out into the glyph and then directed the glyph down over his body—inking it above him from his skull to his toe, magic that urged healing, health, life.

I'd never seen anyone use magic like this before. I'd never seen anyone try. But I could do it. Of course I could do it.

So I did.

Magic spooled out of me and into the glyph. I let go of the kid's other hand so I could catch the power and guide it, weaving and bending the force of it like ribbons of light, of heat, some rough, some slick and smooth, all fast, faster, falling out of me and into the glyph, then over him, then into him, wrapping around his bones, webbing through his muscles, arcing across his tendons.

Heal, I thought. And the magic soaked through him, filled up his wounds, and followed my will, my intent, my glyph, my spell.

The boy gasped, and part of me wondered if this might kill him, and whether it might kill me too since I'd never channeled so much magic before, and sure as hells had never tried to play interior tattoo artist with it. But if I stopped, or worse, if I freaked out, I wasn't sure what the magic would do. Would it stop, collapse, explode? I was pretty sure it would do more damage to him than it was doing now.

I worked on creating an end to the spell. But magic rushed through me like a river raging free of its banks. I didn't know how to cut the ties of magic between me and the ground, or me and the kid. How did you stop something you didn't know how to do in the first place?

I didn't want to disengage too quickly, in case the wild rush of magic lashed back on the kid and left nothing but a burned and charred mess. But I had to let go soon. My ears were ringing and the sheer force of channeling so much magic had gone from feeling good to making me dizzy. I couldn't feel the wind anymore, couldn't feel the rain, couldn't smell the garbage.

This was bad.

I tried tying the strands of magic into knots, to stem the flood, but magic still rushed up through the ground, into me, then out of me into the kid, and then completed the circle by exiting him and wrapping around my hands again. My fingers were getting full, stiff with magic that tangled and wrapped and constricted.

Clearly, I sucked at this. That was no surprise since I had no friggin' idea what I was doing. Knots unraveled, twisted, tangled. I caught at strands of magic and wound them around my fingers, through my fingers, to try to hold them all. But no matter how fast I spooled up the magic, it came faster, rushing up through the soil, through me, into the kid, healing, painting muscle, bone, sinew, his and mine, and then back out through him to wrap around my hands again.

I was about to be in a world of hurt. I could not control this much magic. The magic pouring out of me and the magic pouring out of him collided in my hands, tangled, and burned. I jerked away from the kid, rocking back on my butt, but I wasn't fast enough. Magic crackled, hot, bright. It burned up my right arm like fire in my skin following lines of gunpowder.

I held my right arm away from me and turned my head away from the heat and pain coming closer to my face. Heat licked across my jaw, up my ear, and arced across my temple. I yelled, "Stop, stop, stop!"

A wild thought of stop, drop, and roll before my hair caught on fire flashed through my mind. I flung myself to the side, not caring that wet gravel and blackberries were the best landing I could hope for.

But before I hit the gravel, I hit a very solid chest. A set of arms closed around me and held me tight, my burning arm tucked between them and me, the heat of the fire lessening, cooling, leaving not heat, but pain behind.

I couldn't tell who held me, couldn't smell who held

me—as a matter of fact, I couldn't smell anything. I freaked out about that, then freaked out when I realized I also could not see.

Well, not completely true. I could see something. Everything was really, really white, like someone had just dumped a mountain of snow all around me, or set off a bomb. As a matter of fact, I felt cold and numb, like I was buried in snow, which annoyed me. I'd thought a little bit about how I wanted to die, and freezing to death in an avalanche wasn't even on my top-ten-favorite-ways-to-bite-it list.

Ten involved chocolate and sex. Not one in one hundred involved snow.

And I seemed to remember that I was not in the mountains surrounded by snow, but in the city surrounded by rain. With the kid. Doing magic.

My brain turned over like a cold engine, gave up, and went blank. Then I tried to think again. I was doing magic. Wasn't I trying to avoid magic? Why was that?

"Allie?" A man's voice spoke through the white and I tried to answer, but couldn't feel my lips or tongue.

But the man's voice had punched a hole through the whiteness so I could hear again. Sounds of a city. Sounds of a man breathing hard, like he'd been running. Sounds of rain falling against concrete.

I knew these things should smell like something too, and hoped I might smell the man who was speaking and get a clue of who was with me, but all I smelled was a sort of germ-free disinfectant odor that masked everything.

This was beginning to worry me. I tried to move my hands, tried to blink my eyes, tried to focus.

"Don't fight me, Allie. It's hard enough as it is. Relax."

And that last word brought back to me the owner of the voice. Zayvion.

Color me equal parts amazed and confused. I did not remember being with him. But I had been with a man. A boy. The kid. Cody. I wondered if he was buried in the snow too.

Like a industrial flamethrower in the blizzard of my brain, the memory of Cody and the magic I had used on him burned through my semiconscious mind. I had, or he had, done a substantive draw on magic. I had tried to use it to heal him while a Hound was tracking me. Wasn't that clever of me?

I had to tell Zayvion. He should know a crazy blonde with a gun was headed this way.

"Bon—" And that was all that came out. After that single syllable, my mouth stopped working and I felt like an explosion, or thunderclap, or something loud and nasty had gone off just inches away from my face. That loud nasty sound drenched me in the prickly cool of mint. I could suddenly feel my body again, smell again, see again, think again, and what I thought was that everything hurt.

"Can you stand?" Zayvion asked.

Oh, hells no. With prompting, and some support, I might be able to puke.

I blinked until I could make out his face above me and gave him the dirtiest glare I could muster.

Zayvion scowled. Then he looked up, away from me, and the muscle where his jaw and ear met tensed and his nostrils flared, like he was scenting the wind.

Yes, I was hurting. Yes, I felt sicker than the worst hangover I'd ever had. That didn't keep me from appreciating the fact that Zay was stepping in to help me, and the kid with me, probably at great risk to himself. Plus I couldn't help but notice that Zayvion was a good-looking man. If I'd been up to it, I might even have licked the edge of that jaw to see if he tasted like mint, or what he would do if I bit his ear.

"We have to go, Allie." He looked back down at me. His eyes were brown and warm and understanding. They were also flecked with gold, like back at the diner when he'd Grounded me. I had never seen anyone's eyes look like that, and wondered if it was magic or me that caused it.

I wanted to tell him not to worry. We'd make this work out somehow. I had a good feeling about us.

Had I just said that out loud?

Zayvion's eyebrows notched upward and he lost the serious Zen look. "I do too," he said quietly. "But tell me about that later. We have company."

He pressed his fingers into the back of my neck and the minty feel of his touch rolled down my body in ever-warming waves until I could really and honest-to-goodness feel myself again.

"Mmm," I said. I felt a hundred times better. What was it with those hands of his? "Better," I said. I stretched and yawned.

Zayvion was back in scowling mode, unimpressed by my appreciation. "Now, Allie. Hounds."

Okay, that got through my amazing stupidness. Hounds. Bonnie-with-a-gun. With Zayvion's help, I sat away from him.

"We can't leave him," I said. It came out kind of slurred, but Zayvion nodded.

"Fine. My car's over here. Come on." He stood, helped me stand, something I needed and wasn't proud of, then more or less supported me to his car.

I noticed he was limping a bit and was sure I could feel bruises forming beneath his skin on his arms, stomach, and back. If I could draw magic and paint it through the kid's bones, think of what I could do for a few bruises on a guy I really liked. One little lick of magic should take the sting out of what ailed him. I whispered a poem and told magic to run down Zay's chest, like warm water, like oil, soothing, heating, mending, and leaving health behind.

"Not now, Allie." Zay dumped me in the front seat and slammed the door, breaking my concentration. By the time I had formed a snappy response, he had shut the back passenger's door and was sliding in behind the wheel.

"Wait," I said. "The kid." So much for snappy.

"Got him," Zayvion said. "The cat too." Then he put the car into gear and got us going forward fast.

I rubbed at my eyes with stiff, swollen fingers. I hurt, but in a distant way, as if the hurt wasn't moving fast enough to catch me yet. I looked at my hands. My right hand was an angry scarlet color, like I'd gotten a bad sunburn that went all the way up to my elbow before splitting out into forks of red lightning up to my shoulder. I wondered if I was red all the way up to my temple, where my skin felt burned. I wondered if I had any hair on that side of my head.

My other hand was normalish color except for the knuckles, wrist, and elbow where bands of black seemed to be forming.

"Are you okay?" Zayvion asked.

I pulled myself together and tried to think through the last few events. The afterimages of the magic I had directed, the colors and textures of it painting against bone and flesh—and more, the feel of it coursing through me, filling me and the kid—distracted me for a bit, but I managed to pull my thoughts back. Back to the car, to the rumble of the engine, to the stink of too much garbage in too small a space.

"I'm fine. I think."

"Your hand is burned."

I wiggled my fingers. "I don't think so. It doesn't hurt, it's just red."

"Are you sure?"

"Not really. How is the kid?"

"Breathing. Unconscious. What did you do to him?" He glanced over at me, but I didn't know exactly what I should tell him. Our very strange relationship wasn't making a lot of sense to me right now. Why was he helping me?

Come on, Allie. Think it through. Your dad was killed and you need to go to the cops. Just stick with the simple stuff.

Besides, what I had done to the kid—if I remembered correctly—was heal him. I know I'd tried to needle a permanent image of health and healing on his bones with magic. A lot of magic.

No one used magic to heal someone like that. The amount of magical energy it took to actually heal flesh came at such a high price that it usually killed the user before the patient recovered. Add to that the horrifically failed attempts through the years that had left people maimed, dead, and insane, and magical healing was as much a pipe dream as floating cities.

All of which meant what I'd done wasn't exactly impossible, it was just very, very unlikely.

Zayvion was still waiting for an answer, so I gave him one. "I found him, by the river." I cleared my throat and put a little effort into voice projection so I could be heard over the engine. "Someone stabbed him in the chest. He needs a doctor."

"I didn't see any wounds—blood, but no wounds. I looked." Zayvion geared down, slowing the car. "Are you sure you're okay?"

The stink in the car seemed to be getting worse. My eyes watered and I wondered if I had enough fine motor skills to roll down the window.

"I'm fine," I said. "Tired. Cold. But that kid needs a doctor, that cat needs food and probably a rabies shot, and I need to get to the police."

"Now's not a good time for you to be anywhere in the public eye."

"Why?"

"Because your friend Bonnie spent some time talking to the police. She said she was hired to Hound the hit on your dad."

"So he was killed by magic?" Even though he had told me that might be the case, I did not know how it could actually happen. The idea of my very careful father being touched, much less harmed, by the magic he had been so influential in regulating made zero sense to me. "How? No one can get through his defenses."

"Someone did."

"Who?"

Zayvion glanced at me, those warm eyes still burning with gold. He had tiger eyes, I decided, burning bright.

"Who?" I asked again. "Who could get through to my dad?" Who could match his magical prowess? Who would he even let his guard down for?

"You," he said softly. "Bonnie said it was your signature on the hit."

That was a slap in the face. I was very awake now. "What? Oh hells, she didn't. Who hired her? The cops?"

He shook his head. "His ex-wife."

That narrowed it down to five women. "Which one?"

"I don't know."

I scowled. "Bonnie's full of crap. She'd do anything to make my life miserable."

"Why?"

"Because she and I are in a very competitive business and the last time we went head to head, I won. Also she's a crazy, petty bitch."

He glanced at me, then back at the road. He was taking us through the downtown neighborhoods, heading south toward the highway. I was glad it was still raining. It kept most people occupied with umbrellas and hats and trying to stay dry, instead of looking for a woman on the run.

"The police wouldn't be looking for you if there weren't reasonable suspicion, Allie."

"Do you believe that?"

"Can you convince me to believe your story instead?"

I punched him in the shoulder. "Ow!" I yelled. Stupid, stupid. That hurt. My hand was killing me.

Zayvion acted like he hadn't even noticed I'd touched him.

"Hitting me is not the best way to convince me you are not capable of violence," he said, and I was sure I heard laughter beneath his disapproving tone. "I don't think it would go over well with the police either."

"I did not kill my father. You were there when I last saw him. I accused him of being a jerk, of putting the hit on Boy. I told him I'd go to court to testify against him, and I worked blood magic to make him tell the truth. That was all."

Zay was busy navigating the road. "Even so, the police are looking for you. And they've put out the Hounds to hunt you down and bring you in."

"Why is that a bad thing? I need to go to the cops. I need to tell them what happened. I'm innocent, Zay. I don't want to hide."

The car stopped, and I looked up. We were at a stoplight, and a crowd of people streamed across the intersection through the rain and gray.

"The police have orders to shoot, if necessary, Allie. You're considered armed and dangerous. You were right about one thing—it took a hell of a lot of magic to knock your dad down. More to kill him. Unprecedented," he added quietly.

The light changed and Zayvion moved the car through the intersection, only to slow for traffic ahead. "The Hounds have been approved to Proxy as much magic use as they need to drag you in."

"All the more reason for me to surrender peacefully. I have information that will clear me." I was getting into that uncertain how-much-could-I-trust-him territory. I didn't want to tell him what the kid had told me. That he might know who killed my dad. That he might have been there when it was done. Or at least that's what I thought the kid had said. But until he was conscious and could answer questions, telling him Cody might be a part of it was only hearsay.

"What kind of information do you have about your father's death?" And even though he was quiet, there was that air of authority again. Like he expected people to tell him things because he said so. Like he expected me to do what he thought was best.

And I guess because that reminded me too much

of the sort of things my father used to do to me, or maybe because I'd just had the crappiest day on earth, I suddenly didn't want to do what he wanted me to do.

"Information I'd be happy to tell the police." And not you, not yet, I silently added. "And unless you can give me a better reason than 'you're being hunted by Hounds,' then this is kidnapping, Jones."

Zayvion snorted. We had stopped at another light, another intersection. He turned and looked at me.

"I'm trying to help you." The baffled smile was real and nothing like my dad.

"Why?"

"Because I have . . . friends in the police department. This isn't an average arrest order. Someone wants you gone from public view, locked away, shut up, dead, if need be. Someone wants to kill you, and whoever it is, they have the money, the manpower, the Influence and drive to make sure you are removed from the picture. They think you know who killed your father."

"Why?" My heart was pounding with equal parts fear and anger. Mix in a cup of tired, two spoons of shock, and a heaping portion of way too much magic, and all I could think of was, "Why me?"

"Because you are Daniel Beckstrom's only heir and your father was a very shrewd, very bad man in the world of business and the world of magic."

"Like that's news." I'd grown up hearing about the Hoskil and Beckstrom fight over the patent for the Storm Rods. Grown up listening to the news stories about how my father had outmaneuvered Perry Hoskil, filed the patent in his name alone, and then bought out Perry's share in what was now Beckstrom Enterprises. That action had ruined Perry Hoskil and made Daniel Beckstrom what he was. I'd grown up hearing other, darker stories of my father's magic and business deals too.

But Zayvion had done his job. I was spooked. I always knew my dad had enemies. For some reason, I just never expected to be their direct target.

"Listen, Allie. The police . . ." He stared out the window, thinking. "Anyone can be bought for the right price. Even people in authority positions. It's not safe to go to the police right now. I'll take you anywhere else you want me to. All I ask is that you lie low for a day or two before you approach a lawyer—and yes, I think you should go to a lawyer before you go to the police. Do you have a place I can take you to? Maybe out of the city? Out of your father's range of influence?"

Right. Like I, the girl drifter, would have some out-of-the-way cottage on a sunny shore where I lounged and drank fruity rum drinks, waiting for bad guys to give up plotting my demise. My life was starting to sound like something out of the movies, and I didn't like it one bit.

"My friend Nola . . ." I didn't know if I should mix her up in this. What if he was just making this all up? What if he were the one out to hurt me, out to kill me? He could have killed my father. He was there too.

Okay, now I was just getting paranoid.

"Who?" Zayvion asked.

I swallowed.

"Can you convince me to believe your story?" I asked, "Give me one indisputable reason why I should trust you enough to put my friend in danger."

Zayvion eased out of traffic and turned down an alley. He put the car in park, but left the motor running and shifted his whole body toward me. I was ready for him to punch me like I had just punched him. Instead, I got honesty.

"You should trust me because I'm trying to look out for you. And I don't want you to be hurt, or to die."

He sounded sincere. He looked sincere. Everything about him seemed sincere, but I'd been wrong before. I'd been wrong a lot lately, and people were dying.

"Really? Why not?" I wanted it to come out strong, accusing, but I just didn't have it in me. It came out quiet, sad. Maybe even lonely.

"Because," he said gently. "I care about what happens to you."

He leaned forward, and I thought about leaning away, but then his hand was on the unburned side of my face, and I didn't want him to stop touching me there, even though he paused. His eyes were still brown and gold, still earth and fire, but the heat warmed me, made me feel welcome, wanted. For the first time in a long time I felt like I was right where I wanted to be, with who I wanted to be with, doing exactly what I wanted to do. That electric tingle flipped in my stomach and rushed along my nerves. I brushed my fingers down his long, lean chest and stomach, then dragged my stiff hand around to his back so I could pull him closer.

I was bloody, filthy, and stank of a garbage dump on fire. I was pretty sure most guys would consider that a turnoff in a woman. Still, the need to feel his touch, to savor again the richness of his mouth, the heat of his lips, the strength of his body, pushed all other thoughts aside.

I stroked the arc of his dark cheek with my bloody, bruised fingers and cupped the back of his neck with my hand. I thought I'd have to bring his head down to mine, but that was not the case. He leaned down and kissed me.

Oh, sweet loves, I wanted him. All of him.

I breathed in deeply as the kiss lingered. The electric tingles built up and up and poured through me in a wave of luxurious heat. I opened my mouth to him and he moaned, shifting closer, his knees, the stick shift, and his seat belt all stopping him from making much progress.

I, however, hadn't buckled my seat belt. I pulled my legs up and shifted in the seat so I could face him. He drew his hand down the back of my left arm and pressed his palm against my ribs. With his help, I crawled over the stick shift and then placed my knees on either side of his seat. I eased down across him and straddled his lap.

He was built thicker than I'd expected, and there was barely enough room for me to press tightly against his thighs and chest without my back hitting the steering wheel. It was a cramped space, a small space.

And I liked it.

He smiled, and I noticed I had left a smudge of dirt, or maybe blood, on his face. I touched his face, and hesitated. He did not. He kissed me again, and the pleasure, the want, the sweet hot need for him radiated through me.

Oh, I thought. *Yes. More.*

Zay's hand slid up my thigh. His palm, wide and hot, squeezed my hip and I gasped hungrily. Fire followed his thumb as he stroked down the curve of my hip bone. I moaned for him, for the taste of him, for his touch that was hot and cool, mint and magic licking beneath my skin. I wanted him to fill me, to ride this sweet, hot fire I could not quench. Then his hands were gone, fumbling between us, and I thought he was trying to unzip his pants, or unbuckle the seat belt, so I leaned back.

The car horn blared out—loud, jarring a Klaxon of reality—and we both held very still.

We just stared at each other and breathed hard and didn't move. There were things I wanted to say, like "please don't stop," and "please don't go away," but the suddenness of this, of us, of everything, came crashing down around me.

I was in the middle of a crowded city crawling with cops and Hounds, running for my life, and had decided that taking a quick sex break was a good idea? The practical side of my mind sent off rockets and warning sirens.

If Zay was telling the truth, I was in a world of trouble. The cops, Bonnie, and a bunch of other Hounds were looking for me. They thought I was a murderer.

If Zay was not telling the truth, he himself might be a killer.

That was not a quality I looked for in a man.

And this was not a good way to start a romance. No matter how much I wanted it.

"I can't—" I started.

"Mmm." Zayvion leaned his head back into the headrest and looked away from me, out at the cold and the rain. Finally, he looked back, and his eyes were brown, warm, with barely a spark of gold. He was good. I'd never met a man so in control of his emotions.

"I know," he said. "But you asked me why I didn't want you dead." He smiled and, even though I was cold and shaking with need for him, he was a perfect gentleman and sweetly helped support me as I lifted off his lap and settled back into my empty seat.

I needed an attitude adjustment myself, something to get my mind off him, off what it had felt like to be with him. Sarcasm usually did the trick.

"So. You're saying you don't want me dead because you want me in bed?" I said. I thought it would come out a lot funnier than it did.

"That's not what I said." He put the car in gear again and drove down the alley to a cross street.

"Your kiss said you wanted me in bed." That was better.

"You mean the kiss you started?" Zayvion shook his head. "Maybe that's all you were saying, but I was saying I was open for more than just sex—maybe a real date that didn't involve blood, bruises, that incredible odor you're wearing, or unconscious people in the backseat. But if it's just sex you're offering, I wouldn't turn it down."

"Right. Is there anything else a man really wants from a woman? Wrap it up in pretty words all you want, Jones. You can't tell me you're any different than any other man I've dated."

"Maybe not. But you are different than any woman I've ever known."

Oh. That was sweet too.

"You don't get involved with women on the run from the law?"

He paused before answering. "That, actually, is none of your business. You can't take a compliment, can you? Let me say this as straight as I can. I like you. A lot. Enough to follow you all over this town, even when I'm not getting paid for it—in the rain, I might add. Enough to get you out of town before you're killed, enough to quit my job, and you have no idea how much hell I caught for that. I like you enough to do what it takes to keep you safe."

"You are a cop, aren't you?"

"If I were a cop, would I be taking you away from the police to keep you safe?"

"Who said I need someone to keep me safe?"

Zayvion gave me a who-are-you-kidding glance.

"Careful, Jones."

"Fine. Maybe you don't think you need someone looking out for you, but you're wrong."

"No, I'm not."

"And stubborn. Like your father."

That shut me up. It was just not my day for snappy comebacks. Probably because he was right. The car rattled over potholes and jostled the kitten awake in the backseat. The little thing started mewing and wouldn't stop.

"What's with the cat?" Zayvion asked.

"She belongs to the kid."

"Do you know his name?"

"He was sort of babbling, but I think he said Cody Hand."

I glanced at Zayvion. If his mood had just been warm, flirty, and fun, it had suddenly parked square in the middle of pensive, cool, and serious.

"You know him?" I asked.

He didn't say anything for a long moment. "No." His mouth might be saying no, but his body language was saying oh, hells, yes. His body language might even be saying they were good friends—cousins, pals. Or maybe his body language was saying they were enemies. Close enemies.

"No?" I asked.

"I know of a man named Cody the Hand. He had

a knack for magical forgeries. Landed him in the state pen, I think. But that was seven years ago."

"Anyone who forges, or creates, original art with magic is called a Hand," I said quite unnecessarily. "Maybe this kid is just a regular kind of magic artist."

Zay nodded and the rest of his body language said he wasn't so sure this kid was just a regular kind of anything.

"What? You want me to frisk him for ID?" I asked.

"It wouldn't hurt."

I rubbed at my face, which made both my face and my hands hurt. I tried to work up the desire to touch the kid's garbage-and-blood-soaked clothes again. I wondered if I would feel the magic I'd painted in him. I wondered if it would burn through me again. Trap me. Scar me. "I don't know how to frisk anyone. I'm not a cop."

"It's easy. Just like they show in the movies. Pat his pockets."

He was so not joking.

I twisted in my seat and looked back at the kid. He really did look better. No, he looked fine. His skin was pale, but he had a healthy pink across his cheeks and he was sleeping so hard he was snoring. Didn't look like a mastermind magic forger to me. Looked like a sweet kid who fell on hard times.

I braced my foot on the floorboard and pushed up and around so I was sitting on my knees. I reach around the bucket seat to feel the front pocket of his jeans. No wallet in the first one and, thankfully, no garbage worse than what I was covered in, and no hint of magic. I reached back a little farther to check his other pocket.

The stupid kitten pounced, all claws and teeth and hissing fury, and tore the hell out of my left hand.

I yelled and shook my hand until the ball of fur tumbled to the floor, where it trembled and mewed and looked pitiful.

"Are you hurt?" Zayvion asked.

"No." I lied. My hand looked like I'd lost a fight with a killer rosebush. The cuts and punctures probably weren't very deep, but that cat had been scratching around in filth and garbage.

Great. On the run for my life, I try to do a good deed and now I need a tetanus shot. Maybe something for rabies, too.

Stupid cat. Good things did not come in small packages—mean things did.

I sat forward in my seat again. I tucked my bleeding hand under my tank top, hoping the cotton would help to stem the blood flow, but my sweat, cat piss, garbage, and river water made the cuts hurt more.

"Anything?" Zayvion asked.

"Nothing in his front pockets and I am not rolling him over to pat his butt. Think about it, Jones. What are the chances of me running into some infamous, escaped forger left for dead along the river on the one day I would go down there to stroll through garbage?"

"Amazingly low."

"Exactly," I said. "And besides, he doesn't look old enough to be an infamous forger. He's only a kid."

"True," he said. "And that cat doesn't look like it can do any harm. It's only a kitten."

"Bite me, Jones."

That got a smile out of him. "That sounds promising." He glanced over at me and I met his look, straight on. Dared him to offer.

He looked like he was about to, but said, "I can get the kid to a hospital and have him checked out. They'll run his fingerprints and see if he's on file or missing from anywhere. But first, I'm getting you out of town. You said you had a friend?"

And it wasn't like I could make up a phony address. I really had nowhere to go except to Nola's. And besides, magic or no magic, Hounds, or no Hounds, Nola could take care of herself, and I was tired and feeling more bruised and achy by the minute.

"Head east."

"How far?"

"Burns."

"Your friend lives three hundred miles away?"

"You said you wanted to take me outside my father's range of influence. I don't think he has much pull in cow country."

Zayvion grunted. "Good thing I have a full tank."

I leaned my head against the window. "When the skyscrapers turn into barns, and the barns turn into mountains, and the mountains turn into rangeland, wake me up." I didn't intend to really fall asleep.

But I did anyway. It just wasn't my day.

Chapter Eight

I'd like to say my dreams were troubled. Filled with grief and anxiety-driven images. But I did not dream, did not even feel like I had really gone to sleep until a bump in the road knocked my head a little too hard against the window and I snorted awake.

Oh, so ladylike of me.

Zayvion was a quiet driver. No music, no tapping his fingers, no chewing gum, or yakking on the cell phone. He chuckled when I woke.

I turned my head, my neck stiff from leaning in one position too long. The marks from the tips of my right fingers to my temple were cool and tender, both hands still stiff and swollen, especially the left one with its black bands and cat scratches. Otherwise I seemed very much whole.

"The last skyscraper was at least four hours ago," Zayvion said. "Lots of barns, miles of fences, cows off the road, cows on the road, horses, rusted cars, and a few hundred bars."

"Why didn't you wake me up?"

"I didn't know you wanted to stop for a drink."

"Ha-ha. Were you just going to drive until we ran out of road?"

"No." He glanced my way, looked back at the road. "I thought I'd wake you up once we got to Burns. We're almost there."

It wasn't raining on this side of the Cascade Range, but daylight was sliding into the golden tones of late afternoon. The rangelands spread out around us in wide expanses of dusty green and sun-baked browns, sagebrush and juniper dotting the land all the way out to the roll of mountains on the horizon. It wasn't the wet and green that most people pictured when they thought about Oregon. What few houses we passed were surrounded by battered lawns that eventually stretched out into tracts of land gone brown beneath the advance of autumn.

And yes, we were getting close. Within a couple of miles to the turnoff that would take us up the dirt and gravel road to Nola's farm, which was good. Even though I'd been soaking in it for hours, I still hadn't gotten used to the stink of the garbage. I noticed Zay had cracked his window for a little fresh air. Right now, I wanted a shower more than almost anything in the world.

"It's the first road after we cross the Silvies River."

Zayvion frowned. "Silvies marks the edge of the grid in Burns, doesn't it?"

"You know a lot about magic for a guy who stalks people for a living."

"Call it a hobby," he said.

"Stalking or magic?"

"Both. What does your friend do out here?"

"Farm," I said laconically. "Not everyone wants to live their lives plugged into magic. Some people like to do things the old-fashioned way—electricity, gas, phone, but no magic."

Zay grunted, but didn't look at all convinced. He slowed the car as he approached the willow-lined river.

I'd forgotten how pretty the countryside was. Even though it wouldn't be all that hard to make magic accessible, the people of Burns had voted against it. It felt quieter here, in more ways than one, and made it seem like we were worlds away from the noise, the crowd, and the worries of civilization.

"See that bridge?" I asked.

Zay nodded at the one-lane with wooden guardrails that spanned the river.

"That's the edge."

"Of what?"

"Of your world, Zayvion Jones."

"My world?"

"The magic and stalking world."

We were almost at the bridge and I knew it was coming, the line, the break, the edge where magic flowed up against, and then fell silently over, pouring into the Silvies and never touching the other side.

I was ready for it. Ready for the stomach-flipping lurch as magic released me from its hold and pushed us through to the other side, water and magic rushing beneath us. Zay drove onto the bridge.

I laughed, releasing the pent-up pressure in my chest. I was light-headed and it had nothing to do with holding my breath. Breaking out of the reach of magic felt like pressing around a corner on a really smooth roller coaster. I wanted to throw my hands in the air and yell.

"Oh," Zay said. "Shit."

So maybe he didn't like it as much as I did. Maybe he wasn't ready for the prickly sensation over his skin that felt like every hair was standing up straight.

Maybe he didn't like the weight and pressure of magic drifting away from his head and chest.

Some people didn't like roller coasters either.

"You okay?" I asked.

Zay's hands clenched the steering wheel so tightly that I could see the yellow of his knuckles. "I didn't know."

"That magic wasn't easily accessible everywhere?"

"Why anyone would want to live without it."

We were on the other side of the bridge now, and Zayvion still took it slow, even though the road on this side was in as good, maybe even better, condition than the road on the other side of the bridge.

"Some people choose to live without electricity or indoor plumbing. Some people choose to live without eating meat. Some people choose not to handle magic twenty-four seven, not to gather it, channel it, trap it, harvest it, eat it, breathe it, use it, and hurt for it."

Zayvion nodded. "I didn't say it was a bad thing. I just said I didn't understand before."

"Before the bridge? You have been over bridges, haven't you?"

He gave me a dirty look. Portland was full of bridges—you couldn't go anywhere without crossing water in that city. "I haven't been off the grid for a long time."

"Really? I thought you only came to the city recently."

"I never said that."

"So you've lived in the city for years?"

"I never said that either."

"Zayvion." I was getting annoyed now. "I know you worked for my father, but I don't know anything else about you. Would it hurt to open up and tell me a little about yourself?"

He didn't say anything for a while, and that worried me.

Finally, "There's not much to say. I'm an only child, my parents live on the coast. I've done freelance work." It sounded like a well-practiced book-report recitation. As revealing as a grocery list.

He stopped talking, so I got him started again. "What kind of work?"

He shrugged. "Whatever I could get."

"Spying?"

"If it pays, I can do that."

"You're not answering me."

"Well, I followed you around for your father. I've had a couple other jobs along those lines."

"You're a PI?"

He smiled. "No. You have to go through training for that, report to the regulatory agencies, keep good records."

"Let me guess, you hate paperwork?"

"See? You know more about me than you thought you did."

"I know how you kiss," I said.

"One kiss does not a man make."

"What's that supposed to mean?"

"It means maybe I've got a few tricks up my sleeve you haven't seen yet."

"Well, well. Look at you all confident and strutting. I think getting away from magic has done something to your attitude, Mr. Jones."

"Oh?"

"I think it's made you human."

"Not even close." He took a curve in the road a little too fast and slowed down again. "How about you, Allie? Tell me about yourself."

"You worked for my father. You know everything about me."

Zay glanced over at me, his brown eyes intense. "Everything?"

I shrugged. "He gave you my personnel file, right? Don't look at me like that—I've seen it. My entire life in black-and-white—my strengths, my weaknesses. I was just another asset to him, Zay. Not a person. Not a daughter. Not a woman."

Zay thought about that while the scenery slid by. "So tell me something about the woman."

This conversation was heading dangerously into intimate territory and that scared me. My heart beat harder. "What do you want to know?"

"Why do you Hound so many jobs for free?"

Oh. I didn't realize he'd ask about that. I'd done a lot of free jobs. Mostly for people who didn't have the money, and mostly when it was pretty clear they were being taken advantage of. Every time I sat down to pay my bills I'd ask myself why I did it. It wasn't like I was rolling in the dough and could afford to be charitable. Hells, I wasn't even making my rent month to month. But I didn't do it to get back at my father, though I'm sure he would have disapproved. I guess I did it because I honestly believed it was right to help people when I could.

"Money isn't everything," I said. "Magic isn't either. Sometimes people get confused about that. Sometimes even I get confused about that."

"You, confused? When?"

"College," I said with forced cheerfulness. "Magic and drugs do not mix. Or rather, they mix too well." I'd lost almost a full term to that particular hell. I'd managed to pull myself out of it with the help of a few people I hadn't seen since. I found out the hard way I have an addictive personality. That's bad news for a Hound, and probably why I was always drinking coffee. "Thanks for bringing up *that* particular subject."

"Didn't like college?"

"Liked college. Didn't enjoy being manipulated into being there."

Zay nodded. "I like that about you."

"That I dropped out of college? Did drugs?"

"That you weren't afraid to do what you thought was right, even if it meant failure in your father's eyes. You picked up your life and moved on. More than once."

I felt a blush warm my neck and face.

He, of course, chose that moment to look over at me. "I like that about you too. For such a tough girl, you blush easy."

I scowled, but it didn't help. I just blushed harder. Time to change the subject. "Lots of people get over failure," I said.

"Lots of people don't have such a . . ." He paused, thought something over. "A lot of people don't have a man like your father telling them what they should be. A lot of people can't stand up to that kind of pressure, Allie, can't stand up to that kind of will. You could. You did."

"For all the good it did me, right?" That sounded sullen, so I tried to steer away from the subject. "Do I get an award for good behavior?"

He shook his head and did not look at me. "No," he said regretfully. "You just get this."

"Garbage and an almost-dead guy?"

The corner of his mouth twitched up.

"Garbage, an almost-dead guy, the cat, and me. Not

all bad." He looked over, brown eyes filled with warmth, with sympathy. I couldn't do it. I couldn't hold his gaze without the blush starting to creep up again. I looked out the window.

"Can we go back to talking about drugs?"

"If you want."

On second thought, I didn't want that either. My dark past should stay in the past. I changed the subject. "Nola's is right up here somewhere. A big white house with a huge driveway. On the right.

"There." I pointed out the window. Her driveway was a gravel and dirt affair, wide enough that three cars could drag race down it, and close enough to her front porch that getting groceries out of the car was a breeze.

Zay turned down the driveway and we crawled along it until we came up next to her porch, the headlights shining against the closed door of her garage.

Jupe, a mud-colored brute of a dog that was part Lab, part Great Dane, and all parts of him huge, tore through the side yard from behind the house, barking his big square head off and wagging his tail like mad.

"Jupe!" I called to him. I didn't do pets, but Jupe was big enough to be a family member. Maybe two. Still, I did not roll down the window, and I wouldn't until Nola came out. I wasn't stupid.

"Don't you remember me, boy?" I asked.

"Don't open the door," Zay warned.

"Not planning on it. Nola should be out soon." At the mention of Nola's name, Jupe's ears perked up. "That's right, boy. Go get Nola."

"You speak dog? Wonderful talent. Now *that* might get you an award."

"Shut up, Jones." I did like it better when we were joking instead of talking about serious things.

Jupe just kept barking and running from Zay's window to bark at him and over to my window to bark at me.

Finally, the front door opened and Nola stepped out onto the porch. She was country through and through, from her steel-toe boots to her overalls with daisies stitched down the shoulder straps. She'd let her honey-colored hair grow long enough to pull it back in one braid down her back, but otherwise I caught my breath at how much she looked the same as when I knew her in high school.

Nola whistled and Jupe looked back at her. He wagged his tail and barked. She whistled again, lower this time, and the big lunker of a dog bounded over to her and stood at her side.

I rolled the window down a crack. "Nola! It's me, Allie," I yelled.

Nola put both hands on her hips and leaned forward at the waist, peering through the dust-covered car windows.

I stuck my hand out the window and waved.

"Are you okay, Allie?" I knew what she was asking. Did she need to get a gun, call the cops, or tell Jupe to tear the car apart?

"I'm good. I have someone with me. His name's Zayvion. And another guy asleep in the backseat."

Okay, that sounded seriously weird. "Can we stay for a while?"

Nola shook her head and clomped down the porch stairs. She came around to my window, Jupe trailing her like a trained grizzly. She looked in the window at me and got that worried frown I hated to see on her. She glanced at Zayvion, then back at Cody.

"Come on in," she said. "All of you."

Zayvion unlocked the car doors and I opened mine

while Nola waited until she saw me push my own door open. She flinched, probably from the smell, or maybe from the mess of blood and gunk on me.

"Are you hurt?" she asked.

"Just messy. The kid in the back needs help, though."

She took a breath, then opened the back door.

"Wait," I said. "There's a cat."

But it was too late. Nola had the door open, and Jupe stuck his big bear head in the back of the car, snuffing and sniffing.

The kitten hissed and yowled. Jupe harrumphed and licked his chops. The kitten yowled again.

Served the fluffy little monster right.

"Leave the cat alone, Jupe," Nola said. "It is not a toy. Out of there now. Out." Nola patted Jupe's side. He put it in reverse and got out of the way.

"Is this man hurt?" Nola asked.

I stood up out of the car, and wished I hadn't. Everything I'd been through in the last eight hours came roaring down on me. Sweet loves, I was tired, stiff, and sore. And I really had to pee. My stomach cramped and I realized I hadn't eaten all day, either. All of that hit me in one nauseating wave and I was glad for the cool wind against my face.

"Allie?" Nola said.

"I'll help her," Zay said.

I was working hard not to puke, so I kept my mouth shut. If I could have opened it to talk, I'd have told them I was fine and didn't need any help.

"No, I'll help her," Nola said. "You can take him into the house. If you need me to help carry him, I'll be back out."

A thin, strong arm slipped around my waist and, even through the garbage, I smelled the warm yeast and butter of bread she must have been baking. It should have made me feel more sick, but it just made me hungry.

"Ready?" she asked. "Take a few steps for me."

I opened my eyes. "Hey, I'm fine. Just a little tired."

"Good. I'm getting messier the longer I hold you. Let's get going." Nola smiled, but her eyebrows were drawn down in a frown. She was worried about something. I hoped it wasn't me for a change.

We got in the house, which was warm enough that I wanted to sleep right there in the hall, or right there in the living room, or right there in the kitchen. We stopped in the kitchen, and I sat at her oak table and dragged garbage-soaked shoes across Nola's lemon-clean wood floors.

"Thanks for the money," I said. "I hope this isn't a bad time to visit."

"Nonsense. I told you to come out and visit any time. Here." She put a bowl in front of me. "Chicken noodle soup. Eat."

She wiped her hands and the side of her face on a dish towel and then clomped out of the kitchen the way we came in.

I did as I was told, and was not disappointed. Nola was the best cook I had ever known.

While I ate, I listened to Nola direct Zayvion about where to put Cody. Upstairs bedroom, across the hall from Nola's room, probably, so she could keep an eye on him. Plus, Nola knew every floorboard and creak in this old house. It had belonged to her husband's parents and she'd spent a lot of time here even before they were married. If Cody got out of bed in the middle of the night, she'd know.

Zay and she had a conversation, something that involved doctor and magic and authorities and my name.

It was the kind of conversation I figured I should be involved in, but I just couldn't muster the strength to give a damn. Not with a hot bowl of soup in front of me.

I was done with the soup by the time Nola and Zay came into the kitchen. Zay walked in front of her and smiled a little, like he'd had a couple beers and could feel the buzz. I wondered when he'd had a chance to drink. Come to think of it, he'd been a lot more open and relaxed in the car. Talkative, even. I wondered if it was because of the lack of magic around these parts.

"Sit," Nola ordered. "I'll get you some soup."

"Say yes," I advised.

Zay sat down across the table from me, where I noted he could watch the doorway to the living room, and also keep an eye on the other door that led to the pantry and mud room.

"Yes, please," he said. "Thank you."

Nola put a bowl down for him, then took mine and refilled it. "I'll get you some bread."

"No, thanks," I said.

Nola put the soup in front of me again and got busy with the kettle on the stove. Nola had a clean, modern kitchen. An old potbelly wood stove stood in the corner, but I knew she only fired it up in the winter when the snows lingered. Just because she was magic-free didn't mean she lived without the other modern conveniences.

"This is excellent," Zay said. He didn't slur, so I rethought the beer thing. Still, he looked like he was officially on vacation: kicking back, eating soup, and relaxing. I think the lack of magic was good for him.

Nola pulled three cups from the cupboard. "I don't have coffee on, but I'll make us all tea." Nola never asked; she just told you what she was going to do for you. I'd learned early on in our relationship that if it bugged me, I just had to speak up, and she usually didn't mind changing her plan.

"Have you been drinking?" I asked Zay quietly.

He grinned. "No."

"Then why are you so happy?"

"It's quiet here."

That so didn't make any sense to me.

"No magic," he said.

So I was right. Interesting. Magic was his hobby, my ass. I checked his eyes. Still brown. Just brown, like when I'd first met him, with no hints of gold.

"Okay," Nola said, "which of you is going to tell me why that young man—and you—are covered in blood?"

I looked at Zay and he gave me a she's-*your*-friend look.

Lovely.

"I found him down by the river—the Willamette," I clarified. "He was hurt. I thought he was stabbed. Punctures in his chest."

"We took his shirt off," she said. "Not a scratch on him. Took down his pants too. Other than dirt and a smell that will probably take me days to get out of my sheets, he wasn't bad off below the belt."

"He was hurt," I said. "I thought he was hurt. He wasn't walking very good, wasn't breathing very good." I put my elbow on the table and rubbed at my face. "I don't know, Nola," I said through my hands. "It's been a long day."

She poured water into mugs, put them on the table, and sat in the chair next to me. "I heard about your dad. I'm so sorry, honey."

Oh, great. That was the last thing I needed to hear—my best friend, who had probably heard me complain the most about what a jerk my father was—sympathizing with grief I could not feel.

I nodded, because my throat was tightening around a knot. Maybe it was the soup, maybe it was the tea, or the warmth of Nola's house. Maybe it was because I was away from the immediacy of magic and felt safe in a way I never felt in the city. Whatever it was, I just wanted to sit there and cry. I sat back and pulled my hands away from my face.

"I think you need a doctor, Allie," Nola said.

"I don't need a doctor, I need a shower."

Nola's gaze flicked from one side of my face down to my hands, one of which was red while the other looked like I'd gone black-ink tat-happy around every joint. Then she looked over at Zayvion, of all things, and he shrugged one shoulder. Why in the world would she want his opinion instead of mine?

"Just a shower, Nola," I repeated. "I'm tired, but I feel fine."

Nola nodded. "Even those burns and bruises?"

"Don't hurt."

"Okay, let's get you in a bath. Mr. Jones—"

"Zayvion."

"Zayvion. You'll be sleeping on the couch tonight. Blankets and sheets are in the coat closet in the living room. You can make up the couch while I get her in a bath."

"I don't need a bath," I mumbled. "I'll fall asleep and drown. Just shove me under a shower and hand me a bar of soap. A big bar."

I pushed up away from the table.

"You know where the bathroom is," Nola said. "Give me your clothes when you get out of them. They need a wash. And I'll find you some pajamas. Did you pack before you came here?"

"I tried, but that didn't really work out."

Nola patted my left arm very gently as she moved past me. "After your shower, I want to hear all about it." She tipped her head to point at Zayvion. "Everything that's happened since I last saw you." He kept eating soup like he didn't notice her unsubtle hint.

"After my shower I want to go to sleep," I mumbled.

"And since you didn't pack, you have no right to make fun of my taste in sleepwear."

"Like that would stop me."

Nola paused. "I don't think I have anything left from John that would fit you, Zayvion."

"I'll be fine," he said. "I have some spare clothes in the car."

"Good. Get in the shower, Allie," she called over her shoulder.

Like I was going to do anything else.

Zayvion picked up his empty bowl and mine, and put them both in the sink, manners that spoke of either a strong female influence in his upbringing or a long life of living alone.

For the life of me, I did not know why that man was here, with me, at the only place in the world I considered a sanctuary. But I was glad. Grateful even.

I was such a sap.

I watched as he started the water, rinsed bowls. Relaxed, he moved with the kind of easy grace I'd seen in people who do Tai Chi in the park. Unselfconscious. Comfortable. At home in a kitchen away from the push and pull, the want and denial of magic and city living. Or I could be just hoping he felt that way, hoping he'd like this place and Nola as much as I did. And hoping she would like him too.

Jupe galumphed into the kitchen and bumped my

legs with his ox head. I scratched him behind the ears. Satisfied, he trotted over to give Zay the sniffing of a lifetime.

Traitor. I'd been the one walking through garbage and peed on by a cat. I should be the most interesting person in the room to sniff. So much for loyalty.

I headed down the hallway to the bathroom. Jupe, who usually likes to follow me around when I visit, trotted off after Zayvion, which was actually fine with me. Nola's house didn't just look like an old farmhouse, it was an old farmhouse, and the rooms were on the small side. The bathroom was no exception. If Jupe had decided to hang out while I showered, I would have kicked him out anyway. I needed every inch of space I could get to breathe in there, and Jupe took up acres of exhale room.

I turned on the shower and shucked out of my shoes and clothes. I ached in weird places and itched. The back of my throat hurt, so the Offload from the spell I'd worked on the kid was starting to kick in.

I used the toilet, then washed my hands. I glanced in the mirror and winced at the red mark by my eye that fingered out like thin red lightning, down the arc of my cheek to my ear, along my jaw, then down my neck. At my shoulder it spread out even more, webbing down my arm to finally merge into a more solid red from my elbow to my hand. It was like the mother of all burns, but when I touched it, it didn't hurt, didn't feel hot, didn't feel any different than my non-red skin. My left arm wasn't red at all, just ringed by black bruises that were beginning to look like black tattooed bands around my knuckles, wrist, and elbow.

Maybe I did need a doctor. I'd heard of magic leaving marks, especially back when it was first being discovered and used thirty years ago. But those marks were open wounds that quickly festered, resisted medical intervention, and claimed the lives of the wounded. There had been a lot of trial and error before magic was considered mostly safe to use.

My father had been on the forefront of making magic accessible and relatively safe to the general populace. The iron, lead, and glass lines he patented, the Storm Rods that pulled magic out of the infrequent wild storms, the holding cisterns beneath cities—he'd had a hand in all those things.

So while magic was not harmless, most people believed that if they limited their use, or hired a good Proxy service to handle the price and pain, then the benefits outweighed the cost.

I moved my arms around, flexed my fingers, wrist, elbows. A little stiff, including the stupid blood magic scars on my left deltoid, but nothing serious. No open wounds.

I decided to take a wait-and-see approach. I stepped into the hot water and moaned.

Heaven.

I let the water sluice over me for a good ten minutes, my eyes closed, breathing in the warm and clean of it all. Then I stopped soaking and started scrubbing. All of Nola's things were natural, organic, and nonmagic. Her soaps smelled like oatmeal and honey, her shampoo eucalyptus. I used every soap she had available and came out of that shower feeling one hundred percent warm, clean, and sleepy.

Nola knocked on the door. "Allie?"

I wrapped the towel around myself and opened the door.

Nola handed me a folded pair of sweatpants, a T-shirt, and panties.

"The underwear are new—I've never worn them.

The pants will be too short, but the T-shirt should be comfortable. Want to talk?"

"Sure. Am I sleeping in the coatroom?"

Nola's mouth quirked up. "Yes, you are sleeping in my quaint and comfortably cozy guest bedroom." She stepped into the bathroom and gathered up my filthy clothes.

"Nola—you don't have to. I can get them in the wash."

"So you have more time to think about the things you're going to self-edit before you talk to me? I don't think so. I want every detail. Especially the ones involving that man out there. I'll get these washing and meet you in your room."

She shut the door and I slipped on the clothes she had brought me. The sweats were too short, but I rucked them up to my knees and they were comfortable. The T-shirt was soft, roomy, and had a giant cartoon cow sleeping in a field of daisies on the front of it. Not my style, but I didn't care. I was dry, warm, and grateful nobody was shooting at me.

Still, when I walked out of the bathroom rubbing the towel over my head, thinking short hair had some advantages—it dried fast—I was a little uncomfortable to come face-to-face with Zayvion. It's not like we were dating, not like we'd done anything more than get a little handsy in the car. But still, the sweatpants-slob look is something I usually save until after the first month of seeing someone.

"Um," I said.

"I was just heading to the bathroom," he said. Those Zen eyes were calm, unreadable.

"Right." I moved out of the way, both disappointed and relieved he hadn't said anything about the cow outfit.

"Nice cow," he said just before he shut the door.

Terrif. I padded off to the bedroom, and took a deep breath before actually stepping through the door. The room was small, but if I focused on the one wall that was almost all window, and kept the door open, I was pretty sure I was tired enough I could handle my claustrophobia and get some sleep. I didn't care that it wasn't even five o'clock yet. I was tired.

Nola knocked on the door frame and walked into the room. "So. Tell me what's been going on."

I pulled the handmade quilt down and crawled up to the head of the bed. Nola sat on the foot of the bed. She was still wearing her overalls, but had kicked off her boots. She held something in a towel in her hands, and at first I thought it was a cup of tea. Then it meowed.

"You mean Jupe hasn't eaten her yet?" I asked.

Nola petted the kitten's little gray head. "No. Poor thing. She finished off an entire can of tuna. When did you get a kitten?"

"She's not mine. I found her when I found the kid."

"Talk to me about it." Nola scooted across the bed so she could lean against the footboard and sit with her legs crossed up. The kitten mewed again, and Nola put her in her lap and petted her. The kitten fell asleep midpurr.

I heard the pipes in the old house thrum and figured Zayvion was taking a shower.

"I don't know how to explain it," I said. How was I supposed to condense the last two days—days that felt like months—into something that made sense? Where should I even start?

"How did your dad die?" In typical Nola fashion, she cut right to the heart of the matter.

I told her I didn't know. I told her I'd gone to see

him that day, which she was surprised to hear. I told her I'd threatened to take him to court, which she was not surprised to hear. I told her about Mama and her sons, about the youngest Boy being hit, and the Hounding job that led me to my father. I told her about Bonnie chasing me, and the kid and cat I stumbled over buried in the garbage at the river. I told her the kid had been so hurt I thought he was going to die.

She listened, and only interrupted when things got confusing. She didn't offer opinions, encouragement, or criticism.

Then I hesitated. "This part gets a little foggy. Someone had used magic like a bandage on the kid's wounds and I tried to sort of sustain that spell. I think I might have healed him. With magic."

She sat there and stared at me like I'd just told her I'd vacationed on the moon. "Can that happen?" she asked.

"I'm pretty sure it did."

"Have you ever done that before?"

"No. I'm not even sure I could do it again. It was strange, Nola. When that kid touched me, he did something to—with the way I use magic. To the way I perceive it. Like he took off my blindfold and I could see so much more. See the possibilities of what I could do. . . ." I stared at the wall behind her, trying to find the words to explain the experience and coming up with nothing. I must have stared a little too long because Nola sounded worried.

"Okay, that's it. You're going to see a doctor."

I blinked. Looked back at her. Tried out my winning smile. "I'm fine. I don't feel any different except for these." I held up my hands. "Please don't call a doctor, Nola, I really am okay."

She didn't look convinced. "We'll talk about it in

the morning. What about Zayvion?" How did he get involved in this?"

"Dad hired him to watch me. He said he quit the day I saw my dad." I didn't say the day my dad died. I guess it still hadn't sunk in—that he was gone. It just felt like how it always was between us: him off somewhere hoarding money and power, and me trying my best not to be anywhere near him.

"What do you think about Zayvion?"

I leaned my head back on the headboad. I'd slowly sunk down while talking, so now I was lounging more than sitting. "I have no idea."

"Do you like him?"

"He's a good kisser."

She raised her eyebrows and smiled. "So far so good. Let me rephrase the question. How much do you like him, and how long has this been going on?"

She was my best friend. The one woman who liked me even though I was crazy sometimes. The one woman who kept her feet on the ground no matter what happened. I didn't have to tell her everything. But I usually did. It was strange, but, in a way, she probably held more memories of my life than I did.

"I do like him. But I don't think I should. I'm so weirded out right now, I'm not thinking straight, not feeling straight. He's quiet, Nola. Insular. But he's gone out of his way to help me more than once and hasn't asked for anything in return, which is great and worries me. I mean, real life doesn't work like that. There's a price for everything, you know? And every time I think I have him figured out, he does something, and I'm back at square one again. It's hard to tell who he really is."

"Sounds like he's a lot like you. Does he have any redeeming qualities?"

I scowled at her. "Remind me why I come here?"

"Because I am your best friend, and you know I'm always here for you if you need me. Oh, and you think my opinions are pure gold."

"Gold?"

"Well, you think my opinions are pure something." She grinned and it made me smile too.

"So how about some of that golden wisdom?"

She tipped her head back and stared out the door. She was quiet for a while, her calloused hand still on the kitten's head. She had a habit of not saying anything until she was really ready to give her opinion. I hoped she wouldn't want to sleep on it before telling me how screwed up my life was. I hoped she'd tell me she thought everything was going to work out okay.

She finally looked over at me. "Allie, I think you need to take a little time and figure out what you're going to do next. You have been accused of killing your father. You skipped town with someone you barely know, and picked up a guy who had been stabbed. You didn't go to the police and didn't go to the hospital. That is going to be hard to justify."

"I know. I tried to get Zay to take me to the police, but he said it wouldn't be safe."

"And you believed him?"

I shrugged a shoulder. "I was fried. I couldn't think. He was there when I needed him, though." The memory of his hands on my skin, the mint and warmth of him that I was drawn to like a magnet to metal, rolled through me.

There was something between us. Maybe something more than just a physical attraction. "He helped Boy too. And didn't leave Cody behind. Or the cat. I think that counts."

Nola nodded. "Well, I think you should go to the police. For one thing, you're innocent, for another, you've been chased by that Hound woman and we don't know what she wanted to do with you. I'm not sure what to do with Cody."

I yawned. "I just couldn't leave him behind to bleed. Zay suggested we get him to a hospital and see if he's on record."

"Something else to do in the morning, after he finishes sleeping himself out. We'll get him up and let him eat, then see what he has to say on all this. Now, how are you really doing with your dad?"

Oh, I so couldn't talk about this, because if I did I'd just cry, and if I started crying I wasn't going to stop. "I'm okay. I'm trying not to think about it too much, yet. I don't think I want to talk."

She patted my leg. Even though her husband, John, had died four years ago, the marks of grief still showed in her eyes. I knew she'd understand.

"I'll let you get some sleep, honey. We'll see what we can do to straighten your life out in the morning."

I snuggled down between the blankets, not caring that I hadn't brushed my hair and was going to regret it in the morning. The bed was soft but not too soft, and the blankets smelled of soap and a little like flowers.

"Thanks, Nola. For everything."

"Any time. But let's try a visit with less drama and more shopping next time, okay?" She picked up the kitten and got off the bed, then called Jupe. I heard him clomp across the living room—which was across the entryway hall from my room—and pad through the door.

"Jupe is going to sleep in here with you tonight."

"Why?"

Nola pointedly looked out the door, and I propped up enough to see what she was looking at.

Zayvion had made up the couch in the living room, and was stretched out on it, a blanket tossed over his hips and chest, leaving his bare legs and arms free. His eyes were closed, but I didn't think he was asleep yet.

"Like I can't look after myself?" I whispered. "I've been dealing with him for days."

Nola raised her eyebrows and gave me a long look. "Do you know this man?" she whispered. "Do you know anything about who he is? I've watched you fall into bed with men so fast that you didn't even know their names. And not one of them treated you right."

"That was high school, Nola." At her look, I added, "Okay, okay. And college. And after that."

"And this is now," she said. "It doesn't change my opinion."

"You worry too much."

"I'm not the one with burns up my arm and face, nor am I on the run from the law."

I looked up at her. She wasn't angry, wasn't trying to make me feel bad. She was worried. Deeply. And I was lucky to have a friend who cared that much about me.

"Sorry," I said. "I'm just not thinking very straight."

"I know. That's why I'm thinking for you." She walked over to the bed and squeezed my hand. "Good night, honey. Are you sure you don't want anything for the burns or bruises?"

"No. They really don't hurt."

She walked to the door, and Jupe followed her. "Stay, Jupe," she said.

Jupe wagged his tail and tromped back into the room, made a circuit of the meager space between the bed and door, then sprawled out across the floor. He took up so much room that my chest instantly tightened with the panic of being closed in, trapped.

Nola propped the door open wide, giving me more breathing room. "Good night, Allie."

I licked at my lips, eyed the floor full of dog, and looked out at the not-sleeping Zayvion with all that great space around him.

"Is this really necessary?"

"I think so," Nola said. "Trust me on this." She turned off the lights, leaving me and the beast in the darkness. I heard her stocking feet go through the living room, then up the stairs to the second floor. I listened to her check on the kid in the real guest bedroom, wished she'd put me in that room instead because at least it was big enough for me and the dog, then heard her walk to her own room. Pretty soon I heard her light click off and then the squeak of bedsprings as she settled down.

The dark room was a box, a grave, a coffin. My heart beat clunked along while I practiced calming mantras. I could do this—I'd shared a dorm in college. When I had to, I could handle small spaces. And this room was much bigger than an elevator. Bigger than a bus, a crowded subway, a compact car, a cramped closet, a crate—okay that line of thinking was not helping. I was starting to sweat.

Think positive.

This room was so big, a dozen Jupes would fit in it with me. And if I could just stop thinking about it, I could fall asleep and if I could fall asleep, I could stop thinking about it.

I worked on meditating and relaxing my muscles systematically, starting at my toes. By the time I got to my knees, the dog was snoring. By the time I got to my elbows, Zayvion was snoring.

Great. Like sleeping between dueling chainsaws was going to do me any good. I knew I'd never be able to fall asleep.

Then, of course, I did.

Chapter Nine

Cody wasn't asleep. He kept his eyes closed while the lady he did not know came into the room. She stopped by the bed he was lying in and pulled the covers up closer to his chin. That felt good and made Cody wonder if he should stop pretending to be asleep now.

Wait, the older, smarter part of him said.

So Cody waited. A lot of people had done bad things to him. Maybe the lady was going to be bad too.

She moved around in the room and Cody didn't know what she was doing. Pretty soon, he felt something press down at the bottom of the bed like she had left something there. Then the lady walked out of the room.

Cody waited. He was good at waiting. He thought about nice things, like sunshine and wind, and maybe fell asleep for a while. When he woke up, he tried not to think about bad things, like the Snake man and the death man and the knife and the magic and the pain. . . .

Cody whimpered. He remembered the bad things. The bad things were bigger and stronger than the good things. He breathed and breathed, but it did not make the bad things go away. He had to get away from them. He had to run. But the older, smarter part of him had told him to be quiet. He didn't want to make the older, smarter part of him mad.

Open your eyes.

Cody opened his eyes. He was in a room. A new room. He had never seen it before.

He turned his head. The room was dark, but a little yellow light, like a star, twinkled by the floor and made just enough glow that he could see. There was a window with pretty curtains on it and the wall was covered in rows of little flowers.

Cody liked flowers.

Maybe this was a good place. A place where the bad things couldn't find him. He held still and listened. There was wind outside the window, but not a lot of other sounds. Cody was curious about the outside, but tired, too. The spell the older, smarter part of himself had used on him to make the Snake man think he was dead hurt really bad. A tear trickled down the side of his nose. Cody didn't like that the older, smarter part of him had done that bad thing.

It was a good thing, the older, smarter part of him said. *It saved us.*

"It hurt," Cody whispered.

I'm sorry. You were brave.

Cody sniffed and wiped his nose on the back of his hand. The older, smarter part of him did sound sad. And Cody had been brave. Brave enough to ask the lady with magic inside her to help.

Yes, that had been a good thing too.

Cody wondered where that lady was. And then he thought about something else. Kitten. His heart started hitting the inside of his chest too fast, and his throat got all scratchy and scared. Where was Kitten?

He sat up and looked around the room. More tears fell down his face. Cody was all alone and afraid. Maybe Kitten was all alone and afraid too. He had to find her.

He moved his foot and bumped something at the bottom

of the bed. Something heavy like a blanket or a towel. Cody looked down at it. It was a towel with a lump in the middle.

Cody pushed away the blankets and crawled down to the bottom of the bed because he knew what the lump was. It was Kitten. Kitten was here!

Cody picked up Kitten and brought her back up to the top of the bed. He put her very carefully down on the pillow next to him, close to the window so she could see that they were in a new place too. Kitten didn't wake up, but that was okay. Cody was happy. Happy she was here.

He put his head down on the pillow next to her and petted her soft fur with his fingertips. Everything was going to be okay now. Everything was going to be good.

Then Cody felt a strange tingle grow in his stomach, like bees had gotten under his skin, right where the Snake man had cut him.

But it wasn't bees. Someone was looking for him. Looking with the magic coins. Looking with the bones and blood and bad magic.

Snake man.

Hold still, the older, smarter part of him said. *Don't do anything. Cody. Don't move.*

Cody pulled the covers over his head, hiding Kitten under the blankets too. He held still. He held his breath. He wanted the tears to stop falling down his face, but they fell anyway. The older, smarter part of him was gone, so far away, and Cody felt all alone again. But he held still just like the older, smarter part of him had told him to.

The buzzing got stronger, and spread under his skin. The bees were angry. They buzzed all the way up to his throat because the Snake man told them to. They buzzed around her heart because the Snake man told them to. They wanted to buzz inside his head, but the older, smarter part of him had done something so they couldn't get in.

Cody held still. He tried not to scream, but a tiny, scared sound came out of him.

The Snake man looked and looked. The bees buzzed and buzzed.

It felt like it took a long time. A really long time before the bees flew back down away from his head. Away from his throat. Away from his heart.

Finally the bees stopped being mad. They all went back inside his scar and didn't buzz around anymore and didn't move around anymore.

The Snake man stopped looking.

Cody was alone again.

He was glad the bees were gone. He was glad the Snake man was gone too. But he was afraid they would come back. Come back and hurt him.

It's okay, the older, smarter part of him said. He sounded far away and tired. *Go to sleep. We're safe for now.*

Cody didn't feel safe, but he did feel tired. He made an opening in the blanket so Kitten could breathe cool air better. Then he went to sleep.

Chapter Ten

Someone was staring at me. I could feel it even before I opened my eyes. I breathed in, trying to orient myself by the smells around me. I got a noseful of flower, soap, and dog.

Nola's place. The house was quiet, and no light came through my eyelids. It was night. Everyone else sounded asleep too.

So who was staring at me?

I opened my eyes just enough to see. Darkness and nothing else.

No, someone was watching me. I glanced at the doorway, and in the uncertain light from a night-light by the hallway floorboards, I could see the dark shape of Zayvion sitting on the couch.

Staring at me. He looked like he'd been awake for a while. Alert. Wary. I wondered if I'd missed something.

"Are you okay?" he asked in a hushed voice.

A fleeting memory of a nightmare, bones and pain and blood, slipped from my thoughts. The sides of my cheeks were wet. I'd been crying.

"I'm fine," I said. Except I was alone. Except I wanted someone to hold me, wanted someone to comfort me, even if for only one night. The memory of the kiss in the car made me ache for the taste of him. It would just be one night. One night before I had to pick up my real life and deal with it again. I wondered if he'd say yes.

I sat. "Zayvion?" I whispered.

Light licked amber across the muscles of his arms, bare chest, stomach, and thighs as he stood and silently made his way across the living room. He paused at the doorway, wearing nothing but a pair of boxers. Shadows moved across his face, hiding his lips, but I could see his eyes, burning bright.

"Yes?"

"Would you hold me?" I asked.

"Just hold you?"

I answered him by pulling off my T-shirt. He grunted like I'd just hit him in the stomach. I sat there, half-naked, cold. I wanted his warmth, wanted the safety of his arms around me.

"More than that," I said.

He still stood in the doorway, dark, motionless, and silent, except for the rise and fall of his chest as he breathed more quickly.

After a long pause, I realized I had made a mistake. He was going to say no. Maybe the kiss in the car and the kiss outside the deli had all been one-sided—had all been me assuming there was an attraction between us that was not there.

"I'm sorry," I said reaching for the T-shirt next to me. "I thought you wanted—"

"No," he said, cutting me off. "I do want."

Those words seemed to decide something for him. He finally moved. He let go of the doorjamb he'd been holding onto and snapped his fingers. Jupe lifted his big head and thumped his tail on the hardwood floor.

"Out," Zay said. He snapped again and pointed to the living room. Jupe yawned and dutifully walked out of the room, like he and Zay had been buddies for years instead of hours.

Nola had left Jupe here to guard me, to keep me from sleeping with Zay. Probably because she thought getting serious with a man I barely knew wasn't a good idea. But Nola hadn't had everything in her life go to hell. She hadn't been chased, hurt, accused. She hadn't gotten sick from watching a little boy almost die, hadn't had her father lie through shared blood, hadn't overdosed on magic to try to fix a stranger's stab wound.

She hadn't told her father for the last and final time that she hated him, then had him die on her before she could say she was sorry.

Zay quietly shut the door and padded across the room. He paused and stood in front of me.

Electricity trembled through me. I reached up and placed my palm against his chest, my hand a ghost of ivory against the darkness and heat of his skin. I drew my palm slowly down the tight muscles of his stomach and paused at his waistband.

"I want you," I whispered.

He leaned toward me and I leaned back, lifting the covers so he could come with me to this soft and sacred place. He waited as I tugged off my sweatpants and panties. I waited as he pulled off his boxers. In all the time since he had come into the room, and it felt like hours, days, he had not yet touched me, had not yet kissed me.

And I so desperately wanted him to.

Zayvion lay beneath the covers beside me and finally, finally, drew his hand up my hip, my ribs, and over the curve of my breast. I shuddered in pleasure.

He brushed his thumb over my nipple, paused to circle it gently. I moaned and met his lips with my own.

Desire echoed through me and I trembled with need. I tangled my legs with his and leaned back, bringing Zay on top of me, the weight of his strong, wide body pressing me into the soft embrace of the bed. He lowered his head and gently bit the hollow of my neck. Electricity flickered through me, wicked and warm, pooling between my thighs.

I was hot, needful, hungry.

I dragged my nails up his wide, lean back. I pushed my fingers into the thick curls of his hair, savoring the texture of him, and coaxed his lips down to mine. He breathed gently against my cheek, then finally, finally, his lips cradled mine, soft, hot. His tongue slipped sweetly into my mouth, seeking, stoking my passion. With every stroke of his strong, masculine heat, need rose in me. High. Higher.

The scent of pine, of musk, the salty-sweet taste of him, wrapped me, filled me.

I wanted more. More of him. All of him. I wanted this to never end.

Heat and pleasure stretched me, filled me so full, too full.

More.

I arched up, pressed against him, wrapped around him. The sliding heat of fire licked through me, growing, spreading, pulsing, until all I could feel, all I could want was the aching hardness of him within me.

Yes.

Zay shuddered. Hot waves of pleasure broke and poured through me, tumbling me over the edge of desire and gently down, down to the soft, welcome warmth of his body against mine.

It has never felt like that before, I thought as he lay

against me, sweating and heavy, my legs still tangled with his. *It has never felt so right.*

I might have drifted off to sleep, or maybe I just lost track of time. But I eventually noticed again the ticking of the clock in the living room, the smallness of the room around me, and Zayvion.

He rolled away, leaving a final kiss on the top of my breast before taking up half the bed by lying on his back. I shifted to my side and put my head on his shoulder and my arm across his chest, not ready to lose contact with him yet.

We didn't say anything. Even though his breathing was soft and even, I knew he was awake because I could hear the flick of his eyelashes as he blinked.

And while I did not know why he was still awake, I knew what was keeping me up.

I couldn't believe I'd just slept with him. Not that it wasn't wonderful. Okay—fantastic. But now I didn't know what to do. Nola was right. I had a long history of falling into bed with men before I knew them. And I did not really know Zayvion.

It would be crazy to fall for someone who was hired to stalk me—who maybe still was stalking me. After all, he had a remarkable knack of tracking me down when things went terribly wrong. He was a wild card in my suddenly too-wild life.

Other than stalking and maybe spying, I wasn't sure he even had a job.

He might be following me and doing all these nice things because I was rich. Richer now that my dad was dead. If he got in good with me, he would never have to work again in his life.

Maybe he had this all planned and wanted to get me out here where I couldn't defend myself with magic.

Okay, that was crazy. He'd told me he didn't kill my dad, and I believed him.

Pull yourself together, I thought.

I wished I'd made the dog stay.

I wished I'd gone back to sleep.

"Zay," I said.

"Mmm?"

"I need to ask you something."

He shifted so he was on his side, facing me. "So do I. Let me start, okay?"

"No. Me first," I said. "Are you here because you want the money I'm going to inherit?"

He paused on an exhalation and stiffened. "You're kidding, right?"

"No. I want to know if you want my money, or if you're angling for a hand in the business—Beckstrom Enterprises."

He closed his eyes. When he opened them, all the warmth and laughter was gone. "Is that what you think? That I did this to manipulate you?" He was angry and probably had every reason to be.

"Yes," I said. "No. Maybe." I groaned and flopped over on my back. I couldn't think straight. I pressed my fingers over my eyes. "I don't know," I said through my palms. "It's just happening so fast. I don't know if I can handle this. Us. Whatever we are." Hells, could I sound any more pitiful? "You don't want the money, do you?"

He didn't say anything. I waited, but all I heard was his breathing, slightly elevated, like he was still angry. I finally pulled one hand away from my face and peeked over at him.

Predawn light fingered through the slats covering the window. It was pretty, I suppose. It lent enough light for me to watch Zayvion's expression close down until none of the warmth and passion of a lover showed in his eyes. Until he was calm, controlled, closed. Zen.

"I don't want the money," he said with such quiet and control it actually spooked me. "I don't want control of the company. If this is going too fast, then I'll give you some time to think about what I do want."

He reached over and brushed my bangs out of my eyes. His thumb glided across the mark of magic that curled at my temple, and I found myself longing for the coolness of his touch. Something deep in my bones responded to him, drew toward him whenever we touched.

"What are you?" I whispered.

There was a knock at the door, then Nola's voice. "If you two want to put some clothes on, I think you need to come out to the kitchen and see this."

I didn't know she was awake, hadn't heard the springs on her bed creak, hadn't heard her walk down the noisy wood stairs. Hells. Someone could have walked in and killed me, for all the attention I was paying. Or maybe I'd been paying very close attention to the only person in the house I wanted to see.

Still, it was predawn. Nola had a hideous habit of getting up before the sun, so she'd probably heard all the moaning and groaning going on in here. This old farmhouse had very thin walls. How fabo was that?

I blushed, and was glad the light was low.

"We'll be out in a minute." I pulled the top blanket around me and slid off the bed to gather the sweats and T-shirt.

Zayvion got out of bed, picked up his boxers, and put them on.

I managed to get my sweats on while contorting to hide my decency behind the blanket. Oh, screw it. It's not like we hadn't just been a whole lot of naked with each other a few minutes ago.

I dropped the blanket, turned the inside-out T-shirt inside-in again and tugged it on over my head.

Zay was watching me.

"What?" I asked.

"Do you want your father's money?"

I rubbed at my hair and knew it must be sticking out like a Christmas cactus. I was glad there weren't any mirrors in the room, because I was sure I was a vision of lovely.

"Listen," I said while I rummaged for a robe in the closet. "I know I've had advantages in my life because of my father's money, nice things and good education—especially the education. But when I failed at getting my degree in business magic and dropped out of college, he disowned me. I knew there would be no going back on that."

"Why didn't he hire private tutors?"

"What do you mean? To teach me magic?" I snagged a plain white robe off the hook, and shut the closet door. "No one teaches magic outside the universities. It's too dangerous. If a student does something really stupid, you need a whole crew of people to set Siphons, bear Proxy, and do other kinds of mop-up."

I thought Zay was just testing to see if I had really gone to college. But he was watching me, his nostrils flared like he was trying to scent the truth of my words.

"You never met other users?" he asked. "Teachers?"

And I knew there was something riding on my answer, something important.

"What if I had?" Okay, that was a bluff, but I was suddenly really interested in what had gotten Mr. Zen all worked up.

He shrugged one shoulder, but otherwise was still, waiting.

I was so not in the mood for a game of truth or dare. "I've never met with teachers outside of the universities. Well, maybe in a social setting, but not in a student-teacher sort of way. Okay? Why is that such a big deal?"

"Allie, your father was very powerful in the world of magic."

"And you're trying to see where I fit in all that?"

He nodded.

"I've told you—I didn't fit. Wasn't a part of it—whatever 'it' was. Disowned, remember?"

Zay nodded and looked over at the window, avoiding my gaze. "That's good to know."

What had gotten into him? I hadn't tried to be public with my dropping out and estrangement from my father, but there had been a couple slow news days, so it wasn't like it was a secret.

"What did you think?" I muttered. "That my dad and I were out to take control of all the magic in the world?"

Zay turned to look at me so fast I thought his neck was going to snap.

"Sweet hells, Zay. I was joking," I said. "Joking. What is going on in that head of yours?"

Nola's voice called out. "Allie, Zayvion. Breakfast."

Zay looked down at the floor and rubbed at the back of his neck. I didn't think I'd ever seen him embarrassed before. "Sorry. That was funny," he said unconvincingly. "Let's go get some coffee." He pulled into his jeans and shirt, then escaped the room without looking at me.

Weird. Weird. Weird.

I tied the robe closed and tucked my hair behind

my ears. Maybe I'd been onto something just then. Maybe my father *had* been out to control all the magic in the world. He already owned patents to most of the systems that made magic available. So what else was there to control? Who else was there to control?

I thought about Cody. I thought about him pulling magic *through* me, like I was a flesh-and-blood conduit for it. No one should be able to do that. *I* shouldn't have been able to do that.

And I certainly shouldn't have been able to heal him.

Were there other people who could do things with magic that they shouldn't?

A shiver ran down my arms and the nauseating pangs of panic rolled in my belly. I'd been in so many bad situations lately, even the hint of something going wrong put me full into fight-or-flight mode, and it was exhausting. I shook my hands to loosen my shoulders and neck, and took a few good breaths to clear my head.

Coffee first. Then, if I still felt like it, I could panic.

I walked out of the room and made my way to the kitchen and the low sounds of unfamiliar voices.

Nola, Zayvion, and Cody were all in the kitchen. Zay stood at the stove, drinking from a coffee mug, and looking calm and unperturbed as always.

The unfamiliar voices were coming from a small TV set on the counter. Right now it was some woman talking about foot fungus.

"I'll get you some food," Nola said. "Why don't you sit next to Cody."

I looked over at the kid. His blond hair was damp and brushed down tight against his head. He'd obviously just taken a shower. It looked like Nola had found a spare pair of sweats and a flannel shirt for him. He was about Nola's build, but I did a quick reassessment of his age. Slight of frame and delicate features, yes, but not because he was a kid. I'd put him in his mid-twenties, maybe even early thirties. His head was bent over the kitten in his hands. He completely ignored the bowl of cold cereal on the table in front of him, and, as far as I could tell, everything else.

"So your name's Cody." I sat in the chair across from him where I could keep my eye on Zayvion. "Remember me?"

Cody looked up from the kitten and smiled a bright, lopsided smile. "Pretty colors," he said. He held up his hand and waved it in the air like he was pushing finger paints around. He frowned when nothing happened.

"There's no magic here, Cody," Nola said, and it sounded like she'd been saying that for a while.

Cody stopped waving and put his hands back around the kitten.

"Cody?" I said. "Do you remember me helping you? Do you remember talking to me down by the water?"

Cody started rocking in the seat of his chair.

Oh. I looked over at Nola. "I didn't know," I said.

She nodded. "Well, it should make it easier to narrow down where he came from. I can't imagine someone isn't looking for him."

"I still think we should check to make sure he didn't escape from a penitentiary," Zay said.

He pulled a couple pieces of toast out of the toaster, dropped them on a plate, and layered a thick wedge of cheese between them. He walked over to the table and sat down next to Cody, across from me. Good. Now we could both keep an eye on each other.

"Penitentiary?" Nola asked.

"Zayvion thinks he might have gotten in trouble with the law."

Nola placed a plate of homemade bread, butter, cheese, and apples in front of me. "I'll get you some oatmeal," she said.

"Don't bother. This is perfect, thanks."

She moved over to the stove, poured a cup of coffee, and handed it to me.

"What kind of trouble do you think he was involved with?" she asked Zayvion.

Zay chewed, and slurped coffee. "Forgery. There was a high-profile case a few years back. A young man who committed a string of forged magical signatures. Covered up some pretty big Offloads, Proxy abuses, blackmail, and embezzlement. Landed him in prison."

"Was he mentally challenged?" Nola asked.

Zay shook his head. "If he was, it was never mentioned in the news articles. Still, there were rumors that once he was out of the public's eye, the people whom he had indicted before he was sentenced dealt out their own kind of justice."

"They mentally damaged him?" she asked. "How is that possible?"

"Tried to kill him, but were not successful. It's hard to kill someone with magic. Takes an incredible amount of power, and intense focus and control."

"And the price is too high," I said.

"What's the price?" Nola asked.

Questions like that made me realize she really did live in a world without magic. "Death. If you take a life, you have to give a life."

"Oh." Nola looked over at Cody, who was still rocking.

"And," Zay added, "despite all those risks, they

apparently didn't want to get their hands dirty by killing the old-fashioned way."

"Do you really think he might be the same person?" Nola asked.

We all looked at Cody, who rocked faster and hummed.

"They say he was a genius," Zay said. "An artist who could manipulate magic and make it become anything he wanted it to be."

"Nobody can make magic into anything they want," I said, hoping it was true. "There's a limit to what magic can do, a limit to any user's ability."

Zay shrugged. "Some say magic isn't as cut and dry as people think. It's only been in use for what? Thirty years?"

"Isn't there a name for people who are naturally talented at magic?" Nola sat at the table. "I heard it's rare. Aren't they called Servants or something?"

"Savants," Zay and I said at the same time.

Cody stopped rocking. He looked up at each of us, his blue eyes wide, frightened. Then he dropped the kitten next to his cereal. "Kitten likes milk. See?"

Kitten did indeed like milk and went to town, greedily lapping it up from around the floating cereal.

"Hmm," Nola said. "It might be easy to find out where he came from, but I'm not so sure it will be as easy for you to get him back there."

"Who said we were taking him anywhere?" Zayvion asked.

"I do," I said. "I think he needs to go back to wherever his home is." Wherever he's safe, I thought.

"And if I disagree?" Zay said. "How are you taking him without a car?"

"I'll drag him in with me to the police, and let them take care of him."

Nola held up her hand. "Wait. The news is back on. This is what I wanted you to see."

I glared at Zay and he looked at me, unperturbed. But when I heard my name on the news, I turned to watch.

It is strange to hear your own name on the news. I suppose people might think it's an exciting thing, but really, the news mostly covers tragedies, scandals, and misfortune. Any time your name is associated with one of those things, you were in a world of hurt and probably didn't want the whole world to know about it.

Hearing my name spoken by a reporter, a stranger who did not know me, was weird even though my name had been occasionally mentioned alongside my father's in the media. This time felt very different. This time made me feel vulnerable, exposed, violated.

A picture of my dad next to an intelligent-looking dark-haired woman who I assumed was one of the wives I'd missed out on flashed on the screen. Then the screen filled with a picture of me, from a dedication ceremony I'd attended with my father during my precollege days. In the photo I was smiling and had absolutely no idea what a huge mess my life was about to become.

The news ended with the reporter reciting a phone number, and summing up that I was a person of suspicion in the case of my father's death and any information on my whereabouts should be immediately reported to the police.

The reporter gave the camera over to the weatherman, and I sat back in my chair, acutely aware that Nola and Zay were staring at me.

"Shit," I said. I supposed the only good thing was they didn't say I was armed and dangerous and should be shot on sight.

I expected Zayvion to say he told me so—Bonnie had ratted me out to the cops and they were looking for me, just like he said. But he sat there quietly, which was pretty decent of him.

"Well," Nola said. "I think we need to think this out and make a plan of what to do next. Allie, do you have any ideas?"

"I still think I should go to the police. Turn myself in."

Zay sat back in his chair and watched me from over the edge of his coffee cup.

"I'm innocent," I said. "I didn't do anything."

"Can you prove that?" Zay asked quietly.

"Of course I can."

"You have an alibi for where you were after you and I left the deli?"

I opened my mouth to tell him of course I did, and he could shove it. But my recollection of what had happened from when I left my dad's office to when I woke up at Mama's was spotty at best. Even the deli seemed a little foggy to me.

"I went home," I said.

"Did anyone see you there?" Zayvion asked. "Did you make any calls? Talk to anyone in the halls?"

"No."

"No witnesses. No calls to trace. Not good," he said. "Then what?"

"I left."

"Why?"

"I couldn't stand the smell of the building."

"Doubt that will hold up in court, but fine. Where did you go, and who saw you go there?"

This is where the really big black holes and gaps of time filled my head. The hit I Hounded on Boy had kicked in pretty hard by then. I was hurting and maybe even a little delirious. I was lucky I hadn't wandered around town bleeding out of my ears and singing show tunes. For all I knew I might have done just that.

Or maybe I'd gotten angry and confused. Maybe I'd found my way back to my father's office, managed to ride the elevator without having a panic attack, gotten past his perky, nosy secretary, and somehow summoned the strength to draw enough power, through the protection wards—and cast a killing spell—to kill him.

It just seemed so incredibly unlikely. But it also seemed incredibly unlikely that I couldn't remember nearly a full twenty-four hours—the twenty-four-hour span when my father was killed.

"I can't remember, exactly."

Zay said nothing. He didn't have to.

Nola rubbed her hand between my shoulder blades and gave me a gentle pat. "I suppose this is a bad time to remind you what I think about using magic."

"Yeah, Nola." I managed a small smile. "I know what you think about using it. And right now, I see your point." I looked back over at Zayvion. "So maybe I don't have an alibi. But do they have any evidence that I went back to my father's place? Do they have any evidence that it *was* me who killed him? A security camera? Some eyewitness in the lobby or something?"

"They have Bonnie's testimony that she Hounded the hit and it was your signature on it."

"Bonnie hates me and would do anything to make me hurt."

"Can you prove that?" Zayvion asked.

I rolled my eyes. "Maybe. Probably. We haven't hidden our hatred or anything. People know about it. The bank job she and I handled—all the people involved in that know how she feels about me."

"That would help," Zay conceded, "but it won't change the fact that the police brought in three Hounds to sniff the hit, and that Violet hired a separate Hound independent of them to check too."

"Violet's my dad's current wife?" I asked.

It didn't take him long to figure out I was not joking. He nodded.

"Okay. What did her Hound say?"

"They all said it was your signature, Allie."

Five Hounds sniffing the same hit would find subtle differences if there were any. If five different Hounds said I did it, even I would think I did it.

But I had zero recollection of killing my father. I'd think a person would remember such a thing. I think I would remember it, memory loss or no memory loss. I would have felt it. I would have tasted it. It would still be in my hands, in my lungs.

"How do you know all this, Zayvion? Are you a cop? A reporter? How do you have all this inside information that I don't have?"

"Allie, I've told you all that. Don't you remember?"

That hit me like a punch to the gut. I did not remember. If he had come clean about who he was and what he did and why he was always following me around, it had fallen down the same twenty-four-hour black hole growing in my head.

I opened my mouth to tell him "How about we just pretend I don't remember and you can tell me again," but Cody let out a piercing, childlike scream of glee that reminded me why I never wanted to have a child.

He stood and pointed at the window, and once he ran out of air he filled up again and kept on screaming.

Nola moved around the table and put one hand on his outstretched arm. "You need to be quiet now, Cody. Use your inside voice. Use your words. Tell me what's wrong."

But Cody was not listening. He pushed away from Nola and hurried over to the window, still screaming.

Zay was on his feet and moving toward him now. Even though Cody acted like a kid, he was still a man, and none of us knew enough about him to know what he might do.

Cody pressed his palms flat against the window, then switched so only his fingers were touching the glass. He wiggled his fingers as the pale yellow light of the rising sun filtered through the branches of the willows beyond the road and spilled like ghostly honey across his hands.

He stopped screaming, transfixed by the sight of sunlight on his hands. Then he looked up and through the window. "Sunshine," he said softly. He looked over his shoulder at Nola. "Sunshine."

Wow. The guy really liked sunshine.

Back on the table, the kitten stuck her paw in the milk, slipped, and dunked her face in it. She mewled and Cody reluctantly turned away from the sunshine to retrieve her. "Sunshine, Kitten," he said. "Sunshine." He picked her up, but became confused as to what to do with the milk-soaked cat.

Nola handed him a towel and he dried her feet and face.

"Zayvion," Nola said. "Stay here with Cody, please. Allie, let me get your clean clothes for you. Do you want to shower?"

"All right," I said.

Zayvion cleaned the table, taking dishes to the sink, and I followed Nola to the laundry room.

"What?" I asked her when we got there. Her not-so-subtle attempt to get me away on my own meant she wanted to talk to me without Zay around.

"I've been thinking about everything you told me last night, and I have a couple questions." She opened the clothes dryer, letting out the floral fragrance of fabric softener. She pulled out my jeans, T-shirt, socks, and underwear, and dropped them all in my arms.

"Okay."

"Are you sure Cody had been stabbed?"

I leaned my hip against the washer. "Yes. It wasn't an Illusion, or a scratch that looked worse than it was. I know a bad puncture when I see one. And this one was sealed with magic."

Nola leaned against the dryer and crossed her arms over her chest. "Did healing him have anything to do with the marks up your arm?"

I nodded.

"You don't think you can do it again?"

"Nola, *no one's* ever done that. You can't just pluck magic out of the ground and make it do anything you want it to do. You have to study, learn the shapes it will accept, memorize the glyphs, mantras. It's work—hard work—and it hurts if you do it wrong. It hurts even if you do it right. To just suck up a handful of magic and wave it at someone until they stop dying is impossible."

"Impossible?"

"Improbable. To the extreme," I added.

"So who can manipulate magic that way?"

I knew what she was getting at. "Nola, I am so not a Savant."

"I don't know about that, Allie. You did really good in school."

"I flunked every course. The only reason they didn't kick me out was because my dad owned half the building and staff, and I left before they got up the nerve to tell him I sucked."

"I think you may not remember all the details of college."

I scowled. "It's been recently pointed out to me that my memory isn't all it's cracked up to be."

"And you often lose bits of your memory when you use magic, correct?"

"Yes."

"But not every time?"

"No. And before you ask, I don't know why. I don't know why magic sometimes takes my memory and sometimes doesn't."

"Still, you remember healing Cody, even though you were manipulating far more magic than you usually do."

"Nola, just say whatever you're getting at."

"Allie, you are a Savant whether you want to admit it or not. I know it, Zayvion knows it, I think your father knew it, which is why he wanted you to get so much schooling, and also why he wanted you involved in his business. You have the ability to use magic in amazing and powerful ways."

"Like to kill my father?" I asked quietly.

Nola just looked at me. "Do you really think you could do that?"

"I don't know," I said in a small voice. "I've been really angry at him for a long time."

"And you never killed him. Why would you do so now?"

I rubbed at my uncombed hair. "He put a hit on a little boy, Nola. A good kid who didn't deserve to take the brunt of my dad's business maneuverings. It was like the last, worst thing I could handle letting him get away with."

"Do you really think you could have killed him?"

I thought about it. I'd been angry—furious. Magic never works when you are in a highly emotional state. I knew that was true of everyone, no matter their level of proficiency—no matter if they were dumb to it or a Savant. I'd gone to my dad to make him pay for his actions. But even then I knew Boy had gotten to a doctor and I was sure Mama would make a pretty penny suing my dad for all she could get. I wanted him to pay. I wanted him to stop using money and power as an excuse to do horrific things to people who did not deserve it. But I did not, deep down, want him to die.

"I haven't told anyone this," I said. "Cody said he knew who killed my dad. He said he was there when it happened."

"Did he say you were there too?"

"I don't think so. He was babbling, but he seemed pretty . . . adult about it. Which is strange, considering what we're seeing in the kitchen."

"You haven't told Zayvion that Cody might have information?"

"No. I'm not sure how much I should trust him." I could feel the hot prickle of a blush rise up my face. "I know. Last night I was stupid. But now . . ." I lowered my voice and leaned toward her. "What if Zay just wants to get in good with me because I'm about to inherit a lot of money, and one of the biggest power broker companies in the business of magic? He might even work for one of the corporations that have been after Dad's patents for the Storm Rods for years."

"Or," Nola said, "maybe it's as simple as what he told me. That he worked for your father, and realized he liked you too much to spy on you anymore."

"He told you that?"

"When you first came, and he and I were getting Cody to bed."

"And you think it's the truth?"

Nola tipped her head to the side. "I'm not sure. He seemed sincere. I think we can safely assume he finds you attractive." She paused while I blushed again. "But there's something about him that gives me pause. I think you pegged it when you said he was insular."

"And doesn't that make you suspicious? He must have something to hide."

Nola smiled. "My best friend is pretty insular, and I still think she's a wonderful human being. Even if she does move too fast into relationships, and then panics when things get too serious."

"Oh, that is so not what I'm doing right now."

Nola chuckled. "Why do you think I wanted Jupe to stay in the room with you? I knew you'd do this. You are so predictable."

And there it was, the down side to having a really good friend.

"Thanks," I said.

"Anytime." She patted my arm gently, and then stopped as if my arm were injured. "Are you sure you don't need something for that?"

"No, it doesn't hurt." Which in itself was odd, but I didn't want to think about it. "Nola, if it were you, would you trust Zayvion enough to tell him about what Cody said and go back into the city with him?"

"No," she said. "But if I were you I would."

"Because I'm crazy?"

"Because you always push away men at the first sign they might see that you're vulnerable and use it against you. And you have rarely been right about that."

"So you like him."

She shrugged. "I don't know him yet. But he drove you all the way out here. He knows how to do dishes. He's certainly not hard on the eyes. What I think is, you like him. And you are too afraid to face that."

I rubbed at my eyes with one hand. "No, I just don't want to die because I fall for a pretty smile and a pair of strong shoulders."

Nola gave me a doubtful look. "Is that all he is to you?"

"No," I said quietly. "Listen, Nola. It's different out here on the farm, far away from magic and what it does to people. Magic drives people to do things you can't even imagine. The Proxy laws only came into effect a few years ago—before that anyone could inflict the pain and price of using magic on any random person they chose. People were dying so that a select few could have green yards, or get rid of wrinkles, or eat as much as they wanted and never gain weight. Regulations help, but even the best people can do horrible things when magic is involved."

"Which means good people can do great things, too," she said. "Good people like you, like me, and maybe even Zayvion."

I shook my head. "You are such an optimist."

"Yes, I am. And it isn't a dirty word in my book. Go take a shower. Think about it. I'm going to talk to Zayvion about Cody."

"What about Cody?"

"I think he should stay with me. I'll pull a few strings and see if I can find out where he came from and who he really is. Don't look at me like that—just because I don't use magic doesn't mean I don't have connections. And besides, if he's here, and if he really does know something about your father's death, I don't think it would be safe for him to stay with you until you make contact with the police and get that straightened out."

"I could call your local police station and turn myself in here."

She shook her head. "I'd rather not be on record as being involved in this yet. Cody was stabbed and left for dead. I don't know who would have done that, but I don't want them on my doorstep until I find out what his story is. Besides, the sheriff out here kisses up for any publicity he can get. I think he's angling for a higher office—maybe mayor—and I don't want you, or Cody to become his political platform."

"I had no idea you had such a calculated, conniving side," I said.

"I prefer to call it 'practical.' " She sashayed out of the room.

I took her advice and headed off to the shower.

Nola had a good head on her shoulders and could usually see between the lines of my personal drama and history, and give good advice. But she was wrong about one thing: Zayvion. Maybe he was a good enough guy, and maybe he found me attractive. But every instinct in my body told me that there was more to him than met the eye. And I refused to completely trust someone who appeared out of nowhere so conveniently every time something horrible happened.

He must want something out of this, something out of me.

As the shower sluiced away the musk and pine scent of him from my skin, I found my thoughts returning to his touch, to his lips, to the silent strength of him. And I realized I wanted something from him too. Not just sex. Not just companionship. Something deeper that I could not yet name.

Chapter Eleven

I changed back into my clothes, brushed my hair, and used Nola's toothbrush. The black bands on my left knuckles and wrist were still there. So were the whorls of red on my right. They didn't hurt, not even when I rubbed at them. I wasn't sure how I felt about bearing a lasting, visible mark from magic. It would be a conversation starter, I supposed, but probably not a conversation I'd much want to get into. Which meant if I ever had a social life again—barring I got shot, locked away in jail, or otherwise derailed from trying to live a quiet life—I'd have to make up some pretty good excuses for why I tattooed my left hand and had permanent henna painted from my right eye down to my fingertips.

If things weren't so serious right now, I might have some fun making up stories about it, but as it was, all I could think was that it would really make me stand out in a crowd.

Or a police lineup.

This was not the most convenient time for a drastic makeover.

I strolled out into the kitchen and found Nola and Cody there. Cody stood by the window, kitten in his hands, sunshine on his face. Nola was sipping coffee again.

"Don't you have some farm-type things to do?" I asked.

"Got them done before sunrise. Zayvion's packing up."

I nodded and walked over to Cody. I stood next to him, looking out the window. Nola had a wide porch railed in white wood. Farther out was a length of green grass and flower beds that were done blooming for the year. Her driveway was to the left and just out of view from here.

"Cody, do you remember me?" I asked.

Cody stroked the cat over and over, and I was amazed the little thing had any fur left on its head.

I turned so I was to the side, but in front of him. I was careful not to block the sunshine that seemed to hold him so rapt.

"Do you remember me from the river when you were hurt?"

Cody petted the cat faster, and began rocking from foot to foot.

I tried a different tactic.

"I'm sorry you were hurt, Cody."

After a full minute or so, his rocking slowed.

"You did a good job helping me make you feel better. With the colors and the—"

"Magic," he whispered.

I nodded. "Magic." I waited, letting this agreement settle between us.

"It was pretty," I said, and I meant it. "Beautiful magic. And it made your chest stop hurting. Do you remember that?"

He nodded. "I remember."

I glanced over at Nola. She was wiping down the kitchen counters and listening. Since the slow but sure approach seemed to be working, I waited a while before speaking again.

"You told me you knew a powerful man. Was he my father?" Pause while he rocked and Nola put her dishrag away.

"Mr. Beckstrom, right? Did you see me too?"

Cody nodded, a brief jerky motion.

My stomach churned. I glanced over at Nola, but she didn't look panicked.

"That was good, Cody." I worked hard to stay calm and convincing. "You were good to see us."

Cody rocked.

"You saw us because you were using the pretty magic, right?"

Cody rocked faster.

"Okay." I let the silence stretch out until he was rocking slower again.

"Did you see my dad die?"

Cody stopped rocking and looked at me. His eyes were still summer blue, but they were narrow, as if he were trying to see me through a thick fog.

"The Snake man told me to. I was you. You killed him."

I cannot even explain the weird-creepy chill of hearing him say that. I tried to keep my voice level and soft. "I killed him? Or were you using magic to forge my signature when he died? How did you access that much power, Cody? Where were you? When did you do it? Who is the Snake man? Is he out there?"

Hells. I had pushed too hard.

Cody's eyes went wide with panic. He grabbed at his stomach, over his scar.

"Ow, ow." He moaned. "No, no, no." He looked

like he was going to scream or cry. He pulled the kitten close to his chest, dodged past me, and threw himself at the kitchen door. It banged open and Cody ran outside.

I was right behind him.

He ran down the porch stairs, one hand still on his stomach.

I smelled lavender, sweet and peppery. Nola didn't have lavender plants. I hit the stairs running and made a grab for Cody, but that boy moved fast. He was out of reach, outpacing me, heading toward the middle of the yard running, wild, scared.

"Cody, wait!" I ran after him.

The yard was as wide as the house and stretched out half an acre before it reached the road. There were no trees in the yard, no place for someone to hide.

Jupe tore out of the house, snarling and barking. But I didn't need his warning, because I'd seen it too. A flash of light in the air, silver hot cooling to a burning gold, struck like lightning. But instead of fading, the air where the strike had sliced filled with a flurry of black ash—like a cloud of black butterflies had suddenly appeared. A woman stepped through that wall of flying ash. Solidly built, blond, and stinking of lavender, it was Bonnie. She was reciting a mantra and moving her hands in a very un-Hound-like spell.

Cody ran right toward her. He threw his arms out to his sides and yelled, "Run! Run fast!"

Jupe pounded past me. Even though I had long legs and was in good enough shape to run, that dog was all muscle and instinct. He was gaining on Cody. But Bonnie wasn't standing still; she was headed for Cody too.

I heard footfalls and hard breathing coming up behind me. Risked a glance over my shoulder. It was Zayvion.

"Don't, Allie," he yelled.

Don't what? Catch the only person who knew how my father died? Don't try to outrun Jupe, who was still snarling and barking and about to tear Bonnie and/or Cody into pieces? Don't pound into Bonnie like she was a lump of clay that needed a whole lot of my knuckle prints?

Bonnie reached Cody before me. Bonnie caught him in her arms, and even though he struggled, she chanted a mantra—hard, guttural words—held her fist high in the air, and a flash of copper lightning struck again, struck Bonnie, struck Cody, and sent Jupe skittering back from the wall of ash, growling and yelping.

It was a flash, a slice of heartbeat. Bonnie and Cody were there. Lightning struck. Bonnie and Cody were gone.

Black ashes drifted down like raven feathers and shadowed a perfect circle on the ground where they had just stood.

"What the hell?" I jogged the last few feet to where Cody and Bonnie had disappeared. *Disappeared!* No one could vanish in a flash. No one. I didn't care what kind of spells they knew. The scientific improbability of moving that much mass—and the payment for pulling on so much magic *in a nonmagical zone* so that it shot like lightning from a calm sky—freaked me the hell out.

I tried to pull on the store of magic deep in my bones, but I was too agitated, too angry, too damn scared to think of a mantra, much less speak one. People magically snapping from one place to another was fairy-tale stuff. This couldn't happen. And for the good of the world, I didn't think this should be able to happen. This kind of power in the wrong hands could change the way magic was used and abused. In the wrong hands—and as far as I could tell, Bonnie was the wrong hands since she'd just kidnapped a guy from out of nowhere—this ability would make for dark, dark years ahead.

"Holy crap," I said. "Holy crap, holy crap!"

I was shaking, breathing too hard. But I was thinking fast. Maybe Bonnie and Cody weren't really gone. Maybe she'd just found some sort of way to confuse light so I couldn't see them. For all I knew, they might still be standing right there in the middle of the yard in front of me.

Zayvion came up to one side of me.

"What?"

I held up my hand to tell him to be quiet. And he did. Okay, there were some things I really liked about that man. I tipped my head to one side and listened for breathing other than his and my own. I watched Jupe, who sniffed at the black circle of ashes, but didn't step into them. I inhaled, smelled something like burned wood—the charcoal smell of ashes, fresh air, and a hint of chicken fertilizer.

Zay took a cautious step forward, and he was quiet, working his way around the circle of ashes.

I mentally intoned a mantra, calming, centering, set a Disbursement, then pulled on the magic from my bones. A flare of heat winged from my right hand up my arm to my eye. The magic followed the path of the marks on my arm—but it wasn't a painful sensation. It was a comfortable heat, like thrusting that limb into a warm bath. My left hand felt cool, and that was nice too. Magic, no longer small inside me, sprang from my body quicker than it ever had before, and I had to do some fast maneuvers to keep hold of it, keep focused, and draw it into my senses, especially my sense of smell.

The world exploded into smells. The greasy tang of ashes hit my sinuses and made me choke, coupled as it was with the dusty stone scent of pavement, the thick smell of mosses and rot and fungus from the field, decaying leaves, and decomposing organics from the distant chicken coop. Grass was green, bitter, oily, textured with the cold scent of dew. I could smell the river, tart and rushing with a silty mix of minerals, and I could smell Zayvion, the heavy pine of his cologne warmed and complicated by the stinging potency of his sweat, his fear, his anger.

And his shock.

I glanced at him. He was watching me with as close a look to awe as I'd ever seen on someone.

Oh, right. Magic. This was a dead zone. A magic-free zone. The only way to tap into magic here was to access the network that didn't reach this far—that didn't cross the river.

No one could do that. Unless they carried magic in their body. And no one I'd met could do that, except me.

"Allie?" he breathed.

"Later," I said.

I Hounded the traceries of the spell Bonnie had cast and smelled the copper-burn stink of spent magic coming from the circle of ashes.

The glyph of Bonnie's spell lingered in the air, and it was like nothing I had ever seen before. Not just a cabled line of intricate linked spells, this glyph was jagged, knotting back into itself to form a circle, like an incredibly intricate spider's web, with a black, black hole into which all the threads fell and stopped completely.

This spell wrapped in on itself. There were no trailing lines leading back to the caster. If I hadn't seen with my own eyes that Bonnie had been the one to cast this spell, I would have absolutely no clue who had cast it, where it had come from, or what it had done.

And knowing those things was my job.

"Holy crap," I said again, quieter.

The one thing I did know was that Bonnie and Cody were not still standing in the yard.

"What do you see?" Zayvion asked.

"It's a spell, feeding into itself, and leaving no trailing lines. They aren't here, Zayvion. I don't know where they are, but they are not here."

Zay took a deep breath and rubbed at the back of his neck.

"What?" The scent of him had changed, and with my *über*sharp Hounding senses, I knew his level of fear and anger had just spiked. "Good love, Zay. If you know anything about this, will you just come clean with me? That kid knows who killed my father."

His scent changed again, back to the sugary wash of surprise. He looked up at me from across the black ash circle. I don't know what it was, instinct maybe, but neither of us wanted to touch the ashes.

"He knows who killed your father?"

"Yes."

"Did he tell you who?"

Served me right. If I was demanding he had to level with me, it was only turnabout-fair that I tell him what I knew. Lovely.

"He wasn't very clear, but he mentioned a snake man, and that it was done with magic, and that I did it, or he did it as me." If I hadn't still been hyped up on magic, I was pretty sure I'd feel naked-at-the-table vulnerable for placing my last chip in Zayvion's palm. As it was, I just wanted him to give back as good as he got.

"So he was involved in the hit."

"Sounded like it to me, but before I could get anything more specific, he ran out here."

Zay went back to rubbing his neck. He muttered something and stared at the horizon for a second, long enough for me to consider kicking him in the shins until he talked.

"Allie, I'm breaking a lot of rules talking to you about this, but it seems stupid at this point not to."

"Good. Tell me." I was getting a little tired from holding the level of concentration needed to keep my Hound senses open, but what surprised me was that I did not feel a decrease or lack of magic pouring from within me. The small magic in my bones was a limited quantity, a small flame, and was usually depleted pretty quickly. Not this time.

"I don't know what she did—I don't even know who that woman was," Zayvion said.

"Bonnie."

"Really? Okay. So I don't know what Bonnie did, but I do have an idea what she used to do it."

Anyone could tell she used magic. "Spill it."

"It's a technology your father was developing. A way to make magic portable."

Holy shit. Portable magic would change the world. If magic could be carried in some easy little package, instead of gathered and stored in lead and glass networks running beneath and throughout an entire city, anyone could access it. Anywhere. Even in the dead zones.

"I have never seen anyone use magic to shift mass like that," Zayvion said. "Much less open up a portal or door or whatever that was. I mean, there are stories. . . ."

"How could anyone Proxy the Offload of that powerful of a spell?" I asked.

Zay's mouth became a thin, straight line. "There are ways. They are not legal."

Said like that, flat and unaffected, it gave me the chills.

"Fine. This is technology I could see someone wanting to steal. But who would kill for it?" I asked.

Zay gave one short laugh. "Who wouldn't? This is going to revolutionize everything we know about and do with magic, Allie. This will put someone in a position of worldwide power and influence. It is why we were being so careful not to let the technology get out before laws and enforcement were in place."

"Dear loves, Zayvion, did you just say 'we'?"

"No."

We stared at each other for a moment, but it didn't matter what he denied. I knew what I heard. "You want to tell me how you're involved in this?"

"No, but I know who we should go talk to next."

"Ooh, let me guess. The police? The FBI?"

"Violet."

"Who?"

"Your stepmother."

I groaned. "Run back into the city to the one place the cops, the Hounds, Bonnie, who may or may not still be working for whoever may or may not want me dead, probably have trip-wired and staked out to try to catch me? Great idea."

"It is a good idea," he said. "You just don't know it because you don't know Violet very well."

"At all. Never met her."

He gave me a funny look.

"Listen, I gave up caring after replacement mother number two."

"Abigail?" he asked.

"Yeah, I think so. You know an awful lot about my life, Jones."

"I'm a big fan of the Beckstrom legacy."

I tried to parse out what he really meant behind that and gave up on it. "Well, whatever. If you screw me over, I'll hunt you down and tear you apart. Got that?"

His eyebrows arched up, but instead of looking worried, like he ought to, he was smiling. "I wouldn't expect any less of you, Allie."

I stepped to the edge of the ash circle and knelt. My senses were still sharpened by magic. I leaned over the circle's edge and inhaled with my mouth open. Magic, burned, coppery, and thickened with other metals and oils. Something more too, something I could only describe as slick-tasting hit the back of my throat.

"I don't think that's a good idea," Zay said. "This is untested."

"Where's your intellectual curiosity? Your sense of adventure?"

I glanced up at the circular spell glyph that hovered in the center of the circle just above the level of my head. I reached into the circle and ran my fingers through the black ash.

Not ash. More like feathers. But feathers so delicate that they crumbled, or melted, at the slightest of contact. And also unlike feathers, the ashes felt warm against my fingertips, like menthol soaking in. I had a wild desire to stick my finger in my mouth and taste it.

I opened my mouth, but before my finger could

even get close to my tongue, Zayvion's hand clamped down around my wrist.

"Bad idea. We don't know what that is."

"If you let go of my arm, maybe we can find out."

"Or maybe it will kill you. I'm the guy who doesn't want to see you dead, remember? Don't be stubborn and stupid." His hand was hot and felt good.

"You so aren't winning any points in my book, Jones."

"You'll get used to it."

We had a little glaring match that made me want to throw him down and bed him again. What was it about him that was so irresistible? He was bossy, secretive, maybe even condescending. But he was also thoughtful, kind, and heaven help me, he was looking out for my well-being whether I wanted him to or not. I liked that about him. His tenacity to stick with me, no matter what I got into.

"Fine," I said. "Let go."

He did and I brushed my fingers on my jeans to cover the fact that I already missed him touching me.

I stood and released the draw of magic, pulling the power away from my senses of smell, hearing, and sight. The world snapped down into more tolerable olfactory levels, and I couldn't help but sigh at the relief of normal perceptions.

The strange thing was, I didn't feel as tired as I usually did when I worked magic. And I did not have the feeling of emptiness I always got when I drew upon the magic I stored in my bones.

Zay and I started walking back to the house, and I glanced down at my hands. The left one tingled like it had been asleep. The marks on my right hand looked different somehow, darker, with a gold cast that flowed into greens and opal blues. Working magic had affected the burn. It looked like an amazing tattoo, a spider gone wild, but painted in opalescent tones instead of flat ink. I always wanted to get a tat, but had never taken the time. I was fast growing fond of this scar.

It was probably only a temporary thing, but I might as well enjoy it while it lasted.

"You two okay?" Nola called out. She jogged down the steps of the porch, a shotgun carried, muzzle down, at her side.

She was so my best friend.

"We're fine," I said when we got close enough. "Did you see that?"

She nodded. "I didn't know people could appear and disappear with magic. Doesn't that violate most of the laws of physics?"

"I'm pretty sure it does," I said. "Nola, could you do me a favor and pack some food for Zay and me?"

"Sure. Where are you going?"

"To visit my stepmom."

Chapter Twelve

Nola made quick work not only of packing a picnic lunch, but of somehow stashing enough food in one box to hold us through winter.

"There must be something more I can do," she said. I put the box of provisions in the backseat of Zayvion's car and turned to her.

"I don't think so. Well, I guess if I get arrested and things go to trial, I'd love to have you testify about my character, and what you heard Cody say about my dad's death."

"You are not going to get arrested," she told me. She caught my hand. "Be careful, Allie, and don't do anything crazy. You know how much I hate visiting people in hospitals."

I did know. She'd stayed at John's side for months, and afterward swore she'd never set foot in a hospital again.

"I promise I'll stay as safe as I can. And since Zay refuses to leave me alone, I figure if things get bad, I can always shove him into the line of fire while I run like hell." I smiled, and she shook her head.

"You do like him, Allie. Remember that."

Remember it? It was impossible to forget.

Then she pulled me into a hug that was surprisingly

fierce for a slight woman. I hugged her back. "This won't be the last time I see you," I said, hoping it was true.

"I know." She released me and stepped back, still holding one of my hands. "Be careful and be safe. Come home when you can."

She gave my hand one last squeeze and stepped back. Jupe, the big lunker, pushed his head against Nola's hip, and she rubbed at his ears.

"See you soon," I said. I got into the car. Without a second good-bye, Zayvion backed out of the driveway and headed down the road.

"You okay?" he asked.

I felt a little cold, even though Nola had given me an old denim-and-wool coat of John's she'd found stored away.

"Don't worry about me. I'm fine." I crossed my arms and stared out the window, watching the bare limbs of trees filter the cloud-dampened sunlight. It was noon now. I figured we'd hit the city after dark. And before we got there, I wanted a plan.

"How well do you know Violet?" I asked.

He shrugged. "I've been working with her for a couple years."

"Working with her? Doing what? Did my father know? Why didn't you tell me that before?"

"My employment with her is not something I bring up in casual conversation." He grinned at my scowl. "The things Violet works on are very security-sensitive."

"So there's more going on than whatever we saw Bonnie use today?"

"As far as I know, the things Violet was working on did not hold the potential for transferring mass."

"As far as you know?"

"There are things she wouldn't necessarily tell me. I spent a lot of time following you around when your father started signing my paycheck. And you've kept me pretty busy for a few days."

"So you think Violet knows more than we do?"

"I doubt she knows someone has used her technology to do an instant transfer from one place to another—if it was her technology."

"Good. It will give us some leverage in negotiating."

Zay was quiet for a minute. The bridge was coming up soon, only a few more turns in the road until we were there. "You're going to negotiate with her?"

"Hell, yes, I am."

"About what?"

"Keeping my ass out of jail. Maybe having her pull some strings with the Hounds hunting me. She must know a few of Dad's shadier friends."

"Aren't you afraid she'll cut you out of your inheritance?"

"Oh, the hell with the money. I figure she's named in Dad's will, and has some sort of controlling interest in Beckstrom Enterprises. For that matter, all his other ex-wives might have a piece of the Beckstrom pie. I refuse to play a game of who gets to gnaw at the scraps of fat. Having tons of money—especially money made off of the misfortune of others—isn't my ultimate goal in life. I want enough to cover rent, buy coffee, and maybe hitch a train out of town every once in a while. And I want to not have to live my life wondering if, when I turn the wrong corner, somebody's going to be there waiting to kill me because I have something they want."

"You've put some thought into this, haven't you?"

"Years and years of it. There's the bridge."

"I see it." He tightened his grip on the steering wheel while slowing the car. Then he crept across the bridge.

Midway into the bridge I felt magic, like a curtain of static electricity, tingle and snap over my skin. Then the magic reached deeper, pouring into me through channels I did not know I had, filling me so full my skin felt tight. I'd never felt magic so keenly, so close, so intimate. I stretched my hands up over my head and pushed my legs out. Muscles lengthened, expanded, but still the magic poured in. I couldn't stretch to make room for it all, couldn't think it away, chant it away, push it away.

"Zayvion?" I couldn't hold this much; no one could hold this much magic. And while it didn't hurt, my ears were ringing, my heart was pounding, and my vision was tunneling down. "Zay?"

I was drowning. Magic filled my lungs, rose up my throat, poured out of my mouth, my ears, nose, eyes. I gasped, pulled in some air, but not enough. Not nearly enough.

I couldn't even think clearly enough to cast a spell to use the damn stuff. This was a stupid way to die.

"Breathe, Allie."

It was Zayvion. I thought it was Zayvion. Whoever it was, I tried to follow their advice. Breathed in, even though there was no room in me for air. Breathed out.

"Good. Again."

Great. I didn't know I'd have to do it again. I breathed in, and this time there was a little more room for air. I breathed out, and breathed in again without any prompting.

Each time I inhaled, there was a little more room, a little more space for air, then space for air and thoughts, then space for air and thoughts and, finally, space for air and thoughts and me.

I moaned on the next exhalation, inhaled and tasted mint in my mouth, smelled mint stinging my nose. I blinked blurry eyes that could distinguish only light and darkness. Tears slid cold tracks down my face, pooled in cold puddles in my ears.

I was lying in the front seat of a car. I thought about my little book, wondered if I'd need to check it to see who I was, where I was.

"Cold," I said. "Cold."

"Good." That was Zayvion's voice for sure. I remembered him. Remembered we were driving. I blinked again until I could see his face above me. His eyes were the most amazing gold—all gold—with only flecks of brown. Beautiful. But he looked worried. "Can you hear me, Allie?"

"Y-yes." I cleared my throat, then ran my tongue around in my mouth. You'd think with all that magic filling me up, I'd have lots of spit left, but my mouth felt dry as a desert canyon. I tried talking again. "I'm okay."

Zayvion didn't look convinced. "We're going to wait a little before I agree with you on that. Here's some water. Can you drink?"

Oh, hells yes. I was so thirsty I could drain a river dry and still have room for a few creeks and springs.

He held a water bottle to my lips and helped me lift my head. I drank until he took the water away. The water was good. I could think much more clearly. I even knew where I was—in the car, lying back in the front seat, with Zay still in the driver's seat but leaning over me. From this angle, I could just make out the cloudy sky through the window behind him.

"What hit me?" I asked.

"Magic."

"I know, but I mean, why? Why so strong?"

Zay exhaled. "I'm not exactly sure, but it might have something to do with this." He held up my hand so I could see it. The marks there, the spiderwebbing was now whorls of silver, gold, blues, rose, and greens. I looked like I'd dipped my hand in liquid fire opals, or metallic oil. The marks on my arm had turned the same metal colors as my hand, but there was more of my skin to be seen between the lines on my arm. It didn't look like there were new lines, but rather that the same burn marks I'd had since I healed Cody had gone shades of metallic psychedelic instead of just burned-looking red.

"That's going to be a conversation piece," I muttered.

Zay laughed. "You had me worried."

I looked back at him. He was still leaning over me, and even though he was smiling, the smile faded quickly. "Really worried."

"Kiss it and make me feel better?"

Heat sparked in those tiger eyes of his and he bent his head. His lips touched mine gently, hesitant to press too hard. I opened my mouth for him, and it was all the invitation he needed. It was still a soft kiss, a careful kiss, but I didn't want him to pull away. And he didn't. Not for a long, slow moment.

"Do you know how dangerous it is to overload like that?" he asked me, his lips barely away from mine.

"Yes," I said. "I didn't mean to." I reached up enough to catch his mouth again, and the kiss moved over into I'm-not-hurt territory. He felt good, he tasted good. Minty. Warm. Alive.

I didn't want him to go away. I wasn't sure if I was

up for a full tussle, but a little hand play seemed like a really nice idea right now.

Zayvion pulled away. "You wanted us to take this slow."

"I don't remember saying that." Actually, I did.

He raised one eyebrow and, this close, close enough that if I put my arms up around his neck I could probably get another kiss out of him, I could see that he didn't believe me.

"Okay. Maybe this is a bad time," I said.

"It is."

"So why are you still lying over me?"

"I'm waiting for you to thank me properly."

"For what?"

"Saving your life. Again. I've never met a woman who was so intent on dying."

"Hey, did I ask for your opinion? I can save my own life just fine, thank you. And I don't even know what you did. For all I know, I saved my life just now."

"No," he said. "It was definitely me."

"Prove it."

He drew one finger up my arm, and the cooling ease of mint followed it. It was like the magic in me burned with fire, and the magic in him flowed with ice. I shivered and it wasn't from cold. He felt good. Incredibly good.

Fire and ice. Hell of a pair we made.

"What does that have to do with saving my life?"

His finger paused and the magic within me cooled and flowed out of me, back to the natural store deep beneath the earth. The pressure from holding so much magic and then being released from it spread like a warm blanket over me. I felt relaxed, content. I felt like we'd just had sex.

"I Grounded you." He smiled. "And you liked it."

"I don't need you to do that, you know. I could do it for myself."

"Just say thank you, and we can get going."

"Is that all it will take?"

"Well, that and admitting you are very lucky I am good at Grounding. Very lucky I was here with you just now—very lucky I was with you after you Hounded that hit on Boy—very lucky I was there when you went off the deep end pulling magic to try and help Cody—"

"Heal Cody. And not try. Did."

Zay's smile slipped a little. "Heal? You healed him?"

"I told you that already."

"No you didn't. You said you thought he was hurt, but we couldn't find any evidence of it."

Shit. It must have been Nola who I told. I hated it when I found memory gaps in my head.

"Well, I'm telling you now. I healed him. With magic."

"No one can heal with magic."

"I know. I did."

The smile was gone, the warmth and teasing were gone. In their place sat neutral Zay, calm Zay, Zen Zay. "That explains why it took so much to Ground you."

I didn't know what to say to that. Grounding, or acting as a lightning rod for another magic user while they are using magic, was not an easy thing to do. You had to be incredibly malleable, incredibly pain tolerant, and incredibly calm while you guided magic to exit another magic user, or exit a spell, and flow back down into the earth.

The way magic worked, you couldn't Ground yourself. But having another magic user—someone who handled magic in their own unique manner—step into the exact rhythm and style of your casting and Ground you was so rare as to be generally unadvisable.

People who tried it and succeeded were highly trained specialists and usually lingered around high-powered people, serving as bodyguards. Even so, just because in theory a trained specialist could Ground a magic user, it always caused harm—a double Proxy if you will—to the bodyguard. One Offload, or price paid, for his or her own magic, and another price paid for the magic the person they were Grounding was using.

But Zayvion didn't look like he was in pain, didn't look like Grounding me was causing him to pay a double price.

Of course I'd heard that there were those rare combinations when the two magic users, caster and ground, were so well matched that Casting and Grounding were like dancing the tango, two bodies moving, breathing as one. Still, someone always paid a price.

Maybe Zayvion was just very, very good. Or maybe we were just very, very good together.

"Allie, I am trying to keep you alive. It would be nice to know these kinds of things."

I tried to remember what we were talking about. Oh, yes. Healing.

"Is there anything else you haven't told me?" he asked with a smile. "Any other abilities you've developed? Invisibility? Super strength? Can you crawl up walls?"

"Oh, please. Get off me, Jones." I giggled and accidentally snorted. Sweet loves, I was getting giddy.

"Are you sure? Okay, fine. Fine." He sat up and levered the back of his seat to a more upright position, then levered mine up too.

"You warm enough?" he asked.

"I'm fine." I pulled Zay's jacket off my lap, where he must have put it when I was knocked out. I wrapped it over my chest and shoulders.

"You didn't answer my question."

I shrugged. "There's nothing else I haven't told you. Just the healing thing."

"No big deal. Just the healing thing," he mimicked.

"What is your problem? You don't think I should have healed the kid? Do you want me to apologize for saving his life? Forget you, Jones. I healed him. Deal with it."

"I didn't say you should apologize, but you could have mentioned it."

"When?"

"Before."

"Oh, that's clear. Before what?"

The muscle where his jaw and ear met clenched. "Before we . . . before we went to Nola's."

That was not what he had meant to say. I figured he really meant to say before we slept together. Before we made love.

"I tell you what, man of a million secrets. When you tell me all the things about you and your life that I want to know, I'll return the favor."

Silence. Maybe we were both a little angry. Silence suited me just fine.

It started raining, and Zay flicked on the wipers, both of which squeaked. Miles went by.

Fine. I did not need to coddle man-moods. Instead, I leaned my head into the window, pillowing it with my hand, and tried to think what I should do once we got to Violet's place.

"Where does she live?" I finally asked.

"Who?"

"Violet."

He glanced at me, looked back at the road. "Don't you ever read magazines? Watch TV? Read a paper? How can you not know these things?"

"The last newspaper I read told me my father was dead. And you know what? Maybe I do know this stuff, and maybe I've even known it for years, but maybe one of the last dozen times I've almost blown my brains out casting magic I lost those memories." My voice was rising. I was angry and, sure, frightened. I'd like to see anyone else go through what I'd been through in the last few days and act like a cheerleader.

"Do you know how many birthdays I remember having as a kid? Three. I've seen pictures of all the other ones, but I can't remember them. None of them. Not even the ones when my mother was still around. Don't give me shit for the price I've had to pay to live my life. I didn't get a choice about losing my mind. Magic is a heartless bitch, and she's had me by the throat for years."

So much for moody men. Chalk one up for the moody female.

Zayvion let the windshield wipers have their say for a while. Then, "Sorry. Violet's been living in the condo with your father since they were married sixteen months ago. Before that, she lived at one of the other properties he owns in the city. The condo is downtown."

"I know where the condo is," I grumbled. Realizing just how petty I sounded, "Thanks, though. I didn't know when they got married. I never received an invitation."

"She didn't wear white," he offered. "And I think her flowers were lilacs and daffodils."

"You pay attention to the strangest details. Most men would be scoping the crowd for single desperate drunk chicks."

"That would be Joan, and she was a friend of the bride's cousin. Recently dumped."

I held up one hand. "That's all I need to know about that."

"I thought you wanted to know my secrets."

"I don't need to know who you slept with at my stepmother's wedding."

He grinned. "Okay. Your father looked happy, and maybe a little bewildered. He kept looking over at Violet like she was a puzzle he couldn't quite figure out."

That didn't sound good.

"There's not a person in this world my father couldn't figure out," I said.

"There's you."

I thought about that. He was probably right. My father never understood my motivations, my desires, my needs. He had an idea of who a daughter of his should be and expected me to fill that preassumed role in his life. I'd let him down pretty badly on that account.

But it did make me more curious about his newest wife.

"So tell me about Violet."

"What about her?"

"Do you like her?"

"She has been good to work for. Fair. Intelligent, but demanding, as you'd expect of someone pushing the edge of the technological magic field. She has a dry sense of humor and is blunt about her opinion. Like some other women I know, she's a little too stubborn for her own good."

I let that comment pass. "Do you know if my dad gave her a controlling share of the company?"

Zay glanced over at me. "I thought you weren't worried about the money."

"I'm not. I'm just trying to figure out why she would have married my dad. I mean, money is the obvious reason, but it could also be for some of the patents for magic and tech integration he owns. I could see a woman who was involved in scientific innovations liking the package he could offer her: security, visibility, ability to take product to market, funding, and access to patented technology. Not to mention friends in low and high places."

Zay shook his head.

"What?"

"Did it ever cross your mind that she might have married him because she loved him?"

I laughed. No snorting this time. "Right. Just like his other four money-digging wives."

"Five. Or don't you include your mother on that list?"

"Low, Jones."

"I'll take that as a no, then."

It was the sort of comment that should have made me really angry, and when I was younger I might have even hit him in the nose for it. But I'd had time to think about why my mother married my dad. Maybe it was love in the beginning. I hope there was still love when I was conceived, but for all I know she was in it for the quickly multiplying fortune he was acquiring. I had been told she wasn't living in the poorhouse overseas. Dad paid alimony to all his wives, and I knew my mom was, for the most part, taken care of because of the years she'd spent with him.

Not that I had heard from her since she left.

"Do you really think any woman would marry Daniel Beckstrom without thinking about how good his wealth was gonna look on her?"

Zay shrugged. "Probably not."

"You didn't answer me about the controlling share of Dad's company."

"What about it?"

"Who holds it?"

"Now that your father is gone, you."

Oh, good loves. Just what I needed. "So I am the sole heir to the Beckstrom fortune, minus taxes and whatever the other wives get, and I have the controlling share of the company?"

"Yes."

I didn't know I even had shares in the company, much less enough to swing a vote. Maybe Zayvion was right—I should have read the newspaper more often. "So much for keeping a low profile."

"Well, that, and don't forget the fact that you're indicated in your father's murder."

"I have not forgotten that."

He looked over and gave me a small smile. "Good."

Oh. He was trying to make sure my memories were still there. Decent of him, I supposed. It might get a little tedious to be reminded about what I had not forgotten, but it might be nice to be filled in on the things I had lost.

"It's what, another four-hour drive to the city?" I asked.

He nodded.

"Good. I expect to spend most of that time listening

to you tell me everything you know about my father, his company, my stepmom, and her inventions."

"Really? And if I don't feel like talking?"

"We Beckstroms are known for our knack at Influencing people."

"Influence doesn't work on a Grounder, Allie."

Hells. He was right. That meant I probably couldn't force Zay to do anything against his free will. There was something so satisfying about that, I actually chuckled.

"What?"

"I hadn't thought about it," I said. "I suppose it bothered my father."

"No, it was one of the reasons he hired me—I couldn't be Influenced by anyone and he knew I wouldn't just do what he wanted me to, but would make solid, lawful decision on my own . . . in his best interest, of course."

And it also made sense as to why my dad had hired him to follow me. He knew I wouldn't be able to Influence him either. Like I said, my dad was a thorough, careful man.

"So, what? You're not going to answer my questions?"

"I said I couldn't be Influenced. I didn't say I couldn't be bribed. What will you give me if I talk?"

"How about Nola's cooking?"

"It's a good start."

I unbuckled my seat belt and crawled into the backseat. Nola had packed several sandwiches, home-baked cookies, some cheeses and bread, bottles of water, a container of what looked to be soup, a thermos of coffee, and other foil-wrapped things at the bottom of the box that I didn't bother digging down for.

I pulled out the sandwiches and cookies, grabbed water and the coffee thermos, and crawled back to the front seat.

I unwrapped a sandwich, held it out for Zay. When he reached for it, I pulled it away. "Talk?"

"What do you want to know?"

I handed him the sandwich, unwrapped one for myself. "How long have you known my dad?"

"I've worked for him for about a year."

I noted the slight side step of worked instead of known, but let it pass. "And my stepmom?"

"Worked for her for three years."

"What did you do before that?"

"I agreed to tell you about your dad and stepmom, not to fill you in on my personal life."

"True." I ate my sandwich—chicken salad—and poured coffee for us both. I figured I had a little time. Maybe by the time we rolled into town he'd open up a little and show me a glimpse of who he really was.

The miles passed quickly, and Zay was adequately generous with the information he shared. But every time I steered the conversation to any time before he had worked for my stepmom, he neatly sidestepped the question.

"I get the feeling you would be a lousy date, Jones," I said.

"Not at all. I'm a good date. Talkative, informed on current events. I even still open doors for women—out of respect, not condescension. But this isn't a date. Is it?"

"Absolutely not. I'd expect more than a boxed lunch in a car."

The afternoon light was fading into evening, and the cloud cover that had not lifted all day created an early, false dusk. The drive up the I-5 freeway had shown buildings made of wood and brick with plenty of space around them slowly change to the crowded stone, glass, and iron architecture of smaller cities. Soon those buildings traded up into high-rises and skyscrapers.

Once inside the city limits, I couldn't stop scratching my arm. The concentration of magic here was so high I felt like a string pulled tight and buzzing in the wind.

"You okay?" Zay asked.

I stopped rubbing at my arm with my palm and nodded. "It itches."

"Want me to try?"

I knew what he was asking. Did I want him to Ground me, to drain the magic that filled me so full? It had never been like this before. Sure, I could contain a little bit of magic, but now I felt like a circular river, magic pouring up through my feet, filling me until it poured out of me to fall back down into the ground again. And since I wasn't actually using the magic, I wasn't paying a price for it cycling through me. Except for the itching, that is.

"Here," Zayvion said when I didn't answer.

He put his hand on my left arm, and took a deep breath. The mint-cool poured out from his hand, washed across my shoulders, and cooled down my arm. I put my head back against the headrest and moaned.

"Oh, good. Really good."

He kept his hand there for a little while longer, and when he finally let go, the cool mint lingered.

"Thanks," I said. "And thanks for the other times too."

"You're welcome. This would be a good time for

you to duck down below the window level and try not to use magic at all. Do you think the Hounds can find you on smell alone?"

I reclined the seat until I was lying almost fully back. I was still upright enough that I could see the streetlights go by as we made our way through the edge of the city, heading downtown.

"Bonnie knows me. If any of them broke into my apartment, they probably got my scent. Except the building leaches old magic when it rains, so the stink might have covered my olfactory signature."

"Let's hope so. Maybe now would also be a good time for you to meditate and try to stop glowing like a neon sign."

"I'm glowing?" I held up my hand. In the low light of false dusk, all I could see was my hand. The lines were darker than my skin, but no glowing.

"Not physically. Magically. Think you can dampen the amount of magic you're channeling?"

"I don't know. This isn't exactly something I've had any experience with."

"Now would be a terrific time to try." He sounded worried, and that worried me.

I closed my eyes, felt overwhelmed by the colors and textures and tastes of the magic racing through me, and snapped my eyes open again. Too easy to get lost. I stared at the car's overhead light, which was dark, and whispered a meditative mantra.

Think calm thoughts, I thought. *Think of the magic as air, no color, no taste, invisible. It comes into me like air, unseen, it exhales with my breath, unseen.*

This seemed like a really good visualization so I kept at it. Inhaling the invisible, exhaling the invisible, and carefully keeping my mind clear of any spells or glyphs. It wouldn't do for me to turn the car into a train, or to give Zayvion a set of wings or something. Not that I could really do those things. Or could I? With this much magic at my disposal, I could probably do anything I could imagine.

So long as I was willing to pay the price for it, of course.

"I don't know what you're doing, but it's good, Allie," Zay said. "Just keep doing that for a few more miles, okay?"

Oh sure. Hold the tightest concentration on nothingness that I'd ever tried before while billions of cubic miles of magic poured through my veins. No problem.

I am an "off" switch, I intoned to myself. That didn't work quite as well as the invisible angle, so I went back to inhaling and exhaling unseen magic.

I was aware of the car slowing, then turning a couple of tight corners, pausing, and then entering what I hoped was the gated garage beneath my father's condo.

"You can come out of that now," Zayvion said. "The wards around this place won't let your signature escape."

Yeah, but I wasn't sure the only thing I should be worried about was the Hounds and police outside of the building's wards. No matter how much Zayvion liked Violet, I did not know the woman. It was just as possible she wanted me dead, so the corporation's control would fall to her. But like Zayvion had reminded me, unless I wanted to go to the cops and explain where I had been during my father's death, and that I had no alibi, and also point out that the one person who said he knew how my dad died was mentally challenged *and* had literally disappeared into thin air, I might want to throw my hat in with someone who had power and pull in this city.

And right now, that someone was my stepmom.

I hated trusting people. Especially people who slept with my father. I hated having no other choice—oh, I suppose I could try to get out of the country and be on the run all my life, but I was already getting pretty tired of being chased. I wanted my life back, on my terms. And if it meant being vulnerable enough to ask for a favor or two, I'd just have to suck it up and deal with it.

I let go of my meditative state and the image of invisible magic was replaced by color, texture, smell, and taste again. I hissed. My arm itched like the mother of all rashes.

Mint flowed up from my hand. "Come on," Zay said. "It's more heavily blocked and controlled inside the living area. You might feel better there." He tugged on my hand until I sat up; then he got out of the car.

I got out too, and took the time to stretch. I knew there were cameras in the parking garage. I knew that whoever Violet had running security already knew we were there, and was probably halfway down the elevator to meet us. I looked over at Zay and he was leaning against the car, looking toward the elevator. He knew it too.

Well, at least his story lined up. He did know some of the details of the condo.

The elevator door slid open and a man on the tall, blond side of the spectrum, dressed in jeans and a suit jacket, stepped out.

"Mr. Jones, Ms. Beckstrom," he said from across the parking lot, his voice echoing against the concrete structure. "If you'll leave your things there and come with me. Mrs. Beckstrom is waiting for you."

I snorted. It was all so very overly spy-and-intrigue, it seemed ridiculous. But Zay pushed off of the car and headed toward the elevator, pausing until I came up beside him.

"Kevin. How are the wife and kid?" Zay asked when we were close enough.

"Driving me to the poorhouse. And yourself?"

"Things are looking up."

Kevin nodded and I felt like I'd just watched a conversation from a movie where the words didn't really mean what they were saying but were instead some sort of secret code. "It's a pleasure to meet you, Ms. Beckstrom," Kevin said. "Please follow me."

He used a remote to open the elevator door, and stepped into the mirrored interior.

Elevator. Groan. I hated elevators, hated small places.

Still, I had manners and knew when to use them. I plastered on a smile and stepped into the fun house of horrors. Zay stepped in after me and I tried not to look at him in the mirrors—reflected at every angle—'cause I couldn't believe he looked good so many different ways. His dark curls were hidden by the ski cap. The light reflected by so many mirrors made his cheekbones cut a hard edge beneath his eyes, and chiseled shadows along the line of his strong jaw. But even the sweatshirt couldn't cover the width of his shoulders, nor the long, lean angle of his torso and hip. And while I was trying not to look at him, he was looking right at me, brown eyes soft, wide lips curved just enough that I had the feeling he was enjoying my discomfort.

Kevin, on the other hand, wasn't my type and wasn't even what I'd consider handsome. His eyes were too large for his face, his chin too small. He was the sort of guy you would never expect could kill you in an instant. I knew his type. I'd grown up around guys like him.

Since the two of them weren't saying anything, I kept my mouth shut too, and split my time between trying not to freak out that I was trapped in an elevator, and trying not to look at my reflection, which showed my own dark-haired and tattooed image, trying not to freak out that I was trapped in an elevator.

Instead I stared at my eyes, really looking at what Violet was going to get for a first impression of me.

For one thing, I looked like a woman who needed to learn how to apply her makeup on eyes, cheeks, and lips instead of drawing with kiddie markers down the side of her face and arm. Maybe I should have asked Nola for some cover makeup to blend in the marks the magic had left behind, although I doubted she'd have something that would disguise the marks, now that they'd gone psychedelic on the right and ink black on the left.

Well, I could either be flinchy about Violet seeing me all marked up by magic, or I could hold my chin up and make her think I was happy with how things had turned out so far.

I went for the second option. Chin up. Breathe. The doors would open any second, any second, any second.

And they did. I pulled a rich-bitch-princess move and shoved past Kevin to get out the doors, out where there was air and space and fewer things pressing in so close that I thought I was going to be crushed.

Kevin didn't need to lead me down the halls—I'd lived here. "In the great room?" I asked over my shoulder.

"Yes," he said. "It's to the right."

I kept a pretty good pace, letting the panicked race of my heart settle with the rhythm of my stride. With any luck I'd be calm and collected once I finished off the hallway and made it to the room.

The boys behind me chatted about sports, and this time it sounded sincere. I slowed, and stepped through the high-arched doorway into the great room.

The decor had changed since I was last here—new couches, new tables, new rugs and paintings. But some things were the same—the mantel spanning a fireplace that took up nearly half a wall, and, of course, the entire wall of one-way glass that revealed the city and its lights spread out below.

The other thing that had changed was the woman standing in the center of the room. Or more precisely, the girl.

Violet looked young enough to be a classmate of mine. Her red hair was pulled back in a clip, and she had really good cheekbones. She wore plain but fashionable glasses, no jewelry that I could see except a gold band on her left ring finger. And instead of the top-of-the-line designer dresses I was used to seeing my stepmothers in, she wore a pair of black slacks and a baby blue T-shirt.

"Hello, Allie," she said. "It's good to meet you."

I stood there, frozen, trying to fit her into the idea of being my father's wife. Good loves, she couldn't be even a year older than me. I never thought my dad would be such a playboy jerk as to marry someone who could be his own daughter. How had Zayvion managed to leave that little detail out of the wedding rundown he'd given me?

Kevin moved off to one side, where I knew the bar was, and I commended him on his insight. I so needed a drink.

Zay came up behind me. "Hello, Mrs. Beckstrom," he said.

She smiled briefly. "Hello, Zayvion. I trust it wasn't too much trouble for you to come here this evening?"

"There were a few complications."

"I'm sorry to hear that." Violet tipped her head to the side and looked at me as if I were a specimen that was not reacting as she had expected. "Would you like to sit down?"

"Thank you, yes," Zayvion said. He took a step forward and purposely bumped his shoulder against my arm, breaking the frozen shock I'd been stuck in.

"Um," I gracefully began. "Yes. Thanks."

I got moving across the marble floor, my tennis shoes squeaking until I hit the thick rug that did a fair job of wall-to-walling the room.

Violet sat in one of the reclining chairs and tucked one leg up beneath her. I slowed by the couch farthest from her, but she spoke up. "Please come sit closer. I hate yelling across this room."

I'd always hated that too. Which was cool. And weird. But since I didn't feel like yelling either, I settled down on the love seat nearest her.

She studied my face and hands, a frown making only the barest of creases across her smooth forehead. This close, I could see that her youth was legitimate, and not bought off the operating table or maintained by spells.

"What are those marks?" she asked.

"Oh, I got into a fight with a tattoo artist."

She raised her eyebrows. "Okay, let's take care of this right now. I loved your father. I know the age difference between us is a hard thing to deal with, and if my own father had married someone my age, I'd probably be angry too. However, since I am not going to judge you for how you treated him, I expect you to do me the decency of not judging me for how I treated him either."

Zay was right. She was a blunt little thing.

"Terrific," I said. "Then how about you tell me how much of the corporation you get now that he's dead."

She blinked once and held her breath before letting it out. "About one quarter of it. You have just over half, and the rest of his ex-wives, combined, hold the remaining quarter."

Not enough of a stake in it for her to kill my father. Unless she and my father's other ex-girls were banding together on this.

"I could try to be tactful," I began.

"Don't bother."

Kevin handed me a glass of red wine, and gave Violet a glass of white.

"Did you kill him?" I asked.

She shook her head, took a drink of wine. "I was going to ask you the same thing."

"No," I said. "I've been angry with him for a long time, but not enough to kill him."

"Teresa said you were furious when you left his office."

"Teresa?"

"His receptionist."

"Oh. I was furious. He'd just lied to me about a hit on a little kid I'd Hounded back to him. I told him I was advising the people involved to sue his ass off."

Violet smiled. "He said you were strong-willed. Said you took after Angela."

Wow. I hadn't been compared to my mother in years. And certainly not by someone who spoke her name like maybe they'd met, or maybe they were friends. And what the hells kind of friendship would that be? Violet was old enough to be my sister, not my mother's crony. I took a gulp of wine.

Okay. I had to admit there was one thing money could buy—really good wine.

"How did . . ." I wasn't sure quite how to bring it up. "Who found him?"

"Teresa. She was hysterical and called me first. I placed the call to the police." She took another drink of wine. "It was horrible." Her voice was much softer, and I could see the lines at the edge of her eyes and the circles beneath them. I got to thinking that even though she looked like a natural redhead, and I expected her to have a very fair complexion, she looked a little gray, as if maybe she really was grieving his death.

That would so not fit with my vision of one of Dad's wives. Most of the women he'd married wanted the money and the limelight that came from being on Daniel Beckstrom's arm. But then, why should things turn out how I thought they would? I'd been wrong about lots of things. Zay had said he thought they loved each other. I tried to picture this girl, someone who could maybe have been my friend if she wasn't my stepmom, next to my polished, powerful, stern father, and just couldn't make the image work in my head. Another image came unbidden into my mind—the idea of the two of them in bed together.

There were some things that should never be imagined. That was one of them. I took another swig of wine.

"Tell me what you know about his death," Violet said, "and I'll fill you in on what you don't know."

Zayvion, who had been standing over by the bar with Kevin, walked over and sat on the couch opposite me, settling against the leather cushions with a beer in his hand. Sweatshirt, blue jeans, and a beer. They all looked good on him.

"I hope you don't mind." He held up his beer toward Violet. "It's been a rough couple of days."

"No, that's fine. I want to hear what you know too, Zayvion."

Zay took a drink of beer and gave me a subtle, encouraging nod.

You better be right about her, I thought. He must have gotten the gist of my sentiment because he raised his eyebrows like I was a recalcitrant child.

"Okay," I said. "I found out he died when I picked up a paper at a newsstand down on Third Street. I was on my way to get coffee. The last time I saw Dad was the previous afternoon when I accused him of illegally Offloading into the St. John's side of town."

"St. John's?" She sounded surprised. "How interesting. I've seen the records, and the company hasn't ever used in-city Proxy, and especially not out by St. John's. That's over the railroad divide. In the dead zone."

"I was there. I Hounded the hit. It was his signature."

"Really." She glanced at Zayvion. What I couldn't figure out was why she was all of a sudden so interested in St. John's. "Who did you Hound for?"

"I won't give names. Client confidentiality."

"I think we both need to break a few rules here if we're going to share information."

"Okay, I'm all for that. You start."

She tipped her head. "Did you know that Zayvion was hired by your father to keep an eye on you?"

"Yeah, I figured that out pretty quick."

"And that he worked for me before that?"

"Yes. Tell me something you shouldn't, and I'll spill the rest of what I know."

It was like a game of chicken. A game I was good at, mostly because I had nothing to lose. Violet didn't seem to be a slouch at it either.

"Kevin, will you see that we are not bothered?"

Kevin walked over to the doorway and pressed a button. Even without using magic to enhance my senses, I felt him draw on the deep, rich core of magic over which the condo had been built and he deftly set a Deflection spell. There was nothing in this world I was aware of that could break a Deflection spell of that magnitude and expertise. Respect for Kevin's worth just jumped about a million points in my book. A plain-looking, unassuming, deadly guy who cast magic like the highest-level user was a hard position to fill, but it looked like my dad, and Violet, had hit the jackpot when they found Kevin.

Violet untucked her leg from beneath her and rested both of her elbows on her knees, the glass of wine held in both hands.

"Your father and I met when he became interested in a line of study I was following at a very private institution. At first we argued. He was an intelligent man and had strong ideas about how magic should be made available to the public. I had other ideas. I thought a system with more freedom would alleviate some of the criminal elements of magic use. If we are all equally able to use magic, perhaps we would be less likely to hurt one another with it or for it."

She took a swig of wine, draining her glass. "He agreed to invest some money so I could pursue the application of certain technologies to magic. We were not romantically involved then. That didn't happen for several months, and it was a mutual decision, though I had to talk sense into him when he wanted to end the relationship. You may not believe this, but he was a kind man, if you could get through the business tycoon exterior."

Okay, that just creeped me out. I looked over at Zayvion, but he was looking at Violet.

"In any case, we developed some astounding devices. Disks about the size of your palm that carry enough magic to cast a single spell."

"Portable magic. Even off the grid," I said. "Even in a dead zone."

"Yes. And since the magic is in the disk, and can be more easily accessed by the user, there is very little price to pay."

"So there is no Offload, and no need for Proxies?"

"That's right."

Holy shit.

"Do you realize how much this will change how magic is used?"

"Yes. And apparently, so do other people." She glanced over at the bar where Kevin stood, and I heard the clink of glass on glass, then the sound of wine pouring.

"How do you charge the disk with magic in the first place?" I asked.

She shook her head. "That I won't tell you. Patents are pending. The entire process will change how magic can be accessed and distributed. We both thought, with enough regulation, the disks would do more good than harm. But we were not going to release them for public use until we had laws in place. We had just begun working on the legal side of matters when he was killed."

"Him dying didn't do you much good at all, did it?"

She laughed, one hard, broken sob. "No. Not at all."

I glanced over at Zayvion, who looked his thoughtful, Zen self.

"Do you know a woman named Bonnie Sherman who Hounds for a living?" I asked Violet.

She shook her head. "I don't think I know anyone named Bonnie."

"How about a man named Cody Hand?"

She frowned, thinking. Kevin came over with two full wineglasses and another beer for Zayvion.

"Wasn't there something in the news a long time ago about a man named Cody the Hand who was sent to jail for corporate forgeries?"

"It might be him," I said.

"I know of him. Why?"

"I think he forged my signature on the hit on Dad. I also think he knows who really killed him."

Violet became very still. But it was the sort of distracted nonmotion that looked like she had left her body on neutral while her brain burned through an amazing amount of calculations.

Finally, "Where is he?"

"We think Bonnie has him."

She curled back up in the chair, looked over at Zayvion.

"We were off the grid," Zayvion said. "Out in the country. We had Cody with us. He's been damaged mentally, whether at birth or later in life"—he shrugged—"but he can comprehend simple concepts, and he is aware of magic."

"He was in a field ahead of us," I said, "and a bolt of lightning . . ." I paused. Actually, it hadn't looked like a bolt of lightning striking from sky to ground. Now that I thought back on it, I realized it looked like a shot of copper lightning had come up out of the ground. "Uh, a bolt of some sort of energy shot up out of the ground. It was a copper-colored flash. Then Bonnie was suddenly standing there in the middle of the field in front of him. We were a world away from nowhere, and so far off the grid, electric lights could pass for magic."

If Violet had looked ashen before, she looked like she was going to faint now.

"What happened?" she whispered.

"She put her arms around Cody, intoned a spell, and held one hand up. Then they disappeared."

"Impossible," she said. But her eyes were too wide, and she had a white-knuckle grip on her wineglass. She looked at Zayvion.

"Impossible," he agreed. "But it happened. There was residue left behind in a perfect circle on the ground. Black ash."

"Feathers," I cut in. Halfway through my second glass I was starting to feel the wine. I wanted to stretch out and lie back on the love seat. If someone had offered me a nice lap quilt and a pillow, I'd probably stay right where I was. But I wanted to leave this condo as quickly as was practical. There were too many memories ghosting me here.

I placed the glass on the table next to me so I wouldn't be tempted to swig down the rest of it. I noticed Zayvion had not started on his second beer yet, either. Good. Maybe I'd be able to talk him into driving me home, or loaning me his car for the night.

"It felt more like feathers than ash," I said. "And it melted at the slightest touch."

"You touched it?" Violet asked.

"She tried to taste it," Zay muttered.

"Oh, God, what were you thinking? Don't ever do

something like that! That is an untested, and possibly deadly, matter."

"Hey," I said with a smile, "get off my case. You're not my mom."

"Technically?" At that moment, I realized she and I could maybe be friends one day.

She took a deep breath. "Okay. At least we now know that the disks have been stolen, not destroyed."

"What?" I said. "You knew there might be some of these disks out there?"

Violet nodded. "We had a fire a few months ago at one of the production labs. We thought everything had been destroyed, but there was some doubt. And other . . . things that hinted of a break-in. But the . . . investigation we implemented left us with very little to go on."

"What did you have to go on?"

"A very slight indication that the person, or persons, who broke into the lab may have gone toward North Portland."

"Shit," I said. I didn't like where this was heading. North Portland had more than its share of shady people. You could close your eyes and point anywhere along any of its streets and find a felon.

"Do you have any idea who would do this? There can't be that many people who knew about the project or where the lab was."

"We have ideas, but ideas are not proof," she said, in a reasonable impersonation of my dad.

"So do you have some good reason why we shouldn't go to the police with this?" I asked.

"I already have," Violet said. "They hadn't had much luck tracking the stolen items. It was one of the reasons we were hoping the disks had been destroyed in the fire."

I rubbed at my eyes. I was tired and my head was starting to hurt. There had to be an easy way to figure out who had access to the technology. And to draw some sort of connection between that person or persons, Cody, Bonnie, and Snake man, if Snake man was real and not just some kind of imaginary friend—or worse, a pet—of Cody's, and of course me, and maybe even the hit on Boy that pointed back to my dad and his death. What were we missing?

Nothing besides a suspect, a motive, and some hard proof.

Hells.

I needed to find Bonnie and wring her thick neck. No, I needed to get the information out of her about who she was working for and how she pulled her smoke and mirrors act. Then wring her thick neck. Which meant I needed to Hound her. But not tonight. Tonight I wanted sleep. Tomorrow I'd take on the world.

I also did not want Violet to set a bodyguard on me, or try to force me into staying safely trapped here until things sorted out. It would be easy to Influence her, to break my promise not to use people like my father had. I had used it on his secretary, so I'd already fallen off the wagon. Just one more time wouldn't kill me.

"So it's agreed," I said, pouring Influence behind my words. "I'll Hound around the city for Cody tomorrow."

"Uh, no, it is not agreed," Violet said. "First of all, I cannot be Influenced, so you can stop wasting your time. Second of all, we weren't even talking about finding Cody. And even if we were, I am sure I have far more resources at my disposal than you do. The police are looking for you, Allie. If you draw on magic to so much as light a candle, they'll know where you are and will haul you in for questioning."

Well, hells. There was an angle I hadn't thought of. This secret technology was probably still a secret from the law around these parts. I had not only become a new friend to Violet, I'd also become a new liability if I were caught and indiscreetly questioned.

Still, she could send her men and women off to find the kid, all she wanted. And if they found him and either brought him back here or turned him in to the police, I figured he'd be in pretty good hands until I got done wringing the truth out of Bonnie.

"Sorry," I said. "You're right."

Zayvion turned and looked at me, probably surprised at my apology. I gave him an innocent glance. He wasn't buying it, but covered his scowl by taking a swig of beer.

"Good," Violet said. "Why don't you stay here tonight? There is still a bed in your old room. Or the guest suite is available if you'd rather."

Oh, hells, no.

I said good riddance to this place years ago. I had never come running home when things had gotten tough in the last seven years. I was not going to come running home now.

"Thanks, but I have somewhere else to be."

"Where?" She took a drink of wine. She didn't look like she believed me.

"I don't think I'll say. That way if you're asked you won't have to lie when you say you don't know."

"I don't like you going off alone, Allie. You do understand you're being *hunted,* don't you?"

"Oh, yeah. I have the bruises to show for it." I stood. "Thanks for worrying, but I'm a big girl. I'll be fine."

Zayvion stood too.

"Where are you going?" I asked.

"Thought I'd see you to the door." He put his beer on the table. "Good night, Mrs. Beckstrom."

"Take care, Zayvion. Be careful, Allie. And if you change your mind, the door is always open."

"Thanks," I said. And I meant it.

Kevin walked to the doorway and released the spell with a flick of his fingers, the sort of subtle motion that looked like he was adjusting the ring on his middle finger with his thumb. Oh, this guy was good. Very good.

Kevin allowed us through the door, then followed us to the elevator. He used the remote to open the doors, and I felt my shoulders crawl up to my ears at the small, mirrored space.

"Take it easy, Zay," he said.

"You too," Zayvion said. "And next time the drinks are on me."

They shook hands, and I stood there and broke into a cold sweat. How had the elevator gotten smaller? I'd just been in there. With two men. There had to be enough room for me to step in. But try as I might, and I mighted my best, I could not force my foot to lift and take me one step closer to that mirrored coffin.

Kevin turned and walked back down the wide, *spacious,* marble hall, toward the *spacious* great room.

"Allie?" Zay said.

"What?"

He didn't answer, so I looked over at him. He put one hand on the unmarked, left side of my sweaty face and kissed me. Hard.

Oh. The prickly spikes of panic in my chest melted and a whole bunch of other pleasant feelings took their place. Oh. Yes.

I kissed him back just as hard.

"Elevators can be fun," he murmured against my lips.

I bit at his bottom lip and pulled away. "Over my dead body," I said.

But that kiss had broken my panic and put me in another mood entirely.

I strode into the elevator and punched the button. Zayvion stepped in too, then stood directly behind me. The door closed. In the mirror I watched his hands wrap around my waist, saw the slight smile as he pressed his body against my back, then pressed his mouth against the side of my neck.

It was too small here for this. Too small for him to be so close. And I was going crazy for him to be closer.

His hand slipped down the front of my hip, my thigh, then rubbed up beneath the heavy coat I still wore, up the side of my hip, and pressed flat against my stomach. The heat from his palm pooled at my navel and dripped lower. He bit gently at my neck.

Tingles of pleasure poured out from where he touched me. I closed my eyes, and all I felt were his fingers brushing the curve of my breast, his lips on my skin, and his body, hard and hot, pressed against me.

A soft chime rang out and I opened my eyes. Zayvion was smiling, his gaze on the camera I knew was hidden in the corner of the ceiling. Cameras. I had totally forgotten.

Great. Wouldn't Kevin and Violet get a kick out of watching that?

The elevator door slid open, revealing the concrete parking garage.

"This is our floor," Zayvion said.

"Uh-huh."

He held me a moment more and neither of us moved even though we both knew the cameras were watching us. Then the idea of the doors closing on me again, closing me in, got me moving.

I pulled away from the warmth and comfort of his arms, and strode out into the cold garage. The marks up my arm and neck began to tingle, then itch, like thousands of millipedes were crawling from my temple to my fingers. I rubbed my palm up and down my arm, trying to make the itch stop. I heard Zay's footsteps behind me, and noticed it because he was usually silent as a cat walking on marshmallows.

"So where are you going to stay tonight, and how are you going to get there?" he asked.

Ah. I'd forgotten to let him in on my little plan.

I stopped halfway to the car and clasped my hands together in front of me to keep from scratching.

"Do you mind taking me home tonight?" I asked.

Zay strolled over, his hands tucked in that ratty ski jacket he had loaned me. Nola had washed it along with my clothes, and had done a good job getting the bloodstains out of the fabric. I'd have to ask her sometime how she did it. The way my life was going, I'd probably need to do a lot more of that kind of stain removal in the future.

"That depends," Zay said. "Your home, no. My home, yes."

It was my turn to be surprised. "The mysterious Zayvion Jones is actually going to show me something about his personal life? Are you feeling all right? How many beers did you drink? Maybe you should give me the keys."

"Get in the car, Beckstrom," he said with a smile. "I'm driving."

He had closed the distance between us, and I took

a second to really look at him. He walked sober, he talked sober, he looked sober. He even smelled sober.

"How much of that beer did you really drink?" I asked.

"You saw me."

"I saw you take maybe two drinks."

"There you go."

"Don't you trust Violet?"

He shrugged. "Who says I was staying sober because of her?"

I knew that had something to do with me. I even thought it might be something nice, something thoughtful.

"Thanks," I said.

"You're welcome." He continued past me to the driver's-side door, and I walked around to the passenger side of the car and got in.

Zayvion started the engine and put the car in gear. "But if I am taking you to my private residence, for privacy's sake, I'd like you to wear a blindfold while we're driving around the city."

"Won't work," I said. "I can see through walls, you know."

Zayvion shook his head. But he was smiling, and better yet, he was driving. I sat on my hands so I wouldn't scratch my arm to a bloody stump and tried to breathe away the itching. I also worked hard on dimming the glow of magic Zayvion said I'd acquired.

I leaned back in the chair and watched streetlights soldier by, lights tinged with yellow, blue, or pink indicating the kind of auxiliary spells placed upon them. There were some things worth the cost of Offloads, low-level magics that created a huge amount of good for the entire city. And making sure that there was never a chance for a blackout was one of those things.

From the spacing of the streetlights, and eventually the control towers we drove past, I knew we were on the Burnside Bridge, moving across the river from my apartment and into East Portland. After wandering through a few neighborhoods, he pulled his car into a parking garage beneath what I assumed was an apartment building, and I watched the lights of the garage go by until he parked.

"So are there elevators?"

"Yes. And stairs." He got out of the car, opened the back doors, and dug out the remaining food Nola had packed for us. "This way." He shut the door with his heel and, once I was out of the car, he hit a remote to lock it.

This garage was big enough for maybe a dozen cars, concrete, like the one beneath my father's—I mean Violet's—condo, but unlike Violet's place, where the concrete was smooth as marble, this concrete was buttressed with lead rods that webbed the walls and ceiling. Magic collectors. Which meant this was a newer building, or maybe retrofitted.

"How many apartments here?" I asked as I followed Zay over to two doors, one that had an elevator behind it, and the other that had a symbol of stairs on it.

"A few." He paused to shift his hands around the box he carried, then pulled the door to the stairs open. "I'm on the second floor."

The stairs were also concrete, so too the walls. There were no windows, which I found extremely comforting because, although I couldn't see anyone out there, no one out there could see me either. I wondered if Zay had considered those sorts of security measures when he moved in here.

Four levels of stairs later we were at the door to

the second floor. This door had a small window in it, just enough that you could look into the stairwell, or from the stairs could look down the long hall. Another nice feature if you were concerned about running into people.

He pulled the door open and we stepped out of the cool cold-stone smell of old concrete, and into a softly lit hall with a carpet so plush that I lost two inches in height as soon as I stepped on it. Unlike my apartment building, this place did not stink of old magic. I caught a whiff of curry and the hickory of wood burning, and the thick spice of incense covered by an antiseptic lemon detergent.

To the left of the stairs was the elevator, to the right an umbrella stand. The hall stretched between six apartment doors, and Zay walked to the end, then turned left, down a hall that I hadn't noticed because of the false half wall that made it look like the main hall dead-ended.

Zay walked ahead of me and paused in front of his door.

I'd said before that I didn't think there was a spell worth paying for that could keep a burglar out of your house if they were determined to break in. But I had never seen a spell so artfully cast as the one that covered Zay's door. The great hulking ward was so good, it was hard to actually see the thing. If I weren't trying to keep a low profile, I'd pull on magic and Hound that glyph to find out who made it, then I'd go buy one for myself. This had to be the strongest lock-ward I'd ever seen.

So Zay was more wizard than he seemed. He did the finger-wave bit—similar to Kevin's trick—and the spell unraveled. I could sense the strands of the spell pulling in on itself, like eels backing into rock nooks, so that the way through the door was clear. Zay pulled his keys out of his pocket and unlocked what seemed to be an average lock and dead bolt.

"Come on in," he said. The lights flicked on as soon as he crossed the threshold, and with the magical trappings outside his apartment, I was expecting maybe some superintense magic-user stuff inside the apartment. Maybe an old distillery, crystal, and glass rods people used to try to store magic in. Maybe a potted Honey Spurge, which people used to think was so sensitive to impending magic Offloads that it force-bloomed and withered away minutes before an Offload could actually reach you. Or maybe that all his lights would be glowing in the soft pastels of magic.

But like Zayvion, the apartment was unassuming in its simplicity. Modern lines of brushed metal shelves and furnishings were tempered with thick blankets and a few pillows in warm, earthen tones stacked with woven geodesic block patterns, patterns reflected in the upholstery of the couch and love seat, and the area rug in the middle of the white-carpeted living room.

There were no plants in the room, no clutter, not a thing out of place. It almost had an unused look to it.

"Let me guess," I said. "You don't entertain much?"

Zay shrugged and headed into the living room. "Bathroom's to your right, opposite the bedroom. I'm going to take these into the kitchen," he said from across the room. "Hungry?"

"I could eat," I called over my shoulder. I took off my coat and draped it over the back of the love seat, then made my way toward the bathroom.

"What?" he yelled.

"Yes!" Then I had to smile. It had been years since

I'd shared yelling space with someone, and I liked the feeling of not being the only one in the house who was making noise.

Because I am a snoopy bitch, I glanced in the bathroom—clean to the point of being sparse, very bachelor—but at least there was toilet paper on the roll. I had to pee, but decided to hold it long enough to check out his bedroom.

The door was half open, so I pushed it open the rest of the way and stepped in.

Well, well. So the boy did like some luxury in his life. The bedroom was done up in rich blues and browns, with thin lines of yellow here and there, leaving the impression of dark earth below and night skies above cradling stars or moonlight. The bed took up the lion's share of the room, and dark wood dressers and nightstands filled the corners.

"You like?"

I turned and swung my fist, but Zayvion wasn't dumb. He'd snuck up on me and stopped outside my swinging range. That was embarrassing.

"Damn it, Jones, make some noise, will you?" I grumped.

He had taken off his coat and shoes and was leaning, arms crossed over his chest, against one side of the doorway. He was also smiling.

"So. Do you?" he said.

"Do I what?"

"Like the room?"

"It's fine. I was looking for the bathroom."

He pointed over his shoulder. "That way."

"Thanks." He moved out of the way so I could leave the room. "And yes," I said. "Your girlfriend pick out the colors?"

"No."

Well, couldn't blame a girl for trying to find out a little more about him. "Your mother?"

"No. And to answer your other question, I don't have a girlfriend."

Oh. We were being honest.

I raised one eyebrow. "Good." I left him wondering about that, and used the bathroom—making sure I locked the door first. That man was too quiet.

I made use of the facilities and washed my hands. While I was drying them on a remarkably clean-looking towel, I realized my hand and arm did not itch. The black bands on my left hand remained the same, but they never itched much anyway. I examined my right hand in the bright lights of the bathroom and saw no change. I looked at my bare arm in the mirror, and saw no change there either. Other than the fact that it did not itch, it still had bright metallic ribbons maypoling from nail bed to temple. Pretty, really. And when I traced one line of color along my forearm, I could feel magic stir within me. Much more magic than I'd ever held before.

"What did you do to me, Cody?" I muttered. "What did I do to myself?"

Zayvion knocked on the door. "Food's ready."

"Thanks," I said. I finished drying my hands and walked out into the living room. Now that I was in the middle of the room I noticed that the kitchen and living room were one shared space, with an island separating them. Zay stood behind that island, setting out matching plates that were not chipped.

I strolled over and took a seat on the barstool that faced the island. "So you are either never home and everything you own has been recently unpacked from boxes, or you are a raging clean-freak."

"Napkin?" he offered.

I took the perfectly pressed, perfectly white cloth napkin.

"Which is it, Jones? Explain your freakishly neat house."

"I have a maid come in and dust for me once a month. I know how to pick up after myself. And I'm not home much." He scooped out a serving of homemade lasagna for both of us. "Get the salad?" he asked.

I popped the lid on a plastic container and split the salad between our plates. "Why aren't you home?"

"I work a lot. Late hours." He deposited rolls by the salad. "I don't have any butter for the rolls. You okay with that?"

"With Nola's cooking, I don't need butter. Why late hours?"

He wiped his hands on a towel, folded it, and tossed it over one shoulder. "You are a painfully curious woman. Anyone ever mention that to you?"

"Constantly. Do you moonlight?"

He opened the refrigerator behind him and pulled out two bottles of grape soda. "Out of beer. Soda?"

"Sure."

He handed me a bottle and then sat across the island from me.

"Most women are impressed by how clean my house is. You? Complain."

"I'm not complaining. It's just . . . don't you ever let go, relax, and have fun?"

He wiped at his mouth with his napkin. "Sure. It's in the schedule. Monday, laundry, Tuesday, dishes, and every other Thursday afternoon between one and one fifteen, wild abandon."

"Well, since that line of inquiry is only getting me

sarcasm, I'm going to change the subject. Why doesn't my arm itch here?"

He stopped chewing, then started up again. I kept eating and watched his body language. He was serious Zay again.

"Do you know what those marks are, Allie?"

"I know how I got them. From healing Cody."

"Be more specific about that. Did Cody somehow assist you?"

"Yes. He was chanting a mantra. He held my hands. He . . ." I frowned, thinking. "He reached through me and um, caught up the small magic in me and pulled magic out from the network and mixed them together through me. When he had my hands, it was like I could see magic as colors, textures, and I could see how it could be woven into a kind of healing glyph that I directed over his wound and sent deeper, into muscle and bone."

Zay shook his head, a small smile on his lips. "Small magic in you. I'd wondered. And, I'll point out, you didn't tell me about that either."

I shrugged. "I've tried telling people that I can hold magic, that I have always had a flicker of it in me. No one believed it." Not even my own mother, I thought to myself.

"Well, it makes sense for why you can carry magic now. And why it hasn't killed you."

"But why is it so strong now?"

"I think Cody synched you."

"Synched?"

"Old magic term, back in the days before it went public."

I had cut a chunk of lasagna and paused with it halfway to my mouth. I didn't know magic was discovered more than thirty years ago. That wasn't taught in any of my history classes, and certainly wasn't a common belief. As far as I knew magic had been *discovered* thirty years ago.

Zay negated that fact like he expected me to know it. Expected me to believe magic had been around for a lot longer than everyone thought.

"The problem with synching," he continued, "was that a person could become so in rhythm and tune with magic that they would either become lost to it, or become a part of it. Neither of those things are good. People who are receptive to the frequency of magic can sometimes carry magic within their bodies for short periods. On a small scale, a very small scale, there was some success with this. But anyone who tried to carry more magic than enough for a simple spell—"

"Burned themselves out," I said. "Physically, or mentally. We studied something like that in school, but they called it 'forbidden' and nothing else. They refuse to teach any more about it."

He nodded. "Too many people were harmed or killed trying it. No one's been able to isolate which combination of genetic quirks enables a person to actually house magic."

"You think Cody can hold magic?"

"No. But I think whatever he did to you, or through you, triggered your ability to house magic on a much larger scale. But not without a price." He pointed at my hand.

And for the first time, I felt self-conscious of it. I curled my fingers closer around my fork, and couldn't believe I felt bad. It was just a mark. A burn. I'd been burned before.

But never like this, never with so many colors, never so sensitive, never so . . . beautiful. Did liking a disfiguring mark make me a freak? Did being ashamed of it make me any better?

I scooped a bite of noodles and sauce into my mouth. "It burned," I said. "But it hasn't really hurt, just itches sometimes. Do you think it will fade like a burn?"

"I think that depends."

"On what?"

"On if you ever use magic again."

"Listen, I like Nola and all that stuff she stands for, but I am not going to turn magic-free just because I got a little burn."

"Good," he said. "You have a great ability, Allie. It would be a shame to see you give it up."

I took a swig of grape soda. "I think I can cover the marks with makeup."

"I suppose, but I don't think you should."

"Why?"

"I think it's beautiful. Exotic. Powerful."

I looked up into those tiger eyes and saw the fire burning behind them.

Oh.

"I like the sound of that," I said.

"Good." He went back to eating, but there was a palatable heat between us. I started thinking about that bed of his, starting thinking about those sheets.

"The bands on your left hand will probably stay," he finally said.

"Okay. I give up. How do you know these things?"

I hadn't expected him to answer. I especially hadn't expected him to tell me what sounded like the truth.

"I've studied magic my entire life. My . . . my job involves . . . being aware of all the ways magic can manifest. Knowing how it is used, legally and illegally."

"Wait. Did you just tell me you're a cop?"

"No."

"FBI? CIA? Is there a division of government that oversees magic use?"

"Not exactly."

"So you're part of what? A secret society of, oh, here let me guess, uh . . . Buddhist monks who believe it is their divine calling to run around telling people how to use magic."

"I'm not a Buddhist."

"Well, if you're even half of what I just accused you of being, you are most certainly a vigilante."

"Most certainly?"

"Seems pretty clear to me. Is there a secret handshake to get into your little fraternity?"

"Yes."

I studied his face, calm, neutral. He'd be hella good at playing poker. "Bullshit."

He smiled. "The lines on your right hand and arm won't go away either," he said.

"Okay, so let's pretend that I believe you are a part of a secret society of magic cops."

"Okay."

"And let's pretend I know that magic has been around for hundreds, thousands of years."

"Okay."

"Have you ever seen this before?" I held up both hands, my right hand a webwork of opalescent lines, the left banded in black at each joint.

He reached, took both my hands by the fingers, studied the backs of them, then gently turned them over to study the palms.

"This." He traced the palm of my right hand like a fortune-teller. The gentle strokes sent heat that had nothing to do with magic rushing up my thighs. "This is where magic marked and claimed you. When you use magic, you feel it moving through these lines."

I nodded.

"It is magic's gift to you. This," he said, running his fingers gently between the fingers of my left hand, his touch softly circling each joint, "is where you denied its effort to absorb you. When you use magic, you may lose feeling here first, and if you use it too much, or too quickly, that sensation will travel from your hand, to your arm, and eventually could stop your heart. It is the price you pay for the gift."

"Positive energy." He lifted my right hand slightly. "Negative energy." He lifted my left hand.

"Power and restraint." He drew my hands together. "Very sexy."

Great. I was a battery. Well, at least he had a nice way of saying it.

"Sexy," I mused. "Are you un-slowing down our relationship, Jones?"

"Maybe. How un-slow do you think you can handle it?"

This had to be the lamest relationship I'd ever been in.

"Ground rules," I said. "This is just for tonight. No promises means no complications and no complications means no dumping in the morning."

"I can live with that."

"You still hungry?" I asked. He had not taken his hands off of mine, and still held me as if I were something he did not want to disappear.

"Not for food," he answered.

Oh, baby, sweet-talk me all night long.

I pulled my hands out of his. "Good. I'm done too. Let's go see if your bed's big enough for the two of us." I strutted off, and lifted my tank top up over my head and then off. I don't know what it was about him, but he made me want to get naked in a hurry.

He jogged up beside me and gently drew his hand up my back before wrapping it around my waist and walking with me to the bedroom.

I figured this was going to be hot and quick, maybe a little fun, or a little rough. But Zayvion had different ideas.

He locked the door and walked to the dresser. I, standing alone, kicked off my running shoes and made my socks into little balls that I stuffed inside my shoes.

"Zay?" I asked.

"Mmm?" He opened a drawer and I heard the rattle of matches in a box, then the scritch of a match being lit. He lit the candle on the dresser.

"You want me to help with that?"

"No, I'm almost done."

Okay, so this, maybe, was the downfall of having a perfectionist for a lover.

"You want me to make sure the sheets are smooth—maybe iron them, or think I should dust off your condoms and arrange them in alphabetical order?"

"Is there a problem with how my condoms are arranged?" His back was still toward me, but he had moved on to the other dresser in the opposite corner of the room. Same deal there, match, snick, candle, flame. Rhythmic. Ritualistic.

"Hello? Half-naked woman standing over here," I said.

The muscles of his shoulders twitched, but he still didn't turn to look at me. "Give me a minute," he said. "I'll make it worth your wait. Promise."

"I thought we said no promises."

"You did." He walked past me to the corner and lit a candle there with a new match. He pointedly avoided looking at me. Okay, this was getting weird, though I suppose no weirder than him being a part of a secret society of magic cops. He walked around me, gaze averted, and lit the last candle in the last corner of the room.

"You're really into candles, aren't you?"

He put the matchbox down on the shelf next to the last candle he had lit. "Something like that," he said. He turned off the overhead lamp and the room filled with a soft golden glow. This time when he turned, he was looking right at me, and the fire from the candles reflected the burning passion in his gaze.

"Are you sure there isn't something else you'd like to do?" I asked. "Maybe burn some incense? Wash a couple of windows? Fold some laundry?"

He stalked across the room and stopped in front of me, so close I could feel the heat off his body, even though we were not touching.

"You talk too much," he said.

"That's a great way to get me in the mood."

He stood there, still staring at me, and I thought about reaching out and grabbing him, but this looked an awful lot like a game of chicken and I was determined he touch me first, not the other way around.

"I see you're still wearing a shirt," I said.

He leaned back to make elbow room, and pulled his shirt off.

Hells, he was a fine-looking man. Muscled, not gym-worked, but hard and flat. I wanted to touch him. I wanted to lick him up.

He leaned back in again, but instead of pulling me into an embrace, he very gently pressed his fingers against the mark on my temple. "If the candlelight is too bright, tell me," he said quietly.

He wrapped his right arm around my waist and

pulled me against him, and I got my hands on his back. He drew his finger in some quick pattern against my temple. I gasped at the hot race of mint that flowed into me, warming me, warming the magic in me, making me hot, trembling, hungry.

I moaned, and opened eyes I did not know I had closed.

"There is sensual pleasure in the weight of carrying magic," he said. "Let me show you."

"Yes," I breathed. He bent his head and kissed me.

My world exploded. His lips were warm, his tongue sliding into my mouth and slowly exploring the taste of me, as if I were something wonderful to savor. His fingers traced the whorls of magic on my palm, my wrist, the inside of my elbow, flicking across erogenous zones I never knew I had. His motions were sweet and almost painfully gentle. I squirmed and pulled away from his lips, unable to bear the sensation overload. I leaned my head against his chest, breathing hard as he traced up my arm, then drew heat and the sweet slide of mint across my shoulder and collarbone. His finger caught under my chin and he lifted my head. I wanted him to get out of his pants. I wanted to be out of mine. But I did not want him to stop doing exactly what he was doing. He pressed his leg between mine, and shifted so that his right hand was firmly against my back. He dipped his head and kissed the marks on my neck, sending another shiver of need through me.

I moaned.

He sucked, his tongue exploring the lines of magic that flowed up the curve of my neck.

I closed my eyes, moaned again as his tongue drew up the side of my jaw. Warmth and need spread through me, flickering like fire from my nerves, pulsing through the lines of magic.

He bit—not too hard, not hard enough—and I gasped. I wanted more. I wanted him to never let go.

His mouth drew up my cheekbone and I trembled. Though I was shaking, I ran my hands up his back, his neck. I slipped my other hand down to his belt line. I wanted to feel him. The fire building in me was too hot. He breathed across my cheek, and I could not move.

His fingers teased the lines of magic on the tip of my shoulder, tugging magic up to the surface of my skin so that I felt tight with it, tight with the need for release. He traced the pattern again, his fingers dipping down my cheek, down along the bare, soft skin of my neck. I arched back so I could feel him, feel more of him. I wanted him to release me from this hungry, joyful need.

"Let go," he said over the pounding roar in my head. "I've got you."

I opened my eyes and he kissed my temple, his tongue tracing a pattern there.

Magic welled in me, rising like a tide I could not stop. It filled me, stretched me, rising to his touch, rising to meet him, to wrap around him, drown him, consume him.

No. I struggled not to lose control of the magic. I struggled to hold it still, breathing deeply to try to clear my mind. If I lost control of the magic, Zayvion could be killed.

But his tongue teased and encouraged. He kissed his way back down my cheek, bit at the thin lines of magic that curved across my collarbone and fingered to the edge of my breast. I shuddered.

I couldn't wait. I couldn't hold this much magic; no one could. My body ached with the weight of the magic filling me, magic Zayvion tugged, stroked, sucked, and drew upon in rhythm with his hands and tongue.

We kissed.

"Let go," he whispered against my lips.

I opened my eyes. I couldn't hold on. To the magic, or the need.

I opened my mouth to beg him to give me a minute to catch my breath, or maybe to tell him I wanted this, this abandon of control more than anything in my life. But I didn't have time. I didn't have thought. I didn't have breath. Just one more second and I would explode.

The candles in the room dimmed and I groaned.

Zayvion's hands glowed with the yellow light of the candles. He mumbled a spell in a language I had never heard before. He released the spell, plunging deep into the magic I could no longer contain.

I yelled out, burning with pleasure, throbbing with the joy of him deep inside the power that coursed through me. The world was reduced to textures: soft, silk, the watery touch of air. Reduced to colors: Zayvion's eyes burning tiger-bright, his hands lost in a glow up to his elbows that cast his dark skin in gold light and ink shadows, the room a night sky around us, the deep brown earth holding us strong. Reduced to smells and tastes: sharp garlic and the mild cheeses of our dinner, the pine-sweet musk of Zayvion's sweat, the honey of melting candle wax.

Magic poured out of me, filling the room, and I poured out with it.

This, this was the way I wanted to die, pouring out, losing myself to the glory and power of magic, Zayvion strong and hard inside me, becoming part of the world, and then becoming all of the world.

But I was still human enough, still me enough, to want more—to want to take Zayvion on this ride with me.

I didn't have to cast a spell, didn't have to concentrate. I wasn't just a woman with magic anymore. I was magic. What I desired, magic became. And I desired Zayvion to experience this joy.

I poured magic into him. Zay groaned and breathed hard, his eyes half closed. We stood, holding each other tight. We still hadn't finished undressing, but that didn't matter. How could the mere pleasure of flesh compare with this, with me feeling him inside my whole body?

Zay groaned again, and I knew he could feel this, feel me around him, feel magic pouring hot and fast into him.

"Come with me," I said, or maybe I only thought it. "We can be everything."

I kissed him, and he kissed me back, hungrily.

Zay drank me down, and I poured out magic, whipping magic around us like ribbons in the wind, spooling from my fingers, from deep within the earth, from deep within me, into him.

And still it didn't fill him.

I pulled back enough to look in his eyes. They still burned bright, but there was something else behind that. A darkness as calm and deep and endless as the night sky. I could pour as much magic as I wanted into him. He was a lightning rod, a man who could Ground me and the magic I sent into him, and pour it back to the earth from which it came.

"Oh," I said. This was so much more than I thought, he was so much more.

If I was the battery, he was the grounding wire. I could throw magic around all I wanted and he'd never loose his hold on me. We fit, so neatly a part of each other, magic to magic and soul to soul.

"What are you?" I whispered.

"What do you want me to be?"

This had such lovely possibilities.

I drew my hand up his butt and rocked my hips to remind him I was also a woman of flesh and desire. Still, magic poured through me, through him, to the earth.

One corner of his lips quirked upward.

"More?" I asked him.

"Think you can?" he asked.

"Try me."

Zayvion kissed me, softly, and the magic swelled between us.

"Bed," I said.

We made it to the bed, though I needed some help getting there and getting my pants off. I was dizzy with power, light-headed to the point of little specks dancing at the corners of my vision. But I didn't want to let go of the clear rush of magic streaming through me. I wanted to make love to that calm, strong man, and try to break his calm, strong focus.

Once we were on the mattress and sheets—both of which were soft—the room seemed to spin a little and stopped only when Zay was above me, his eyes dark, dark windows into eternity.

He wasn't just Grounding me, he was sucking the power through me, swallowing me down faster than I could refill, and drinking up more. I ached with the speed of the magic rushing through me. Ached with it, and loved it.

Time to fight fire with fire. I concentrated on holding the magic tightly inside my body, not letting any of it, not a taste, not a glimmer, not a thread of it escape me.

Zay jerked and moaned, and his body, which was naked now, thank heavens, responded to the sudden deprivation. He lowered against me and we kissed. I wanted to feel him inside me in every way, magic and flesh, but I made him work to get my mouth open, made him work to release my hold on the magic, and then, when he had done so, with as much patience as I could tolerate, I gave him all of me, and he gave all of himself in return.

He was hot, sweating, hard. My heartbeat thrummed, pounding in rhythm with the pulse of his mouth drawing magic from the lines against my collarbone, the hollow of my neck. Sliding waves of pleasure rolled through me, and I tangled my fingers in his thick, curled hair, pressing his head closer to my skin. He drew my hands up and above my head, lacing his fingers with mine. The heat of my right hand and chill of my left were uncomfortable so close together, but his hand cradled between my palms felt strong and solid and warm.

Magic coursed through me in waves of heat and ice, wrapping around his hand, wrapping around his body as he lowered against me and paused. I groaned. The weight of him between my thighs and against my hips and breasts, and the pressure of magic beneath my skin, begging to be released, turned every breath into an additional, aching pleasure.

He bent and gently licked my right nipple, and I luxuriated in the nerve-hot sensation.

Yes. Now.

Need shuddered through me as he licked my left nipple, then nipped, and sucked at the magic that filled me and filled me.

He was no longer Grounding me, no longer drinking the hot, fast flow of magic from me, and I was filling too full, too fast. The ache was unbearable. The pleasure immense.

I trembled, gasped for air.

"Ground me," I begged.

Zay plunged within me, within the magic, and I cried out in joy.

I arched against him and rode the pulsing waves of hot, silken pleasure, emptying of magic, emptying of hunger, emptying of need.

We kissed, a little sloppily, a little slow, and didn't stop until the heat of magic, the heat of our passion, pooled into a sweet warmth between us, until our heartbeats slowed, until we could breathe again.

I rested curled against him, warm and languid. The magic within me was quiescent, satisfied. And so was I. I had never felt anything like that. I now understood why some people willingly paid painfully high prices to use magic during sex.

But this had been more than a dime-store sex toy or three-step spell. Somewhere during the wild storm of magic Zay had called up within me, we had joined together, manipulating the give and take, the flow of a massive amount of magic.

And I felt absolutely no ill effects from it.

"How come I don't hurt?" I asked.

His chin was tucked so his lips were near my ear. "What do you mean?"

"We used a lot of magic just now. A lot. And we did not set a Disbursement spell. So why aren't we paying a price for it?"

His breathing caught, and I counted three strong beats of his heart against my chest before he spoke. "Soul Complement," he said, as if that explained everything.

I pulled back so I could see his face. "What is that supposed to mean?"

"Didn't your father teach you anything?"

That kind of question usually made me defensive. But here, in his arms, I had no desire to put up my guard. "Other than how to balance a checkbook? No. Is it a magic term?"

Zay took a deep breath and stared at the wall behind me. I figured he was trying to decide what to tell me, or maybe how much.

"Listen," I said. "You probably have lots of reasons to be all secretive and such. But my life has been changed by things I don't understand. It would be fabulously decent of you to let me in on all this."

He still didn't say anything, so I tucked back into the warmth of him. "Would it help if I promised not to tell anyone?"

Still nothing.

"Scout's honor?" I offered.

"Are you a scout?" he asked in the kind of voice that told me he was smiling.

"Not that I know of. But for you, I'd totally get started on that."

He shifted, drew his hand down my hip and thigh, and I pulled back so I could see him again.

"There are terms among the Authority," he said.

"Wow. Why don't you start with authority? Authority of what?"

"Magic."

"Really. Magic experts? Are there magic lectures? Magic bake sales? Magic bingo night?" I had a bad habit of making jokes when something startled me. The idea that there really was a group of secret magic worshippers scared the hell out of me.

He made an exasperated sound and rubbed his face. "Do you want to hear this or not, Scout?"

"I'm sorry. Go ahead."

He looked back down at me. "There are terms among the . . . people who use magic. A Magic Complement is someone who can either support or aid another caster, or whose magic style and ability are similar to another caster so that complex spells, like Grounding, are possible between them."

He could Ground me without it seeming to hurt him. "You and I are Magic Complements?"

"Yes."

"And that's why we can manipulate so much magic without burning out?"

"Possibly. There are other ways two magic users can work together. Besides being a Magic Complement, there is also a Magic Contrast. A Contrast is someone whose magic style and ability are at an opposing stance with another caster. Contrasts can often achieve even more power or control when they work together. The conflict of magical styles can bear strange advantages. But there is always a grave price to pay for that kind of magical interaction.

"Complements can also achieve a lot through working magic together, and there is usually a smaller price paid. There are many degrees of Complement and Contrast. You and Cody are Complements on some levels."

"That's why he could pull magic through me?"

"Right."

"So what is a Soul Complement?"

"The highest joining and expression of two magic users manipulating magic as one."

I swallowed to try to find my voice. "Does that happen very often?"

"It is believed there is a Soul Complement for each person who uses magic."

"Believed?"

His voice softened. "So few find each other. Fewer still risk death to discover if they can cast magic in perfect complement. It's hard to prove if there is a Soul Complement for each person." He paused, golden eyes studying me. "There have been some throughout history."

"And there's us," I said.

"And there's us."

He didn't look sad or excited about it. Just calm. Patient. Waiting for me to say something.

What did one say to someone who had just told you that they may be your perfect soul match? Predestined companion. Yang to your yin, and all that?

"I think this might get a little complicated after all," I said.

"Mmm." He reached over and gently brushed my bangs away from my face. "Want to ask me anything else?"

I laughed. "Not yet. Let me think this over, okay?" And there I was, asking him to give me time, to take it slow. He didn't seem to mind.

"Sure."

I rolled over and pressed my back against his warm, wide chest, and he wrapped his arms around me and held me tight.

After what felt like a long time, he said, "Allie?"

"Yes?"

"I didn't expect this."

"What?"

"You."

I was quiet, thinking about that. I hadn't expected him either. Hadn't expected to care for him. To need him. Maybe even love him. "Are you sorry?" I asked in a small voice.

"No."

I couldn't help it. I sighed. "Good. Neither am I."

I slept soundly and deeply, which was rare for me. First of all, I had a million thoughts spinning through my head. Second of all, when I'm first sharing a bed with someone, I wake up all night long, forgetting and remembering that I have someone in the bed with me. But Zay's sheets were soft, his body warm, so warm we had to drape the sheet between us so we didn't stick together, and his steady breathing lulled me. If he snored, I did not notice.

A beeping alarm clock, however, I did hear. Zay rolled away from me and turned it off.

"What time is it?" I asked.

"Five thirty."

I groaned. "Why would anyone want to get up at this hour?"

"Well"—Zayvion rolled toward me—"I can think of some good reasons." He kissed my lips, even though I had severe morning breath after the lasagna. I gave him points for being brave.

"What sort of good reasons?" I asked innocently.

"It's a good time to read the paper," he said.

"Uh-huh." I wrapped my leg over his hip and scooted closer to him. "What else?"

"Sometimes I get in a run before breakfast."

"So you like to work out first thing in the morning?" I asked.

"It's a good way to get the blood pumping."

"Then by all means, you should work out." We kissed, and I savored the feel of him against me. I was sleepy, warm, and sated. We took some time kissing before getting into the full swing of things. But then,

I'd always been told it's best to stretch before any strenuous activity.

It was fun sex, casual sex, the kind of sex that didn't have anything to do with magic, Complements, Contrasts, commitments, or complications. Just warmth, togetherness, and pleasure. I thought it was a perfect way to start the day. From the look in Zay's eyes, he thought so too.

When we finally rolled away from each other, I stretched out on my back, arms over my head, toes pointed, and moaned. "So good."

Zay put his palm on my bare stomach and kissed my breast. "What are you making me for breakfast?"

"Ha-ha. Who's the guest here? I expect coffee and homemade eggs Benedict to be waiting for me when I get out of the shower."

"How about cold cereal?"

"Do you have milk?"

"No." Zay absently ran his fingers up my stomach, then down over my hip bone. "I could see what else Nola packed."

I grinned. "Perfect. Now, if you'll excuse me."

I rolled out of bed, away from his teasing hands. I suffered a twinge of modesty when I realized I didn't have a robe to cover up with. No matter. It was still dark in the room, and I liked to think I had a pretty healthy body image. Just in case, I kept my shoulders back and sucked in my stomach as I headed toward the bathroom. Good body image or not, posture could do wonders for a woman's figure.

"Save me some hot water," Zay called.

I crossed the hall into the bathroom. My little stroll had cooled me off and I was prickly with goose bumps. I opened the clean chrome and glass shower door, and turned the hot water on high. I opened a couple cupboards—one was apparently a medicine cabinet, as it had one bottle of aspirin and an extra bar of soap in it. Another held towels. Neatly folded. Of course.

A good, thick steam was fogging up the room, and I stepped into the shower, added a little cold water, and took my time savoring the heat.

Unfortunately, my only choice of soaps were both heavily scented with pine. Another reason why Zay always smelled like a walking forest.

Smelling like a car freshener wasn't exactly a goal of mine, but since I didn't have any of my own bathroom stuff, including deodorant, toothbrush, and lotion, it looked like I was going to do with or do without.

And I was so beyond the finicky-girly stage of life. I thought it might even be kind of nice to smell like him.

I washed up and thought about the meeting with Violet. The disks being stolen during a break-in and fire seemed a little hard to swallow in the light of day. More likely there was someone on the inside, maybe even someone she was trying to protect who was behind the theft.

Could it be some of the Authority that Zay had mentioned?

Secret society of magic. I couldn't begin to count how many ways that freaked me out.

It was just as possible that Violet might be looking for some way to dodge the corporation's claims to the disk research and development process so that she could either sell the patent or put the technology, and herself along with it, up to the highest bidder.

That kind of tech—portable magic—would go for billions. Violet could be assured whatever kind of life she most desired.

But she'd had that with my dad. Or at least she said

she did. The Daniel Beckstrom I knew was not beneath marrying a woman for her mind, then dumping her as soon as he got her intellectual property signed over in his name.

Violet was a smart woman. She may have decided there were more benefits if she were the widow Beckstrom, instead of just another discarded ex-wife.

That made sense, but now that I'd met her, I had a harder time fitting her into the money-hungry, calculating, black widow category. Intelligent enough to pull off that sort of a scheme? Sure. Willing to actually kill my father? I didn't think so.

Which left me with the break-in-and-fire story for the missing disks. And somehow Bonnie, and whoever she was working for, and Cody fit into this mess.

I dunked in the water, and rubbed at my face. I needed to find Cody. If he really was there when my father died, then he could finger the people behind it. And since I'd healed him and practically bathed in his blood, I was confident I could sniff him out of the city. Where I found Cody, I'd find Bonnie.

I finished rinsing, gargled some hot water, and rubbed my palm over my itching arm.

I turned off the shower and toweled dry. My arm felt like fire ants were swarming over it.

"Damn it." Scrubbing with the towel only made it itch more. Maybe it was irritated by the soap. The ribbons of color seemed brighter, and my unmarked skin was pink from the heat of the shower. Cold water? I thought about turning the shower back on, but spotted a bottle of hand lotion on the sink. I pumped lotion into my palm, sniffed it. It smelled like beeswax, and didn't have heavy perfumes. I spread the lotion over my hand and arm and shoulder and face, careful not to use my fingernails. Much.

Nope. My arm was on fire, hot to the touch. Maybe I was having an allergic reaction to the soap. Worse, maybe I was having an allergic reaction to the magic I carried. I didn't even know if that was possible.

Peachy.

My clothes were on Zayvion's bedroom floor, so I wrapped the towel tightly around me, tucking the corner in at the top. The towel was short and barely covered my butt. Another joy of being a tall woman.

What I needed were my clothes and some anti-itch cream. Or Zay's fingers.

Bingo. If he could Ground me and ease the pressure of the magic trying to push out through my pores, I might even be able to think straight. Might be able to meditate, regain my control, and figure out what was making my arm itch, itch, itch.

I strode out of the bathroom, into the living room. "Zayvion?"

But it was not Zayvion who stood by the couch. It was a plain-looking man, an unhandsome man. Not Violet's man, Kevin, but someone like him. A man you would never notice in a crowd, someone who calmly paused to decide exactly how he was going to kill me before he muttered a mantra and drew his palms toward each other, pulling magic up from the earth and from the building's storage. Like most magic users, he did not draw it into his body, but worked a liquid silver glyph between his hands.

All this in less than a second.

"Zay!" I yelled, hoping to give him time to catch the guy after I died.

I drew on the magic in me, and whispered a mantra of safety, of shielding. The first one that came to mind was a stupid little spell—one that can be used against rain when you forgot your umbrella, or sharp rocks if you were wading through a pond. It was not strong enough to ward off a magical attack.

Like wings of fire, magic spread inside me, filled me. A trailing salve of power rushed down my arm.

The man brought the tips of his fingers together, then pulled them apart, releasing the glyph.

Magic is fast. Spells cannot be tracked while they are being cast, but can be seen after the fact, like an afterimage burned in the air. I did not see the glyph that wrapped around me, but I could taste it on the roof of my mouth—thick and sharp, like a chemical burn—and I could feel it, cold as a frozen wire squeezing my throat.

I ran my hand over my neck and magic spooled from my fingertips, burning into the cold wire. I unknotted the glyph, and it broke in a shower of blue sparks.

The man pulled a gun.

A gun.

And pointed it at me.

There were spells that could be cast to cause a temporary muscle cramp, say in a gunman's hand. There were spells that would momentarily blind a person. There were even spells that could make a person sneeze uncontrollably.

Any one of those would do me fine right now. But I couldn't think of one of them. I couldn't think of a single spell. It was like the world had suddenly stopped making sense, but had slowed down so much that all I could do was stand there, frozen in shock, wondering why the world had suddenly stopped making sense, and wishing I could think of some way to save my life.

Magic cannot be cast from a state of confusion or high anxiety or emotion. I was burning with untapped power, and I couldn't do a single thing.

So instead of fighting the emotions, I gave in. I got angry.

Death by bullet? Oh, hells no.

I charged at him.

He lowered his gun, the idiot, and took half a step back, but I was six feet of pissed-off, adrenaline-pumping woman, and if I was going to die, I was going to take him down with me.

I rammed my shoulder into his sternum. Air blasted out of his lungs, the gun exploded once, twice, so loud, so close I wanted to scream, did scream, as we careened across the room into the door, me clawing for the gun, him pulling his hand away. I breathed in the scent of him—iron and minerals—overwhelming, like old vitamin pills.

The gun rang out again, and this time I screamed in agony. The left side of my body felt like it had been blown apart. The world went white-hot. I tasted blood in my mouth.

The bastard had shot me.

Suddenly, my mind was very, very clear. I convulsed down to the floor, landed on my knees, my hands over the side of my stomach, gushing blood all over Zayvion's perfect white carpet. I thought of a mantra, but the blood, the pain, made it hard to stay calm, hard not to just scream and scream in rage.

I recited the mantra, through the blinding pain, through the blinding fear. Recited it through tears pouring down my face, recited it even though blood made my fingers sticky and slick.

The bastard raised the gun, level with my head.

"Good-bye, Allison Beckstrom."

I looked up into his eyes. If he was going to do it, I refused to look away.

This was not a game, not a lark, not make-believe. I was about to die. I hated that.

He jerked the gun up and pointed it past me.

It was Zay behind me. I hoped it was Zay. Then I hoped it wasn't because whoever was behind me was about to be shot. The man's finger tightened on the trigger.

But there was no explosion, no bullet.

Magic is fast.

You cannot see it coming.

I had focus. I had deadly concentration. I was overflowing with magic. I was also in pain and could not think of a spell.

But I wasn't just a woman with magic. I was magic. Who needed a spell? I told the magic to make him stop, make him go away, make him not be there.

Magic poured out of me, hard, fast. A second pain, a fire on an open wound. Too much. Too hot. I screamed. But I could not make the magic stop.

Someone else was screaming, someone else was chanting. The room spun. And everything went black.

Chapter Thirteen

Cody did not like this place. It was dark and small and smelled like mice. His back touched one wall and his feet squished up against a door that would not open.

He was all alone and scared. Kitten was gone and probably didn't like him anymore. He had thrown her away in the field, because he didn't know what else to do. He had told her to run fast. Run away in the green grass, in the sunshine, away from the bad lady and bad magic and the bad bees buzzing and angry inside him.

He shouldn't have thrown her away. She was his friend. His only friend.

He wished the older, smarter part of himself would come back, but he was gone too. Maybe he was mad like Kitten.

Cody rocked and rocked and tried to be brave. If he was brave, maybe the older, smarter part of him would come back. Maybe Kitten would come back too.

His head knocked against the wall of the tiny room and hurt but Cody didn't stop. Cody didn't know how long he rocked. A long time, maybe.

Then he heard something. Footsteps. Someone was walking on the other side of the door that would not open. Not little footsteps like Kitten. Big footsteps. Footsteps that belonged to a man.

Cody rocked and rocked. He wanted to go away. Far away. Fast, fast, fast.

The footsteps got louder. Stopped. The door clicked.

Cody held still. He held still in the dark and didn't scream. He was too scared to scream. Too scared to move. He didn't want the door to open. Didn't want anyone to find him.

But the door did open. And standing there, so big, too big, was the Snake man.

"Aren't you something, Cody?" he said in his snake voice. "I don't know how you survived. A death for a death is the price. Why aren't you dead?"

Cody couldn't talk. Cody couldn't tell him that the older, smarter part of him had done something, something special with the magic in the coins, something special with the magic in the little bone. He couldn't tell him that the older, smarter part of him had found a way so they wouldn't die. And he couldn't tell him that the lady with magic inside her had made him all better again.

"You don't know, do you?" the Snake man asked in a sorry voice that was not sorry. "Well, maybe we'll find out together." He smiled, but it was only on the outside. Inside he was hating. Hating Cody.

Maybe if Cody sang a song the Snake man would go away.

"Snake man, Snake man, bake a cake man."

But the Snake man did not go away. He reached into the little room. Cody wailed, wishing the older, smarter part of him would come back. He wasn't brave all alone. He was too small to be brave. Too small for anyone to hear him. Too small for anyone to care.

Chapter Fourteen

There is something wonderful about silence, about blackness. For one thing there is no pain. For another there is no fear, just gentle drifting and casual ignorance of reality's harsh light.

But silence cannot stretch on forever. Sounds punch their way through, muffled at first, a man's voice, a name. My name. And the sound of my name carries so much more—it tells me who I am, and that I am not dead just yet.

I wonder if I'm breathing. Inhale.

Air, light, sound, taste, smell, and pain—hells, the pain—chew the silence to shreds and I am awake.

"Damn it, Allie, breathe. C'mon, babe. I can't do this. You can't do this to me."

I opened my eyes—okay it took a few tries—but I finally got them open. I felt like I'd just spent the last month in a meat grinder.

"There." Zay's voice was shaking, his words coming out too fast. "Good. Good. Don't give up. Don't go away. Stay here. Good. Good."

I blinked. I was going to open my eyes again, honest to goodness, but the silence was so easy, so soft, so empty.

Zay swore and dug his hands into my ribs, sending

off shock waves of pain. "No. Fuck it, Allie. Come back to me."

If I had fallen into a vat of hot mint, I couldn't have felt more permeated with the sting of it.

Ow.

The darkness skittered out of my reach, all of its soft, welcoming nothingness covered by a warm, wet layer of mint. And the mint flowed toward me, gently forcing me to step back, to turn, to remember I was not breathing and that was bad. To take a breath.

I opened my eyes.

Zayvion's face, ashen-green, sweat glittering in the tight black curls across his forehead and running wet lines down his cheek, hovered over me.

"Look at you and those beautiful eyes. Good job, babe. You're doing really good. Take another easy breath. Perfect." He smiled. "I am Grounding the hell out of you, Dove. You need to let go of the magic, let it rest, let it fall back into the earth. Can you do that?"

Oh sure. And after that maybe I'd show him my amazing high-wire trapeze act.

"Just keep looking at me."

I blinked, but this time I could open my eyes again.

"Good. I'm going to talk you down into a trance, all right? I'll be right here. You'll be safe. You'll be warm. Comfortable. You're safe with me."

I listened as he droned on, and every so often reminded me to breathe. And then he guided me to feel every part of my body from the top of my head to the soles of my feet and told me to exhale and envision all of the magic pouring out of me into the ground.

I did. And I was awake. For real this time.

Zay was still above me, still sweating, still shaking, and still looking a little sick around the edges.

"Hey," I tried to say. It came out breathy and all vowel.

"Hey," he said. "How are you feeling, babe?"

Oh, like I could do cartwheels uphill.

"Bad," I said. "Turd." I'd meant to say "tired" but it didn't come out right. Zay didn't seem to notice.

"That's okay. That's good," he said. "I'm going to help you sit, then get you to bed. Ready?"

He didn't wait for me to answer. The room spun. Eventually I figured out it was me moving, sitting up, and not the world doing a lazy Susan.

Smart, I are.

Zay sat there with me, anxiously brushing my hair away from my face until I looked back into his eyes again.

"I'm fine," I lied. "Help me up."

With him doing most of the heavy lifting, I was on my feet and, with his arms supporting me and his voice a constant babble of encouragement, I was across the living room, down the hall, and lying back thankfully, so very thankfully, on Zay's bed. The strange thing was I didn't have on any clothes.

He fussed with my pillows, and I realized some of the moisture on his cheeks wasn't sweat. It looked like he had been crying.

"Zay?"

"I'm here." He lowered closer to me.

"What's wrong?"

His face went blank, still, frozen. Then he hung his head. "Nothing," he said. He laughed, choked, then looked back up at me. "Everything's okay."

"Something's wrong," I said. "Zay. I don't remember." I hated saying it, but I had a really bad feeling I had missed out on something big.

"You were shot. Do you remember that?"

I remembered pain. I remembered terror. Anger.

"Right here." Zay gently cupped my left side, just beneath my ribs. "I think the bullet went all the way through, but I haven't gone looking for it yet. You bled pretty hard."

"Bled?" It seemed that unless Zay had stitched me up or cauterized the wound, I should still be bleeding.

He nodded. "You healed. Like you did to Cody, I think. Magic closed the wound. Does it still hurt?"

I felt his finger brush downward from the top of my rib cage, lost feeling for some time, then felt his finger again toward my hip bone.

"It's numb," I said. As a matter of fact, I was feeling a bit numb myself.

"Who shot me?"

"A hit man named Dane Lanister. Do you know him?"

"No."

"Are you sure you've never seen him before?"

I raised my eyebrows. "As sure as a part-time amnesiac can be." Oh, good, the shock was wearing off.

Zay grinned. He leaned down and kissed me, not hard. I tried to kiss him back, but was too damn tired. He tasted like salt, sweat, tears, and the bitter tang of fear. Even so, he tasted good, familiar.

"Did you catch him?" I asked when he had pulled away.

"No," Zay said. "You were pouring magic at him in a spell I have never seen before. Do you remember that?"

I shook my head.

"I had cast a Holding spell at the same time." He gave me a long, level stare, like maybe that should mean more to me.

"And what happened?"

"Do you remember Bonnie disappearing with Cody?"

"In the field?"

"Right."

"So Dane—the man who shot me," I said, "disappeared?"

"Yes."

Which meant either Zay and I had created just the right combination of spells to physically move mass—a preposterous notion—or he had one of those stolen disks, a less preposterous notion.

"Who is he?" I asked. "Who does he work for? How do you know him?"

"I don't know who he's working for right now, but I'm guessing it's the same person Bonnie's contracted with."

The person who has the disks. The person who has Cody—the only person who saw who killed my father. The only person who could clear my name.

"How do you know him?" I asked again.

Zay stood and walked over to his dresser. He dug out a sweater and pulled it on over his long-sleeved T-shirt. "I've seen him off and on in my . . . career."

"How magnificently vague of you."

Zay tugged a stocking hat down over his head. "Thank you."

"He tried to kill me. I deserve a better explanation."

"There are more than one faction of magic users who do not follow the law, Allie. You've run into some—you've Hounded long enough to know what some people are willing to pay in exchange for power. The kinds of things they are willing to do."

"Cut to the chase. We both know there are creeps and hustlers out there. Are you talking about black-market magics?"

Zay pulled his coat off a chair. "More than that. Dane runs with a pretty influential group. I'm not going to tell you their name."

"Why? So in case I'm captured they can't torture the information out of me?"

He gave me a long, silent stare.

"Oh. Well, isn't that nice. So you're talking serious psychopaths? Why would they want me dead?"

"I don't think it's only about you, Allie. It's about who gets to control the tech—or maybe who gets to control your father's company, which controls the tech. You just happen to be in their way."

"Violet isn't involved in this, is she?"

"If she is, she's on our side."

"We have a side?"

"Damn right we do."

I pushed the covers off my legs and broke out in a sweat. Hells, I was tired. Still, I pushed up so I was sitting, and the covers slipped off. Oh yeah. I was naked. I tugged the blanket up over my chest and held it there. I was suddenly very dizzy. That was enough aerobics for the moment.

"Where are you going?" I asked.

"To call in a few favors. You can't stay here long. Not after the amount of magic you poured out. I set some Diversion spells, which should confuse anyone hunting you for about an hour." He glanced at the clock on the nightstand. "This won't take me long. Rest. When I come back, we'll need to leave on foot. Think you'll be able to do that?"

"Which part? Resting or running?"

"Both."

"Is there an option C? Take a vacation somewhere sunny, and drink a lot of rum until the world unfucks itself?"

Zay paced over to me, pulled the covers back over my legs, leaned down, and kissed me. He was trembling a little. Tired, I figured, or hurting. I wasn't the only one who had thrown a lot of magic around.

"It's good to have you back. Be here when I come home." Then he turned and left the room.

Even tired, even burned out, I could feel spells unweave as Zay left the room. I heard the dead bolts on the door snick shut.

I suppose he meant well. My knight in ski-coat armor and all that. But I was not about to stay here and wait for him to find some way to save me. Because as soon as that Diversion spell wore off, anyone looking for me wouldn't have to wonder where I was. They'd know, because I glowed.

I was tired of running. I wanted to be one step ahead of this problem for a change, instead of a mile behind. And the only thing I had on my side was Cody. If he had indeed seen who killed my father. Instead of waiting here to get found out, I was going to do a little hunting of my own.

First, though, I needed clothes.

It took a while, but I put on my bra and jeans, a sweater of Zay's, and a pair of his socks too. While I was at it, I borrowed a stocking hat out of the half dozen he had in his sock drawer and put that on.

Then I sat on the edge of the bed and indulged in my new hobby of breathing heavily and waiting for the room to stop spinning.

C'mon, Allie. Suck it up and get moving. I bullied myself to my feet, waited for the vertigo to pass, and walked out into the living room.

Blood. Everywhere. Blood covered the carpet in a wide, wet pool. Blood painted the wall and the side of the couch.

Holy shit.

I pressed my hand over my side, couldn't feel the pressure, but could feel the edges of a scar. So much for wearing a bikini again.

Okay, I'll be honest. I wanted to cry. There is nothing so freaky as seeing your own blood poured out like spilled cans of bargain-basement paint. There is nothing more sickening than realizing that your world has changed so much that people have actually tried to kill you. It made me feel vulnerable, and threatened to freeze me with fear. Where could I go that I would be safe? There was nowhere in this world I couldn't be found. Not here. Not my apartment. Not even Nola's. At any moment, around any corner, there could be someone with a gun pointed at my head.

I stared up at the ceiling and inhaled and exhaled, fighting down panic. I was good at fighting panic—I rode elevators—and had a healthy aptitude for denial.

When panic stopped squeezing my throat and I could breathe more evenly, I looked away from the ceiling. I refused to look at the floor or walls or furniture covered in my blood.

I was light-headed but I walked over to where the coat I had borrowed from Nola hung, checked it to make sure it was clean and that it had my little book in the pocket, then put it on.

I buttoned it up and went around the other side of the couch to avoid getting my shoes wet. I paused at the door. Zay had cast a hell of a spell. It practically vibrated out of the walls. He'd walked through it. There had to be a way to unweave it enough so I could get through it without breaking it, because if I broke it, I'd be a kill-me-now neon sign.

The very idea of drawing on magic, even a thin tendril of it, made my stomach turn. Every inch of me felt raw and empty. I was pretty sure the ability to cast magic had been blown out of me. I didn't know how long it would take me to recover from that.

Using magic to unlock the glyph was out of the question. Maybe he had it set so that anyone crossing it from the outside in would be stopped, but anyone crossing it from inside the room to outside would be okay.

Nothing to do but try. I put my hand on the doorknob, unlocked it, slid the dead bolt. Turned the handle. The door opened. I couldn't sense a change in the spell. I put my fingertips in the doorway, didn't feel any changes, put my whole hand, then my arm through so my hand was over the threshold. Nothing.

The ward was set outside in, bad. Inside out, good.

Thank you, Zayvion Jones.

I stepped through to the hall and shut the door behind me. The building didn't smell so good anymore; the heavy odors of people living too close together hit my sinuses and made me feel like choking. It was probably just an aftereffect of channeling so much magic—my senses were blown open. The lights in the hall seemed too bright, and a moth in the ceiling light sounded like a jumbo jet.

Of course, for all I knew, I could be running a fever, or bleeding internally from the wound. Just because the hole had closed didn't mean the healing had worked any deeper. I pressed my arm against my side, trying to decide if it felt squishy, or in any way like there was more fluid under the skin. Swollen, which, I supposed, was to be expected. Internal bleeding?

How the hell should I know? I was not a doctor.

But I was walking okay, tired, dizzy, but not in excruciating pain. That had to count for something, right?

The doors on either side of the hall were shut and I didn't hear any noise through them. Even though I couldn't remember the moment I was shot, I figured gunfire would stir a few people out of bed. Unless they had all gone to work already. Or maybe Zay had fancy noise-dampening spells too.

Possible.

There were two doors at the end on the hall. The stairwell and the elevator. I had to pick one. I wanted to go down the stairs. But I didn't want to wear myself out. Hells. Elevator, for the win.

I could do this. I'd done elevators a lot lately. I was great at elevators. And not one had sent me plummeting to my death. Yet.

I pressed the button and walked to the side of the doors, so I could see someone getting off the elevator before they saw me. The bell dinged and the doors opened. I waited for someone to step out. Listened for movement. The door started to close again, so I got moving and stuck my hand against it to hold it open. The door reopened and, sure enough, the elevator was empty.

I stepped in. The coffin closed down around me.

Strange how it never mattered how badly you hurt, you could still feel another pain—like the morphine needle when you'd broken a bone. And no matter how tired I was, I could still manage enough adrenaline to freak out in an elevator.

I pressed L for luck and leaned against one wall, the brushed bronze of it cool against my cheek. I stared at the numbers as they slowly blinked downward, broke out in a sweat, inhaled through my nose, exhaled out my mouth. The sound of my breath was accompanied by a high, panicky moan. I thought about calm rivers, summer days, soft sunlight. It didn't work.

I wanted to run out the doors when the elevator opened to the lobby, but I couldn't move that fast. Like wading through a bad dream, I pushed myself to walk across the elevator floor and finally, finally made it into the lobby.

My heart pounded too fast for so little exertion. Panic probably had something to do with it. I gritted my teeth to keep from making any sound. I could do this. I just needed to get outside. To get some fresh air.

I heard sirens and didn't care. I just wanted to get to the door and get outside. The door was glass and iron and let in the cool gray light of a slate-sky morning. Seeing that cloudy light made me feel better. The world—the real world with sun and wind and cars and people who didn't break into apartments with guns—was right out there. I pushed through the door, out into the cold, out into the wind, out into spaciousness with no walls and no ceiling and no guns I could see, and took deep, gulping breaths. I shivered and wiped the sweat off my face. Eventually I realized the sirens were growing louder.

The sirens were real. There were more than one. There must have been a bad accident. I glanced around to get my bearings, and checked out the name of the apartments: Cornerstone. The building and street weren't familiar. Sirens kept getting closer, louder. Maybe it wasn't an accident. Maybe it was the gunfire and somebody had reported it. Maybe they were coming for me.

I kept my hands tucked in my pockets and my head down as I walked toward the street corner. The cross street was Stark, and that helped some. I knew which side of town I was on—the east, on the other side of the river from my apartment and downtown.

But I wasn't planning on going to my apartment. I was planning on Hounding Cody. I just needed to sit for a couple of minutes and get my strength back.

I waited on the corner, watching traffic go by as sirens grew louder. I did not want to be standing on a corner if those sirens really were out looking for me. I either needed to get walking, duck into a building—all of which looked to be shops, offices, or apartments—or I needed to catch a ride.

I dug in the coat pockets. Nola had stuffed some money in them, bless her heart. I hailed a cab, got one to stop on my third try, and ducked in just as the blue and red lights of a police car—two, no, three—came down the street. The cab waited for the police to pass before pulling away from the curb.

"Where to?" he asked.

I had no idea where to go, but I knew the one place I could hide better than anywhere in town. The one place Violet had said their leads had sent them when they were looking for the disks.

"St. John's."

As he turned into traffic, the sirens stopped. I glanced back. Sure enough, they had turned up the street toward Zayvion's apartment.

Maybe someone had reported the gunshots.

Maybe Zayvion had lied and turned me in. A chill rolled over me. Would he do that? Hells, I might do that if someone bled all over my rug and left bullet holes in my walls. He might be telling the truth about working for a secret society, but that didn't mean he wasn't human. There was bound to be some sort of reward for my capture. If not on public record, then somewhere, behind closed doors, with the corporations that wanted the tech, and the people who wanted me out of their way to get it.

Could I be more suspicious? It made me feel guilty thinking Zay might do something like that, but I'd been used, influenced, tricked, and betrayed so many times in life, it was hard to trust.

He'd been there for me, my conscience whispered. Every time things had gotten really bad, Zay was there. And now I was breaking my promise to stay put and wait for him.

Maybe I was pushing him away like Nola said.

Well, if those police were looking to arrest me for killing my father, then maybe it was better I didn't drag Zayvion down with me. I didn't think our relationship was far enough along to be in the aiding and abetting stage.

Or maybe that excuse was just another way to push him away. Push away a man who'd put his life on the line for me. Someone who'd nearly gotten shot because of me. Someone who was trying to look after me.

I rubbed at my forehead. It made my head hurt. I didn't know what the truth was, didn't know how my life had spiraled out of control so quickly. What I did know was that I needed to find Cody. And since this whole thing had started when I Hounded the hit on Boy, that's where I was going. To Mama's. If my dad really had set an Offload on Boy, then there was something going on between Mama and my father, or maybe Beckstrom Enterprises and Mama, that Mama was not sharing with me. And I wanted to know what that was. I wanted to know if maybe she too had played me for a fool and tried to use me to get at my dad.

It occurred to me that she could have agreed to let Boy be hit, agreed to call me to Hound him, and been pleased to send me on to my father's office in a rage.

I had thought Mama's anger and fear were real—that she was truly concerned Boy would die. I thought the news of my father being behind the hit had been a surprise to her. I thought I'd read her right.

But it was a hell of a coincidence that the one day I visited my father in seven years was the day he was killed. And whoever killed him knew I'd be there, and forged my signature on the hit. Mama was one of the people who knew I'd been there. So was Zay.

I was the queen of suspicion today. Go, me.

Raindrops, fat and heavy, splatted on the cab's windshield, then a few more fell. Pretty soon morning had dipped into a darker gray and it was raining pretty hard. I was really happy I'd taken one of Zay's hats. Really happy I had a warm coat. And as soon as the cab crossed the North Burlington railroad track, I could have sworn I'd just taken a painkiller. My shoulders relaxed, my neck stopped hurting. I didn't know what it was, but I always felt better coming up to this side of town. And even that was making me feel suspicious right now.

"This is it," the cabbie said.

"Thanks." I pressed a ten into his hand and got out of the cab.

Rain bulleted down, and I impressed myself by jogging across the street. I kept close to the buildings, taking advantage of their overhangs as much as possible. The air smelled of oil, the rot off the river, and the chlorine-clean smell of rain doing no good to wash away the musky decay of wood and asphalt and sewage.

What I didn't smell were the spices and grease of Mama's restaurant. What I didn't see were lights in her windows. What I didn't hear were the sounds of her voice, hollering orders at her Boys.

Maybe barging in her front door wasn't the best way to go about this. Time for Plan B.

I ducked into the alley beside her restaurant and took a minute to think about what I should do. Maybe Mama's was closed. Maybe she was visiting the youngest Boy, at the hospital. Maybe I needed to come up with a plan that was something more than "demand Mama tell me the truth and find Cody and get him to the cops."

One thing I definitely didn't need was to stand out here in the cold and rain much longer. Hat and coat didn't mean I was pneumonia proof.

The dark clouds were going black fast, and the wind was starting to gust. The rain shower picked up speed and the temperature dropped. I could see my breath. We were in for a hell of a storm. The change in air pressure, or maybe temperature, made my right arm ache, and stung in the old blood magic scars on my left arm.

I heard the subaudible growl of thunder in the distance, and felt a strange echo of it in my bones. I felt like a string resonating to a distant orchestra. There was magic in that storm—wild magic—and it was coming fast.

The wind shifted, coming hard off the river. A gust filled the alley with a strong peppery odor. I sneezed and looked over my shoulder. I needn't have bothered. I knew who was standing there, smiling at me, drenched in lavender. Bonnie.

And yes, this time she had her gun out for show and tell.

"Allie! It's so great to see you. We're gonna go take a walk, 'kay?" She smiled her bright, cheerleader smile and waved her gun like a pom-pom at me. My stomach clenched and my legs felt weak. Looking at that gun was like getting a drink of the hooch responsible for the hangover from hell. I might not have a good memory of being shot, but my subconscious did, and my body did too—a sensory memory of the smell of metal and gunpowder, of someone standing in front of me with a rod of cold steel in their hand, of pain, of terror.

I seriously needed to figure out why I thought going to North Portland was ever a good idea.

"Bonnie," I said, trying to get my voice down an octave. "How's it been going?"

She looped her arm in my arm, and locked down tight, so we were side-by-side like the best girlfriends ever. She held the gun in her right hand, waving it around while she talked. All she had to do was bend her elbow and the muzzle of that gun would be buried in the ribs I had not been shot in yet.

"Oh, it's just been fine. Just fine," she said, like we were talking kids and husbands in the aisle of a supermarket. "Got some new clients right now, and the office boy is working out. Oh, I did a little job that the police are very happy about." She leaned her head in toward me, so she could lower her voice and press the gun against my jacket. "A murder case. Very high profile. Crime of passion. Between family members. It's been all over the news. Maybe you've heard about it?"

"I haven't had time to keep up with current events."

She chuckled and started walking toward the back of the alley, and I had no choice but to go with her. "It is so *good* to see you. And how about you? Where have you been keeping yourself, rich girl?"

"Around," I said as she marched me down to the back end of the alley. "Tried to take a little vacation in the country, but that went to hell."

"I love the country! Fresh air, cute animals." Wave the gun, jam it in my ribs. "Your friend Nola sure has a nice place, don't you think? Hope she's doing okay."

A thinly veiled threat. At least we'd gotten that out in the open. And while I was scared, I was also feeling morbidly pleased about the situation. I had a feeling Bonnie was going to take me to where Cody was—or at least I hoped so. She was the last person I'd seen with him.

I decided it was the perfect time to work on my optimism and look at Bonnie as one psycho bitch of a silver lining. I couldn't get Cody and his testimony to the police, or a lawyer, or maybe the FBI, if I didn't know where Cody was.

And if she wasn't leading me to Cody, she was either dragging me off to the police, where at least I'd get my one phone call—and I figured I'd use it to call Violet and see if she could release some of Dad's blood-hungry lawyers—or she was taking me to whoever hired her to find me in the first place.

"I'm sure you know all about the country," I said as lightly as I could. "Didn't you just make a special trip out there?"

Bonnie laughed, and I mean she threw her head back and cackled up into the rain.

They say it only takes a tablespoon of water to drown a person. I was hoping they were right. But Bonnie didn't drown, which was an amazing shame considering the size of her mouth.

"Sure I did! I took a special trip just to go see an old cow farm."

Chicken farm, but I didn't bother to correct her.

She turned down the road less used that ambled up behind Mama's place. I figured the place had a back door, but had never felt the need to go snooping for it.

The truth of the matter was, I was getting pretty tired. I was cold, wet, hyperaware of every smell, texture, color, and change of light. The storm was looming, heavy as a migraine closing in. I just wanted to sit down somewhere quiet and dark and warm, and wait for the storm to pass. So when she turned toward the back door of Mama's, I was grateful.

"Now, we're going to take care of you real nice. Promise. We're just so excited you came by." She opened the back door, and the spell woven over the door hit me like a barrel full of bricks. I tasted blood at the back of my throat, and the last thing in the world I wanted to do was walk through that door. I hadn't felt a threshold spell that strong since Zayvion's place.

"Come on in. Don't be shy," a man's voice said. "We've been waiting for you."

I swallowed blood and blinked hard. I knew that voice. And when he turned on the lamp next to him, I knew I shouldn't be surprised, but damn it, I was.

James, Mama's slick-as-a-snake Boy stood there, grinning at me. But what surprised me more was that next to him stood another smiling man. And that man was Zayvion Jones.

Chapter Fifteen

Betrayal sucks.

My heart felt like someone was in my chest kicking it with steel-toed boots—and that someone was me. How could I have I trusted him? How could I have liked him? Stupid, stupid heart. When I got out of here—and I was so going to get out of this so I could see Zay's ass in jail—I swore I would never fall for, never trust, and never care for anyone again.

It was going to be all about me from now on. I was going to look after myself alone, and the rest of the world and all the people in it could go to hell for all I cared.

Who needed this kind of grief? Who needed to find out, again, that someone they loved was just a back-stabbing bastard who played me for all he could get?

He had used me.

And I let him.

I didn't know which made me angrier.

Bonnie shoved me through the glyphs and the door. I felt a hot ribbon of blood pour from my nose. I wiped at it with the back of my left hand. Thunder rolled, still quiet, but coming closer.

"So how's this going to work?" I asked.

Zay stayed right where he was, the far side of a

room that was some sort of storage behind the kitchen. Wooden shelves were stocked with cans, boxes, and bags of things you'd expect to see in a restaurant. The doorway, where Zay was standing, opened to a narrow view of a chopping block and countertop. I was pretty sure that was the kitchen behind him.

James strolled over to me, took my right wrist, and pushed up my coat sleeve. He whistled. "Zayvion told me you survived the visit from my business associate this morning. I'm sorry how that turned out."

I bet he was. I was, after all, still alive.

"Zayvion also told me you had been burned and could no longer use magic, but I didn't believe him." He grinned, showing me all of his dental work. His breath smelled overwhelmingly sweet, like cherry candy. Blood magic. Probably mixed with something else, maybe cocaine or speed. Great. The man was raging.

"My apologies," he said to Zayvion.

Zay shrugged.

Okay, so if Zay told him I couldn't use magic, maybe he wasn't completely on their side either. He knew in intimate ways just exactly how well I could use magic, and how well we used it together. Soul Complements, and all that. Maybe he was working another angle. One all his own.

I tugged my wrist out of James' hold. Fact one: my arm hurt. It was quickly going from ache to throb. Fact two: I refused to let anyone get handsy with me. Fact three: despite the ache, my arm was also starting to itch, which meant I might still have some sort of chance of drawing on magic if I needed it. One look at James' happy, glassy eyes and sweat-covered face and I was pretty sure I'd need it soon.

Thunder rolled somewhere over the city, and James pointed toward the door to the kitchen.

"Why don't we step inside. Maybe I can get you a drink?" he offered.

"Water would be fine," I said. I walked across the room, James in front of me, Bonnie and her gun behind me. Zay just watched with a neutral expression, pulling the Zen act.

"Bastard," I said as I walked past him.

"I told you to stay there," he said, plenty loud enough for James and Bonnie to hear. "You could be in a nice holding cell right now, telling the police a story about people who disappear into thin air and plot to overthrow your father's fortune, and that you have no alibis for your whereabouts when he was killed. And you know why you aren't? Because you are too damn stubborn to do anything anyone tells you to do."

My mind went blank. Then it filled with fury. I leaned back and punched him in the face with everything I had.

Zay's head snapped back and hit the wall behind him. He yelled and grabbed at his nose and slid down the wall. I stepped up to swing at him again, but Bonnie caught my arm and shoved the gun so hard against my spine I could feel a bruise spreading. My fist hurt too—I was pretty sure I had broken my pinky, but that pain, I had to admit, was way worth it.

"Funny," she said, "but stupid. Do that again and I'll shoot you."

Zay got on his feet and those tiger eyes of his were really burning now. If I weren't deeply in hate with him, I might think he didn't look all that angry. I might even say he looked pleased. That he was happy

I'd done that. That maybe he was trying to tell me something else with that look, something secret.

"Bitch," he said.

Well, that was no secret.

"Fuck you, Jones."

Bonnie shoved me toward the kitchen. I couldn't tell if Zay followed, because he was too damn quiet for me to hear and the thunder was close enough that it had gone from an intermittent rumble to a deep growl. Besides that, Zay was only a small part of this surprise party. My heart sank as I saw Mama's other Boys, four of them in total, leaning against the kitchen counters, and over there, rocking on the floor in front of the refrigerator, was Cody. Mama herself stood in the middle of the room, looking angry and worried.

Oh. Hells. I was so screwed.

I quickly went through my options. Trying to get out of this alive was priority one. Trying to get out of this alive with Cody was priority two. If they wanted to negotiate, I'd negotiate.

I pushed panic down, and grabbed hold of my confidence. I could handle this. I was a Beckstrom, and if there was one thing we were good at, it was Influencing people to get our way. If ever there were a time for me to give in and act like my father, this was it.

James was at the sink and strangely true to his word, filling a plastic cup with water for me.

"Hello, Mama," I said. She looked away and would not make eye contact. Wasn't that interesting? Maybe she wasn't the center of this affair after all.

I gave each of the Boys a look. Like matching statues of didn't-give-a-damn, they looked back at me, and made no other move.

James walked over and handed me the cup of water. "Here you are." He strolled back to the sink and leaned against it, his arms crossed over his chest.

I was glad he hadn't filled it all the way to the top, because my hand shook and my pinky was so swollen it made it hard to keep the cup steady. I did my best to cover all that, and took a sip. I was thirsty enough I could drain the river. Both of them. But I wanted to have something in my hand I could use to delay my responses—it was an old board-meeting trick I'd learned from my dad—so I resigned myself to the fact that I might need to make this cup of water last a very long time.

The lights flickered, a blink of darkness. The storm was coming.

"The situation is fairly simple, Ms. Beckstrom—may I call you Allie?" James asked.

"No."

He smiled. "Good. As I was saying, Allie, there is only a small thing I need from you, something Zayvion has assured me you will have no quarrel with."

"Really? I don't recall hiring Zayvion to speak for me. Is this a legal matter? If so, we should both have lawyers present to protect our interests." I tried putting some Influence behind my words, but was too shaken to do much good.

"Soon," he said. "But first I thought you and I could talk. Come to an understanding. An agreement. Like family."

Okay, that got me. I blinked and looked harder at him. He didn't look much like any of the women my father had married, or at least none whom I could remember. And he was the polar opposite to my dad—shorter, darker, thinner. The person he most resembled was Mama.

"Family? How exactly does that work?"

His smile flashed into a grin. He looked like an animal about to strike, something hungry and quick.

"Snake man, Snake man, bake a cake man," Cody whimpered.

Oh, hells no.

Snake man. The man who killed my father. The man who somehow made Cody forge my signature. The man who threw a spell strong enough to kill someone and had apparently not paid the price for it. Holy shit.

Cold sweat spread over my skin. I took a drink of water, hiding my reaction as best as I could. If he could kill my dad at a distance and still be alive, I figured he could kill me close-up. I glanced around the room, looking for an escape, a weapon. But gun-happy Bonnie was still behind me. I assumed Zay was too, since I couldn't see him. I couldn't see a knife, a fork, or a heavy pan within reach. For a working kitchen it was painfully clean of any dangerous implements.

"You and I are kindred spirits," James continued. "You hated your father. I hated your father. You wanted him dead. I wanted him dead. You wanted his business to stop taking advantage of the poor and the innocent, like my poor little brother, and I wanted his business to recognize the original creator of the Beckstrom Storm Rods and pay back the money he has made off the technology he stole."

I put two and two together and came up empty. "You wanted my father to pay Perry Hoskil for the storm rods? Perry Hoskil has been dead for ten years."

"I know," James said. "Perry Hoskil was my father."

Which meant Mama had slept with Perry Hoskil. I glanced at her. "Mama?"

She looked up, pressed her lips together, and nodded.

It didn't make sense. Why would Mama go along with James in this crazy scheme? But at least I was finally able to see all the holes in the puzzle. James was the bastard child of Perry Hoskil. There had been a fierce court battle years ago over who had proprietary ownership of the patents and production of the Storm Rods—the technology that had allowed magic to be harvested not only from the rare magic-charged storms, but also from the reserves of magic that pooled deep in the earth. The two men who claimed they had the rights to the rods were partners in the invention of the technology. Those men were Perry Hoskil and my father. But my father had gone behind Hoskil's back and filed the patent in his name alone, claiming proprietary ownership of the technology.

Perry Hoskil had lost the case. Most say he was bribed out of pursuing further litigation. Most also said he took to drinking and drugs, and he was found years later, dead of an overdose in some garbage heap on the worst side of town. Maybe on this side of town. Maybe even right here where I was standing.

I didn't think anyone knew he had a son. But then, I wouldn't expect Mama to share that information with the world.

She had shared it with at least one person though—James.

"Okay," I hedged. "You want to sue Beckstrom Enterprises for royalties due. I still think you need a lawyer for that."

He was no longer smiling. "I've talked to dozens of lawyers. I've talked to judges. They won't do shit for me." He paced over to where Mama stood and back to the sink. "They say there is no winning back that money. No getting the money due me. No getting back the technology that is rightfully mine. Beckstrom has had the law tied around his filthy fingers for years, and there isn't a lawyer he can't buy off." He paused and smiled at me. "Couldn't buy off. Things are different now, aren't they? Now that Daniel Beckstrom is dead."

If he was waiting for a reaction out of me, he didn't get it.

The lights flickered again, three quick times, and I only had to count to ten before I heard the answer of thunder. My arm was really starting to ache, and the ache was spreading. The closer the storm came, the more I felt like I was coming down with the flu.

"But now that you're here," James said, "you can see that a little justice is finally served."

"I'll do what I can," I said, trying to sound reasonable. "But I'm under suspicion for killing him, and until my name is cleared, you may not want to do business with me."

"It will be a very short business relationship," he said. "You sign over your shares of Beckstrom Enterprise to Mama, and you can go your own way and live your life."

The lights flickered again, throwing the kitchen into darkness long enough that the other Boys were looking a little worried.

I counted to eight. Thunder.

"You'll still have to convince Violet's lawyers that I didn't sign my shares over under duress," I said. I was stalling, looking for an out. Waiting for a good bolt of lightning to really knock the power out for more than a second. "People think I killed my father.

They are not going to honor a contract I sign when I'm not in my right mind."

"You'll convince them that you've snapped out of your killing passion. That you regret your hasty, terrible actions. You'll turn yourself in to the police and declare you want to pay back your father's debt to the Hoskils. Then you'll live a nice long, unpleasant life behind bars."

"And if I talk?" I knew there had to be an "or else" in there somewhere. I didn't really care what it was. But I needed time. The itch and ache in my arm were growing worse, like needles of fire stabbing through every pore. I didn't know what kind of tricks James had up his sleeve, but I could hold magic within me. A lot of it now. And I was banking James didn't expect me to be able to use it here.

He walked toward me, stopped just out of arm's reach. "This isn't a game," he snarled. "There are a lot of lives on the line, a lot of people tired of Beckstrom's stranglehold on magic. Tired of hard-and-holy Beckstrom saying who can use magic and how and why and when.

"No more. We will wage war, bring it to the streets if we have to. You are nothing but an inconvenience to these people, and to me. You will sign your rights over to Mama. Zayvion will turn you in to the police. And I will hold a gun at that young man's head until I hear you are safely locked away. Your other option is to say no to me. Instead of killing you with magic, like I killed your father, I will kill you right here with my bare hands, for fun."

The lights flickered and went out.

I swung for James in the darkness, missed, and heard Bonnie swear. I ducked and made a blind run for Cody. Thunder roared, so close, so loud, that I did not hear the gunfire that threw the room in staccato light.

Someone hit me from behind and I fell to the floor, slamming my head and shoulder against the cupboards. I knew who it was—could recognize the pine scent of him no matter how dark the room was, knew his body intimately. I pushed him away. He felt like deadweight.

Lightning flashed, pouring through the single window of the room. In one moment I saw Zayvion, facedown on the floor, unmoving, a dark pool spreading out from under him. He had thrown himself at me and gotten a bullet in the back of the head. Panic threatened to freeze me.

No. No. No.

I caught a glimpse of Cody pressed against the refrigerator, curled in a ball, his hands over his ears, before darkness fell again. I rolled away from Zay's unmoving form and threw my body over Cody's. The spark of gunfire lit Bonnie's face. Her laughter, and the sound of bullets, were swallowed again by thunder.

She stopped shooting. Probably to reload. I got on my knees and whispered a mantra. Magic lifted, painful, but clear and pure from deep within me.

I was incredibly aware of everyone in the room. Cody's terror, all the Boys' anger, Bonnie's fury. James was halfway across the room and coming to kill me. I was also incredibly aware that Zayvion was not breathing.

There was one other person in the room—Mama. To my magic-filled eyes, she glowed with pure, untapped magic. North Portland magic. St. John's magic. Here. Magic no one knew existed. Magic shielded by an elaborate Diversion glyph so old it mimicked the natural geology around it perfectly, hiding, cloaking the pure store of magic beneath this part of the city. Someone was maintaining that spell. And that someone was Mama.

Maybe James had threatened to expose the unharvested magic if Mama didn't go along with his plan. No, if James knew about magic beneath St. John's, he would have sold off rights to it to the highest bidder. The idiot was killing people for bits of silver and didn't even know he was sitting on a gold mine.

Lightning and thunder rode each other's backs, and I knew I had to make a choice—use magic to stop James, to stop Bonnie, to stop the Boys. Use magic to save Cody. Use magic to heal Zayvion.

I never was very good at making snap decisions. So why choose one thing? Why not do it all?

I pushed up to my feet.

Light, I thought, and magic rose to my command. The room flooded with a harsh white glow. A glow that radiated from my right hand, and made it feel like it was on fire. My left hand was already numb, and the lack of feeling pushed up to my elbow so that my whole arm hung useless at my side, but I didn't care. I was determined to stop this mess once and for all.

Stop, I thought, and that worked too. Magic spooled out of me to wrap around everyone in the room and hold them still. Even Zayvion's blood stopped flowing. I could feel the labored pressure of his heart trying to beat, the strain of his lungs trying to fill.

I was burning up, too raw and too hurt from the last time I used magic. But there was a pleasure in the pain, a siren desire to use the magic before it used me up. And I could. I could heal Zayvion. I could crush James' throat, blind Bonnie, knock out the Boys, force Mama to tell me everything she knew. I could do anything. Anything I wanted.

And all I wanted was for this not to be happening. For Zayvion to be alive. Maybe for one last chance to tell him I really thought we were good together and wished we could have made it work. To tell him I had hoped he would be the one person in my life who wouldn't betray me. To tell him I hoped he had an explanation for being here, being a part of James' plan to take over Beckstrom Enterprises and kill my father, and that maybe he was still on my side.

I hesitated. Heard sirens between the explosions of thunder. Watched as Bonnie squeezed off the last bullet, watched as it sang true toward my heart.

Heal or kill?

I guess Zayvion had it right when we first met. I just didn't have killing in me. No matter how much I wanted to.

Heal, I thought, and I poured magic into Zayvion, guiding the bullet out of the wound in his head, guiding the magic, like ribbons of thread, ribbons of energy, to knit flesh, to mend bone, to whisk away old blood and soothe swelling. Fast, faster, before the magic consumed me, consumed the last of my mind, my memories, my soul. Fast, faster, before the bullet reached me, piercing my flesh. Fast.

Lightning struck, so close I felt the heat of it lick beneath my skin, and shuddered with a heady mix of agony and pleasure. I was too hot, too cold. Then pain bulleted through my chest. I fell.

I couldn't feel my hands. I couldn't see the magic anymore. I couldn't move. But I saw Zayvion open his eyes. Saw his lips form my name. Saw him push up from the floor and reach for me.

And I saw Mama turn to James and hold up a hand filled with the magic of St. John's. Saw her wield a very complex, very strong Holding spell. Hopefully, she'd take James in to the police. Hopefully, she would make sure Cody got somewhere safe. Hopefully, she would do the right thing.

Zay reached me. He touched my face, though it looked like it hurt him to do so. *I love you,* his lips said.

And I knew he did. I loved him too, despite it all.

Don't go, he said.

But I did not know how to stay. The storm was in me, taking me apart, pulling me away.

This, I decided, was a pretty good way to die.

Magic filled me and filled me, and like a dam filled too full, I broke. I was swept up and up until I rode the storm clouds, free and distant from all the world and pain below.

Chapter Sixteen

"Allie?"

It is strange to hear your name when you think you should be dead.

I tried to answer.

"Allie?" Same voice. A soft voice. A woman's voice.

"Allie?" Nola. That was her name. Nola was looking for me.

I moved my mouth (I had a mouth!) and opened my eyes (eyes!). Light, low and yellow, shone on Nola, on Nola's pretty face above me.

She smiled and her eyes watered. "Welcome home, honey. Drink some water." She put a straw to my lips, without asking—typical Nola—and I drank. That was an exhausting thing to do, and I fell gratefully back to sleep again.

It is a weird thing to wake up in a bed you don't remember falling asleep in. Daylight was filtering in through the shades on the window, so I at least knew what bed I was in—Nola's cozy guest room. I could not remember getting here.

As a matter of fact, the last thing I remember was getting up and wanting a cup of coffee. Because it was my birthday, and I was twenty-five today. And since

I was miles from where I last remember being, I was going to assume I'd had a hell of a night, drank my ass off, and ended up out here at Nola's partying.

My head hurt like I had the granddaddy of all hangovers, and my mouth tasted horrible. I couldn't remember anything about my birthday though. I rubbed my hands over my eyes, caught a flash of colors.

My right hand was ribboned in peacock-feather colors of metal, and my left hand was tattooed around every knuckle. A faint memory flickered at the back of my mind, but I could not draw it forward.

Hells. Lost memories meant I'd been using magic—maybe Hounded too hard and had my short-term memory pay the price for it.

What kind of idiot was I? Add to that the IV tube in my left arm, and it was pretty safe to assume I'd really done something stupid.

Nola walked into my room with an armful of sheets.

"Morning," I said.

She jumped and had to catch the sheets before they hit the floor. I grinned.

"Allie," she said. "You're awake!"

"Yes. What's got you spooked?"

Nola put the sheets down in the spare chair and hurried over to sit on the bed next to me. Her tanned skin was flushed red and her eyes looked bloodshot, like maybe she hadn't gotten much sleep lately.

"How are you feeling? Don't try to sit. Let me get you water. Do you know where you are?"

Okay, now she really had me worried. I'd never seen her rattled.

"Slow down," I said. "One thing at a time. I hurt some. Did I use a lot of magic recently?"

She nodded.

I exhaled in relief. "Okay, that explains the memory loss. Is today still my birthday?"

"Oh, honey." She brushed my hair back from my forehead and her cool fingers felt good. Why did I wish they felt like mint?

"Your birthday was three weeks ago."

"Wow," I said. "Did I have a good time?"

Nola laughed, but she was crying too. "No. It was a miserable birthday."

"Except for my cool tattoos?" Making jokes when I'm scared and the world is falling apart, and I can't remember anything and just want to cry, is one of my strong suits.

"Tattoos?"

I held up my hands.

She pulled a tissue out of her pocket and wiped at her face, then blew her nose. "Those aren't tattoos, honey."

I knew that. I just wanted her to tell me what they were, because I had absolutely no idea.

"I'm going to get you water, and you are going to drink. You are also going to try some broth. While you do that, I'll try to help you remember . . . remember everything."

"I don't want any broth," I said.

"Too bad. And Jupe is going to stay here and keep an eye on you until I come back."

I looked over and, sure enough, the big ox came trotting into the room and rested his head on the edge of the bed.

"Stay," Nola said, to me as much as the dog.

I was so glad she was bossing me around, because it meant she thought I really was going to be okay. But I wasn't as convinced. I felt sore, inside and out.

Emotions flooded through me—fear, anger, sorrow, loss—in a confusing wave. Even though I hate crying, and had no idea why I wanted to cry right now, I could not stop the tears that ran down my face.

It made me angry that I was crying for no reason, or maybe for a reason I couldn't recall. And being angry only made me cry harder.

Stupid, stupid, stupid. If I'd had the strength, I'd pound the walls. But I couldn't even muster the energy to sit up.

When I heard Nola walk toward the room, I averted my face and stared at the curtains. I wiped at my cheeks with my strange, multicolored hand, a hand that did not look like my own. Sorrow tightened my chest, but I took three deep, calming breaths. I could do this. I could survive finding out what I didn't know anymore. I could survive losing bits of my life, and bits of myself. I'd done it before and been okay. Mostly.

"Let's get you sitting," Nola said. She leaned over me and I looked up at her. Even though I figured my eyes were puffy and red, and my cheeks and nose were all blotchy, she did not say a word about it. She didn't make comforting noises, or tell me she was sorry. She was just her normal, strong, matter-of-fact self. "You're not broken," she said, "just a little bruised."

She was the best friend ever.

It hurt to sit, hurt more to stay sitting, but with Nola's help, I managed.

"You okay?" she asked.

I was shaking, sweating. "I'm good."

She put a tray over my legs and set a cup of broth, a spoon, a straw, and a carefully folded white napkin on it. There was something about the neatness of the napkin, pressed cloth, spotless white, that tickled the back of my mind. Then the sensation was gone.

"So." Nola kicked off her boots and sat on the bottom of the bed, leaning against the footboard. Something down on the floor mewed. She got off the bed, and sat back down with a little gray kitten in front of her. The kitten picked its way across the quilt, exploring the folds and batting at the ridges.

Cute. I didn't know she had a cat.

"Where shall we start?" Nola asked. "Your birthday. Do you remember me calling and telling you to come out and visit me?"

I frowned. "I don't think—no, I don't think so." I picked up the spoon and was surprised at how heavy it was.

"I left you a message because you weren't at your apartment. You later told me you were Hounding a hit up in St. John's."

The room got hot all of a sudden and twirled like a merry-go-round. I wanted to puke. I think I dropped my spoon. Somewhere in that gut-wrenching chaos were my memories of St. John's, but no matter how far into it I leaned, I could not snag the bronze ring and retrieve them.

"Here now," Nola said.

She was above me. I was lying again, covered in sweat. But at least the room had stopped spinning. She put a cool cloth on my forehead and I reveled in the simple, soothing pleasure of it. Okay, maybe I wasn't feeling as good as I thought I was.

"You're fine," she said. "I'll go slower. We have plenty of time to straighten this out. Plenty. Sleep now. Sleep."

And I did.

The next day, or at least I hoped it was the next day, I woke early. Tendrils of anxious dreams slid away, leaving me with nothing but a hollow feeling of loneliness. My arm no longer had the IV hooked to it, so I decided to go take a bath.

I pushed the covers back, levered up, and rested a while before making my way slowly, hand on the walls for balance, into the bathroom. I sat on the edge of the tub and rested until I stopped trembling, then finally stood and stripped naked.

The image in the mirror was a shock. Whorls of metallic ribbons marked me from temple to fingertip on my right, rings of black banded my fingers, wrist, and elbow on my left. The blood magic scars on my left deltoid were slashes of red.

A ragged, pink scar as wide as my hand puckered just below my ribs on my left, and a thumb-sized circle sat just below my collarbone.

Wow. So much for wearing a bikini.

I leaned against the sink and stared at my eyes, trying to fit this reality of the new me with the knowledge of the old me. My eyes were still pale green like my father's, I still had short hair, though it looked like I needed a cut soon, and I was a little on the thin side. Still, I was me.

"This is it," I whispered. "This is me now. I can deal with it."

There was a knock on the door. "Allie?"

"I'm going to take a bath," I said.

"Need any help?"

I did. And I knew Nola would be happy to be of assistance. But what I needed even more than her help was my life back, or at least a sense of normalcy. And that meant sucking it up and taking care of things myself as much as I could.

"I got it so far."

She waited outside the door. I took a deep breath and made it back to the tub. I crawled into it and eased down onto the cold ceramic. I turned on the spigots until the water poured out hot.

"I'll get breakfast started and bring you some towels," Nola said through the door.

"I can do it," I lied. Luckily, she was already gone.

Turns out I did need help getting out of the tub, getting dried, and getting dressed. I also needed some help back to bed. Even so, I felt pretty good about my accomplishment for the day.

I leaned back against the pillows Nola propped between me and the headboard of the bed, and breathed hard until my heart stopped beating so fast.

"A couple more days like this, and I'll be ready to run a marathon."

"How about you get through a meal without passing out first?" Nola said.

"Spoilsport."

She smiled. "I have oatmeal for breakfast. What kind of tea do you want?"

"No coffee?"

"Let's start with tea."

"Fine. Do you have mint?"

Nola frowned. "Mint? Are you sure?"

"I think so. Why? Don't I like mint?"

She shrugged. "You've never asked me for it before, but maybe you developed a taste for it recently."

I thought about that, tried to remember if I drank mint tea, but no clear image came back to me. What came to me was an emotional memory of the comfort, ease, and pleasure mint could offer. For whatever reason, I liked mint and I missed it. A lot.

"I guess," I said.

Nola patted my leg and strolled out of the room.

She spent the rest of the day giving me back what memories she could. Not much of it made sense, but I carried an unconscious knowledge, an afterimage of it all deep in my subconscious. My emotional memory was intact. I remembered the grief, the anger, the fear, the pain, if not the actual events themselves.

My father had died.

I'd been shot. Twice.

Accused of murder.

Cleared of that accusation by Mama's and Cody's testimony.

I had drawn upon magic so hard that it had been permanently burned into my skin, my bones.

I healed someone.

I'd totally missed out on my birthday. No presents, no party, no song.

I had missed my father's funeral.

And I might even have fallen in love with a man named Zayvion Jones.

I had done so much, and lost it all.

Nola didn't seem to think it was something out of the ordinary for me to deal with, but I didn't think I had ever lost this much memory at one time before. That magic I'd done—the last thing in Mama's kitchen that Zayvion had apparently told Nola about—had nearly killed me.

If you used magic, it used you too, and I had used the hell out of it, probably without setting a Disbursement. It was just my luck that my price had been twofold, physical pain—a coma—and massive memory loss.

I hoped I had made the right choice. I hoped that if I still knew what I had known then, I would make the same choice.

Wishing I'd done something different—maybe not used magic so much, maybe not gone up to St. John's, maybe not gone to see my dad, maybe not tried to help Cody—would only drive me insane. And most of the time I felt too close to crazy already.

About a week through my recovery, when I had graduated to the couch and could get around the house slowly on my own, I sat in the living room and picked up my little blank book.

Nola was in town, talking to some people about becoming a caregiver for Cody. She felt strongly that getting him away from any place that had magic would be best for all concerned. And from what she'd told me about him, I agreed.

I opened the book. The first few pages had my name, birthday, and medical allergies listed. Some other things too, like the number for the police, for the hospital, my address, and Nola's. Filling most of the pages after that were the notes I had taken before my birthday.

From the date of my birthday forward were only a few sparse notes outlining Mama's call to me, the Hounding job I'd done on Boy, the trip I'd made to see my dad. My hands shook at that, and my throat felt tight, but I kept reading. I had notes that covered the blood magic Truth spell my dad had lied about, my suspicions about Zayvion, my desire to go to the police and testify against my father.

And that was it.

Nothing more.

All the rest of the pages were blank.

I thumbed through them, all of them, looking for any other note, any other word.

Blank. Blank. Blank. Dozens and dozens of stupid, white, empty pages. Why hadn't I written more? What was wrong with me? I always kept good notes. Always. Why wasn't there something in there about the magic marks? About healing? Why wasn't there something in there about how I really felt about Zayvion?

I threw the book across the room, and immediately felt stupid for doing so. I rubbed at the headache behind my temples.

So I'd screwed up and hadn't taken notes. *Deal with it,* I told myself. Freaking out wouldn't put words on the page. Making a vow to do better from now on might do some good.

And I could start now. Write that I am angry I didn't keep better notes. Sounded like a dumb idea, but then I decided that I should do it. Every detail I wrote down was one more bit of my life I got to keep.

I got up, retrieved the book, and found a pen on the coffee table. I sat back on the couch and opened the book to a clean page. Maybe I should start with waking up here.

So I did.

After about a half hour, I heard the crunch of tires on gravel. Nola was home.

She unlocked the door, letting in the clean, cold smell of rain and dirt. She strolled in carrying a bright blue bag with a bow on it.

"Happy belated birthday." She dropped the bag on my lap.

Before I could say anything, before I could worry about how to thank her for doing such a wonderful, thoughtful, kind thing when I was feeling so sour and petty, she said, "You're welcome. Open it."

I sat up straighter and grinned. "Thank you." I pulled tissue paper out of the bag and peeked in it. Whorls of colors, of thread—no, yarn—filled the bag.

"Yarn?" I lifted out a skein each of pastel orange,

rose, blue, purple, and green, colors that mimicked the marks of magic on my hand. Two long wooden needles, and several other short wooden needles with a point on each end, including a couple tied together by a plastic cord, remained in the bag.

"Yarn and knitting needles," Nola said happily.

I pulled out the long needles, and tried to intuit if I had ever held anything like them before. They didn't feel familiar. "Do I? Have I ever?"

"No. Not at all. I've chosen a new hobby for you to learn. We can knit together. You'll like it."

I raised one eyebrow. "I think I should be the judge of that."

She chuckled. "I knew you'd say that. I'll teach you the basics, then I thought maybe we could try to make you some nice gloves."

"Why do I need gloves? Are you putting me to work around here?"

"No." She gave me a serious, almost sad look. "You can't stay out here forever, Allie. You need to go back to the city. Back to your life there. And if you find out you don't like it, you know you can come back until you decide what you want to do next."

"You're kicking me out?" I meant it to sound funny, but it came out sort of small and sad.

"You'd get bored soon anyway, and curious about what you left behind. I know you. You don't like to leave things unsettled, and a lot of things are unsettled. Your dad's business, your relationship with your stepmom, your Hounding business." She paused. "And you need to settle things with Zayvion. He stayed here by your bed for two weeks. I think there are things unsaid between you."

"Really? Is that why he calls? Why he stops in to see me now that I'm conscious?" He had done neither of those things, and apparently it annoyed me even though Nola didn't have a phone so, technically, he couldn't call.

Nola pressed her lips together, then stood. She pulled something out from behind a vase of flowers on the mantel. It was an envelope. She handed it to me.

My name, in writing I did not recognize, was on the front.

"He left you this."

"Have you read it?"

She shook her head.

I stared at it for what felt like a long time. "I think I want to know what he has to say to me face-to-face."

"Are you sure?"

I was sure. Very sure. "If he has something to say to me, I want to watch him say it. I need that. I deserve that."

Nola patted my knee. "I agree. But you don't have to go anywhere today. Maybe when the gloves are done you'll be ready to wear them to your favorite coffee shop. Then, after you settle back into life in the big city, you can get in touch with him."

Talking about Zayvion stirred feelings in me I was not comfortable addressing. I was so ready for a change of subject. "Did you take a class to become wise and all-knowing, or were you just born bossy?"

"Both. Now are you going to stop complaining and try something new"—she pointed to the skeins of yarn—"or are you coming out to help me clean the chicken coops?"

"When you put it that way, how can I turn down knitting?"

"I'll get my needles," she said. "We can do a little before lunch."

She jogged up the stairs to her bedroom and the

kitten padded into the room. It eyed the skeins of yarn and mewed. I pulled out the end of a string and dangled it over the edge of the couch. The kitten belonged to Cody. Nola said she'd found her out in the field the day after Zay and I had left.

"How did it go with the attorneys?" I said, loud enough for my voice to carry.

"Good," she yelled down. "We're closer to convincing the authorities that Cody would be well served out here." She headed back down the stairs, a tapestry tote in one hand. "The sheriff has decided to get involved. He says it's because he's concerned for all of the citizens under his jurisdiction. I think he sees a golden opportunity for some media exposure."

The kitten bounded all of six inches and attacked the thread dangling in my hand.

Nola made a sour face and plunked down on the couch next to me. "I don't like the sheriff's interest, but his involvement was like pouring grease on gears. It looks like I might even have Cody out here as soon as this summer, if all goes well."

"And if it doesn't?" I asked, tugging back on the string and fishing the kitten up onto her hind feet.

"You know me. I am not the kind of woman who gives up on the people she cares for."

Oh. She meant me, too. "Thanks," I said.

She pulled out two long, wooden needles and a ball of light blue yarn. "Ready?"

I tossed the skein of yarn under the coffee table for the kitten to chase, then picked one of my yarns, the mint green–colored one, and nodded. "Let's do this."

"Good. First, make a slip knot."

Nola had an annoying habit of being right.

About two weeks later, when she and I had both

finished a set of gloves and knitted matching scarves, I knew it was time for me to go. The rains of September were now November sleet, and the ground stayed frozen all day.

It was time for this bird to fly south. Well, north and west, really, to Portland, before the snows made it hard to get over the pass.

I made some phone calls. First to my bank, and found out I'd had a sizable deposit transferred into my account at the beginning of the month. When I asked them to trace it back, they said it was from Daniel Beckstrom's estate.

And yeah, that creeped me out. Even dead, my dad was trying to influence my life. And at the same time, it was probably one of the nicest things he'd ever done for me. I was so damn broke right now, not to mention the new debt for the hospital stay before Nola and, as she told me, my stepmother Violet bullied people to get me transferred out here, away from magic, and into Nola's capable hands.

Of course, I had not forgotten I was late on rent. Months late now.

I called my landlord, and he had my apartment locked up. Hadn't sold my stuff because my stepmother had made out a check to cover rent through next month.

I'd have to pay her back, maybe even thank her for that. If I ever talked to her again.

But what really sent me back toward the city, more than the threat of snow, more than the restlessness, was magic. Even though there was no magic here at Nola's, I still carried a small magic within me. Except it wasn't small anymore. At night it shifted within me, slow and gentle, stretching, stroking, growing. I felt pregnant with it, heavy with it, but unlike what I imagined carrying a child was like, magic filled my whole body: my bones, my muscles, my organs, my skin. I could smell it. Taste it. See it. Hear it.

It made me ache in a strange and pleasant way, like a hunger I could not sate.

And somehow I knew the answer to that hunger was in the city.

Nola drove me to the train, stood in the icy rain, and held me tightly. "Be careful. I'll call you when I get the new phone installed. Then I expect you to call me every day."

"I'll try," I said. We'd come up with a new plan of me calling and telling her about my day. Sort of a backup to my little book and the computer at home. "If you ever want to get out of the dark ages and maybe actually buy a computer, I'll send you e-mail too."

Nola rubbed my back one last time, then let me go. "I'll think about it. Good luck, honey. I'll see you soon." She climbed back into the truck with Jupe.

I picked up the new backpack she had given me and the duffel that had some extra clothes I'd bought, my knitting stuff, and Zayvion's letter in it. I wore a warm, knee-length coat I'd bought in town, and the gloves and scarf Nola knitted. I wasn't so much trying to hide my marks as just trying to stay warm against the bitter cold.

I got on the train and waved to Nola and Jupe. It was time to try to make my real life my real life again. To do that, there were a couple of people I needed to see. And one of those people lived in St. John's.

In my old life—the life I remembered—things had a way of going wrong a lot.

It looked like my new life was going to be a lot like my old life.

I stood just inside the doorway of my apartment, and could not force myself to take one more step.

What my landlord had been reticent in telling me over the phone was that my apartment had been ransacked. My living room looked like it had been hit by a hammer-happy demolition crew. Everything was ruined.

He hadn't reported it to the police, which was no big surprise. The surprise was that there was another smell in my room more powerful than the stink of old magic. I had smelled it before—iron and minerals, like old vitamins—but I couldn't remember who or what smelled like that. I broke out in a cold, terrified sweat. Who or whatever belonged to that smell had scared the crap out of me. Were they, or it, here? Had they or it recently been here? I didn't hear anyone in the apartment. I didn't sense anyone in the apartment.

Magic stirred within me, pushing to be free of my tenuous control over it. I breathed through my mouth, trying not to smell, trying not to freak out, and trying to think calm thoughts so the magic would not slip my grip. Coming back to the city—back to where magic flowed beneath my feet, filling me up and pouring through me to the ground again like a circular river—had been hard.

So far, I could control the magic, or at least let it flow through me and not use it. So far.

I exhaled, and told the magic to rest, to be calm, slow, like a summer stream. That helped some. Enough that I could look around the room and see how much of my physical life I'd lost—most of it.

But I still could not force myself to step in—into the stink of old magic, into the panic-inducing odor of iron and old vitamins.

I needed out of here. Fast.

I left the room and locked the door behind me. I took the stairs down and strode out into the chill of late afternoon. It wasn't raining for a change, but it was going to be dark soon. I wanted to yell. To rage at the entire, stinking, unfair world. To hit someone. Anyone.

Magic lifted. Sensuous heat licked up my arm, promising power.

No. The last thing I needed to do was something magical.

I tipped my head back and stared at the gray sky, trying to get a grip. I counted to ten. Twice. I thought calm thoughts.

Then I tried to be reasonable. I had nowhere to go, but I was not sleeping in that dump tonight.

I hailed a cab and let my nose—literally—lead me to several apartment buildings to the west. It meant a couple of extra hundred a month in rent. I'd find a way to swing it. I couldn't live in that crappy apartment anymore. It was time for a new start. A blank slate.

The third apartment complex I tried was called the Forecastle. The building didn't stink of magic, had no elevators, and was renting out a third-floor one-bedroom. What more could a girl want?

It was only five o'clock, still close enough to normal business hours that I didn't feel bad pounding on the manager's door.

It took a minute, but I finally heard footsteps, then the lock being turned.

"Yes?"

The manager was a heavy man, bald, wearing jeans and a button-down shirt. He smelled like chicken broth, and he was short. Short enough that his wide, round face was level with my boobs.

Great.

He stared at my chest, but I had to give him some credit because he managed to pull his gaze up and actually look me in the eyes.

"I'd like to rent the one-bedroom, and I'd like to stay in it tonight."

"It doesn't work like that, lady. I'll need to do a credit check, get some references. Why don't you come back tomorrow." He took a step backward.

He was going to slam that door in my face. I was going to be stuck with nowhere to go tonight unless I wanted to sleep in my wrecked apartment, or a women's shelter.

Oh, screw that.

The one thing we Beckstroms did well was Influence people. And even though I'd sworn off using it, I felt justified in breaking my vow. This was an emergency.

"Please?" I put a little Influence behind my words, just the slightest amount, because I wasn't sure what all the magic coursing through me would do.

What it did was sting. My right arm felt like I'd just wrapped it in Band-Aids and ripped them off all in one go. My left arm felt heavy and cold.

I drew a sharp breath.

Well, that hurt.

I tried again, more carefully. "My apartment was broken into and I can't stay there. My credit isn't all that great, but I have money in the bank that will do first and last, and a month in advance if you need it." That was better. Just the barest breath of Influence behind the words. My arms didn't hurt as much. I concentrated on only Influencing him to give me the benefit of the doubt, not to fall senseless beneath the power of my words.

"My name's Allie Beckstrom," I added.

That got him moving.

"Oh," he said. He studied my face more closely, then nodded and nodded. "Oh. I didn't recognize you. Come in. We'll get the papers filled out and I'll show you the apartment."

He opened the door and I stepped in.

"Bad couple of months you've had," he noted casually as he dug through a messy stack of papers on a desk. "With your father and all."

"Yeah," I said, "it has been."

I looked around the room and noted a couple photos of men and women in police uniforms on the wall, including one of what seemed to be a younger version of the man in front of me.

"Are you a police officer?" I asked.

He pulled out a clipboard and clamped some forms onto it. He handed me the clipboard and dug around on the desk for a pen.

"Was. Retired. You thinking about renting for a year? I can give you a break on the price if you agree to stay that long."

I kind of liked the idea of renting from someone who would know how to look out for trouble if it came.

"A year sounds good. I can use all the breaks I can get." I took the pen he offered and began filling out the form. I was happy to discover that I could complete it without having to refer to my little book.

He showed me to the apartment, a moderate-sized but well-kept place with windows that looked out through the branches of the trees lining the street, and over the busy street itself. Not much noise came through the windows, even though I noted a bus stop just a few blocks up the hill.

I liked it.

I spent the first night of my new life sleeping on the floor, curled up beneath my coat, duffel bag under my head for a pillow, happier than I had been for days.

The next day I took the bus to St. John's.

I didn't know why, but crossing the railroad track always put me in a better mood. There was something good about this rotten side of town. Something invisible to the eye, but obvious to the soul.

I stepped off the bus, and waited as it drove past before crossing the street. It was raining lightly, a misty sort of rain, and I kept close to the buildings, using their awnings to try to stay dry. The air stank of diesel, dead fish, and the salt-and-hickory smell of bacon and onions being fried.

A shadow moved in the doorway to my left, and I glanced over expecting . . . someone. There was no one there. Except for an abandoned shopping cart, the doorway was empty.

Great. This was not the place to be if I was suddenly going to get all jumpy and start second-guessing myself.

Suck it up, I told myself. *You can do this.*

I tucked my hands in my coat pocket and walked up the two wooden steps to Mama's door.

The clatter of dishes being washed rang out from the kitchen and the moist heat of the restaurant wrapped around me. At the tables to my right and left were an even split of men and women, maybe ten in total. No one I knew, or at least no one I remembered.

Ahead of me, with his hand still beneath the counter on his gun, was Boy.

Nola told me I'd been shot. Once by a man Zayvion said broke into his apartment. Once by an old Hound enemy of mine, Bonnie. She did not mention me ever being wounded by Boy, but Zayvion had given her only sketchy details about that night we'd all met in the kitchen.

It wasn't like I could go through my life jumping at shadows. Or guns.

I could do this. I had to do this if I wanted my life to be mine again.

That bravado got me across the room and standing in front of Boy.

"So," I said, pleased that it came out low and casual. "Is Mama here?"

"Allie girl?"

I looked to the right.

Mama stopped washing a table, wiped her hands on a towel, and strode over to me.

"Why you come here?"

"I need to ask you a few things."

She glared at me, but I stood my ground.

"Fine." She caught my elbow and walked me toward the door, as far away from Boy and her patrons as she could get.

"You don't belong here, Allie girl. Not now. Not anymore."

I wasn't convinced I'd ever really belonged here. But I'd always felt welcome. And even though Nola told me Mama had finally gone to the police and told them about James' killing my father and putting the hit on Boy, it was apparent my welcome was worn through.

"Maybe not," I said. "But I never thought you would just stand by and let James hurt Boy like that. How could you look away while he suffered? He was just a little kid. He could have died."

Mama pulled herself up, gaining maybe half an inch on her five foot two frame.

"You think I know what James does?" She was angry. It was the first time I had ever heard her call any of her sons by their name. "You think he tells me the things he does? Tells me the people he does it with? You don't know. Don't know what it is like for family to hurt family."

"Try me," I said. I was an old pro at family hurting family.

"When you say your father was the one, I believe you. But you were wrong."

I so wasn't going to let her blame me for this. I gave her a cool stare.

"James was wrong for what he did," she said. "Too much pride, that Boy. Too much greed. My heart bleeds that he hurt my Boy. And kill your father."

There it was. Admission. No apology, but at least she had the decency to acknowledge that she thought James had killed my dad. I just hoped she would speak her mind like this on the witness stand.

"But he is family, you know?" she said. "Family. Still, I do what is right. Tell police. Watch them arrest my Boy, take him away in chains. And my heart bleeds for him. For my poor, prideful Boy."

"Is that the only reason you turned him in? Because it was the right thing to do?"

Then she did a strange thing. She looked away, looked at the floor, looked uncomfortable. "Yes."

She was lying. I could smell the sourness of it on her. And when she looked back at me, her expression clearly stated that she would say no more.

I let it go. Maybe Nola could tell me more. Maybe Zayvion too, if I ever found him. Or maybe someday, when we both had time to recover our lives, I could convince her I was someone she could talk to.

"Is Boy home from the hospital yet?" I asked.

She laughed, a short, sharp bark. "Where have you been, Allie girl? Boy come home month ago. He is strong. Back in school."

"Good," I said, and I meant it.

The hard edge in Mama's eyes eased. "Yes. Good. You go. This no place for you now. No place for your *kind.*"

She stepped up to me, touched my right hand. The magic beneath my skin settled at her touch, the constant, roaring pressure of it eased.

"You find your place," she said. "Who you are. Who you should be. You find your people. Family."

She turned. "Go," she said over her shoulder. She strode off into the kitchen and started yelling at one of her Boys to clean the floors.

Boy with the gun still had his hand under the counter. I decided not to push my luck with him or his gun, and left. Mama was right about one thing. I had some searching to do. To figure out who I was. And who I intended to be.

I stepped outside and walked as quickly as I could through the rain to the curb. I wasn't feeling very well, the mix of smells suddenly too strong for me to stomach. I was tired too, which wasn't much of a surprise. My stamina still wasn't all that great.

Rain poured harder.

I could walk a few more blocks to the bus stop. But a cab was pulling through traffic, and I waved and whistled and caught the driver's attention. He did a passable, if illegal, U-turn, and pulled up beside me. By this point, rain was pounding down so hard, I couldn't see the buildings on the other side of the street. I reached for the door handle.

A man's hand reached down at the same time, and I was overwhelmed by the heavy stench of iron and old vitamins.

"Allow me, Ms. Beckstrom."

I jerked away and stepped back. The man wore a hat and long coat, but was plain-looking, totally forgettable in a crowd. I knew his type. I'd grown up around them.

And I knew his smell.

This bastard had tried to hurt me. Somehow, in some way I could not remember.

"The war is coming," he said. "Time to choose your side."

Before I could do so much as think about drawing on the magic within me, before I could even whisper a mantra, or scream for the cops, he opened the door, left it open, turned, and walked away.

What in the hell was that all about? War? What war?

The cabbie powered down the passenger window. "You getting in, lady?"

I could say no. There was a chance that man had somehow booby-trapped the cab. Or I could say yes, get in the cab, and get the hell away from here.

I voted for speed over certainty.

I climbed in the backseat, and shut and locked the door. Going to my new apartment might be a bad idea. Maybe he'd bugged the car. Maybe he knew the license plate and was following me.

Yeah, well let him follow me. He'd get the surprise of his life if he showed up at my apartment, because I would kick his ass with every ounce of magic I had in me. The war didn't have to come to me; I was more than happy to go to it if I had to.

"The Forecastle."

The cab moved out into traffic, and even though I watched, I saw no other sign of the man. I paid the driver and got out in front of my new apartment, walked inside, and waited awhile, dripping on the floor, looking out the window at the street. Wet trees, wet buildings, wet shops. Wet people walking up the hill with wet grocery bags. Nobody stopped. Nobody looked my way.

Maybe that had just been some sort of warning.

For something I could not remember.

Great.

I headed up the stairs to my apartment. I was so very done with not knowing what the hell was going on. After hiring some movers to bring my few unbroken possessions to my new place, I'd go out and start looking for answers. And I had a good idea of who to ask first—Mr. Zayvion Jones.

Chapter Seventeen

I found Zayvion at the deli we'd had lunch in, and smiled at remembering that we'd had lunch there. He was sitting toward the back of the room, maybe at the same table we'd sat at, staring out the window at the gray, rainy street, his bowl of soup untouched, his coffee cup full. He did not look up as I walked in.

The sight of him, the smell of pine, did good things for my memory, shook loose a few flashes—his smile, the taste of garlic on his lips, his eyes, burning bright. I was pretty sure I'd had it bad for this man. Might even still have it bad for him.

I walked over to his table, and got halfway there before he glanced up.

His face blanched and his eyes went wide. "Allie?" he whispered, like I was a ghost he didn't want anyone to know he could see.

"Zayvion, right?" I asked.

"Yes." He got back a little of his Zen and stood. "Please. Please, sit down." He held out his hand toward me, but didn't touch me as he held his other hand toward the seat. I felt like visiting royalty.

"Thanks." I eased down, careful of the scars over my ribs that still hurt, especially in the rain, especially in the city where magic pooled and flowed.

He sat across from me, and I watched as he worked really hard to clear his face of all expression. While he was doing that, I was trying to fit him to the stories Nola had told me. That he had saved my life more than once. That he had tried to save me in the end. That we had been lovers and I had almost killed myself to save him, even though I thought he had betrayed me.

That last part just didn't sound like me. I wasn't the type of person to give myself up to grand, noble sacrifices.

And this Zayvion looked like he hadn't shaved in a couple days, and like maybe he had been wearing the same T-shirt for too many weeks in a row. This Zayvion looked like maybe he'd been spending too much time drinking and not enough time sleeping.

"How are you?" I asked.

His eyebrows shot up and he let out a nervous laugh. "I've been okay. How are you?"

"Tired," I said, "but that's getting better every day. Nola told me everything she could."

"Memory loss?" he asked. "I'm sorry."

I shrugged and pushed my anger about it away. "Things happen. You use magic, it uses you, and I've been magic's bitch for a long time." I gave him a weak smile, and he nodded encouragingly.

"Do you remember anything?" he asked.

"Flashes. A few images. A lot of strong emotions without a lot of clear ideas as to why I feel that way."

"But Nola told you about your father?"

I nodded. "And about Cody, James, Bonnie, and Mama. She told me about the, uh . . . Violet's research," I said a little more quietly, aware that the disks were still largely unknown, and as far as I knew, not entirely recovered. "And that James is up on murder charges. He's just the tip of this tech-stealing thing, isn't he?"

Zayvion blinked and sat back. He did a good job of covering his surprise, and even did a good job lying. "No. I don't know what would give you that idea."

What gave me that idea was Mama refusing to look me straight in the eye. What gave me that idea was the ominous war-is-coming bastard who opened the cab door for me. What gave me that idea was Zayvion being so quick to deny it, even though I could smell the lie on him.

Fair enough. I could play along until I figured things out. I had lost my memory, not my brains. I dropped the subject and moved on.

"Nola told me Cody cleared my name," I said. "She's trying to get a judge to allow him to come live with her on the farm. She has his cat."

"I didn't know she was doing that," he said. "I think that's a good idea. Really good."

I did too—it would keep him safely out of the reach of magic, safely out of the reach of people who would try to use him like James had. Maybe safely out of whatever may or may not be about to happen in this city.

"She told me my father's funeral was a few weeks ago, while I was still in the coma."

"It was closed casket," Zayvion said. "All his ex-wives attended except for your mother. There were yellow roses and red peonies everywhere. Violet cried."

"So you remember the details of weddings and funerals, eh? Any hot girls there?" Oh. I remembered him telling me about a wedding. About daffodils and lilacs. Whose was it? I chased the memory, dug around in the dark goo of my mind. Nothing. Just the knowledge that he'd said something once.

"You remember me telling you that?"

"Not when you did, but that you did." I rubbed at my forehead with my fingers. I was wearing the mint green gloves I had knitted, and the yarn made a pleasant scritch across my skin.

"I'm impressed," he said. And I knew that he was.

"No hot chicks?" I asked again.

He glanced out the window, glanced back at me. "I couldn't—wasn't looking."

Oh.

I pulled the letter with my name in his handwriting out of my purse and slid it across the table. The envelope was still sealed.

"Whatever it says in there," I said, "I want to hear it from you."

Zayvion put his fingers on the envelope, turned it over, and looked at the unbroken seal. I watched him. It was comfortable here in the heat of the deli, the smell of rich, roasted coffee, the spice of cinnamon and the salt of vegetable soup filling me up. I knew I could use magic if I wanted to figure out what Zayvion was really feeling. I had tried accessing magic once—when I Influenced my apartment manager—and it had been easy. But it stung like salt in a cut, and that actually made me happy.

Sometimes it is good to know your limits. Good to know you still have limits. It makes you human. And I wanted to stay that way.

Zayvion swallowed, and when he looked back at me, his eyes were a little red. "Allie, don't. Don't make me do this."

I waited.

He rubbed his face. "You are so damn stubborn. Fine. The note says I'm sorry about how it all turned out. That I'm sorry you and I got involved and that I can't risk you . . . can't risk a relationship in the . . . in the kind of work I do. There are people out there, Allie. Bad people. Still."

"Like the guy who smells like vitamins?"

"Who?" he asked.

"Plain-looking killer. Knew my name?"

Zay was quiet a moment. "That could be a lot of people."

Oh, and just how terrific was that?

Why it was fan-damn-tastic. Who didn't want lots of plain-looking killers who knew their name hanging around town? We could have a big ole plain-looking killer party.

"Great," I said. "If he happens to stroll by and I point him out, would you tell me who he is?"

"Probably."

And somehow I knew that was the closest, straightest answer I was going to get out of him.

"You were saying?" I said. "About the letter?"

He glanced at the street, then back at me. "It says I hope you'll understand why we can't see each other again, and that you'll forgive me someday."

"So you wrote me a Dear John note?"

"Allie, you were in a coma."

"So you write the woman who is your lover, who is in a coma, may I remind you, a Dear John note? I get hurt and you dump me? What the hell?"

"You dumped me first," he said. "You punched me in the nose."

"Yeah? Well, I healed you, right? With some kind of big, amazing light show, Nola said. I so took you back again. And how do you repay me for saving your life? You dump me."

"I didn't want to—you were dying—I didn't, couldn't." Zayvion threw his hands up in the air and growled in frustration. "You are impossible. I'm trying to make the right move here, Allie. I'm trying to do the smart thing. You almost died. Instead of staying to protect you, I went up to Mama's to try to get Cody. To get him away from . . . from James. I put my . . . my job before you. Before the woman I . . . the woman I didn't want to die."

"You were there when I needed you," I said. "Every time. You're the only person in my life who ever has been."

"Did Nola tell you that?"

"No. I figured that out all on my own."

We sat there, looking at each other and not saying a lot of things.

Finally, I spoke. "I am giving you a chance to change your mind about us, about what you wrote in the letter. A chance for us to try this again. And if you don't want to stick it out with me, fine, I don't blame you. I haven't had the easiest sort of life lately. I'll leave you alone. No hard feelings."

I'd never seen him look so conflicted. Or at least I didn't think I ever had. "Allie," he pleaded. "Things aren't as safe, as stable as they look. I want you safe. I want what's right for you."

So do I, I thought. But I had no idea what that was. My head told me trusting him would be an incredibly stupid thing. He was steeped in secrets, half-spoken truths, and behind-closed-doors dealings. It could take years before I saw the real man behind that masquerade. I didn't even know what he did for a living.

But my heart told me he was right, he was safe, he was home.

It was confusing being me.

"Okay. Until I figure out what I think is right for me, I want you to do me two favors."

"If I can."

There he was again. Zen-Zay, the man of a million secrets. The man I knew I'd be a fool to trust.

"I want you to stick around, at least until I get a chance to point that jerk out to you."

"Which jerk?"

"The one who opened the cab and talked about a war that's coming."

Zay suddenly became very, very still. I could feel the magic shift beneath him, could feel him drawing upon it.

"What war?"

"That's what I want to know." And I guess I looked convincing, because he blinked and sat back in his chair. He looked out the window again, and I could see the muscles in his jaw clench, could see the rope of muscle down the side of his neck strain. He was angry. Or worried.

"I'd love to have you show me who said that to you." He said it in a low, soft, and dangerous voice. But when he looked back at me, he seemed calm, as if we were discussing tomorrow's rain. "What is the other favor?"

"I could really use a cup of coffee."

That got a smile out of him, and I liked the look of it. Even scruffy and underslept, he was a damn handsome man, with those tiger-bright eyes, arched cheekbones, and kiss-me-baby lips. I wanted to reach across that table, grab him by his shirt, and find out what his mouth tasted like.

A wisp of memory, of mint, came to me.

"All you want from me is a cup of coffee, Ms. Beckstrom?" he said.

"No," I said, "I want more. Maybe a lot more." I looked down at my hands, because I needed to look away from him to catch my breath. When I was composed, I glanced back up and said, "How about we start with coffee, lunch, and dessert?"

He leaned forward and gently caught my gloved hands in his. "How about we do."

And I realized this, *this* was what I'd been looking for. It might not be the only place for me, or the best place for me. I had a feeling it wasn't the safest place for me. But for now, for today, it was right where I wanted to be.

Read on for a taster of the next instalment in the Allie Beckstrom series:

Magic in the Blood

Coming in January 2012

Chapter One

I dunked my head under the warm spray of the shower and rubbed shampoo into my hair, wondering where my next Hounding job, and paycheck, were coming from. I hadn't been using much magic since I got back to town, and the bills were piling up. It was time to get on with my life, time to get on with tracking spells again.

I heard a distant pop, like a lightbulb blowing, and all the lights in my apartment went out. I opened my eyes just as a stream of soap dripped into them.

"Ow, ow, ow."

Outside, the wind howled past my bathroom window. We'd been having some bad storms lately—plain old windstorms, not wild magic. Probably a tree or landslide up in the west hills had knocked out the line or blown a transformer, throwing this part of Portland into a deep early-morning darkness. The wail of an alarm from a nearby business started up, and then an answering siren, and then two, joined in on the noise. A couple car alarms got busy.

I rinsed as much of the soap out of my eyes as I

could, turned off the shower, and stumbled out of the tub. I hit my shin on the toilet bowl.

"Ow!" I groped for the sink, found the cool surface with my fingertips, and looked over my shoulder at the single frosted window behind me. No light, which meant the magic grid was down too. There were backup spells to power the streetlights in case of blackout—spells the city paid the price for. Weird they hadn't kicked in yet.

I felt my way along the sink, the wall, the light switch, and the towel hanging on the back of the door. I knew there was no one in the room with me, no one in my apartment. Still, I did not want to be alone and naked in the dark.

"Allie," a voice whispered so close to my cheek I could feel the cold exhale.

I bolted out into the hallway and turned. It was so dark I couldn't see anything.

I traced a glyph for Light in the air in front of me, completely forgetting to set a Disbursement for the pain that magic was going to put me through. Pain, I could deal with later. Light, I needed now.

The hallway, hells, the entire apartment, lit up like sunlight on snow.

I was not alone.

My dead father stood right there on the yellow ducky bath mat in front of my shower. It didn't look like death had done him any favors.

Sure, he still wore a dark business suit—I'd rarely seen him out of business dress—and he was clean shaven and gray haired. Other than that, he looked like a hastily drawn interpretation of himself—his skin too pale, his green eyes gone so light as to be white. Dark, dark shadows caught beneath his eyes and pooled in the hollows of his face. He scowled. He was angry.

Angry at me.

Well, apparently death didn't do much for a person's mood either.

He stretched out his right hand, traced the first strokes of something in the air—maybe a glyph—and then moved fast, faster than any living person, until he was standing in front of me, close, so close his hand pressed against my forehead.

I raised my arms to keep him away, push him away, make him stay away from me. I could smell him—or maybe it was just the memory of him—and taste him, leather and wintergreen, on the back of my throat.

I yelled, tasting more wintergreen as he leaned in closer, all ice and bone—cold and damp against my naked wet skin. The Light spell flickered out, probably because I was too busy panicking to concentrate, and magic does not tolerate that sort of thing.

The apartment plunged back into blackness. I could still feel my dad's hands on my arms.

I ran backward, scrambling to get away from the cold and wintergreen of his angry touch. My back hit the hall wall and I had nowhere else to go.

"Seek," he whispered against my cheek.

Streetlights snapped on—the city's spells finally kicking in—and poured blue light through the windows.

My dad was gone. Cut off midsentence like a dropped call.

Holy shit.

I gulped down air, shaking with more than cold, and

backed into my bedroom, needing to be dry, dressed, covered, protected, safe, and the hells away from here as quickly as possible.

I'd been groped by a ghost. My dad's ghost.

My hands shook, and my heart beat so hard, I couldn't breathe. My dad touched me. And I'd been naked.

I fumbled into a pair of jeans, my bra, a T-shirt, and a wool sweater. Then socks and boots. I picked up the baseball bat I kept near my bed. I didn't know if a baseball bat would work on a ghost, but I was willing to find out.

I stood there, breathing hard, the bat over one shoulder, and stared through the empty hallway at my empty bathroom.

"Dad?" I asked.

Nothing.

Let's just go over the facts: I'd seen a ghost. My dad's ghost.

And he had seen me. Touched me. Spoken to me.

Okay, that was so far down Creepy Lane that it had intersected with Scaring the Hell Out of Me Avenue. I hated that avenue.

I shook out my hands, switching the bat from one to the other, and tried to calm my breathing. *Take it easy, Allie*, I told myself. *Ghosts aren't real.*

Yeah, well, that felt real.

Maybe seeing him was some sort of weird leftover guilt from not being there when he died. Not being there for his funeral or his burial. No, I know I wouldn't have gone to his funeral even if I'd been able to. I was still angry at him then, angry that he had let his hunger for money and power hurt everyone in his life, including me.

As a matter of fact, I was still angry about that.

The lights in my apartment—regular electric—weren't working yet. I didn't want to pull on magic again for light because when you used magic, it used you right back. There was always a price—always a pain to pay. Why give myself a headache when I could just light a candle? Problem was, my candles were all the way across the apartment in the living room.

I strode into the hallway, bat ready to swing. I looked in the bathroom—no one there—and walked (not too quickly, I'll add) over to the side table next to my ratty couch. I put down the bat and found a box of matches. I lit several candles on my bookshelf, on top of the TV, and on the little round dining table by the window. For good measure, I pulled back the curtains, letting in as much light from the street as possible.

Blue light from the streetlamps caught in the whorls of metallic color that ribboned around my fingertips and up my arm and the side of my neck to the very corner of my right eye. It was still strange to see the marks magic had left on me—brighter and more iridescent than tattoos. Stranger to feel magic heavy inside me, a constant weight that moved and stretched beneath my skin.

Even though my right arm didn't itch anymore from the magic flowing through me, my left arm, banded black at my elbow, my wrist, and at each knuckle, was always a little cold and numb when I used magic too much.

I wasn't sure what all of it meant—because no one I'd talked to had ever seen anything like this, like me. People who try to hold magic in their bodies die from it. Horribly. And I'd done my best to stay away from doctors who might be curious enough to want to take me apart to find out why I wasn't dead yet.

I rubbed my arm—the right with the whorls of colors—and scanned the street below.

Rain and wind? Yes. Ghosts? No.

The last room to check was the kitchen. There were no windows in the kitchen, so I picked up a candle in a glass jar and paused in the entryway to the kitchen. My apartment door stood to the right of me, my kitchen lost in shadows ahead of me. I lifted the candle. Yellow light pushed aside blocks of shadow. Nothing.

The phone rang. I jumped so hard, wax sloshed over the candle's wick and smothered the flame.

The phone rang again, and a wash of cold sweat slicked my skin. It was just the phone.

It rang again.

I didn't want to answer it.

Another ring.

Could ghosts use the phone?

Okay, now I was being ridiculous.

I put the candle down on the half wall between the kitchen and foyer and jogged to the phone in the living room. Caught it on the fourth ring.

"Hello?" I said, my voice a little too high.

"Allie Beckstrom?" a low male voice asked.

I recognized that voice. Detective Makani Love had spent a good deal of his childhood in Hawaii and still hadn't lost that particular rhythm to his words. Plus, I could hear the ring of phones behind him and then another voice, female, and likely his partner, Lia Payne. I think the police department had stuck them together for a laugh—Love and Payne—but they'd turned into such a good team, they hadn't asked to be reassigned.

"Hey, Mak," I squeaked.

"Is everything okay? Are you okay?"

I swallowed and worked hard to get my voice down an octave or so.

"Yes. I'm fine. Just, uh . . . kind of startled when the phone rang. Is the power out over there?"

"No," he said. "But we heard part of town was down. You dark?"

The lights flicked back on, and my computer on the desk in the corner room hummed back to life.

"Not anymore," I said. "It just came back on. So, what's up?"

"We need you to come down to the station to give your statement regarding the death of your father."

Oh.

I'd never filed an official report. See, I'd been there the day my father died. I may even have been the last one who saw him alive—except for his killer. But since I'd spent the next several days being chased by the people who killed him, I hadn't had a chance to actually talk to the police about the last time I'd seen him.

Well, the last time I'd seen him alive.

I wondered if Mak believed in ghosts.

"Can it wait until later? I haven't had breakfast yet and was hoping to hunt down some leads on Hounding jobs this morning."

"No. It's been long enough, yah? You've been back in town, what, a week now, almost two? That's patience on our side, you know. We need you this morning. Can you get here in an hour?"

"Will there be any decent coffee in the building?" Love and I weren't best buddies, but I usually ended up going to him when I worked Hounding jobs that involved someone doing something illegal. He and Payne were two of the few police officers I knew who were cross-trained to handle magical crime enforcement.

"Oh, sure. Best coffee in the city, yah. Dug a pit this morning, roasted it with my own hands over the fire. Fresh just for you."

"Right." I glanced out my living room window and through the bare tree limbs that spread across my view of the street and buildings on the other side. It was six o'clock on a late November morning and still dark. Rain gusted sideways past the window, flashing like gold confetti in the headlights of slow-moving traffic crawling toward downtown Portland, Oregon, and the freeway beyond. The police station wasn't all that far from my apartment, but I didn't have a car. The bus ran every half hour and would take me straight to the station doors.

It was doable.

"I'll be there in about forty-five minutes."

"Good. And, Allie?"

"Yes?"

"Don't leave town. And be careful."

A chill ran down my arms. Why would he say that? I wouldn't skip town. And I was always careful. Well, as careful as the situation allowed. "I'll be there in forty-five."

I hung up the phone and scowled at it. Okay, maybe

he had a reason to worry about me not showing up. I'd gotten myself into some weird stuff a few months ago, not that I remembered much of it. My friend Nola, who lived three hundred miles away on a non-magical alfalfa farm in Burns, had taken me in afterward. She tried to tell me what she knew about the days I no longer remembered and the weeks that had gone by while I'd been in a coma. But her information was sketchy too.

The one thing that had become abundantly clear to me was just how much memory I had lost. It still gave me nightmares.

I glanced over at the table by the window. The blank book where I wrote everything just in case magic took my memories was there. I walked over to it, flipped it open. The most current pages were the basic itinerary from the last few days—me settling into my new apartment, the phone messages from my father's accountant I hadn't returned. The sandwich shop I discovered a couple streets over that made really good paninis (I give the salmon rosemary five stars), and the name of a song I liked on the radio.

But as I flipped back toward the front of the book, I found the blank page. The corner of it was worn from me going back to it so often in the last few weeks. Right there on that blank page I should have written everything that happened to me between when I last saw my father alive and when I woke up at Nola's farm a month later.

Blank.

No matter how hard I stared at it, the notes I should have written were not there.

Things I really wish I could remember, like what

had happened between me and a man named Zayvion Jones. I remember him hanging around St. Johns neighborhood in North Portland. I remember him asking me out for lunch, and I remember him going with me to see my father.

What I didn't remember—the things my friend Nola had said happened—was falling in love with him, so much so that I'd sacrificed myself to save him.

It just didn't sound like me.

Slow to trust, slower to love, I couldn't figure out how I had fallen for him so completely in such a short time.

I shut the book and pressed my fingers against my forehead. Magic is not for sissies. Sure, it can do a million good things—keep cities safer and hospitals going, and even just make a bad paint job look good—but it always comes with a price.

Sometimes magic makes me pay a double price—pain for using it, and loss of memory. Yeah, I'm just lucky that way. It was almost enough to make me want to give it up altogether. Almost.

The phone rang again, and I looked through my fingers at it, trying to decide if I really wanted to talk to anyone else this morning. It might be a Hounding job, which would mean money, or, heck, Nola checking in on me.

I picked it up.

"Hello?"

"Hello, Allie." A woman's voice this time. I searched my memory and came up with nothing—see how annoying that is? "I'm sorry to call so early, but I've left a few messages on your cell phone and thought I'd try to catch you before you went out for the day."

I flipped my book open again. Who had been leaving me messages? Just my dad's accountant, Mr. Katz. I glanced at my cell phone—no light at all. The battery was dead, blown. I'd had it only a couple days, and it was currently plugged into the charger.

I'd had zero luck with cell phones lately. Any electronics that worked through a line, like my computer, seemed to hold up okay, but anything wireless self-destructed when it saw me coming.

"Allie?" the woman said.

"Yes," I said, still trying to place her voice. "My cell isn't working. You might want to leave messages here on my home phone."

"Do you want me to have Mr. Katz set you up with a new phone?"

And that's when I knew who it was. Violet. My dad's latest wife. She had a young voice, and from the newspaper articles Nola had shown me, I knew she was about my age. I think I had met her, but that memory was toast too.

"No, that's fine. It's still under warranty. Sorry I haven't gotten back to you. Why are you calling?"

She hesitated, just a pause, an inhalation, but it made every instinct in my body rise up.

"Are you in trouble?" I asked.

She exhaled with a sort of laugh. "I'm fine, just fine. I was hoping you might want to get together for lunch today. I haven't heard from you since before the coma. You didn't contact me when you came back into town. I know we've only met once, but . . . well, since you weren't able to come to the funeral . . . and there's still so much unfinished business with Beckstrom Enterprises and your role in managing the company . . .

I just thought . . . I don't know. I thought we might want to get to know each other a little better. Talk about some things."

My dad had been married six times. Years ago I'd stopped trying to make nice with the women who attached themselves to and were discarded by my father. Which is why I surprised myself by saying, "Sure. Let's do dinner instead, if that's okay. I have a lot of things to get to today."

Violet sounded just as surprised. "Oh. Good. Dinner's fine."

We settled the time and restaurant—not one of the exclusive swanky spots in town, but Slide Long's, known for its seafood—and then we said our goodbyes.

I stared at the phone for a minute, trying to sort out how I felt about getting to know her.

I guess I was a little curious but mostly just lonely. My best friend lived three hundred miles away. The man I was supposed to love was nowhere to be seen. I didn't even know any of my neighbors.

And my dad was dead.

I wondered when I'd stopped liking being alone. Maybe somewhere in the days I couldn't remember, I'd given up on the solitary woman bit and had actually let people into my life. And maybe I had really liked it.

Or maybe I just wasn't in my right mind. Which might also explain the whole ghost-in-the-bathroom bit.

Well, whatever. Right now I had to get down to the police department and tell them what I knew about the day my dad died. After that I'd scout around town and see if there were any Hounding possibilities.

I picked up my journal and quickly wrote that I was giving a statement and had dinner plans with Violet. I paused, wondering if I should write that I'd seen a ghost. Common sense won out, and I simply wrote: *Saw Dad's ghost in the bathroom. Not fun.* And hoped that would be that.